THE RULING PASSION

Previous novels by David Pownall

The Raining Tree War, Faber, 1974
African Horse, Faber, 1975
God Perkins, Faber, 1977
Light on a Honeycomb, Faber, 1978
Beloved Latitudes, Gollancz, 1981
The White Cutter, Gollancz, 1987
The Gardener, Gollancz, 1990
Stagg and His Mother, Gollancz, 1991
The Sphinx and the Sybarites, Sinclair Stevenson, 1993
The Catalogue of Men, Picador Macmillan, 1999

THE RULING PASSION

a novel by
David Pownall

First published in 2008
2nd impression September 2008

ISBN 978-1-84289-050-9

Printed in Great Britain by Biddles, King's Lynn

Herbert Adler
PUBLISHING
www.herbertadler.co.uk

For Jeff, Kate and Girls

The ruling passion, be it what it will,
The ruling passion conquers reason still.

Alexander Pope
'To Lord Bathurst'

CHAPTER ONE

July, 1303. Saint Johnstone, Scotland

William Wild, the Irishman, could hear the argument going on in the tent beside him. Someone was getting it in the neck. The King's high-flown Spanish swearing was notorious – taught him by Eleanor, his Castilian queen, and the foul-mouthed servants she brought with her from Spain. Since her death, the King had gravitated into a sour formality, conscious of his dignity and the dignity of others. He no longer swore from daily habit, only when ignited by extreme frustration. Tonight, some unfortunate had got him into this state.

William Wild thought all these outbursts – which, though always alarming, were getting more sombre and ritualistic – might be unconscious requiems for the dead queen, the woman Edward had worshipped (*all* he had worshipped in this imperfect world). Edward missed her as if she'd died only yesterday. Sometimes he talked as if she hadn't died at all.

Eleanor had once told the Irishman how the Iberian Visigoths used swearing in this way in centuries past – flattering the dead by insulting the living, hoping to summon them up. When fighting the Romans they had professional execrators out in front. Behind them were priests imploring the ancestors to rise and come to the aid of the tribe.

The victim suffering the lash of the King's tongue was having his mother's milk polluted, the testicles of his sons eaten by rats, the wombs of his daughters filled with the seed of plague-victims, his father's grave submerged under the defecations of enemies.

He's not so bad tonight, the Irishman estimated. The flow is moderate. But if it's going to be a session, I should have had a drink before I came.

On entering the presence, all William Wild received was a dark look. "Sit down, you old whore – keeping me waiting," Edward muttered. "Why didn't you save me from that useless time-waster?"

The Irishman sat straight-backed, mouth slightly open as if caught in the act of saying something intelligent.

Edward rubbed his eyes, chin lowered. "Something has to be done about

Ned," he said flatly. Lacing his long fingers together, he studied his nails, frowning. "He can't go on as he is."

William Wild passed a hand through his thinning hair, letting it rest on his bald spot. "Edward, forgive me. I'm completely in the dark. Has Ned done something to upset you?"

"It's what he hasn't done."

"Then perhaps you'll let me into that secret? What hasn't he done?"

"He won't grow up."

On firmer ground, William Wild took time to make a point – no male deliberately avoids growing up. To mature as rapidly as possible is the ambition of every youth.

Edward nodded, holding up a hand.

"Thank you for that, Willy. Before you go any further, it's not only Ned who worries me. I'm sixty-four. I should have been dead years ago." The jokey light in the King's eyes faded, replaced by a flat, opaque fatigue. He paused, rubbed his neck, averting his eyes as if embarrassed. "Now and again, I forget where I am and what I'm doing."

William Wild saw how tired the smile was and his heart fell.

"Spare me any platitudes. I've been trying to work out what's lacking in Ned's character," Edward mused, rubbing his neck again. He frowned as if a thought was giving him physical pain. "He's my blood," he went on, thrusting his legs out and lying back in the chair. "We must have some things in common in our natures, though I can't see it. Anyway, Willy," he grimaced kindly as he spoke, "if you had any idea what to do about Ned, you'd have told me, wouldn't you?"

William Wild raised the question – was there anything specific the Prince of Wales had done or not done, other than being slow to mature?

"In all your chats with the boy over the years, trying to give him shape, you must have had your doubts," Edward said. "Well, my doubts have taken over. I don't seem able to drum up any confidence in him at all." He paused, clearing a space on the map-strewn table as a servant entered with a tray. "I'm surprised you've never mentioned any misgivings of your own."

The Irishman waited until the servant left. "These doubts," he said cautiously. "Could you explain a little further?"

"It would be unfair to let Ned loose on the people as he is."

The Irishman's mouth went dry. There was a note in the King's voice he hadn't heard before.

"You know my son better than most," Edward said. "Be candid with me. He's nearly twenty now. As a man, how d'you find him? Or *can* you find him?"

The Irishman was disturbed. He answered in what he hoped was a chatty, informal way. "We're not as close as we were…which I greatly regret…" Upset, he trailed off into his own thoughts, unwilling to share them.

"Regrets are what I'm talking about, Willy," Edward said intensely, leaning forward. "Dangerous regrets."

"There's plenty of time for him to improve."

"Less than you think," Edward muttered. "I told you. I won't last that long. Ever had a blackout?"

William Wild was silent again. The energy and strength of this man were extraordinary, but forty years of warfare and struggle had taken their toll.

"Are you sure they're blackouts – not just nodding off?" he asked.

Edward's face darkened. "Stop grasping at straws, Willy," he rebuked him. "I was thirty-five with a lot of experience under my belt when I became king. Even if I live on a while, Ned will be at least ten years younger when he comes to the throne. The thought shakes me."

William Wild made a cheery attempt to lighten the atmosphere. "At first, you didn't take being king seriously, remember? Didn't even bother to return to England, you were having such a good time with Eleanor, travelling. Think about those two years when you didn't come back. Quite remarkable, really!"

There was an uneasy pause. Edward laughed. Tension went out of his face. "I let them get on with it. And they did. No need for me, only the *idea* of me. But what's the idea of Ned?" The tension returned and he drank, drumming his fingers on the edge of his chair. "I'd been away a long time. But they knew what I was like. And they know what Ned's like – only too well – know his flaws – which are not like mine."

The genuine sadness in the King's voice aroused William Wild's instinct for self-preservation. This gloom was disturbing – a cause for anxiety. A new state of mind for Edward meant new politics, fresh dangers. Also, it ran counter to character for the King to be evasive, not fully articulating what was on his mind. William Wild had the sinking feeling Edward wanted someone else to do it for him.

"How did a man like me have a son like him?" Edward exclaimed, suddenly angry and bewildered.

"How did a man like your father have a son like you? The weak produced the strong – and the strong produced the weak."

"See! You think he's weak! You agree with me."

"He's a disappointment *to you.* It doesn't matter what I think. Like your father was weak, your son is weak. You're the strong bridge between."

The King's head wobbled, great grey beard jutting out. He held his jaw, blinking. "Hold on, hold on! You're going too fast!"

"Who'd have guessed a success like yourself would come from a failure like your father?"

"This isn't the time for going too far, Willy," Edward warned. "I don't like to hear you running down my father."

"Whom you saved…and betrayed, when you had to. But he always forgave you. Perhaps you'll have to forgive Ned for not being like you."

Edward shuddered. An argument was going on within. Even at this age, volcanic violence could result from exercise of his surging indignation. Above all, this was a man who made war, and settled the questions he asked himself through war. William Wild knew he was taking a risk, and had the scars to prove it, but the case the King was making was full of pitfalls.

"When necessary, you had to act for your father," William Wild reasoned calmly. "You had to fight his battles. You had to sort out the consequences of his failure."

"In some ways, that's true enough, I suppose," Edward admitted. "But it doesn't help me now. I've done everything I can to prepare Ned…"

"Of course you have – very conscientiously and carefully. No one can deny that. But let's imagine if you abdicated and Ned became king…"

"What?"

"From retirement, you could sort out the consequences of his inevitable failures and put him on the right road."

Edward sat bolt upright and laughed. "What a fantastic arguer you are, Willy. Round and round the houses you go. But you're missing the point."

"What's that?"

"Perhaps you haven't noticed, but I change. I adapt. I take a note. That's how I've survived."

Arrogance, wilfulness and cruelty had been tempered in Edward over the years. A great lawgiver had evolved from a great lawbreaker. From accounts William Wild had heard, the man opposite had been a nightmare of a youth.

"I don't believe Ned has the power to change. That's what worries me more than anything else. I've had four sons – any one of the other three, if they'd lived, would have made a better king. Ned can't be taught. There's something unalterable in him."

William Wild drew in his breath. "To say he can't be taught is going too far," he protested. "You're pronouncing his doom before he's got going!

Nineteen is nothing! Give him a chance!"

"I'm not talking about schooling. Ned's already made. I've had that feeling about him since he was very small. Since he was born! He'll always be himself – and that self just isn't good enough. You can't add to it, or take anything away. I call him weak, but what I'm describing is also a strength – in the right place, which isn't on the throne of England."

"Well, this is a shock to me. I didn't know you had such a low opinion of him. You've hidden it very well, I must say."

"What else would you expect me to do?"

William Wild spread his hands in a gesture of confusion. "If you insist he can't change, can't be taught, then what's the remedy?"

"We've solved problems before, you and I."

William Wild saw the grim, intent look on Edward's face. It made his heart plunge. Men whose opposition, greed or awkwardness made them obstacles to the King's will had fallen to the Irishman's knife in the past. It wasn't work he liked. But to shed royal blood was unimaginable.

"He's unfit to govern because he can't govern himself," Edward went on, relentlessly. "What can I do? What's right in a case like this?"

William Wild passed a hand over his forehead, hiding eyes of hazel colour filled with consternation. "You're deliberately overstating the case," he said steadily. "I don't believe you're as anxious as you say."

"Can I, in any conscience, foist Ned on the country simply because he's my son? You weren't in England for the civil wars. It was my childhood, my youth. D'you think I want to leave the country condemned to suffer that kind of chaos when I die?"

Eyes on the ground, the Irishman left his agreement to some of this unsaid, but then only a prophet in the throes of an uncontrollable revelation, or a raving lunatic, would speak out on the issue of whether Ned was fit to rule. He had to be king one day. What quality of king would only be discovered when the weight of the crown was on his head.

Come what may, Ned must inherit the kingship.

First blood must follow first blood. It was the law, ancient and incontrovertible.

William Wild went off to bed. Edward stayed up, thinking about his son and himself. Because my father was such a fool, he mused blackly, I was taught nothing of fatherhood. It's been a guessing-game. Kingship and fatherhood have nothing to do with each other – and I've had to teach myself both. Hence my mistakes. Hence a boy with his head in a jar. Hence, at sixty-four, the earth is shaking beneath my feet.

He pondered on the problem, prowling around his tent. The child, the child – he was bliss, so beautiful, the perfect child. Edward went through important phases of his son's development, seeing patterns he should have noticed in the boy's growth. Too much had been left to luck, to others, to time. But all education is imprisonment, he thought, quoting William Wild, the Irish know-all. All education is oppression. A natural thing grows by inner laws, not the laws of men.

He walked out of the tent and up the hillside. The night was dark, velvet and summery, a Scottish night with midges and a moon.

Bodyguards followed him, mute, moving quietly.

He cursed himself for his lack of courage as a father. A melancholy sound came out of the back of his throat. Pausing in his walk, he lifted his big, heavy head, looked straight ahead, and went absolutely still.

Seen from a distance, he could have been a standing stone.

Overhead, the moon was as pale as the drooping lid of his right eye.

Below, a muffled drum was beaten. He wondered why a drum was being beaten in the middle of the night. What's the danger? Whoever was beating it had not yet found the rhythm.

A breeze came across open ground, ruffling his abundant steel-grey hair.

With all I know, I failed to bring this boy up to be a man. Do I know what a man is? Is it anything to do with being a king?

If only his mother would walk up and take my hand like she used to.

Or be in the air around me, like she used to.

He strained to catch her colour, her warmth, to inhale her perfume. For thirteen years he'd stared into mists, fogs, clouds, corners, shadows, hoping for her female ghost.

A ghost would be better than nothing. Better than the vacuum she left behind.

Her blood is a presence in the boy, he told himself. She's there, in his veins. When I look at him I see her, but I can't love her in him.

He is Eleanor's son. She's keeping him to herself.

More of her blood went into his making than mine.

The trance broke. He caught his breath, heard his heart beat drum-like down in his throat. It was his own heart he had heard earlier. The realisation frightened him. It was too loud, too strong. It could burst. He could die.

At that instant, Ned would be king, ready or not.

With a start, he noticed how far the moon had moved since he glanced at it. He'd been standing still for quarter of an hour. It had seemed only seconds.

Turning on his heel he walked towards the men shadowing him. Hurriedly, they moved aside to let him pass.

With greater vigour in his step he came off the hillside and down into the English camp, passing through the ghostly town of tents, a decision erected in his mind. The risk had to be taken. Ned must learn in spite of himself.

❧

Next morning, William Wild rode out of the English camp at Saint Johnstone with Ned and a dozen mounted archers. Overnight, the King had ordered a foray into the western wilderness of Strathearn.

Seldom completely taken into his father's confidence, Ned didn't have to look far for the true purpose of the expedition. *Foray* meant anything one wanted it to. Going into enemy territory so light-handed was a risk. It appeared to hazard the life of the heir to the throne. This was no foray. Something was pre-arranged to happen. In all probability, the area was safe, very recently brought under English control. It was an old trick the King played – setting traps to test Ned out. The most likely scenario was a mock ambush by English troops dressed in kilts.

Ned disguised his lingering apprehension by playing the clown – making his horse dance over the heathland, showing off to the archers who watched him with hard eyes. He saw how they looked at him. Their lives were also endangered. But he knew they had an inkling of the King's odd educational methods for his son. Mental decoys, games and camouflage had been Ned's lot since he was fifteen. King Edward's court was famous for it.

The Irishman couldn't detect Ned's nervousness. The teacher in him found it difficult to interpret these signals once he was feeling affectionate towards the lad. Any fondness blinded him. Having known Ned from birth, and nurtured his mind, he felt a possessive tug of heart. He wasn't sure Ned was being given enough time to grow into being his own man.

Although there was no physical resemblance between Ned and his mother, she was present in his make-up, shining in his playfulness – the very quality the Irishman and Edward had loved so much in both woman and child. When Eleanor died at forty-four, the King had lost that side. The playfulness in the boy annoyed him.

He's undeniably a certain kind of fool, William Wild reasoned as he watched the prince cavorting – he may even have a touch of the holy fool. But he's a healthy, high-spirited young man. He doesn't judge people too harshly. Having only a shadow of a moral sense, he's no hypocrite. No intellectual…or spiritual athlete either. He loves life in a singular way. He has virtues – some of them unusual for a man of his background.

Lulled by the warmth of his own thoughts, the Irishman drifted into nostalgia. He'd enjoyed Ned's childhood. Often he'd been asked to put his regular duties aside and act *in loco parentis* while Edward and Eleanor travelled abroad, sometimes for years at a time. William Wild had been in charge of Ned's early education, beating off the crushing attentions of tutors and confessors, introducing the child to a wider world.

The mood was broken by Ned whooping exuberantly and galloping off towards the trees. Beyond was dense woodland. The Irishman called out to him to be careful but was ignored. So be it, he mused. He doesn't care. That's his secret and his strength. And don't tell me there's no value in that. He never imagines danger – which means he'll never be afraid.

Having disappeared into the wood, Ned suddenly burst out again, standing in his stirrups, waving strands of flowers, shouting: "Honeysuckle for each man!"

Riding over to the archers he presented blossoms. "Behind your ears! It'll improve your ugliness no end!" he teased. Finally he gave William Wild a flower.

"Smell that, Willy! Is there anything sweeter?" he said with a smile. "But perfumery can't get the essence out. Isn't that odd?"

"We should keep together," William Wild said, glancing into Ned's broad, open features, and the far-seeing bright blue of his eyes. "Don't keep charging off on your own."

They rode on, the prince chatting and joking with the archers. Soon they entered the wood, which was full of birdsong. Two scouts had been sent ahead. One of them was waiting in a glade.

"Plenty of tracks, sir," he reported to William Wild. "A man is following the newest for a while. This close to the camp, it could be some of our own foragers."

"We'll wait to see what he finds out," the Irishman said, dismounting.

"Oh, come on, Willy, we've only just set out!" Ned chided him. "Let him catch up with us."

The archers had already followed William Wild's lead, knowing it made sense. Ned got off his horse, frowning with annoyance. He leant against a tree, arms folded, sulking. A few minutes later the archer who had been following the tracks returned with a horseman dressed for the hunt, carrying a feathered hat. Behind him rode a squire whose outfit was only a few degrees less flamboyant than his master's.

"Piers!" Ned cried, rushing forward.

"Go easy," the hunter said, laughing, as Ned tried to pull him from his saddle. "Willy doesn't look all that pleased to see me."

The Irishman regarded Piers Gaveston with a cold eye. "I wasn't banking on you coming along," he muttered.

"Of course he's coming!" Ned declared. "We need him."

"Well, dear Willy?" Gaveston drawled. "That seems to be decided. So glad we'll be working together." He gave the prince a firm chuck under the chin, but kept his focus on the Irishman, quizzing him with bold eyes. "Ned has to be shepherded a little, don't you think?"

"Did you get permission from the King to come with us?" William Wild asked levelly, matching the challenge with a stiff look.

"He was rather busy so I couldn't talk to him," Gaveston replied offhandedly. "But I left him a message. I'm sure he won't mind."

"My orders are very specific. They don't include you coming along, I'm afraid."

"But my orders say he must!" Ned yelped, an arm round Gaveston's neck. "I can give orders too!"

William Wild shrugged and turned his horse's head to go back the way they had come.

"Where are you going?" Ned demanded.

"To ask your father to sort this out."

"Why does it matter so much if Piers comes with us? What's the problem? He's a better soldier than anyone here."

"I am, indeed," Gaveston said, winking at the archers who were in a huddle a distance off, observing the scene. "Isn't that so, boys?"

A surly grumble of consent arose from the archers. They had all watched the young Gascon unhorse opponent after opponent at tournaments and defeat everyone who faced him in real combat. Feared in the ranks as a magician in arms, he was doubly protected by Ned's open and honest adoration.

"It pains me to have to say this in your presence," William Wild explained in a low voice, leaning down to speak into Gaveston's ear, "but the King excluded you from the party *by name*."

Gaveston frowned, shook his head in feigned wonder and disbelief, then gave a brief smile. "To be so particular about such a trivial issue is sad in a great man – but they can be small-minded when they like. Oh well, one can only marvel. Off you go. What a disappointment. Goodbye, Ned."

He embraced the prince, who was holding his head in his hands, rocking to and fro and moaning. "He has to come, he has to come."

"You can tell me all about your adventures when you get back. I'll have to find something else to do, I suppose."

As Gaveston put his foot in the stirrup, Ned erupted into a tantrum, eyes bulging, face inflamed. "Willy, you're an officious old bastard!" he shouted. "He's my best friend and I need him with me!"

There's the old man's blood coming up, William Wild thought to himself. When you get down to it, they're not so different.

Gaveston's horse shied from the uproar. His master held its head down and leapt agilely back in the saddle.

"Don't go!" Ned cried, stumbling after him. "What happens if I get killed out here and never see you again?"

"You do talk the most dreadful shit, sometimes!" Gaveston called back over his shoulder, savagely driving his spurs into the horse's flanks. "Look after him, Willy, or you'll answer to me!"

Ned refused to speak to William Wild once Gaveston had gone and the journey was resumed. Instead, the prince spent his time with the archers, regaling them with stories of the Gascon warrior's conquests, voice deliberately raised when he wanted William Wild to hear. The tales would sound outlandish to any ordinary listener – as if the exaggerations originated in myth – but William Wild knew there was truth in most of them. Piers Gaveston was a superman of sorts, attractive as a god, absolutely fearless, indifferent to criticism of any kind. Ever since coming to Court as a ward of the King, he had shared quarters and schooling with the prince, and enthralled him.

The Irishman knew Ned's hero-worship could not all be put down to infatuation. If ever a youth was shaped to rule other youth it was Gaveston. As Ned often told him to his face – he was the model of natural superiority. William Wild would have qualified that praise to *unthinking* superiority – a variant of mental inferiority. He had watched as the Gascon charmed everyone with his good looks, airy arrogance and achievements, and Ned lived his life through him, especially in deeds of war and sex.

A development of the prince's character which disturbed the Irishman was Ned's increasing appetite for the base and lowly. He only wanted to shine in the mundane world where he had a clear field. After meeting Gaveston, Ned began to take pleasure in descending from his social pinnacle and bestowing friendship on underlings. The serious endeavours of chivalry and excellence he left to his friend. But if Gaveston defeated a great champion, it was Ned's victory. If Gaveston seduced a famous beauty, it was Ned's triumph as well.

By these means, reasoned the Irishman privately, Ned had ended up at nineteen isolated not only by his education and status but also by this strange vicariousness. He was enslaved by a blind, pubescent adoration of a star.

Ned was unprepared for power because power had already had its way with him in its most frightening form – the power of love.

But William Wild was a man governed by reason. As Ned's unofficial guide to life, his nose had been put out of joint by the rise of Gaveston. Once on the scene, the prince listened to no one else. This had made the Irishman jealous – therefore his opinions were not to be trusted, even by himself. Even without the King's intense pressure to do so, he would not admit his reservations until certain.

Two further factors had appeared late-on during their discussion the previous night. They were the direct cause of the foray into Strathearn. Ned was commander of one of the King's armies – having never killed a man – and betrothed to the daughter of the King of France – having never bedded a woman.

King Edward had churned through his failings as father, teacher and guide and seized on these oversights. At the age of fifteen he himself had been properly blooded as a matter of course, given a prisoner to kill during his first battle, so he could get the feel of it.

He clearly remembered the occasion – the shock and excitement of taking life. It had changed him.

But somehow, in all the careful planning of Ned's education and training, this simple act of initiation had been forgotten. The fault probably lay in the increased sophistication of the times.

Also, the gambit of introducing an experienced woman into the bed of a boy early on – which had been the manner of Edward's own initiation – had fallen into disuse, thanks to the rise of Courtly Love as a code of sexual conduct for the high-born.

In spite of serious misgivings, faced by Edward's enthusiasm for having found the key to the problem, William Wild had acknowledged these points might have some validity. His acquiescence was a tactical error. The King decided promptly to fill these gaps in Ned's basic education. The boy must kill. The boy must have a woman. The educative process would be best taken care of in wilderness, far from public view.

"Bring him back to me a man," he said, an arm round the Irishman's shoulder. "And, if you do succeed, I'm afraid you'll have to change your ways and accept my reward. This time I won't take no for an answer. Your fastidiousness won't work. If you save the nation you'll have to accept an earldom."

William Wild did a circuit of the tall grey stones which stood around the camp made that summer evening on the banks of the River Earn. The sky was beginning to darken and a moon hung in the south. One of the archers was watching over his horse as it drank, the animal standing knee-deep in the shining river, early stars high over its bowed head.

A proverb, obvious in truth from the day it was coined by some primordial ostler, came to mind.

What if, having been led to water, this horse wouldn't drink?

A chill descended as night's blackness ran through the wood and encircled the fire, making the men around it into shadows. Ned's self had no more substance than those shadows. He would flow with the changing dark. Edward might think he perceived something rock-like in his son, but no lad of nineteen was carved in granite. If asked for an appropriate metaphor to convey late adolescence, the Irishman would suggest a brimming cup, life already running down its sides – strongly made for the most part but likely to break if dropped from too great a height.

The Irishman knew his own reputation for being treacherous to everyone except his king – this tough, successful *nonpareil* of kings. Their relationship occupied a sphere of its own – viewed with distrust, envy and bafflement by the rest of the Court. It was strange he'd thrived in royal service, having once failed in his duty at a critical moment. His downfall was expected but never came. The failure itself seemed to be the source of his success.

He'd been given this impossible task, the initiation of Ned, because there was no one else deep enough in the minds of father and son to do it. To call it trust was inaccurate. It was more like being an extension of Edward's paternal and regal panic – and Edward was a man who never panicked. From now on, William Wild was inside the King's final secret. The blood hadn't worked. The inheritance of fire, strength and talent wasn't there.

Not a man of noble origin, having inherited nothing himself, William Wild was nevertheless not opposed to the privileges of birth. The way he saw it, his own prosperity was ruled by his magnificent connection with Edward, who'd come by his great power by the luck of who he was. To William Wild, his life was part of a secondary power emanating from that, and, therefore, an inheritance of fortune. Until he was in his mid-thirties he'd lived by his soldier's arm, garnering a rag-bag of esoteric learning. Having served with sword and spirit in the Magreb, he'd first joined Edward – then heir apparent – in Acre thirty years ago, and been with him ever since.

Not understood by anyone beyond the two men themselves, and being the cause of much speculation, was the Irishman's refusal to accept honours and preferments as a result of his close friendship with the King. He was satisfied to remain his captain of bodyguard, the job he was originally hired to do. Boldwood, a small estate in the Wye Valley, was the only gift of magnitude he'd ever accepted, pressed upon him by Queen Eleanor when she knew she was dying.

CHAPTER TWO

At dawn, William Wild was awakened by the corporal archer. Without speaking, he beckoned the Irishman to follow him to the bivouac built for the Prince of Wales. On the way over, the corporal pointed to the line of tethered horses. At one end stood a tall mount clad in a heavily embroidered saddle-cloth and a smaller horse wearing a reduced version of the same.

"They weren't there last night, though I seem to recognise the art-work," the corporal said, stopping several yards away from the bivouac. "I reckon we've got a visitor. Will you have a look in or shall I take a gander?"

William Wild sighed and shuddered simultaneously.

"We posted a sentry, of course?" he asked wearily.

"That was me, sir. We were briefed to look out for trouble from the west. I was keeping my eye on the river, upstream. It's possible the ripples hypnotised me. They can if you stare at them long enough. His lordship must have come in from the other side. Didn't make a sound."

William Wild turned away. In order to avoid the confrontation sure to emerge from the bivouac, he took the corporal a little way into the trees and slapped him hard several times.

"It could have been an assassin who got past you!" William Wild said, giving him an extra slap. "The next time you doze off on sentry duty, the ripples will be on your back."

"All I can say in my own defence is a genius got the better of me," the corporal said, having not flinched from the punishment. "He's so clever! During the Flemish war, one night for a bet he walked through the French camp in full armour, got his leg over the Duke of Montmorency's daughter, then strolled out again."

"You're a gullible idiot!"

"Yes, sir. I expect so. But I'm not the only one."

"Let the men sleep until this is sorted out. I don't want any more ructions like yesterday," William Wild muttered, walking through shapely birch saplings towards the river, the corporal trailing behind. Gaveston's defiance had created a complex problem. In terms of the King's order, he, Captain Wild, was the leader of the expedition. The prince's position had been left vague – if being the titular commander of half the English army can be called vague. The King had told his son to co-operate and be guided, but Ned would never lift a finger against his hero.

As he wandered along the bank, William Wild toyed with a knotty concept in moral and religious thought, mooted by the Persian, Abu'Ali Al-Husayn Ibn'Abd Allah Ibn Sina, author of *Kitab ash-shifa*, the longest book ever written, who, pondering a section of Aristotle, proposed that, on the one hand, true responsibility for any decision never reposes with an individual who has no power to enforce it, and, on the other, the taker of a decision creates the servanthood attendant on its taking.

Which left the Irishman's mind coasting gently until he saw the splash of pale bodies in a pool ahead.

Crouching behind a bush he studied the scene.

Ned was teaching Gaveston and Hector, the young squire, breast-stroke, holding their chins to keep them afloat.

"Use your legs like a frog!" he was saying. "You've seen frogs. Bend then push. Bend then push."

"Don't let go of me," Gaveston pleaded. "I'm out of my depth."

"You'll never be a good swimmer if you're afraid to put your face underwater."

"Don't let go of me! I can't touch the bottom."

"It looks as though, in spite of everything you said, the wonder-boy has joined the party," the corporal whispered over the Irishman's shoulder, having crept up behind him.

"If you want to stay on the right side of me don't keep stating the obvious," came the frosty reply as William Wild left the cover of the bush and set off along the bank.

As he approached the beach of stones that was the access to the pool, Ned spotted him.

"Oh, do leave us alone, Willy," he called.

"I have my duty to do."

"Well, do it somewhere else."

"I can't continue with this situation. We have to go back to camp."

"Don't be such a spoilsport."

"I refuse to go against your father's strict orders."

"Oh, to hell with fathers!" Ned shouted.

The corporal shouted to William Wild to come quickly and see what was coming down the river.

From beneath towering, dark clouds of a summer rain-storm to the west, round a distant bend overhung with trees, a swarm of rough, bowl-shaped hide boats came rotating in the current, bumping into each other, colliding with rocks. Paddles flailed in the air like the legs of overturned spiders as the drenched occupants endeavoured to keep in the mid-stream.

"Will you look at that!" the corporal breathed.

"They'll be on top of us in a few minutes. Go and rouse the men," the Irishman ordered.

"The lads will love it," the corporal laughed as he retreated down the bank.

William Wild ran back down the bank towards the pool waving his arms to attract Ned's attention to the danger.

A high blade of rock got in the way of the bathers seeing upstream. All Ned saw was old Willy Wild intent on causing trouble over Piers again. Still holding the learners up by their chins, he called out: "Go away! Stop being such a pain."

"Scots! In force!"

"Where? I don't believe you. You're just saying that."

"No time to argue! Hurry up! There must be more than fifty of them!"

Ned immediately struck out for the bank, leaving Gaveston and Hector to shift for themselves, whereupon they both started floundering and crying for help. Hearing Gaveston's panic-stricken yells, Ned swam back and grabbed him. One of the coracles was ahead of the main flotilla and shot through a narrows, entering the pool. Having no weapon, William Wild picked up stones to hurl, but he held his arm when he saw the stern, black-clothed, hooded occupants who paddled hurriedly past, ignoring them.

"Monks!" Gaveston shouted. "Fucking monks in boats, would you believe?"

Soon more coracles were pouring through the narrows in a jumble, paddles clashing as the light craft span. The men in them made no sound, intent on navigating the rocks.

As the surprise effect lessened with each craft passing, Ned and Gaveston woke up to the fact young Hector had disappeared. The prince plunged back into the pool and started duck-diving to look for him while Gaveston raged up and down stark naked on the shore.

When the last monks had gone through, William Wild heard shouting from further downriver as the archers began pouring volleys of arrows into the coracles. Running as fast as he could along the bank, he arrived in time to see the men in the last coracle frantically trying to fend off a hail of shafts with their paddles, only to collapse one by one as arrows struck home.

Aghast, William Wild sank to his knees in the grass, cursing his ill-luck. By flashes of white and red beneath the dark cloaks of some of the stricken men, he'd recognised who they were.

The archers were killing Poor Knights of Christ. Thirty years ago he'd been one of these soldier-monks himself.

Although many of the coracles had been swept away in the current, a log-jam of dead and wounded men had built up in the branches of a fallen tree a few hundred yards further downstream. Under William Wild's supervision, the archers waded in to retrieve their victims, laying them out on the bank.

Like a man in a trance, the Irishman walked amongst the dead and wounded, knowing in the workings of his perverse destiny there would be someone to recognise him, even in this wilderness far from the Holy Land.

The commander was amongst the five survivors brought out of the water. A massive, black-haired Scot, he raged against the blindness and stupidity of the archers. Poor Knights, Templars, could be impartial in wars, having safe-conduct guaranteed by both sides. This had been agreed by King Edward, he bellowed.

Once the Irishman saw the commander wasn't someone he'd known during his service, he did what he could to comfort the man. Apart from roaring that the unit was heading for Saint Johnstone to see King Edward, who would immediately behead the perpetrators of this bloody shambles, the Scot called down God's wrath on the clods who had killed the servants of Christ while they were about His legitimate business.

During this mayhem, the prince and Gaveston were in their own world of grief. Young Hector's drowned body had floated into the branches of the fallen tree. Gaveston wouldn't let anyone else touch it but brought out the corpse and sat on the bank holding the boy across his knees, saying over and over: "What the hell am I going to tell his father?"

William Wild set the archers to work excavating a burial pit in the loam of the woods. While he was pulling flat stones out of the river shallows to protect the mass grave, he heard a voice calling in Arabic from the huddle of wounded, using his old vow-name.

"Theo? Can that be you?"

With a heart torn between anguish and pleasure in equal parts – having recognised the voice as a lost friend – he went over and submitted to the past. He couldn't help the guilt, nor the anger and self-recrimination which came over him as he knelt to embrace the wounded man. Grey with age, thin and wasted, Gualberto was still detectably the comrade he had last seen in Acre on the September day in 1272 when Edward – then the heir apparent – aborted his crusade and pulled out his troops, sailing west to Sicily – the Irishman, then known as Theodosius Flanagan, with him.

"When I heard Acre had fallen, I was sure you must have been among the dead," the Irishman whispered in Arabic. "I was told no one survived."

"Oh, you know how hard it can be to catch me," Gualberto said with a tight grin, "and a good Templar always retreats with his assets. Some of us got away. Though I think an English arrow has managed what the Muslims couldn't."

"We'll get you back to camp," William Wild assured him, examining the arrow in Gualberto's thigh. "This doesn't look too bad."

"Am I to assume you'd prefer me not to mention how we know each other?"

William Wild nodded.

The conversation in Arabic was drawing the attention of the archers, who were in an apprehensive, resentful mood. All men of the Welsh marches, once they had decided the language wasn't the tongue of the Scots, a traditional Celtic enemy, they allowed their guilty anger to make them suspicious. William Wild caught their darting looks and told his friend they would find time to talk once the mess of the massacre had been tidied up.

Several of the wounded died while the archers were scraping a shallow grave-pit in the woods with broken branches. A badly injured serjeant was in great pain, with no chance of surviving.

William Wild had him moved a short distance away from all the activity, then asked Ned to come over.

"This old soldier's had enough. He wants to be put out of his misery," he said, pressing a knife into Ned's hand, who stepped back, holding the knife as if it was red-hot. "I'm not sure what you mean," he said.

"It would be an act of mercy."

"Then be merciful, Willy. I'm too busy dealing with Piers at the moment. He's terribly upset about Hector."

"Come on, Ned," the Irishman insisted. "This happens all the time in war. You know we have to help each other out."

"Then you help him out."

"I'm sorry, Ned, that's not good enough. It's something you should be able to do."

There was a cold pause. Annoyance moved across the prince's features.

"That's not the sort of thing I should be doing," he said eventually. "I'll get back to Piers. Here's your knife back, thank you."

Refusing to accept the weapon, William Wild drew himself up to his full six feet and gave Ned a severe look. "Warriors are brothers. I shouldn't like to feel ashamed of you, Ned."

"I don't care if you're ashamed of me. I'm not a cut-throat."

"I'm not asking you to do anything reprehensible."

"Isn't betrayal of trust reprehensible?" Ned retorted. It was on the tip of William Wild's tongue to tell him the reason for the request but the serjeant suddenly convulsed. A moment later he sighed and went still.

"Well, that's the end of the argument," Ned said, stepping over the body and starting to walk away.

"That's right, don't get your hands dirty," William Wild jeered, following him.

"Shut up, Willy!"

"Look around you! Lend a hand."

"D'you think I don't know my father put you up to this! You're the one who should be ashamed!" Ned retorted, grabbing a broken branch off an archer, and scraping furiously at the common grave being made for the dead.

"You don't think he's got a point?" the Irishman said, moving alongside him, dodging the clots of black leaf-mould being thrown up.

"He had to do it when he was your age. Why shouldn't you?"

"My father's crass ideas do him no credit, and the fact you've conspired with him makes you the worst kind of hypocrite! If all we're good for is cutting each other's throats, so much for civilisation!"

"You can't keep running away," William Wild mumbled, chastened, but trying to hide it. "There's more to being a king than having everything done for you."

"Don't you presume to lecture me! Does being a king mean teaching your son to be a common butcher?"

"I thought you were interested in lowly, common or garden tasks, Ned. I see you often enough with a spade in your hands."

"That's different," Ned muttered, his eyes downcast. "I'm not listening to what you say any more, Willy. You mustn't bother me.

Keep out of my way if you know what's good for you."

Tossing the broken branch aside, Ned went down and sat next to Gaveston who was grieving over the body of Hector. They huddled together like parents over a child, arm in arm, heads bowed, until the pit was ready and the dead had been dragged over and laid side by side within. When William

Wild suggested Hector should be interred along with the others, Gaveston erupted.

"I'm not leaving him here! He's got to have a proper burial, not tossed into a pit with all and sundry!"

"To share a grave with so many holy men is surely a privilege, my lords," the commander chipped in sardonically, having overheard. "Even though their deaths were caused by cretins, this *all and sundry* bled for Christ in the Holy Land."

"He must have a beautiful tomb!" Gaveston declared, ignoring the interruption. "He comes from good family."

"If that's what you want, that's how it shall be," Ned agreed, putting an arm round his shoulders.

Turning from the consolation of his friend, Ned told William Wild the foray was over. "We're going back, Captain Wild. The farce you cooked up with my father is finished," he said with an odd, lofty sourness, "and I'll remember what you tried to make me do."

Using some of the coracles to transport the wounded, the party followed the river down, picking up more dead from where the current had taken them, burying corpses as they moved along.

When the Templar commander was certain Ned was no less than the Prince of Wales, it fuelled his indignation rather than moderated it. By now he was hallucinating noisily, his ravings interspersed with obscenities using Gaveston's name. As the coracles floated eastwards, the horsemen plodding alongside on the banks, Ned had to listen to broadside after broadside of common scandal about himself and Gaveston bellowed over the water.

"We lost Jerusalem because of sodomites like you!" the commander ranted. "Why should the Divine One favour nations led by perverts? You're our sin, our foulness and corruption!"

After more of this kind of thing Ned went to William Wild and demanded the commander's mouth be stopped.

"He's mad with pain," William Wild said. "That arrow's inches from his heart. Try to ignore him. Ride on ahead until you're out of earshot."

"Piers will kill him if he carries on."

"Whether we like it or not, he's under the papal protection – and he tells me your father is expecting him."

"Do something, Willy," Ned insisted. "It's too humiliating."

"We should be back before nightfall. He's probably going to die before long. Can't you put up with it until then?"

"My father will be told you allowed me to be insulted and defamed and did nothing!" Ned said, sullenly. "Along with the other business, I can't help thinking we're not friends any more."

"Ned, please appreciate my position. What can I do?"

"You've let me down," Ned replied with a lowering look, turning to ride off and report back to Gaveston. "I used to think you were on my side, but evidently I was wrong."

Calling a halt, William Wild had the coracles brought into the bank and moved Gualberto in with the commander, asking him to do what he could to check the man's crazed outpourings.

"Surely you realise the man's mad?" Gualberto said. "He's like this most of the time, injured or not."

"How does anything get done?"

Gualberto shrugged. "In his lucid moments, when he forgets what's happened to us, that we're essentially a comic show, spiritually redundant, he manages to regain some of our affection. We look after him. But he's not alone in his madness. Our contempt for those in power has got deeper since you left. These days no Templar cares a fig for the son of a king – or a king, if it comes to that. We've become completely cynical. As for faith...well, that's a free-for-all."

"Later, later," William Wild said soothingly. "We'll find time to catch up once all this is sorted out."

"You were the last of the serious ones. Once you'd gone we didn't amuse ourselves with that sort of thing. Not that the Templars ever had much to offer the mind. Sometimes I wondered if accountancy and theology had been twinned in some infernal university."

The commander grunted and spat blood. Red bubbles appeared on his lips, sliding into his beard. He breathed heavily, inflating his massive chest with the shaft sticking out of it. His roar of pain bore a fresh bout of insults, including a curse on Edward of the English, father of a diabolical deviant infamous throughout Europe, friend of Satan himself.

When the noise subsided into a whimper, Gualberto turned to the Irishman. "You know how bankers feel about the people who have to borrow from them?" he said with a solemn wink. "This is what we've become. Sad, isn't it? When you think how we used to be...such brothers..."

Another tirade from the Scot on the same seditious theme broke off what Gualberto was saying. Suddenly, in mid-sentence, the noise stopped. The giant Templar went quiet, gaped and fell back.

As William Wild bent over to listen for his heart, a big black-haired hand grabbed him by the scruff of the neck.

"The barb's not yet fettled that can kill McHunter," the commander hissed into his ear, cranking himself back up into a sitting position. "Sorry to disappoint you! Now, take me to that cunt of a king of yours. That impecunious spawner of depravity is expecting me to save him from bankruptcy."

CHAPTER THREE

During the nuptial negotiations between Paris and London in May that year, the Prince of Wales refused sight of his prospective bride's portrait.

Ned argued that since he was being forced to marry it didn't matter what she looked like.

His hand had been hawked around Europe since he was four, involving several diplomatic impasses and breakdowns. By the time the bethrothal to Isabella was agreed (envoys made his promises for him in Paris), Ned was market-hardened in this respect. Although he obeyed his father, he was now of an age when the separation between personal feelings and duty had opened up a free field where he could love where he liked.

A few hours before the foray party returned to camp, King Edward received a special messenger from King Philip, Isabella's father, with another portrait of the girl – bigger, and better painted. The French diplomat heading the mission made a firm request on his master's behalf, verging on a demand – the prince must study this likeness very closely and become acquainted with the detail. In the course of the meeting, King Edward discovered his son's refusal to look at the first picture was known in Paris, provoking speculation as to whether this young English prince had any inclination to breed.

The foray party entered the English camp while the Frenchman was exercising every subtle power of eloquence, every ambiguity, hint and enigma he could, in order not to say what he had to say. The King's patience was already running out. When he was told William Wild was already back from Strathearn with casualties, he cut short the interview and went out in his mood of annoyance to meet the day's second embarrassment.

Striding downhill, he ran into the commander who was being carried on a stretcher. Before any courtesies, McHunter tore into the crass inefficiency of the English army and its lack of intelligent leadership. While this barrage was going on, Ned and Gaveston enacted a sombre, theatrical show, approaching the King with the body of Hector carried aloft, making what they thought was a moving plea for the best of tombs to house the boy's bones.

Experienced in the handling of bad news, William Wild remained at the back. When the King's temper snapped, there was no person or protocol to stop the assault on Ned. Shaking with rage, the infuriated father grabbed his son by the shirt and shook him with tremendous force. Ned did not resist or fight back, but hung in his father's grasp like a rag doll, being swung this way and that, head lolling, while Visigothic blasphemies and curses poured from the King's lips.

Everyone – including the French diplomat with the picture under his arm – stood and watched. Gaveston, his expression sphinx-like, folded his arms and looked unmoved.

"And you, you simpering whoreson!" Edward roared at him, flinging Ned aside. "Why can't you leave this fool alone? I sent an order confining you to camp!"

"I never received it, sire," Gaveston replied steadily.

"Don't lie to me!"

"On my honour, sire, I never received it," Gaveston replied, looking straight into the old king's staring eyes, standing his ground. "I would never disobey Your Majesty."

"What an artful whore you make! I've had enough of this bitch-on-heat behaviour between grown men! What's up with you?"

"Speaking to me like that is unseemly," Gaveston said bravely. "It achieves nothing."

"Are you the expert on being seemly? You could have fooled me!" Edward said, his anger going down a few notches as Gaveston refused to be browbeaten, looking straight into his eyes. "Is it seemly to trail after my son wherever he goes?" he almost whined. "Why did you follow him?"

"Because I thought he might be in danger," Gaveston replied coolly. "Sending him out with such a light escort was very ill-advised."

"You dare to criticise me?"

"To the west of here we have no control, sire. It's enemy country."

"Is that so?" Edward muttered, harnessing his indignation. "If you weren't my ward, I'd feed you to the birds. You're going back to Gascony! You can give your family headaches for a change."

"Whatever Your Majesty ordains," Gaveston said with a bow that managed to avoid any hint of submissiveness. "It will be pleasant to see my people again."

Ned ran down the hill, howling.

It was nightfall before William Wild was called upon to give the King his report on the failure of the foray. By that time, not only had McHunter made a demand for huge damages but the corporal archer had been hanged. King Edward let the Irishman know how near his own neck had been to the rope. "You were in charge, Willy," he said. "If I hadn't been cheered by the belief Ned must have played some part in all that blood-letting, I might have sacrificed you."

Eyes cast down, William Wild remained silent.

"Are you telling me Ned wasn't involved? He did nothing?" Edward asked incredulously.

The Irishman nodded.

"How does he always manage to avoid it?" Edward muttered, distractedly plucking at the skin on the back of his hand. "There he is, right in the middle of a massacre! What was he doing? Twiddling his thumbs?"

When he was told his son had been playing in the river with Gaveston and Hector, Edward groaned. "That's it!" he announced. "I give up."

"If that means you're giving up such crude tactics for Ned's education, I'm all for it."

"You were meant to smooth out any crudeness, Willy. That's why I chose you for the job. You've failed me." The King's cold, quelling eye ran over the Irishman's face as he spoke. "If you had doubts, you should have spoken up."

"You're right. I should have refused," the Irishman confessed, "but you seemed to have lost faith in Ned completely. I felt I had to do something."

"Well, I've got even less faith now."

"You can't afford to keep making mistakes with Ned," the Irishman said abruptly. "Everyone's got faults."

Edward waved a hand dismissively. "If he's not swimming, he's digging holes in the ground. If he's not digging holes in the ground, he's rowing the ferry while everyone laughs at him. All the boy does is make a fool of himself." The King's frown darkened, then slipped away into a brief laugh and a shake of the head. "It's a mystery to me how he got this way."

"Why shouldn't he be interested in ordinary things? True, Ned hasn't got what you might call a serious side...yet," the Irishman ventured. "But, like you, it will probably arrive when it's needed."

"That's not enough. I've got to know for sure."

"Ned doesn't recognise problems. He looks the other way.""

"Why? He was never taught that by me."

"Like everyone of that age, he only cares for what touches him," the Irishman went on. "He has his own ideas on what's worthwhile."

He paused, hoping the essence of what he was saying would emerge without having to state it too openly.

Believe in your boy. Help him through. Remember how hard it is to find a self that works.

Edward sat silently staring at the Irishman, drooping eyelid in a frozen wink. "I've had enough of him," he intoned dully after a while. "God save my soul, I've turned against my own child."

"You'll get over that."

"Of all the disasters I have to deal with, he's the worst. What am I going to do? Tell me, Willy – what am I going to do?"

"Well, for a start, we can try to get into his mind. What did you care about at nineteen? Think about that."

The question failed to penetrate the old king's misery.

He shrugged, played with his long beard for a while, then slowly shook his shaggy white head.

With his son unworthy of hope, and Death running round his mind, he couldn't imagine having ever been nineteen.

The recuperating Templars were quickly absorbed into the life of the camp. After protracted surgery, during which he was told several times to prepare for the end, McHunter's arrow was removed from near his heart. Within days he was wearing the barbed steel head hung round his neck, a reminder of the day of infamy on the Earn. Of his fifty men, only four survived. Few were offering themselves as recruits for the Templars these days, it being generally known how disfavourably Philip the Fair, the powerful French king with the Pope in his pocket in Avignon, viewed them. Their dark-spirited autonomy as Europe's power-brokers and bankers was no longer envied. Some pundits considered them doomed – others saw them as the model for the future, provided the organisation could adapt to changing times.

None of these speculations affected McHunter's drive to enlist replacements for the men he had lost. Having worked his way up from servant to high executive in the structure of the Order, he had no spiritual existence beyond its limits. From the moral high ground he occupied as a much-wronged leader unfairly stripped of his manpower by blundering English incompetence, he secretly tempted the well-born young men in Edward's army to sign up so he could build his unit back to full strength.

On his last night in camp before setting out for Dundee and a homeward voyage to Bordeaux, Piers Gaveston met with the commander. He was told how exactly he fitted the requirements of a Poor Knight – his driving, high spirit and fearlessness, his refusal to be put down, his indifference to danger, his inner, secret piety.

Interested but wary, Gaveston articulated the rumours he'd heard about the rocky future of the Templars.

"Oh, you don't want to listen to that kind of stuff," McHunter snorted. "Although it's a good idea to keep your ear to the ground, don't get it full of shit."

Gaveston commented that the Templars seemed to have more enemies than friends these days.

"In our business there's only a hair's-breadth difference," was the answer.

Gaveston mentioned talk he'd heard of heresy and religious malpractice.

"That's just people getting confused," McHunter assured him. "Our interests naturally involve Islam."

The Gascon brought up the stories of the Poor Knights' vast wealth compared to the bankruptcy of the European states.

"Why d'you think I was coming to see King Edward? He wants a loan to pay for his Scottish war. Without our help he'll have to call it a day and go back to London."

"You're saying there's no substance in these speculations about your future?" Gaveston asked.

"King Philip is bluffing. He owes us more than he owns. There isn't a potentate who isn't in our debt. They can't make war or keep peace without our help. And we need cocky, gutsy youngsters like you who can stand up to them once we've trained you in our ways."

"I'll think it over," Gaveston said, making ready to leave.

"The English have misrepresented you. The rumours are wrong. You're a fine fellow. I like you a lot."

"It would be fair to warn you I know nothing about money except how to spend it."

"Don't worry. We can teach you religious banking."

Gaveston brushed a strand of golden hair from his face. "Schooling has never been my strong point," he confessed. "I don't like it much."

"When you get down to it, figures are there to obey you. Perhaps you'd prefer your membership not to be made public?" McHunter asked, changing tack as he saw Gaveston's distaste for the idea of having to be taught something new. "That can be arranged."

"You mean be a spy?"

"If I was an ambitious young fellow with a kingdom in my sights, I'd be looking for backers. You know how unreliable, how fleeting, emotions are, especially in the hearts of spoilt princes. One minute you're the number one beloved – the next, you're nothing but a nuisance."

Gaveston smiled. Ned apart, he had been hero-worshipped by the entire cadre of royal wards at Court for three years, ruling the classroom through the playground, undermining the tutors' labours by his physical brilliance. To all the boys, he was the fount of good-time wisdom, best sportsman, sexual athlete, ace drinker, expert in all things joyous and dangerous. When the time came, these acolytes having matured into positions of power, he would be able to command loyalty at many levels of influence.

"I can't imagine myself ever becoming a nuisance to anyone," he said with a frank smile. "Most people seem to like me. But I'll think over what you've said and let you know my decision."

King Edward's grand strategy for the subjugation of Scotland hinged on taking Stirling Castle that summer. It was the focus of remaining Scottish resistance, lynch-pin to the domination of both the Highlands and the Lowlands. The decision to abandon the strategy for this year (*re*-conquering the Scots was essentially an annual event) emerged, or rather crept, from the black day on the Earn.

That failure undermined the old king's self-confidence.

He wasn't used to insuperably obdurate problems. Stirling Castle had been built in order to be so, but King Edward believed anything built by man could be broken down, including sons.

He had built Ned very carefully, layer by layer, experience by experience, preparing the prince for power. But he hadn't realised this structured education had failed to enter the part of the boy's brain where a strong, unusual self was hiding.

Ned and Stirling Castle became twinned in the monarch's mind, confusing him emotionally.

There was no military logic in not taking Stirling. He had the power to lay siege to the great stronghold and a high chance of success. But any confidence in the rightness of his decision-making had been sapped by his son.

As always in his campaigns to bring the Scots to their obedience, Stirling was the task challenging him more than any other. The English army had dragged itself five hundred miles for the purpose. Arrangements had been time-consuming, cumbersome, and complicated – akin to the long, patient labour of bringing up a child. The imagined achieving moment when an empowered, responsible adult arises was now rhyming in his deeper mind with the fall of a towering fortress – two polarised but desirable events, both suddenly out of the question.

The old man allowed these tensions and visions free play over the ruins of his plans. Defeatism stalked his lonely hours. He became morose, talked to himself incessantly, and drank a lot of wine.

On the day he first let slip to his generals that he wasn't all that bothered about conquering Stirling that summer, he felt an urge to apologise to his son – the first time King Edward had ever felt inclined to apologise to anyone.

In the thrall of this unfamiliar compulsion, he got up earlier than usual and went round to Ned's tent. Servants were busy tidying up after a messy binge, working between young men dormant where they'd dropped. Ned was not amongst them. The King was told the prince hadn't slept that night. As the sun rose he'd gone to join the woodmen.

The sound of the axe was in the air. King Edward followed it until he entered a glade dominated by an enormous beech tree. Taking turns with another axeman, Ned was chopping it down.

Edward remained in the cover of the trees, watching. The boy was impressively strong and graceful, his movements beautifully co-ordinated. The woodmen stood at a distance with some bleary-eyed, ribbon-strewn revellers, observing him with admiration.

Ned knows what he's doing, King Edward thought proudly. Was there ever a time I had that expertise? All those expertises? Digging, laying bricks, cutting timber, essential manual skills. Why have I scorned to learn these crafts myself?

Ned called to his fellow worker to stop swinging his axe.

"Stand away!" he said. "I'll finish it off."

Unwillingly, the woodman retreated. It seemed the man had something to say but he'd thought better of it.

Ned attacked the tree with strong, sustained blows. It began to creak and sway. As the woodmen backed further off, one or two held up warning hands. A rough voice cried out: "I told you to watch out, Your Highness."

The great beech crashed directly onto where Ned was standing, shaking the earth. A fork low down on the main trunk slotted exactly over him, saving his life. The prince stepped away, picking leaves out of his hair and laughing.

This was how fortune often favoured Ned – by gaps appearing in ill-fortune. But although, at this stage, he had never had an accident, he was the undoubted cause of many.

"You were lucky. That was a close shave," the King said in the way of a prelude to an apology, taking Ned's arm as he led him away from the glade.

"Dear, dear Ned, I'm very sorry about the other day. I shouldn't chastise you in front of other people. Please find it in your heart to forgive me."

"I forgive you, father," came the ready, genial reply.

"Thank you, son," Edward said. "While we're talking, may I say how I'd like more help and understanding from you? It isn't really a criticism. We should be working together as a team. That way we'll learn from each other. I think it's so important."

And he embraced his son, kissing him on both cheeks.

"Of course I think it's important, sir," Ned replied as he gently disengaged – broad, handsome features beaming in the afterglow of his exertions. "Does all this mean Piers doesn't have to leave?"

The apology in the forest was not private. Wherever the King went, others had to follow, ears flapping. Ned's standing in the English army rose from nothing to something when the news got out that the King had said he was sorry. Anyone able to extract an apology from old Longshanks must have a lot of guts. There was hope for Ned yet – but, on the other hand, every English soldier could see a crisis looming as a result. The English army had waded through blood and ash to penetrate deep into Scotland, hostile territory, destroying everything in its path. Now it was in danger of isolation, its lines of communication and supply threatened. To have its commander's fundamental personality overturned by a family problem weakened its position. Ned had made his father no longer invincible.

The camp became a sad, quiet place as rumours thickened. Soldiers crept around thinking the worst. Everyone noticed that the apology had not relieved the King's dark mood.

William Wild was summoned most nights to attend Edward in drinking-bouts to kill the pain of depression. As Christendom's greatest warrior sat moodily pouring Bordeaux down his throat, the Irishman was forced to listen to hours of slurred sentimentality oozing out of the wreckage. Much of it involved Eleanor, Edward's dead Castilian queen.

"As I said to Ned, it's all very well you objecting to having your love-life arranged for you, but bear in mind your wonderful mother," the old man keened one midnight. "Ours was a dynastic union if ever there was one – she was only eight and I had to wait years before I could go near her – but I adored that woman all her life."

Vague, mute smiles were employed by the Irishman to deal with Edward's maudlin ramblings. He nodded slightly and cleared his throat, knowing it was a *session*.

Edward plunged on. "Once I'd clapped eyes on that girl no other female ever attracted me. I can't claim to have been faithful ever after, Willy – to be faithful you have to be tempted to stray. I was simply never tempted. I was a one-woman man. You know what she was like. You were in love with her yourself."

William Wild dipped his head in a gesture of qualified agreement.

"Sort of," he murmured. "In a manner of speaking."

"You'd have done anything for her, wouldn't you?"

This time, a fractional movement of the lower lip was enough to signal assent.

"When she brought you to me in Acre you were on your last legs, pulled out of the harbour, beaten up to within an inch of your life," Edward reminisced. "But even half-dead you could talk, Willy. You had the gift of the gab."

"I was in a lot of trouble."

"Wasn't she lovely?" Edward sighed. "And kind. She could see good in you like you can see good in me. We all need people who can see good in us."

The Irishman inhaled the aroma of his wine, filling his lungs, sitting up straighter, then emptied the vessel in one go.

"I've always admired your decision not to take second-best and find a woman of your own, Willy. You're safer sticking to whores."

William Wild held out his cup for more wine.

"When I married again, Willy, I thought there was a chance it might be just as good as it was with Eleanor. Lucky with one arranged marriage, I thought – let's try another. You can still fall in love at sixty. But I didn't. I couldn't. Eleanor still rules our hearts, eh, Willy? You can say as far as love is concerned you and I have had it, haven't we? It's all over."

No gesture of assent was needed. The King's tears did it all.

Few treaties with the French had been as complex as that signed at Montreuil four years before. In a double contract, the grieving widower, King Edward, was to marry Margaret, sister of Philip of France, and Prince Edward, his son, was to have Isabella, the French king's daughter.

Ned now had a stepmother young enough to be his sister, and a three-year-old half-brother, Thomas, next in line to the throne after him.

"You don't regret your decision never to love again?" Edward said, leaning forward, blood-red wine streaking his hoary beard as if he'd been hit in the mouth. "Dying childless is hard."

"The instinct to repeat myself has always evaded me," was the reply, delivered coolly over the rim of the cup. "With the world as it is, what's the point of only living for the next generation? That's why we never get anything done. Never fulfil ourselves. Living for the kids is a trap."

Edward frowned and scratched his head, then laughed uncertainly. "You've lost me. But I shouldn't pry into your private feelings. You sound bitter. Eleanor always thought you'd make a wonderful father."

"Why, I don't know. All I seem to do is talk."

"That's not so, my old friend," Edward reproved him with a fond, crooked grin. "You know how to act."

The Irishman glanced into the King's flushed features, searching for any suggestion of irony. Edward laughed.

"Come, Willy, I'd never accuse you of being an actor. I was remembering how quick you were sucking poison out of that knife-wound of mine."

"If you'd died, the rest of the army in Acre would have torn me to pieces. As your bodyguard, it was my fault the Assassin got through."

"The point I'm making is you're not all talk. You saved my life. Not only that, you proved your selflessness."

"Well, what I had to do, and where I had to do it on your person, made it more appropriate for your wife to take the credit," the Irishman said. "Besides, it made a better story, and she deserved some recognition. How many other women went on crusade with their husbands – and had babies out there?"

The full force of this memory was too much for the old king – with tears flowing into his tangled, grey beard, he saw glittering, cruel deserts, ornate ceremonies of death, the orgiastic sharing out of plunder, sun-blotting flights of vultures, broken towers smeared with blood, ruined citadels, fallen churches, and, holding the centre of this ghastly vision of defeat, his human oasis, Eleanor.

After leaving the King, William Wild went to join his friend Gualberto beside the river. Sultry from a hot summer's day, the night air moved in a slight breeze off the water.

"Well, I suppose I should explain what happened to me so long ago in Acre," William Wild said. "Thanks for keeping quiet."

"Does the King know?"

"I've always been honest with him."

"Well, he must love you. Harbouring a deserter from the Order is no laughing matter," Gualberto said, gingerly laying his injured leg flat. "You don't have to explain anything if you don't want to."

"No, I need to tell you."

"Perhaps I don't need to hear. You've done very well, Theo – watching your comings and goings with the King has made me envious – he obviously thinks a lot of you."

The Irishman picked up a pebble and threw it into the river. "Let me tell you something about the King," he said with a lop-sided grin. "I'm his friend – according to his plan for having a friend he's not supposed to have – someone from the other side of the fence. He adored his wife. According to his plan it was best to fall in love with the woman he was forced to marry. That way he could not be defeated by her. Every move he makes is calculated for its effect on his kingship. An artist of his power, he does everything by design. His only natural, impulsive action is to wreak havoc if the design falls apart. Then look out. He's a killer."

Gualberto looked shocked. "This sounds like ingratitude!" he remonstrated. "Don't you like him?"

"Possibly I don't like him, much – but I love him. I'm able to do that because his plans fail. When he's picking up the pieces, then he's a man." The Irishman threw another pebble. "Get out of the Templars while you can," he said with sudden gravity. "If we're talking about friends – they don't have any left."

"Unlike you, my friend, vows bind me," Gualberto said coldly.

"Vows made to a corrupt body like the Templars are invalid."

"Mine was made to God."

" Vows are made to the self. Selves change. Look at us. Is the old self the same as the young self?"

Gualberto laughed. "Still the same old Theo chasing his tail. Nothing is sacred except the sacredness of nothing? You still believe that? You see, I haven't forgotten everything we used to talk about."

William Wild took this as his cue to bring his old comrade up to date with his doings.

CHAPTER FOUR

You never really knew me, Gualberto. Nobody did. In those days, I never knew myself. When you're looking for God you've no idea who you are. Those who seek the omnipotent make themselves impotent.

Talkers and tinkers – that's the blood I come from, frequently spilt. My family drove me mad. They never had the power to question their misery. The priests of Ireland make a special case for simplicity of mind. They're castles of ignorance with death on guard in the gatehouse.

When you and I met as novices in Cyprus, I'd already spent many years on the road, searching for the undertruth. I wasn't alone. There were flocks of penitents, punishing themselves for being the dregs of the universe. In all the wayside camps, I picked up fragments of thought – the offhand chat of religious men. On the edge of the firelight, I listened, hoping for some help.

Unlike you, Gualberto, I didn't become a Poor Knight to make a living. In Ireland it had occurred to me there might be something in a warrior religion that made sense. After all, we men spend most of our lives fighting. We're expected to go out and get killed. What chance does the meek Jesus have when all his followers adore the sword?

I became a Templar to take a closer look at Islam.

Why not go over to the enemy entirely? Lend my sword to the Sultan of Egypt? That was not my purpose. I wanted to get near – but not too near. I'm a green, rather misty man from a green, rather misty country. The desert is not my home.

In case I might be captured by the Arabs I went so far as to have myself circumcised. For a full-grown man, this is not to be recommended, believe me. Staining my skin with walnut-juice, I went to Mecca. But you must understand, I was only *looking.*

What did I encounter? Hordes of half-starved pilgrims punishing themselves for being the dregs of the universe. They were exactly the same as Christian pilgrims. Some mornings I woke up and I wasn't sure whether I was in Europe or Arabia.

Although it was a rough journey, my only serious trouble involved reading. The heaviest item in my bag was Averroes' *The Incoherence of the Incoherence.*

I was caught by the religious police skimming over a few of the more difficult sections in a public place, but I managed to talk my way out of it.

In Mecca I saw Templars moving around without any attempt at disguise. I saw them standing in the sacred fields of sacrifice amongst the lambs, towering over men making their most important act of religion.

This impressed me.

I didn't imagine they were unifiers of the two great religions, but it occurred to me no Muslim could stroll around Rome with such freedom.

Gualberto, I believed I was close to something I had been looking for, this undertruth I've mentioned. Those confident, powerful men, so at ease, so fearless, right at the heart of the enemy, had a secret I wished to share.

I can see from your expression I must have mentioned this to you in the old days. I'm sorry if you find it annoying. As a child, I was very alarmed by the world I was born into, and what I was expected to believe. I had an uncle who lived in the absolute centre of Ireland. He told me the undertruth is never revealed. He said any truth shown in a flash isn't worth the shine on a harlot's bangle.

The goodness in the mind's onion-world is found by peeling.

Oh, God, did I tell you that as well?

Forgive me. Age writes its own book and keeps going back over the pages.

Further downstream, Ned was stripped to the waist, helping Scots prisoners build a weir by the light of the moon. As they worked, they sang.

Without the Gaelic language, Ned could only hum – but he did this loudly.

"No wonder people doubt he'll ever make a king," Gualberto said as he watched the scene with the Irishman. "He's far too good-natured. But all this mixing with the hoi-polloi won't do. D'you think it helps him forget who he is?"

"No," William Wild replied. "He's more at ease with who he is than most people."

"Then let me re-phrase that – *what* he is."

"They're the same thing. Who he is is what he is."

"Then how can he behave the way he does?" Gualberto asked. "Look at him!"

Ned was showing off, carrying a big flat stone over his head, threatening to splash the exhausted prisoners for a joke. Overseers stood by, arms folded, whips dangling, as the Scots hesitated, heads down, unsure and embarrassed.

"Alright, Gualberto, let's take a few steps back, and examine his behaviour. What is he doing, exactly?"

Laughing, Ned stopped his horseplay and tossed the stone onto the pile making the weir.

"He's having fun with them?" Gualberto offered. "But he doesn't realise they're not having fun with him."

"Let me give you an interpretation – one you might not grasp at first, but bear with me," the Irishman said, getting to his feet and beckoning his friend to follow him down the bank towards the site for the weir. "Unlike us, the fortunate ones, Ned's life was effectively over before it began."

"How so?"

"The last of his older brothers, Alfonso, died ten years before Ned was born. For a decade, England had no heir."

A smile flicked across Gualberto's lined face. "The English might have had a king called Alfonso? That would have been popular."

"When Alfonso was born, an elder brother was still alive, so he wasn't expected to be king," William Wild explained. "His Spanish mother was allowed to name him. The first male child of the marriage was a John, after the King's grandfather, the second a Henry, after his father, then Edward gave up and left it to Eleanor to name them. Anyway, that's immaterial. Ned was the fourth son, all the others having died. He was born when his mother was thirty-eight. He saved the day for Edward."

"Lucky for the queen," Gualberto mused. "The marriage might have been annulled if she hadn't provided an heir to survive him."

"That's where you're wrong. Edward would never have got rid of Eleanor. His plan for being in love *for ever* was too successful. He'd completely convinced his heart. But for ten years it seemed hopeless. Nothing but girls."

Gualberto looked across to where Ned was lifting up another stone, muscles and tendons in his broad shoulders flexing impressively.

Covered in mud, his hair bedraggled, he seemed happy.

"Look at that physique. He's a god," the Irishman mused. "For over-the-hill parents, he was a divine gift."

Gualberto made a sound of thoughtful but slightly puzzled assent, then made a remark that women believed having children late was hazardous. "Hidden weaknesses and flaws in the child seem to be the main concern," he added.

The Irishman let this comment ride without a response, allowing Ned to confound it by straightening his superb arms beneath the dripping stone, pectoral and stomach muscles bulging.

Picking up the cue of the silence, Gualberto laughed quietly.

"So much for the opinion of women! But why d'you say his life was over before it began?"

"Can you imagine the fuss that was made of him?"

"I can!"

"The saviour of the nation. In many ways, from first cry he was a king, with his own mystique."

"You're overstating the case, as usual. He was just a baby."

"He didn't have to do anything...just *be*," William Wild continued. "Future power was his being."

Gualberto threw his hands in the air, delighted with the idea.

"He believes this?"

"He doesn't have to. He *is* it."

"Doesn't he take any notice of history? Murdered kings lie everywhere you look!"

"He drank power with his mother's milk. He's relaxed inside himself. He doesn't care about things outside. He lives in the cave of his own feelings. Any emotion or whim he has possesses absolute validity."

"Ah, now I know why you understand him so well. You're exactly the same."

"No, I'm not. I'm aware of all my imperfections. Ned has a sublime indifference to his. In a way, he has great integrity."

"I find his boyish enthusiasms heart-warming, in some ways," Gualberto observed. "Think of the saints. They were like that, essentially. Look at him now, pitching in with the lads, lending a hand."

"Ned doesn't help anyone," William Wild replied. "Ned simply does what his spirit suggests."

"And what he wants to do is always unprincely and mundane,"

Gualberto pondered. "D'you think seeking the mundane is a form of protest against his destiny?"

"No. It's simply what he is. Ned is mundanity elevated beyond its natural sphere. Kingly behaviour isn't what his father does, or any other king – it's whatever Ned does."

"Well, I think that's fascinating," Gualberto said, "if a little frightening in a future ruler. Are you the only one who's noticed this distortion of the soul – for that's what it sounds like?"

William Wild paused, shocked by the use of the phrase. It stopped him assembling an answer. Having never expressed himself so clearly and forcibly on the subject of Ned's mind to anyone before, he couldn't be certain why the pattern of the idea had suddenly emerged.

The Irishman lightened his tone.

"Ned's the only one ever to undermine his father's confidence," he said. "Take it from me – that's an achievement."

"You didn't help by stuffing the boy's head full of odd ideas by any chance?"

"He never quite got the hang of thought."

Ned saw them standing on the bank and tossed the stone he was carrying into the water, grinning as it made a huge splash. As he waded out, step by step, he adjusted his expression. By the time he was beside them, his face was hang-dog.

"Can't sleep for worrying about my friend, Piers," he said, flinging himself down on the grass. "Sending him to Dundee with no escort! The road gets cut off by Scots ten times a day. If he gets caught, and they realise who he is, they'll crucify him."

"Your Highness has been helping with the construction of the weir," Gualberto observed with the air of a practised sycophant, some irony nevertheless filtering through his tone. "Was that interesting for you?"

"Working alongside those fellows was dismal," Ned replied with a grimace. "They lack a sense of humour."

"From what I understand, they're all unredeemed hostages," Gualberto said, maintaining his obsequiousness. "Their tight-fisted families refuse to pay ransom for them, so it looks as though they'll all end up being hanged."

Ned snorted a half-laugh, flicking his golden hair back from his eyes. "Well, that's very mean of their families," he quipped with a grin.

"The ruin of their country has incensed the Scots," Gualberto continued. "To them such wanton destruction seems reckless, cruel, and ridiculous. What good can come of it? Loathing the English as they do, some families won't pay ransom, even if it means losing their loved ones. Others have had their property destroyed and their money stolen. They can't pay."

Ned looked hard at Gualberto, annoyed by both the deadly calm of the overview and the probing question. "The day-to-day workings of the hostage system don't concern me," he sniffed absently, his eyes roaming over the other side of the river.

"Do we take it you agree with the policy of reducing Scotland to a desert?" Gualberto persisted, his air of deference still intact behind a courteous smile. "How can that benefit the English? Some might argue it doesn't make sense."

"Oh, you Templars know everything, don't you?" Ned murmured, lifting his lip in a sneer.

A voice hailed sentries on the other side of the river.

A horseman emerged onto the cleared ground on the opposite bank. As he started fording the river, well-placed dents in his shield were visible in the moonlight.

"Is that you, dear Ned?" he called. "Have you been waiting for me?"

Ned leapt to his feet, face alight with joy as he ran down to the river's edge. "Yes, it's me, Piers! I've been here for hours!"

"Oh, what a time I've had," Gaveston shouted across with a laugh, urging his horse through the water. "Thousands of Scots to deal with. Between here and the coast they're out in force. Try as I might, I just couldn't get through."

CHAPTER FIVE

The unauthorised return of Piers Gaveston was disobedience on the grand scale. Everyone in camp was astonished by the Gascon's heedless arrogance. The veterans muttered this was yet more proof Longshanks was losing his grip.

The excuse Gaveston gave was a blatant lie – the road to Dundee was not in the hands of the Scots and everyone knew it. King Edward had either to swallow his pride and allow the offender to remain, or throw him in prison. Execution – the proper penalty for such flagrant disobedience as far as the army was concerned – was recognised to be impossible. Gaveston was the King's ward and Ned's heart-friend.

Merely sending him away was no longer an option. He would always come back, believing himself protected from the King's wrath. If he was to be separated from Ned, then the sentence of exile would have to be formal and legal. In order to avoid this extremity – which would be an admission to the world in general how serious the matter had become – Edward decided to outmanoeuvre rather than force the issue.

The King was aware of his own lack of imagination in human relations. His people were a mystery to him, except in terms of his power over them. A subject is not a psyche. The niceties of battlefields, law courts, and tax systems came more easily to him than mutual feelings. Again, he couldn't bring himself to consult anyone but William Wild. That way the Church would be kept out of it. Religion would only effeminise the issue.

Despite his recent failure in the wilderness, the Irishman found himself entrusted to find the means of manoeuvre. He knew this time his counsel must enable Edward to make a comeback as a strong military leader and concentrate on winning the war. He was told by Edward to put the dilemma in its proper place – to establish it as a light matter removed from any parity with war and serious politics.

William Wild went away and thought hard. He went for long walks, made notes, read a few books, tried out ideas in his head, slept on them, wiped the slate clean, started again, honed a few ideas down, put them in order. He decided the King was wrong. Ned's friendship with Gaveston was not a minor problem compared with war or serious politics. It was more important.

After intense intellectual effort, he gave advice both subtle and psychologically sound. When Edward first heard it mooted, he was incredulous. What kind of king would abandon the main objective of a war because a boy had not emerged from a childhood crush?

The Irishman argued that Edward's ageing mind had fallen into a weakness of thought. Ned's feelings and Stirling Castle were joined together. If the siege happened to be unsuccessful it would suggest Ned could never change. Edward should work round the great Scottish fortress and work round Ned.

The conversations between Edward and the Irishman were long and arduous. Several times, the adviser was thrown out with his advice. The King thought about bringing in his best officers of state to pick their brains on the issue, but they were all Churchmen, likely to run off to the Vatican with the whole story. Ned's infatuation would be buried under a mountain of Scripture, papal bulls and moral interference.

After days and nights spent in discussion, the Irishman's opinion prevailed. Edward covered his decision by saying recent military moves had decreased Stirling's strategic value. An announcement was made on 23rd July. The campaign to conquer Scotland had been totally restructured. The King was to take the cream of the army northwards (including Piers Gaveston) on a wide punitive sweep, bringing the Scots to open battle if possible, laying siege to towns and castles, destroying the harvest so the Scots would have nothing to eat in the coming winter.

The prince was to remain at base camp, in charge of supplies and administration.

This task was no sinecure. Until now other people had done the donkey work for Ned, leaving him as a gilded figurehead. But left with only a garrison force of two thousand to protect it, the camp at Saint Johnstone was vulnerable to attack by the Scots. Keeping it intact was crucial to the survival of the English army.

"Give them both hard jobs, real jobs, and they'll have to stop thinking about each other," William Wild had suggested. "Let both of them risk their necks."

"Ned's sure to let me down. He'll lose Saint Johnstone for me," moaned Edward. "

"Put him to the test. Give him real authority. Make him work."

"But he doesn't know what work is. He'll always expect other people to do it for him. You'll have to stay behind with him, Willy."

"My place is by your side."

Edward's eyes suddenly gleamed. A mirthful twitch shook the loose curls of his beard. "I've had a better idea. Instead of pushing Piers away, I'll bring him closer *to me*. I'll have the best sword in the army as my bodyguard."

The English army advanced the twenty miles north-east to the port of Arbroath and took it without a fight on 30th July. While the wrecking and rapine went on, King Edward strolled along the sands, chatting to Gaveston. At frequent intervals, messengers came with news of the absence of treasure and goods in Arbroath. The inhabitants had moved out weeks ago, taking everything with them. The old man would nod to indicate he'd understood, but make no comment, continuing his pursuit of the Gascon's mind in the manner William Wild had recommended. "Trivia. That's the way. Trap him into making a personal commitment to you," he'd recommended. "He's got the mind of a playboy."

"These wavy ridges the tides make on the sand appear every day," the King said carefully, bending down to stroke a delicate ridge of glittering particles. "But they're never still. They change. What d'you think of that?"

"Very little, sire."

"You see how the gulls ride the air so effortlessly? Would you like to be able to fly?"

"I've never thought about it, sire."

"They say the influence of the moon determines the state of the tide but no one knows how it's done. Would you like to know how it's done?"

"If it would help you."

"Me? Where knowing things is concerned, I appear to be beyond help."

At this ambiguity, Gaveston allowed his expression of baffled but polite interest to waver.

"The moon does affect me," he ventured to say. "When it's full, it makes me feel quite odd."

"We'd better keep an eye on that, then."

A messenger on a lathered horse raced over the sand to tell the King Brechin Castle ten miles up the road was invested with Scottish troops. When the King's herald had demanded the stronghold be surrendered, a defiant reply had been received.

The King nodded and broke a beautifully sculptured ridge in the wave-line with his ironshod toe.

"Good. Our siege engines need the exercise," he declared, releasing his hold on trivia. "I've got a new heavy-duty trebuchet that needs trying out."

The Gascon's eyes lit up and he gave a little yell of delight.

"I love trebuchets!" he enthused.

King Edward put an arm around his shoulder and gave it a bone-crunching but affectionate squeeze.

Sir Thomas Maule stood on top of the tower of Brechin Castle and watched the English army fanning out after crossing the South Esk river. He believed the fortress to be impregnable and was confident that it could withstand a long siege. Like all the other Scots leaders, he had expected the English to move south-west against Stirling, not north against smaller targets. He understood why Arbroath had been secured, for its port, but Brechin? What was there in Forfar to draw Edward so far away from his base?

All that summer, Maule had thrived on a diet of anti-English jokes, many of which he had made up himself. Lately, his favourite theme concerned the antics of Neddy and Perrot, a pair of fey lads who constantly defied King Edward's authority. In many of these comic constructs, the duo secretly fought for the Scots, admired for their gigantic genitalia. The most recent product of Maule's imagination ascribed the change in the English master-plan to Neddy forcing his indulgent old dad to go north so his Gascon boy-friend could eat *phallus impudicus,* a highly-prized fungus which thrived in the forest of Monthreathmont.

English barons with heralds rode up ahead of the main army to deliver another demand for surrender. Maule dealt with this from slits in the lower gatehouse, making the plenipotentiaries wade the ditch to listen to him. First of all, he told a few of his jokes, including the one just described, then issued a ringing defiance which made the Englishmen wince.

"You tell that murderous old bastard from me, Brechin Castle is a jagged stool lodged up his arse which he'll never be able to pass," Maule thundered, "and if the stupid whore hasn't got the wit to work that one out, tell him to ask his son and his love-mate. Those dung-punchers will know what I'm talking about."

For the rest of the day, the besieging army established its positions around the castle. Maule watched as the artillery train brought up the siege engines and parked them out of arrow-shot. He expected some form of riposte to his insult before the light went that day, but nothing happened. The English sorted themselves out and relaxed. He saw them taking walks along the river.

As the dusk came and the fires glowed in a great ellipse around the castle, Maule couldn't help feeling disappointed at the lack of an immediate response.

A sortie on his defences before nightfall would have set the tone for the next couple of months – a sharp, bloody repulse teaching Edward a lesson. Brechin would survive a six-month siege. The siege engine wasn't made that could batter down its immensely thick walls.

But he hoped Edward wouldn't give up too easily, thereby denying him sport. For a few months there could be great war entertainment for the Scots. The siege wasn't likely to last beyond October because the campaigning season was brief in these far northern climes. Then the English army would have to go into winter quarters, which would mean a humiliating return to Saint Johnstone, leaving Brechin undefeated.

The next morning Sir Thomas Maule was up early, hoping for some action. He was surprised to see the enemy already drawn up, banners fluttering. Yesterday they had marched the twelve miles from Arbroath, the dust of the road on their backs, shambling at leisure rather than striding. Now they looked washed and tarted up, as if awakened to the seriousness of the challenge.

Sir Thomas Maule was a far-sighted man. When out hawking, he could spot quarry a mile away. The viewing platform erected beside the new slinging-machine the English had brought with them – he calculated its throwing-arm must be at least fifty feet long – contained a crowd of dignitaries having breakfast. The detested Edward Longshanks was clearly visible, towering above the rest, and – could he believe his luck? – beside him were two fair-complexioned youths arm in arm.

Never a man to comfort his enemies, except by challenging them to accept the bitter truth about themselves, Maule, by his savage insult, delivered conscientiously by the English envoys, inadvertently saved the Prince of Wales. If Edward had not been in such a frenzy against Sir Thomas's insult when Ned appeared in Brechin with the supply train from Saint Johnstone – in absolute defiance of his father's orders – the tigerish, protective love which surged up in the King would never have been aroused. As it was, Maule had triggered an explosion of paternal feeling, even when Ned's first words on seeing his father were: "Is Piers around?"

Instead of blaming Ned for making the insult so potent, Edward ceremoniously brought the two youths together, re-uniting them in a show of his favour in full view of the castle. Also, while the Bishop of Chester was blessing the great trebuchet – including the counterweight made from lead off the local church roof – Edward told him to give a benediction to the boys as well.

He then gave Piers the privilege of christening the mighty siege-engine.

Hector, the name of the young squire drowned in the Earn, came immediately to the Gascon's mind.

Edward then swore a great oath that he would catapult Sir Thomas Maule's head over his own castle walls as soon as it became available.

CHAPTER SIX

Sir Thomas Maule was kept waiting while the great war-machine was being blessed. From dawn till noon, he sat in a chair on top of his tower, cauldrons of oil in a permanent rolling boil either side of him, watching the rituals.

"The English are doing what they do best," he said to an aide at his side, "farting about and dancing round their vices."

During a pause in the pageantry, Edward's head of artillery, Jan de Groot, was told to increase the size of Hector's first projectile. De Groot – who was also the designer of the giant sling – protested that the load would break the arm.

Edward told him *his* arm would be broken if he didn't obey.

While a suitable missile was being fashioned by stonemasons, an apology was sent to Maule for keeping him waiting.

"My lord king offers single combat between his best man and yours for the sake of some entertainment while we're preparing ourselves," the herald added. "Do you have anyone who can stand up to Piers Gaveston? The King knows you've heard of him."

Maule called his best warriors to him for consultation. He found their responses to the challenge matched his. Although Gaveston was the butt of everyone's scorn, held in contempt *as a man*, no one dared fight him.

Scots don't fight sexual witches, was Maule's reply to the King, we fuck them or burn them.

Hector didn't hurl his first stone until mid-afternoon. It weighed two hundred pounds. Jan de Groot watched on his knees, a prayer on his lips, as the long arm was released, the counterweight crashing down. All his mathematics and knowledge of timber under stress told him the arm must break, but it didn't.

The missile whirled three hundred and fifty yards in a perfect low trajectory, smashing into the gatehouse a man's height from the ground. The wall shook. Dust arose. As it cleared, Sir Thomas Maule came out of a little door beside the drawbridge, a towel over his shoulder. He examined the point of impact, turned and looked pityingly at the enemy, shook his head, then wiped the wall down.

The defenders cheered, laughed and applauded.

Sir Thomas took a bow, then sauntered back through the door.

The stonemasons' waggon delivered the second missile to the artillery team, who rolled it into the sling pouch and adjusted the ropes.

As the ballast-box of lead crashed to the ground, up went the arm again. The ball of solid rock flew through the air, striking the wall twenty yards to the left of the first impact, and five yards higher. Before the dust had settled, Sir Thomas appeared again, waving his towel. This time he had to clamber up an inclined breastwork to reach the spot. While elaborately wiping down the stones he shook his head and sighed very loudly. On all the parapets above him, his men went mad with delight, dancing and waving their weapons.

Sir Thomas nonchalantly picked his way back down the breastwork. As he dawdled back to the door, hand on hip, he whirled the towel around his head.

Jan de Groot was summoned to attend the King.

"You're never going to create a breach if you don't keep hitting the same place," Edward said. "Can't you be more accurate?"

"It will take us some time to get the feel of the machine, sire," de Groot replied. "We need to establish the distance pattern."

"And those walls are very thick," Ned offered brightly.

The King turned to Gaveston.

"Any advice you can offer, Piers?"

"I don't like sieges, sire," Gaveston replied. "I'd much rather give battle out in the open. But if we're stuck with a siege, well, a frontal assault would be my choice."

The King appeared to give this proposal deep thought, walking up and down and stroking his beard.

"You're absolutely right, of course," he said eventually, "but we're in no great hurry. I have to think of the casualties. I don't want to waste my men."

The strategic discussion petered out, giving Jan de Groot his chance to explain how a supply of standardised missiles which would follow identical trajectories had been prepared for Hector at the previously reckoned maximum weight. But the King's genius had proved this weight to be an underestimation. However, with the short time they had at their disposal, the stonemasons hadn't been able to produce uniform missiles at the new maximum.

"As I don't propose to make a fool of myself trying to batter down the entire curtain wall," Edward declared, "you can tell them to take all the time they need. No one's going anywhere – especially Sir Thomas Maule."

Later that evening a three-day holiday was declared for the English army. Although a state of alert was to be maintained, the men were encouraged to find recreation.

In the fine August weather, the men played games, sported, swam in the river, revelled and made music. As all the Scots in the area had either fled or taken refuge in Brechin Castle, it meant soldiers were free to go the few miles east to Montrose and enjoy the five-mile beach between Scurdle Ness and Saint Cyrus. Horse and foot races were held along the sands.

Edward took the opportunity to toothcomb the heavy costs of war with the Bishop of Chester, Walter Langton, who doubled up as treasurer of the Exchequer. They were joined by McHunter who came up from Saint Johnstone with offers of credit from Frescobaldi, an Italian bank linked to the Templars. Calculations and account-making went deep into the night.

Meanwhile, Sir Thomas Maule sat sweating on his tower between the cauldrons, towel around his neck, waiting. His pipers played beside him. His drummers drummed. Though his banners hung limp in the hot, still air, his heart remained high. Let the English work, play, or bugger each other, he said to his men, they will never bring us down.

Part of the King's new policy with his son was to trust him to carry out important tasks. On the last day of the holiday, Ned was sent to check if the stonemasons had produced the right munitions for Hector so the bombardment could start up again. Jan de Groot was down with a sick fever and couldn't accompany the prince. Ned wandered over to the stonemason's yard, took off his shirt, picked up a hammer and chisel and started working alongside them. The men, under pressure, were nervous and nonplussed. No one had the wit or courage to tell the Prince of Wales what he must do – that every projectile had to be exactly the same.

Instead, the stonemasons let him continue, keeping an eye on the missile he was working on so it could be put to one side.

Ned's enthusiasm for the job mounted as he worked. Most men would have got bored and tired with such hard labour, but his interest grew as the sphere took shape. He insisted it should be weighed and measured in exactly the same manner as the other missiles. It was at this stage someone should have spoken up. Some optical defect made the prince incapable of envisioning the perfect sphere. His missile was detectably egg-shaped.

When the time came to transport the missiles to the trebuchet, Ned walked alongside the ammunition sledge, his hand proudly on his handiwork having carefully scratched a cross on the surface to identify it. Later that night, the foreman of the masons tried to explain to the delirious Jan de Groot what had happened, recommending that the prince's missile be removed. Convinced he'd relieved himself of the responsibility, the foreman then withdrew to enjoy the few hours left of the holiday.

At the recommencement of the siege, all the missiles launched by Hector struck within a circle of five-yard diameter. King Edward was delighted. His only displeasure came from Sir Thomas Maule's antics. Doggedly, in spite of the new accuracy, he came out of the little door and wiped down the wall after each shot.

The bombardment worked very slowly. The structural damage appeared slight, but it accrued. Because it became possible to guess where the missile would bounce to afterwards, Sir Thomas became increasingly bold in his defiance, not retreating to the little door after each shot but standing closer and closer to the target area, insolently guiding the ball down with waves of his towel.

The importance of the occasion brought Jan de Groot from his bed of pain. Shivering with fever, affected by double-vision, he stood beside Hector, his heart gladdened by the consistency of the machine's performance now it had the right ammunition.

As his missile was rolled into the sling, the Prince of Wales strutted over, put his foot on it, turned to his father and announced this one was made by his own hand. He asked if he could have the honour of firing it himself, which was granted.

Ned's ball flew into the air. At the end of its trajectory a touch of outswing developed, deceiving Sir Thomas so he was caught, unawares and splattered against the wall like a mosquito.

In this manner, at an arm's-length of fifty feet, Ned slew his first man.

After the fall of Brechin, Edward marched northwards bringing fire and sword to small places. The tonic effect of Ned's initiation into life-taking was felt during the army's rampage through Moray and Banff, reinforcing the old king's opinion that it was only the lack of primal experiences that had held back his son's development. Kincardine, Aberdeen, Macduff, Elgin, Kinloss, the villages and settlements of the mountains and lakes to Boat-of-Garten in upper Strathspey, all witnessed deeds of blood performed by the Prince of Wales, not in combat, but in common butchery. Under his father's approving eye, Ned went up to his elbows in blood.

Fired by his son's progress, hope regenerated, King Edward decided not to withdraw south of the border at the end of the campaigning season. Instead, he would keep up the pressure on the enemy by maintaining the English army in Scotland right through the winter. If no surrender was received by spring, the siege of Stirling would open with the daffodils.

Turning south at Mortlach on 6th October, the army headed for winter quarters. The spoiling of Kildrummie, Fettercairn, Dundee, Scone, Gask and Dunblane took Edward to Dunfermline on 5th November, where the army settled down. Ned stayed at the new camp for three weeks, then set out for Saint Johnstone. His faults had not been alluded to since Brechin.

The friendship with Gaveston ended up not only intact but stronger for being protected by the King himself.

As Ned embraced his father in farewell during the first snowstorm of the winter, the old man's frame was shaking, whether from cold or emotion, Ned could not tell.

"It will be hard living up here until the spring," Edward whispered into his son's ear, "but it means I'll have time to think over what I've learnt these past few months. We are different, you and I, but our blood's closeness has power. Half my life was spent in great, wasteful foolishness, yet I denied you a few years of the same. I've been a very mean old man. Now I understand how you must be allowed to be yourself in order to be a king. One cannot exist without the other. From this day forward we act together in all things."

When the prince arrived at Saint Johnstone, William Wild was given leave to return to England for three months. He reached his small estate at Boldwood in the Wye Valley on 6th December, relieved to catch sight of chimney smoke from his riverside house rising in the frozen air.

Initially, it proved difficult to purge Scottish political and military affairs from his mind and enter into the life of the farm, which was slow-moving at that time of year. Valmai, his Welsh concubine, had given birth to identical twin daughters during his absence – his first offspring. Valmai was an imaginative, energetic woman who knew William Wild's history: wanting to create a legitimising aura over her offspring, she had one child christened Eleanor, the other, Leonora, the Spanish form of the name. At first, William Wild considered this an enormous impudence but later grew to like the idea.

At Christmas-time, Gualberto came to visit on his way to South Wales on treasury business, bringing news of the activities of the independent Scottish rebel William Wallace in Strathearn. With the English presence in Scotland now entrenched throughout the year, a *modus vivendi* treaty was being edged into existence, which Wallace was threatening to wreck, in spite of the willingness of the other Scottish leaders to compromise.

On a sharp, clear morning, as the entire household rode along the Gloucestershire bank of the river towards Tintern Abbey to attend the Christmas mass, William Wild looked up at the steep, forested slopes of Wales rising beyond the opposite side, meditating aloud on frontiers.

"It occurs to me, Gualberto, all these barriers, though real, and fought over, owe their existence to the idea of what God cannot do," he mused. "Both William Wallace and the King should be told this."

"And what can God not do?"

"For a start, he cannot impose limits upon himself – whereas we can. We take oaths to do or not to do, we make promises, we obey restrictive laws. We pour our life-blood into making borders. This river, for instance, is only a drain but it means more than that on a piece of treaty-paper."

Gualberto leant forward in the saddle and covered his ears. "On my way to mass, I refuse to listen to anything that taxes my brain," he said. "Today, God can do anything."

"He cannot change Himself. He cannot make the sum of the angles of a triangle be not two right angles…"

"Alright, alright! Now you're making me suffer!"

"He cannot control Time because he is outside Time. But Time is his limit, his frontier. Although he cannot fail, the existence of Time is his failure. He succeeds because of Time, in which all things happen and all men are born. So Time might be the greater god."

Gualberto looked over his shoulder, gesturing to his friend that he could be overheard. "Carry on confusing yourself, by all means," he whispered, "but don't spoil the feast by confusing your dependants."

William Wild frowned and pulled his hat on tighter as a wind swirled down from the ridge. They rode along in silence for a while until Gualberto invoked memories of other journeys they'd made together.

"It doesn't matter where you are, Willy, this valley, other valleys of sand and rock, barren places as hot as hell, you're the same, the same then as you are now – an overthoughtsman," he jibed. "D'you remember persuading me to be a Muslim for a day? We kept the timetable of prayers, you mullahed me mightily. What was that preposterous thing you said? Islam was better because it was *younger*. In terms of your nonsense, Willy," Gualberto laughed, poking his friend in the shoulder, "that was a high point."

"If one religion emerges from another, doesn't it imply superiority of some kind? As for the value of youth, I rest my case over there," William Wild said, pointing to Valmai who was striding alongside them, her babies slung in Persian shawls on the backs of servants behind her. The woman's eyes flashed moodily bright and wild; her hair was tied up with silver, jewelled strands into a kind of crown; her pliant body moved with animal authority, graceful and lively. Valmai walked with the assurance of one whose beauty belonged on both sides of any border.

As William Wild watched her, a rich purple in her dress drew his mind to the desert. A comparison between Valmai and Gaveston entered his head. In a mental play which he would never have shared, he – a man of sixty-five – deprived himself of Valmai, and gave her to the Gascon, who was her equal in age, of equal beauty, her natural mate.

Even a man as blithely self-centred as Gaveston would fall in love with her.

The dangerous bond with Ned would be broken.

Then he remembered the abyss in Gaveston's mind. No woman would ever bridge it by her beauty – no man either unless boundless power, wealth and freedom were in his gift.

"Wherever I look these days," William Wild confided to Gualberto, "I see Ned, and the effects of Ned. I see people biting their fingernails, praying the old king will live for ever. I'll spend the whole of mass looking at the poor who'll be ruled by him. I pity their trust in the means that created him. I pity us because we know just how ramshackle those means are."

"Were these the arguments you put to the King when you were defending Ned? I think not," Gualberto taunted.

In lieu of an answer, William Wild told his friend the story of the day Ned deserted the camp at Saint Johnstone and went to find Gaveston in Brechin – unforgivable insubordination, by any standards – made worse by the camp being threatened by the enemy in strength. But because Ned was so obviously incapable of controlling his need to be with Gaveston, William Wild had bowed to the inevitable, accepting responsibility for the camp's defence himself. This was disobedience on his own part.

"I knew I was in the wrong, and he was in the wrong, but I had to think of the camp," the Irishman continued. "All I asked Ned to do was take a letter to the King outlining the situation and requesting reinforcements. It was never delivered. When I asked him about it later he said he'd forgotten. He told me to my face – as soon as he was with Gaveston everything had flown from his mind, including the lives of three thousand men. Fortunately, the Scottish force couldn't be held together because of the harvest and they melted away, but if they hadn't, the camp would probably have been overrun."

"Wasn't the King outraged when he found out?" Gualberto asked incredulously. "Surely he couldn't blame you for it?"

One of the twins began to cry. The servant jogged a little to soothe her back to sleep, running ahead of the party through the frosted grass. William Wild was silent for a while, watching the scene with pleasure. Then he sighed and turned back to Gualberto.

"Edward never knew. When I heard about what happened at Brechin, and Ned being back in his father's good graces, I decided to keep the whole episode quiet," he explained. "If a man finds real faith in what he's compelled to believe in, how unkind to feed him anything that contradicts it."

The sound of Tintern's bells rolled up the valley, bringing to the Irishman's mind a memory of Eleanor and Edward as he had known them twenty years before on the day Ned was born.

Here was another miraculous baby – another child worshipped as a saviour, lying in the crib with its secret tight in its little fist.

Loving one instead of all had put Ned's saviourhood in a much lower class than Christ's. He would save one man only – for himself.

The dark thought died as Valmai drifted across to touch her breast against his foot in the stirrup and smile up at him in a way that always shook his heart.

CHAPTER SEVEN

Whitsuntide, 1306. Westminster

Ned shifted on his knees, leaning forward on the handle of a sword which was supporting him. He was in the fourth hour of keeping vigil in Westminster Abbey in preparation for being knighted the following day, 22nd May 1306, along with a thousand others from all over the country – the biggest dubbing ever to be held in England.

The pain in Ned's knees was acute. He'd run out of prayers in the first hour, then started to reminisce aloud to keep himself from falling asleep. Gaveston sat beside him on a stool, lending him half-an-ear as he dozed.

"My father is a great actor, you know, Piers. Although he says he holds the art in little respect, he can do it better than anyone. Inside him, he's got characters to choose from – outfits hanging in a wardrobe. Except the clown. He can't play the clown, which is his great weakness. Of all the shows I've seen, nothing compares with the performance he put on ten years ago. He had a dais built outside the palace so he could stand there and let everyone see him cry. He can weep at the drop of a hat. If anyone can do that, watch out. They're capable of anything. The whole sham was for the sake of war, so the Church, the nobles and the City would stop complaining about taxes and let him go to Flanders to fight the French. I had to stand on a box for everyone to look at. 'If I don't return from fighting those who thirst for English blood,' the old fox said, sobbing, 'crown this lad king.' I was thirteen. The shock of seeing my own father put on such a display was bad enough, but the worst part was seeing people taken in by it. One minute they hated him, the next they were eating out of his hand. When he left the platform they cheered and cheered. They knew he'd been acting. But he'd been acting *for them.* That's what they love, Piers. They'll forgive anything as long as they know it's for them. As my father took me down off the box he whispered in my ear: 'Your destiny has been made public, young man. While I'm away, see you live up to it.' All this happened at the time we first met. You'd been taken on as a royal squire. As soon as I saw you, a poor refugee who'd escaped from France, I knew what freedom looked like. When my father insisted on taking you to Flanders with him a month later, I asked him to take me too. But he refused because I was his regent, which was a farce. What could I do at that age? I wanted to be with you. I wept. But those were real tears. No acting."

The King had arranged this mass knighting to raise money for yet another Scottish campaign. John Comyn, a stooge king Edward had installed after the surrender of Stirling two years ago, had been murdered by Robert de Bruce. The device of making money from knighting – the families of the candidates were charged a hefty fee – was cooked up by Edward's financial advisers.

To purify this pragmatism, Edward announced that the thousand new knights would be a corps loyal to Ned, his twenty-two-year-old heir – brothers-in-arms bound by vows harking back to Camelot. In the minds of this generation of English knights, there would be a Round Table at which all disputes would be settled honourably. At Ned's call a host of devoted warriors would obey the summons to protect him, the spiritual descendant of Arthur.

King Edward's own knighting at the earlier age of sixteen had been a small affair by comparison, hardly noticed because a civil war was raging. He had always seen it as a lost opportunity to gather souls about him.

The candidates in the abbey were supposed to obey the great nocturnal silence of the Benedictines, but the dark, soaring air was laden with chatter as friends and relatives helped the youths through the tedium.

Monks entered the choir to perform a night office. Their singing struggled to rise above the noise.

More people came into the church. Voices were raised. Someone blew a trumpet. There was laughter. A fight started somewhere. The Benedictines sang on, but the music went askew because monks on the north side of the choir couldn't hear their opposite numbers on the south.

"Aren't you tired, Piers?" Ned asked, glancing at the figure squatting on the stool. "You don't have to stay."

"I'll see you through," came the mumbled reply.

"Why it had to be done like this, I don't know."

"Aren't you the man who loves to rub shoulders with all and sundry?" Piers retorted grumpily. "Your father probably did it to please you!"

Ned let the remark pass.

For a while no word was exchanged.

"When this is all over, I thought we might go down with Willy and stay with him in Gloucestershire," Ned said eventually. "Did I tell you he'd married his Welsh whore? The old man gave him hell. Called him an old fool."

Gaveston's lack of response was lost in the commotion now filling the great church. Unaware his friend had finally succumbed to sleep, Ned carried on talking, forehead pressed against the pommel of his sword, staring at the stone floor.

"He sees it as a betrayal of my mother's memory. He thinks Willy should have stayed faithful to a woman he couldn't have. That's the way the old man is. He hands out the responsibilities – you do this, you do that! Even now, while he's dragging himself around half-dead, he's trying to force people to feel what he wants them to feel. But you know me, Piers. I won't have it."

Ned muttered and fumed through the hours of darkness, raking over all his resentments while Gaveston slept on the stool.

As first light came through the stained-glass windows, touching the throng with weak rainbow colours, Ned leaned over and grasped Gaveston's hand. "Don't you worry. When he's dead, the first thing I'm going to do is set you up properly. So far I haven't been able to help much."

Disappointed when this declaration was received in silence, Ned gave the hand a shake, but Gaveston slept on. When Ned realised, he sighed and put an arm round his idol's shoulders.

At six in the morning, the crush in the abbey was so great the monks weren't able to get back into the choir to sing Prime. An appeal was sent by the abbot to the King, asking for help. Ten huge war horses were brought over from the palace stables and led through the west doors of the abbey. The enormous beasts immediately responded to the crowd – which they took for an enemy army – whinnying and crashing their iron shoes on the flags, barging the mob aside, clearing a way through to the high altar.

The monks followed the horses, tucked in behind, stumbling over piles of fresh dung shed in the animals' excitement.

Ned ended his vigil, muscles stiff and sore from the long hours on his knees. He woke Gaveston and together they left the abbey guarded by a ring of men-at-arms, joining an even greater crowd.

Outside, Ned elbowed himself space against the wall to urinate.

Someone shouted: "Why don't you hold it for him, Gaveston?" Laughter greeted the crack. A scuffle followed as the tired bodyguards flailed uselessly at the crowd.

"Thanks for seeing me through the vigil," Ned said to Gaveston over his shoulder, ignoring the abuse and the disturbance. "I've been thinking – we've known each other for ten years, near enough. When I catch the old man in a good mood, I'll ask him to give you my countship of Ponthieu."

Gaveston gave a short, scornful laugh.

"What's so funny?"

"He'll say no."

"It's mine to give. I inherited it from my mother. She would have liked you. You're her sort of man – very like my father must have been when he was young." Ned laughed at the thought, oblivious to the crowd. "Why shouldn't I give you some of my lands if I want to?"

"If you really want to give me Ponthieu, that's not the way to go about it," Gaveston replied. "If *you* ask him, he'll refuse. Get someone else to do it."

Inside the abbey the Benedictines had reached the five psalms for the dead.

❦

At the magnificent Whitsuntide dubbing banquet, under cover of music played by eighty minstrels, Ned asked William Wild if he would approach the King on the matter of giving Ponthieu to Gaveston. The Irishman was drunk but not that drunk.

He refused, giving as his reason that he was currently out of favour.

"That won't last long, Willy. He loves you better than anyone else – certainly better than his own son!" the prince said. "Do it for me."

The Irishman knew there was no point whatsoever in attempting to persuade Ned against the idea of the gift but he also knew it could be a mortal blow to Edward's new hopes. The request would drive him mad. It had to be proposed in such a way that the last three years of patient acceptance of Ned's infatuation with Gaveston didn't appear to be a mistake. A very specific man was needed for this job.

"Ask Langton."

"Langton? He hates me. He's my worst enemy."

"Your father knows that. If Langton takes your part, he'll listen to him more than anyone else," William Wild replied. "All you've got to do is persuade Langton."

"My father wouldn't have anything to do with me for months because I shouted at Langton once. And the man loathes Piers!"

The Irishman saw two stuffed swans being carried through the hall. From where he sat, it looked as though they were swimming between the tables.

"He's your father's most trusted councillor. If Langton gives your proposal support, it stands a chance."

Ned frowned impatiently. A servant appeared and asked him to return to the high table to eat.

"Then I'll ask Margaret, my stepmother…or one of my sisters. They're on my side. Women understand friendships – why some matter so much. Piers and I have been close for ten years, Willy. That's half my life, near enough. My father doesn't grasp that, does he? The way people care for each other escapes him. Look at the way he's treated you!"

William Wild caught the fierce glance of the old king from across the hall as another servant was despatched to bring the prince back to his place.

"When he criticised the woman I chose, he was only thinking of my posterity," the Irishman explained, "forgetting how I don't care to have a posterity in the same way as he does. Besides, he's starting to take me back into favour – otherwise I wouldn't be here."

"Then you're in a position to speak to him for me!"

William Wild held up his hands. "Ned, here's something you mightn't have considered," he said sagely. "You're off to the north to fight another Scottish war for your father in a few weeks. He's been forced to accept that he hasn't got the strength to lead the army any more. Bringing Scotland to heel means more to him than anything else. Win that war and he'll give you whatever you want. And, if Piers has a hand in the victory, more the better."

"Oh, Willy," Ned sighed with exasperation. "You know what those campaigns are like. Sheer slog. There's no guarantee we'll get anywhere. Piers needs Ponthieu *now*. I want him settled."

"If Piers performs some notable service during the war, who knows, there might be a few Scottish estates going begging."

"I don't want to give Piers anything up there. He's a Frenchman and he'd like something in France," Ned replied with petulant force. "Come on, Willy – don't let me down. Speak to my father for me and I'll be forever in your debt. Think of the future."

The Irishman caught the inference, marking the frustration in the prince's reddened eyes. It was remarkable how this man, with an entire world being ceremoniously tooled to turn on his axis, had one single thought in his head.

"I've given you my best advice," William Wild said evenly. "An emphatic victory against the Scots would definitely do the trick. Failing that, try Langton."

But it's not my best advice, the Irishman thought as Ned seethed, stamping his foot in disgust, golden spurs tinkling. The best advice would be not to ask at all.

"One gets very tired of being told how to live," Ned said bitterly, waving aside the servant who was desperately trying to get him away. By this time, awed anticipation had descended on the whole company as they watched the prince defy his father. "Piers and I were going to come down and see you in your sty with your Welsh harlot, but we've changed our mind. I'll remember this, Willy."

Ned strode away, head in the air. The eyes of all the guests followed him. Before sitting in the chair on the right hand of his father, he deliberately swerved to a table several ranks down, bent over Gaveston and lightly stroked his cheek.

A sound, half sigh, half groan rose from the guests.

With the heir finally in his proper place, the King swayed beside the swans, a gnarled, jewelled hand on each. The richness of his robes could not mask the exhaustion in his eyes. His age was a grey cloud around his head. The erectness of his figure was suddenly lost. He buckled, putting his weight on the swans, which moved under his hands. An involuntary moan of pity filled the hall.

Edward steadied himself, shaking his head slowly. There was a hush as he carefully lifted up the pinion feathers on both sides of one of the stuffed birds with his fingertips, spreading out the great wide wings.

"Look, an angel at my table!" he exclaimed.

A puzzled silence followed, then a deep buzz of concern.

Edward raised his other hand to hush the guests, then swore on the swans never to personally draw sword again except to recover Jerusalem. When he died, he went on, Ned was forbidden to put his father's corpse in a tomb until complete victory over the Scots had been attained.

The general sadness swelled up again. In the murmur ran the threnody – only age and the mind's failing powers can bring down such a great warrior, such a great king.

"The avenging of any injuries done to God and the Church and myself by any who do not love us, I leave to my heir, who will be the second Edward," the old king announced, eying Ned. "Stand up, my son, so all can see you."

Ned obliged, smiling broadly, opening out his arms.

"This is the king we have made for you," Edward said, pointing a long finger at him. "Other monarchs envy me my glorious son. In God's name, hopeful of His mercy, I ask you all – when the day comes, be loyal to him."

When the festivities were over, William Wild caught Edward in a generous mood and obtained formal forgiveness for marrying his concubine. He also obtained permission to return home to the Wye Valley for another six weeks before joining the army. By mid-July he was to report to the King on the northern border. From here, the King would oversee yet another invasion.

Edward confided to the Irishman that the funds for this war would have to be strictly controlled. Bankers and finance men were dominant in his life. He described a deal he'd agreed whereby the Exchequer was raising money by selling off the lands of Robert de Bruce, the Scottish usurper, and his adherents in advance of their defeat.

"But these fiscal geniuses aren't my kind of people, Willy," he said sombrely. "They lose me. I need an old familiar face. Someone I can moan to."

Crossing the Severn on the Irishman's way home, the ferry capsized and he got a soaking. Pneumonia resulted, followed by complications.

When the time came to begin his journey northwards, word arrived of an early English victory. If the news had been bad, William Wild would have gone to join the King, setting the risk of death aside.

As it was, he sent a messenger to explain his failure to appear on the given date, requesting a further month's extension of leave.

The messenger arrived at the King's headquarters in Saint John, Perthshire, on the same day he was told his son's army – one day's march ahead – was performing merciless cruelties on the civil population. These exceeded the norm to such an extent, Ned was called back to headquarters to give an explanation of his conduct.

William Wild's man from the Wye Valley was in a queue at the provost's tent waiting to deliver his message when the Prince of Wales rode in sharing a black charger with Gaveston, both men daubed with blood. Their small party had been ambushed in the wild country between the King's headquarters and the army twenty miles ahead.

Even the spectacle of his son's wounds – which were slight – did not sidetrack the King. Hotly, in front of several churchmen, including Walter Langton, he demanded to know why such mindless brutalities were being performed in his name.

"Hold back, Father," the prince replied, raising a hand. "Don't be so quick to believe the worst of me."

"D'you deny mutilating girls, opening the wombs of pregnant women, torturing the blind and infirm?" Edward cried. "I have it on the word of priests you've done these things."

"Why judge me without hearing my side?" Ned complained, slipping off the saddle. "Doesn't it matter that I've been cut? Chased ten miles? We were lucky to get here at all."

"Never mind your scratches! You swore your oath as a knight to defend the weak and helpless barely two months ago! The next I hear, you're killing people you're supposed to protect!"

"They were succouring the enemy, sire," Gaveston slid in.

"Who asked you?"

"You should listen to what Piers is saying," Ned remonstrated, giving the Gascon a hand to dismount. "He's only telling you the truth. We had to make an example of someone."

"What good is teaching lessons to those you then murder?" Edward muttered, grey head sinking into his shoulders. "Beware that kind of ridiculous sin."

"It is war, Father – war as you taught me."

"Against infants? Against cripples left to till the fields?"

"Against anyone in the way," was the barefaced reply. "And what would you do? Leave Scots alive behind our lines?"

The old king shuddered, gazing round at the churchmen who maintained chilled, distant expressions. "I didn't teach him this, as you know. What's happened to his sense of honour, why it's reached these depths, I can't even begin to guess."

"Is this all you called me back for – to quibble over a few details?" Ned asked, head cocked to one side.

"What kind of Christian are you?" Edward thundered suddenly. "You make me feel ashamed!"

"I'm as good a Christian as any other," Ned retorted, eying Langton. "But if it pleases you, our Bishop of Chester, here – whom I'd like to talk to on another matter entirely, when he has a moment – will hear our sincere confessions."

On returning to Boldwood, the messenger recounted the story of what he had witnessed. The man kept referring to the presence of Gaveston as if he could not understand the man's *function.* Who was he? Wherein lay his power? Was he a wizard? How could he safely beard this king, so famed for the ferocity and speed of his wrath, and get away with it? He described how, as the old king railed, Ned and Piers kept up a stream of babyish sighs, raising their eyes to the heavens, and tenderly wiping blood off each other's faces in a dumb-show.

"They were laughing at him," the messenger added. "It was a sight you'd rather not have seen."

CHAPTER EIGHT

William Wild's request for an extension of leave was refused. He was instructed to join the King as soon as possible. No explanation was given.

Still weak from his illness, the Irishman set out for the north with Valmai to nurse him through the two hundred miles of the journey. He had objected to her accompanying him at first, but consented when a doctor told him his chances of survival were very low. As wife and lover, she had the right to share with him what time he had left.

As they travelled, they talked and gossiped to keep the Irishman's mind off the discomfort of riding in a bumpy cart over bad roads. Valmai was interested in the bond between Ned and Gaveston. She asked questions about their behaviour. Having lived all her life in a valley dominated by a great monastery, she was familiar with passionate male relationships and knew how powerful they could be.

"These feelings can't be destroyed by anyone outside. Only the men concerned can control them, if they have the will," she said one morning as they were passing through the Cheshire plain near Nantwich. "Amongst the Cistercians these affairs were too strong to last more than a couple of years. Then they burnt themselves out. Tell the King not to worry."

"No, you tell him. He'd like to hear it from a woman," William Wild groaned as the cart went over another bump in the road. "Advise him on what to do if his son breaks up with one man and then goes off with another, and another, and another, as they do. Don't forget, I was with the Templars. I know how it works between men. They're bound to a wheel."

Valmai was silent for a while. She remembered how the small community where she'd lived near Tintern was always subject to rivalrous affections between monks of power. Logic and justice had no place in these interplays. The enormous abbey, built to enlighten the love of God, sheltered a second love twisted around God's like a vine.

"Perhaps it's an enchantment," she suggested. "You tell me Gaveston's handsome, a star of the tournament, every boy's hero. People grow out of that kind of adulation by the time they're twenty."

"How will the King know if that's the case?" William Wild retorted, feebly irascible. "He tells me he's dying. Ned's marriage hasn't taken place yet. Edward must be desperate to get it settled before he dies. And do we know if Ned will go through with it when he's king? He might take it into his head to be a bachelor and live openly with Gaveston."

"He wouldn't dare do that," Valmai said, shocked at the thought. "People would be disgusted!"

"It may be my fault," William Wild muttered, staring out over the flat country. "When he was fourteen I told him about Socrates, who would have got rid of his nagging wife and lived with a young man if he could. The greatest thinker of all preferred men. Ned might have found that encouraging."

"None of the fourteen-year-old boys I've met cared about philosophers," Valmai said to comfort him. "At that age, all they're interested in is chasing rabbits. Now put it out of your mind. The prince is like he is through no fault of yours."

The Irishman told her the story of the foray into Strathearn three years ago and the King's panicky thinking behind it. He explained how one of the essential initiatory experiences Ned hadn't had was subsequently provided at the siege of Brechin and how the prince later developed a strong taste for it. But achieving the long-term effect of killing fellow-beings had not been straightforward.

"As I mentioned to Edward at the time, trusting butchery to have a benevolent effect on anyone is an odd approach," he said morosely, "and the same applies to sex with women. It's just as bad if it's only with whores and no finer feelings are involved."

Valmai noticed tiny red bubbles coming from the Irishman's nose and told the driver to stop the cart.

On the roadside, with hedge wrens singing in his ear, breath short, terror of death galloping through his brain, William Wild kept talking. As Valmai cradled his head in her lap and his heart floundered, he spent what he took to be his final minutes bemoaning the fact all the philosophers – Greek, Roman, Arab, Church – had been unable to come up with a useful explanation of homosexual love, or guidance for those who struggled with its problems.

"Why is everyone so evasive about it?" he muttered. "Christ said nothing on the subject. Mahomet left it to one side. Even Aristotle had nothing useful to offer – but it's always been around."

"Don't you go plaguing yourself with Aristotle at this time, my lovely," Valmai crooned, tears filling her dark-blue eyes.

The Irishman clutched her by the collar of her dress, drawing her closer.

"Think of the millions of men deprived of women," he hissed. "Armies! Prisons! Monasteries! What are we saving all that manhood up for? Christmas?"

Partly to calm his delirium, Valmai asked if she should send for a priest to give him extreme unction. He waved the idea aside.

"Why did I wait so long to fall in love?" he breathed. "To have children with a lovely woman is life's garland. Does it ever occur to you that perhaps I was once a homosexual?" He pressed her hand to his lips. "I've told you what it was like in the dormitories of the Poor Knights."

"Oh, that doesn't worry me," she replied soothingly. "You should be thinking other thoughts at this time, *cariad*."

"I don't honestly know whether I was a homosexual or not! I'm tormented by the thought," the Irishman moaned, trying to lift his head. "I have to get out of here. I can't see a thing!"

Valmai held him down as he feebly attempted to get out of the bed in the cart. "Quiet now," she said, watching the blood drain from his face. "Don't trouble yourself any more."

"Can't abide fatalism, even from you!" he babbled, falling back, eyelids fluttering. "Oh, Valmai, Valmai, I can't stand it. Poor Ned. If we find something to love, should we be deprived of it to please anyone? Anyone at all?"

Valmai suddenly seized him by the shirt and shook him, violently. "Ned, Ned, Ned! D'you ever think of anyone else?" she cried, eyes flashing. "You're dying. What about your own children?"

William Wild stared at her, blood streaming from his nose.

His eyes went dim.

"Have you got something important to say to me?" Valmai said, holding onto him. "If you have, then now's the time to speak!"

He frowned hard, sighing. "There was something but it's not all that important."

"Even at death's door you'll cling to falsehoods. Be straight with me," she pleaded, cradling him in her arms. "Isn't there something about you and Spanish Eleanor? Something about you being someone's father?"

William Wild looked at her. "Is that what it was?" he slurred, eyes filming over. "I can't see it matters now. What a bright light! Call this music? The Whirling Dervishes are back!"

He slid into a dream. Fierce and jealous gods frowned down on him from desert hills, gods he'd loved and cast aside, watching him sweat out a dance with death.

❦

After his meeting with Ned at Saint John, Walter Langton, using powers delegated to him by the Pope, granted the prince a special dispensation for cruelties and bloody offences committed in pursuing the King's enemies.

Before absolution was given, Ned had to listen to a moral lecture. He sat in front of the small, bald bishop, nodding in all the right places, not disputing any of the points raised against him. In the heat of the moment, he had allowed these gory abominations to take place – the worst by his own hand.

Langton mentioned how uncharacteristic this behaviour was in the prince – how he recalled a reticence to shed blood in earlier days. Ned looked at him, puzzled, and said nothing.

As soon as the dispensation was firmly in place, confirmed by a blessing, Ned got up from his knees and said he wished to raise another matter. He asked if the bishop would speak to the King on his behalf, requesting permission for him to give the countship of Ponthieu to Piers Gaveston.

Langton could hardly believe his ears. His disapproval of Gaveston was known to everyone, including the King – also, after the quarrel between himself and the prince, he had maintained a distance at which their mutual dislike could be diplomatically handled.

"Why don't you ask him yourself?" Langton asked.

"It would be better coming from someone he trusts."

"He doesn't trust *you*?"

Ned grinned and shrugged. "Do fathers ever trust sons? Will you do it for me? I'd be most grateful," he asked winningly. "It would help a lot."

"This is a very odd proposition," Langton said, putting his fingertips together. "So odd, I'd like to know more."

"More? More about what?"

"If I had something to ask of your father, it would be strange if I approached his son with a request to do it for me."

"Why?" Ned demanded.

"We've had our differences in the past."

Ned frowned, looking into the churchman's patient features.

"Oh, that? All forgotten," Ned declared airily. "Well? Will you or won't you?"

Langton thought for a while, avoiding the prince's affable gaze. "I like to have good reason if I'm to stick my neck out," he said eventually. "So far, I can't see one."

"I can help you there," Ned replied with a frank, boyish grin. "The day will come when you'll need my favour."

Langton glanced quickly into Ned's eyes, nodded and folded his arms – a silent acknowledgment of the point made. He would have preferred to let the cold moment pass, but his nature was such he couldn't quite concede. "If you're asking me to do this," he said archly, "and your power is so much greater than mine, can it be you know it's wrong and you want me to take the blame?"

"Wrong?" Ned echoed. "What's wrong about a gift?"

"Then, I repeat – if it's not wrong, I don't see why you shouldn't ask him yourself."

Ned stood up and towered over Langton, glaring down at him, the grin still in place.

"Without my favour, you'll have no future. Think on that."

Langton studied Ned's mask of fixed geniality for a few seconds before accepting – conveyed by an emphatic sigh, indicating he had no choice. "A final question, if you'll permit," he said, as a waspish afterthought got the better of him. "Could it be you've fallen out with your friend and want to turn the King against him? That will be the effect, I assure you."

Ned stared, eyes blank as two blue pebbles, a flush rising up his neck. "As far as I'm concerned, you've made me a promise," he said forcibly. "Let me down at your peril."

Ned spent the rest of the summer with the advance army in pursuit of the Bruce, who went from castle to castle, drawing the English deeper into remote areas after him, retreating from each place at the last moment, creating maximum frustration and annoyance.

When the small Scottish force retreated onto Mull in late September and the English had to follow Bruce as he hopped from island to island of the Hebrides, Ned was glad to be recalled to headquarters. He returned with several successful minor sieges to his credit, but no Bruce tied to his horse's tail. Twenty-two young knights who had become bored by the frustrations of the campaign left the army and returned to England without permission.

"So much for the loyalty of your friends, Ned," the King said, reading down the list of deserters, the Irishman by his side. "Willy, instruct the sheriffs to confiscate all their lands and goods." He paused his finger going to the end of the list. "And who's this bringing up the rear? Piers Gaveston. Well, well."

Ned hung his head.

"Was he the ringleader?" Edward asked roughly.

"It wasn't a conspiracy," Ned mumbled. "They just drifted away because it all became so tedious."

"And you just let them!"

"The weather was terrible. It poured down every day. We were in fog most of the time. I couldn't keep track."

"The elements are so inconsiderate," Edward mocked. "Your pals were full of enthusiasm when the going was easy, carving up old women and babies. But when it dared rain *on them,* poor darlings, well, that was too much. Strange how the weather didn't slow Bruce down. What a sad and sorry tale this is, eh, Willy?"

The Irishman gave a rueful, admonitory smile to Ned. Sallow and gaunt, he was slowly recuperating from his brush with death near Nantwich two months ago. After the crisis, Valmai had edged her comatose husband up the western side of England a few miles a day. By the time they reported to the King, the patient was so emaciated Edward was smitten with guilt at having put his old friend's life in danger.

"When are we going to make a man out of you, Ned? I can't conquer Scotland with boys," Edward said sourly, glancing at William Wild again for support. "Campaigning isn't the way I'd choose to spend summer at my time of life but it has to be done."

Ned's shoulders slumped. He looked out of the window.

"We don't need Scotland," he whispered. "You use it as a whipping-boy for mother's death. You take it out on the Scots. That's when this annual invasion started – straight after she died. You should get over it."

"What?"

"Let the Scots keep their swamps! It's an obsession of yours I don't share."

"Hear this, Willy? Have you ever heard such nonsense?" Edward said, appealing to the Irishman for support.

"Piers says the country's not worth having," Ned continued. "You can't grow anything. The people are too backward to be of any use…"

By bringing Gaveston into the argument, Ned brought his father close to a fit. Edward walked over and stood shoulder to shoulder with the Irishman, tranquillising himself with the physical contact of his old friend.

"Leaving your hero's perceptions aside for the moment, Ned, have you got anything further to say about these defections?" the King said through gritted teeth. "What was the real reason your comrades deserted you?"

Ned avoided his father's gaze. "If they say I gave them permission, don't believe it. They just went off in dribs and drabs."

"Well, isn't that what they are – dribs and drabs?" came the sardonic reply. "And when your friend Gaveston gets back from disporting himself in French tournaments with big prize-money and doing deals on the side for the Templars, he'll be fined everything he's gained. I'll leave him with nothing."

"Is that where he is – in France?" Ned asked in apparent innocence. "I haven't heard from him in ages."

"You bald-faced liar! He's based in Ponthieu! You lent him the castle!"

"Did I?"

"You know damn well you did! And the rest of the defectors insist you released them!"

"Oh, no – that's quite untrue. All I said was…"

"I know what you said, you treacherous half-wit! You said you'd run off as well if you could!"

"That I deny, absolutely. I did my best to hold them together. I was always reminding them of their duty to you. But they all got completely bored chasing that coward Bruce who wouldn't stand and fight!" Ned wailed, also looking for support at William Wild who kept his head down, pretending to check through the list of defectors. "I couldn't promise them things would get any better so they ran away."

Edward sat, easing himself down with the aid of a wall. His movements were slower these days, his speech thicker. The meeting with Ned was taking place in the chapter house of Lanercost Priory near Carlisle where the King had settled for the winter. From there, next year's campaign against the Scots would be launched.

"It hasn't been a good season," the King said, leaning his head against the cold, red sandstone. "Everyone is laughing at us!" The bitterness in his voice was flat and thin. "Are we to assume we've seen the last of Gaveston? He'll stay in France? I can forget about him?"

"Well, I wouldn't say that. He promised me he'd come back when he'd won enough money to keep him going," Ned said ingenuously. "He has hardly any income. The only way he survives is by winning prizes and what I give him."

A shiver passed through Edward's frame. "Ned, my dear son," he said, knotting his hands together in his lap. "This isn't the way for a military leader to conduct himself. One doesn't let troops go home because they're bored. War is boring! It's a soldier's duty to be bored! Ask me! Forty years in the saddle! But bored or not, before I die I'm going to bring the Scots to heel. I'm going to tame them like I did the Welsh. It's the only way you'll have a chance of keeping the kingdom together. D'you hear what I'm saying?"

"Yes, Father," Ned replied without enthusiasm, "though I have to say, losing those people didn't make a scrap of difference."

"Never mind that now. The Scots know about my state of health. They'll be foxier than last season, more reluctant to fight a pitched battle. You'll have to get in there and flush them out."

The King paused, breathless, sunken eyes beseeching his son to grasp the urgency of it all. Ned smiled, nodded, then asked if he could go now.

"You will listen to me!" Edward yelled, voice cracking. "The country you inherit has to be secure. That is my last task. To achieve that, I have to stop looking after you so much. From now on, Willy – who has always spoken up in your defence – is going to keep an eye on you for me."

"That's alright, Father."

"He'll be your watchdog."

"Yes, Father – if you feel I need one."

"Use him as a go-between. Hide nothing from him. He'll check your expenditure. Keep an eye on your behaviour. Remind you what your objectives are. We have to do better, Ned."

"We will, Father. May I go now?"

Edward fell back, exhausted. There was a long silence as he took time to recover.

"Come here," he said after a while, conjuring up a fond smile.

Ned obeyed. Long arms reached out, muscles, once hard, now trembled as the prince's head was pulled down for a kiss.

"Bless you, my dear son" Edward whispered, holding onto him. "You're very precious to me. But you must do better in binding people to you. Don't concentrate so much on one man. He isn't everything."

Ned went south with William Wild. In early December Gaveston returned from France and they met joyfully at Dover. Together, they visited Canterbury and Langley, spending Christmas at Northampton with Queen Margaret, the King's French second wife and her young sons, the prince's half-brother.

Ned's companions during these festal wanderings were the defectors from Scotland. While they were celebrating their reunion, the King pardoned them – against all good advice. William Wild despatched a report to Edward on the response to this generous act. "The news came at an unfortunate time. They'd been drinking for days. The cry went up – if Scotland be bad next year, we'll do the same, and be pardoned again – by Ned, our new king for his dad will be dead."

The Irishman's report arrived when the King was ill, being nursed by the Black Augustinians of Saint Mary Magdalene at Lanercost. When he recovered, there was a mountain of administrative work waiting for him. Fortunately for Ned, the report was never seen by the ailing king – as most of Willy's reports weren't. Believing William Wild had the measure of his son, Edward kept the issue aside as much as possible – much as he'd been able to do when leaving him in the same care as a child.

If he had bothered to read what William Wild was writing to him over the months of December and January, it wouldn't have gladdened his heart. The old king had become a figure of fun in Ned's circle – a comical relic of the previous century. Although power remained with the father, the future was with the son. The young men scented more sophistication, more romance, more *plesaunce,* and less Scotland. A better time was just around the corner.

When the prince was called back to the north in late January to attend a parliament in Carlisle, he was ordered to stay with the Benedictines at Wetheral, a few miles away in the Eden valley. Edward was now very ill. The last person he wanted to see was his exhausting son.

William Wild become a frequent visitor to the King's bedside – riding over from Wetheral to give his reports verbally and staying a few days at a time. The news he brought the King was generally not one of hope. Ned and Piers and company were being a trial to the monks, incapable of being serious, ignoring all pleas to conduct themselves decently. This catalogue of loutish inanities – which the Irishman disliked relating – was relieved when a visitor arrived in the north with an ingenious solution to the problem of the heir-apparent.

Peter the Spaniard, cardinal-bishop of Santa Sabina, had been appointed papal nuncio in England. He was due in Carlisle in February, ostensibly to back up the continued peace between France and England and the completion of the marriage contract between Ned and Isabella. William Wild picked up a rumour via Gualberto, that the nuncio was also interested in dynastic matters closer to home. Ferdinard the Fourth of Castile was in delicate health and without an heir. None of those in line to be king of Castile was acceptable to the papacy. There was one, however – the son of Ferdinand the Third's daughter, Eleanor – who was. And that was Ned.

Would Ned be happier as the King of Castile, where nobody knew him? All the Spanish kingdoms were notoriously despotic. Criticism of any monarch was mercilessly crushed. Ned would be able to live as he liked, with whom he liked. The crown of England would be the price he'd have to pay.

On the day this dropped into his lap, Edward was laid low by bronchitis. William Wild sat by the King's bed, sweating and shivering with an illness of his own. The Augustinians brought in a couch and laid it alongside so the two sick old men could talk.

"You must be convinced our cause is lost," Edward coughed. "Bringing me bizarre proposals like this!"

"You've always said the Spanish side is dominant in Ned. Perhaps he'd be happier there," the Irishman insisted. "Why not send him over on a state visit – let them have a look at him?"

The King called over to an infirmary canon washing the windows, the hood of his robe discreetly pulled up so he wouldn't overhear.

"Hey, you! Get this old madman out of here!" he wheezed. "He's making me worse!"

Nonplussed, the Augustinian picked up his bucket, unsure what to do.

"Oh, leave it," Edward croaked, waving him back to work. "We're telling each other fairy stories, aren't we, Willy?"

Disappointed not to have aroused interest in his scheme, the Irishman pulled a wry face. "I don't understand why you're dismissive of the idea. At least, it's a way out," he said.

"Getting Ned to fall in love with a woman like I did is the way out," Edward insisted. "It can happen."

"Edward, your son is surrounded by young men fucking every female they can find over at Wetheral. Every farm girl for five miles is being drafted into the abbey and all Ned does is watch."

"Watch?"

"Yes…remotely…without interest."

"And Gaveston is at it, and Ned doesn't mind?"

The Irishman nodded. "It doesn't mean anything to Ned. It's not that he doesn't like women," he said. "In fact he likes them as people more than most men. And your wife and daughters are on his side."

"What does that mean – on his side?"

"They accept him as God made him. They don't see why he shouldn't be king *as he is.*"

Edward scratched his beard, looking puzzled. "You've discussed this with them?" he asked.

"It's all they talk about. It's all anyone talks about!"

"Christ's ears and eyes! I'm lying here in a dream!"

"It's a public issue."

"My friend," Edward said, addressing the canon who was standing on the window-ledge in order to reach the top section of glass. "The religious life being what it is, you've probably been ruled by a superior with a weakness similar to my son's at some time or other. Can such men be trusted?"

The canon made a piteous bird-like noise, pleading with his eyes to be left alone.

"You see how unpublic an issue it is really, Willy?" the King muttered. "They'd rather not have an opinion. I don't care what the women think. I don't care what the country thinks. All that matters to me is – what does King Philip think? And, going on from that, what will this girl Isabella be able to do with Ned? She's the one who'll have to deal with him. Haven't you guessed Peter the Spaniard's main reason for coming here?"

The Irishman looked more uncomfortable than he was already.

"Philip of France wants to know if my son is going to be able to fuck his daughter and give her children," Edward said, raising his voice so the Augustinian couldn't help but hear. "If we can't convince the Cardinal-Archbishop that Ned's up to it, and he runs back to the Pope with the news non-consummation is on the cards, the marriage won't take place."

The washing of the windows became frenetic.

"That's why Philip's been dragging his feet over fulfilling the territorial clauses of the contract, handing over the castle lands and properties agreed. I did my part straight away and married his sister. But that was a side-issue. It's Ned who matters. He carries everyone's hopes. At the moment it's water in a basket."

William Wild lay on the couch, head propped up on one elbow, teeth chattering with fever. "Then you might as well tear up the contract," he said, wiping sweat from his face. "Ned's a man-lover. He's never going to change."

"You hear that?" Edward bellowed in anguish as the canon scuttled across the room, desperate to remove himself. "This whore is telling me my son's an irredeemable sodomite! You must know as much about that as he does, both of you having been locked up with brothers in dormitories of depravity! Tell me about it, first hand, *please!* We have to find a cure somewhere!"

The canon stopped at the door, water slopping from his bucket.

Looking back at the King he wondered whether the request could be at all serious. Was this his moment to speak his mind and influence history? There were things he could say – stories he could tell – but he thought better of it. Parental shame was to blame for the King's outburst. Later, the window-cleaning canon would pray for the King's soul and the King's pain.

He backed out, bowing frequently, carefully closing the door behind him.

CHAPTER NINE

Carlisle, made of stone the colour of dried blood, blasted by salt winds from the Solway, ruined by Scottish raids, trampled over by huge English armies on their way north, was the capital of border warfare. Every building was either damaged, or in the process of being rebuilt. When the retinues of the men summoned to attend the King's parliament of January 1307 swelled the population, the few streets around the castle and cathedral became mud-slides. Many in the town were sick, famished or mad. Beggars, whores and thieves clustered around the doors where visitors stayed. Because life was so unhygienic and uncomfortable in the town, Edward's physicians had advised him to winter at Lanercost Priory twenty miles to the east where, though the chances of a Scottish raid were much higher, his chances of survival would be better.

On the 20th of the month, Walter Langton arrived at the cathedral of the Holy and Undivided Trinity, the only building big enough to house the parliament. He was to represent the King, who was too ill to attend.

The great church was full of scaffolding. Cold winds blew through the choir, which was under reconstruction after a fire. Arches were deformed and twisted by subsidence caused by a drought which had caused a local famine. Blocks of stone, loosened by severe frosts, had tumbled onto the floor, cracking the flags. The rubble remained where it had fallen. People in the cathedral had to wend their way between the piles of masonry. In the smoky half-light a few knights, churchmen and merchants who had bothered to make the journey so far north for the parliament shivered in furs around braziers.

William Langton took in the dismal scene. His heart fell. No good could come from such a depressing start. Not enough members had arrived to make a meeting worthwhile. It was an insult to the King so few people had turned up. He postponed the meeting, but asked the members present not to leave Carlisle.

This parliament was crucial. If a majority didn't attend, a claim could be made later on that any measure agreed at Carlisle didn't have full backing.

The King needed money for the campaign against the Scots – a cause which had become profoundly unpopular. Only a few powerful magnates with private armies continued to support it because they stood a chance of gaining vast new estates if the conquest was successful. Elsewhere, there would be sullen, bitter resistance to the King's demands. The country in general was sick of the Scottish wars and the poverty created by them. Middle and small landowners, the City, the Church, were being stripped of their wealth so King Edward could feed his obsession. Now the old man was on his last legs, clinging to his dream. If the opponents of the war could tactically withhold their co-operation for long enough, he would die – and take his dream with him.

Whatever happened afterwards would not be in the mould and manner of this king, they reasoned. His son was effectively his opposite. If that meant the end of twelve years of fruitless military expenditure, they would rejoice in the difference. Besides, those future times were so uncertain, so different, it wasn't worth preparing for them. Ned would be an experiment.

From the look of the weather – heavy, overcast sky, snow flurries and a freezing north wind – and to give laggards time to arrive, Langton calculated it would be best to wait another five days before restarting the parliament. When, having announced the postponement, he attempted to mix with some of the members, he found them so sour he wondered whether any of them would bother to return.

Langton's duty was to go back to Lanercost to tell the King what had been done in his name. As he passed through the shattered town with all its scars, defacements, filth and human misery, he realised what an error of judgement it had been to hold the parliament in Carlisle – even though it was ostensibly for the sake of the King's health.

The real running cost of Edward's war was everywhere to be seen. Who, in his right mind, would be inclined to vote a penny more for its continuance?

With these dark thoughts in mind Langton encountered the men he would least like to meet up with on the road to Lanercost – Ned and Gaveston, accompanied by William Wild. Langton remembered the prince was supposed to have attended the opening of the parliament. It had slipped Langton's mind as most things connected with Ned tended to do.

"Aren't you attending the talking-shop?" Ned called out as they drew abreast. "I assumed you'd be virtually running the show."

Langton explained the situation.

"Well, if that's the case, what better time for us to go and see my father about the other matter?" Ned said breezily. "I want to sort it out as soon as I can. We're all here. Let's go and do it now."

Langton shifted uncomfortably in the saddle, sleet in his eyes. The last thing he wanted was to deliver double bad news.

"I wouldn't say it's a good time at all, Your Highness," he declared, shaking his head. "The King will be disappointed the parliament hasn't got off the ground. Waiting another five days isn't going to improve his temper."

"I'm not prepared to live my life according to my father's temper. As Willy here will tell you – temper is for children, not adults."

"If there's to be the remotest chance of success, I recommend we choose another time," Langton persisted, tilting his hat forward to keep the sleet off his face.

"We won't do that. No more prevarication. You've already upset our plans by not doing as you promised."

"The King has been extremely ill!"

"All he has to do is lie there and listen! We want this business settled so Piers can go over to Ponthieu and take possession before we both have to go into Scotland again."

Langton was glad the bad weather in his face was masking his annoyance. The prince was talking like a father or a husband. Suddenly, he was disgusted. He thought of the King, racked by sickness, daily battling for his life, plagued by one squalid problem – a problem the King seemed not able to face any more.

Through the sleet spattering from the brim of his hat, Langton saw a crowd had left the eastern gate and gathered where the two parties had met. They were standing silently, crosses made of twigs in their hands, eyes lifted to the riders. Famine being commonplace, no one in the company took any particular notice of these starved, skinny wretches until they surged forward and blocked the road.

Many in the crowd were old soldiers, too weak or injured to travel, left to fend for themselves after previous campaigns. The will to get out of the hell of Carlisle had left them. Women of all ages, some with infants, boys and girls, made up the rest – many so far gone in poverty and disease their gender was indistinguishable.

"Get them out of the way!" Langton shouted to the men of his escort, tightening his rein."

"In the name of Christ," a man with an unaligned top and bottom lip said from under Langton's horse, holding onto his stirrup. "Do not deny Beholders a sight of Piers Gaveston."

A strong gust of hail drove everyone back towards the gatehouse for shelter, the man still hanging on. Once behind the walls, Langton prised the man's hand off his stirrup.

"What is this about?" Langton demanded above the howling of the wind through the gatehouse arch.

"False angels."

Langton manoeuvered so his horse blocked Gaveston's view of the man, and bent down, a finger to his lips.

"Beholder? What's a Beholder?" he asked, holding out his cloak to give the man shelter.

As the man replied, his unaligned lips worked against each like millstones. "Felix the prophet of Dash set us a penance," he replied. "We must confront the false angels. If Gaveston's here – who makes such a fool of our prince – we must look upon him."

The storm heightened. There was no refuge other than walls. The horses became terrified at the screaming of the wind and had to be held. Everyone dismounted and huddled together, taking what shelter they could between the animals and each other.

Langton found himself surrounded by the Beholders who pressed their twig crucifixes against him. Glad of their protection against the hail, he crouched down, looking into the circle of eyes around him.

"Is he here?" the man with the millstone lips demanded. "Point him out so we can look upon him."

"You'd offend him."

"We must do so."

"Reverences of holy places and the relics of saints are one thing – staring at people, another," Langton said, a smile on his face.

"Felix says let the dead revere the dead!" the man with the millstone mouth exclaimed. "We look at the living – the moving handiwork of God and the Devil."

"Aren't the dead the completed work of God, whereas the living are unfinished?"

There was a pause. Langton observed the momentary dimming of the man's fanatical bright eye.

"I'll have to talk to Felix about that one," he said after a while.

"He is a great thinker. He says the living are the true church of Christ."

Langton chuckled to himself. Lashed by a wind full of ice, cowering with beggars and princes under the bellies of beasts, he was charging up his brain to enter a disputation as if back at college.

"Staring at *sinners* – for that's all he is, like the rest of us – cannot be a penance," he said triumphantly. "It is mere gawping, gawping at corruption!"

"Beauty is the balm of God," the millstones intoned, rocking on his haunches. "It cures the soul, which is what a good penance does. If we only have each other, all we see is ugliness and misery which leads to the sin of despair. That makes us worse. No light shines. No desire is kindled. We are already within the power of death. Thus is your case overturned, my lord."

Langton put his hands over his ears and shook his head, laughing. "If this is your prophet's message, he must be mad."

"He is! Mad with the world!"

The Beholders started chanting the list of false angels Felix their prophet had given them, including Italian boys in the retinue of the papal nuncio, Peter the Spaniard, due in Carlisle shortly, and various personages summoned to attend the parliament.

"This priest of yours knows the world which drives him mad," Langton commented. "These are important people. How does he know so much? What kind of a man is he?"

"He lives beside a waterfall of learning – a refugee from power and glory. His day is yet to come. That's what he says about himself."

"Well, he certainly sounds an interesting man. I must meet him. Get him to come to Carlisle."

Millstones seemed doubtful. "He says he only likes to be looked at when there's good reason," he declared. "But I'll ask and see what he says."

As the storm started to subside, Langton went over and positioned himself beside Gaveston so the Beholders could see who he was.

The famished gang acted discreetly, quietly, religiously, casting one bold look each before moving off into the streets.

To Langton, a man of orderly, conventional mind, this was strangely humbling. If the times were less knotted and strained, it might have been on his conscience as a churchman to have Felix investigated – but greater questions of state pushed the issue aside.

The Priory of Mary Magdalene at Lanercost was already full of the King's household and government officers and clerks – two hundred people in all, crammed into every available space in the priory. Shanties had been erected in the cloister, packed with shivering scribes. There were factotums in the vestry, servants bedded in the cellars. The canons wandered through this maze of humanity in abstracted pain – their vocation suspended. When the King moved on they would cease to be part of a war-machine and return to their prayers.

The Prince of Wales with forty riders appeared at the gates of Saint Mary Magdalene's needing food and shelter. Fermin, the prior, accepted them with due resignation. There was no room, but welcome and charity would have to be stretched further.

The north and south transepts of the church had been used as extra dormitories since the King's arrival in October. During the worst of the snowstorms, the nave was used as a stable. An ass had foaled. Fermin enjoyed this Bethlehem in reverse, the ass giving birth under Christ's roof. He was a man who searched for meaning.

Fermin knew more than enough meaning would descend on Lanercost when a great king died within its walls. No matter how many visitors poured through the gates, or how sparse the rations were, nothing could detract from the significance of what was about to happen. Fame would arrive.

As he received the Prince of Wales and ushered him to the warming-house where the King lay, Fermin was deaf to the chatter of the throng who came along with him. He had no idea where they would sleep or what they would eat.

The canon appointed as chronicler for these times was summoned to take up a listening-post in the roof of the warming-house. Being naturally inquisitive, as well as conscious of history, Fermin would have preferred to do this work himself, but he was a big man, not the right shape for cramped corners.

At the door of the warming-house, Ned held up his hand and ushered Langton in with an encouraging smile, asking he should do his work on the issue of Ponthieu straight away. Then he firmly shut the door and led everyone else away.

The King was sitting wrapped in furs close to a big fire. The smell of singeing filled the high room. He listened to Langton's report on the parliament in silence, staring into the flames.

"Postponement was a mistake," he grumbled when Langton had finished. "No matter how few you had there, you should have made a start and got things going."

"Sire, the numbers were pitiable. I had no alternative."

"Five days! Five days for them to put their heads together to say no. I should have gone myself."

"No, sire. That would have been humiliating."

Edward laughed grimly. "I can't be more humiliated than I am now. They *thought* I was going, didn't they? And they still didn't turn up."

Langton blamed the atrocious weather. He painted a picture of people struggling through snow and ice to get to Carlisle from every corner of the country.

"Alright, alright… life's hard for the rich, I know," Edward grumbled bitterly. "From now on I must know who arrives in Carlisle. Put a watch on the gates. In five days' time I've got to have a workable parliament that can vote me the money I need."

Langton bowed. The King sank a little lower in his cushions. Outside, the wind was howling.

"You can go now," Edward murmured. "You must be soaked."

Langton took a deep breath and took a step back, out of the range.

"My lord king," he said hesitantly. "I am sent – unwillingly, as God lives – on behalf of my lord, the prince, your son, to ask, in his name, for permission to promote his knight Piers Gaveston to the countship of Ponthieu and give him all the lands thereof."

There was no explosion of wrath, only a deep groan. "I can't believe what you're saying. Who are you to dare ask such things?" Edward asked, his eyes screwed up tight.

"Sire, I had to."

"If you're unwilling, why do it? What's the matter with you?"

"The prince insisted."

"Then we'll see him together. Go and get him immediately."

High in the roof, the chronicler squirmed deeper into the recess. Prior Fermin's instructions were to obtain *ipsissima verba*, the actual words used. Everything said by the doomed king in his final dealings with life was to be recorded. This would be a considerable feat of memory for the monk in the roof. It was impossible to use pen and ink while squeezed into a space a terrier might have for a kennel so he had to remember it all, word for word, then get back to his room as fast as possible to write it all down.

Langton returned with Ned.

The old king levered himself out of his chair and beckoned them both to come closer.

"On what business did you send this man?" he asked Ned.

"That I might be able, with your assent, to give the county of Ponthieu to my friend Piers."

"Who gave you Ponthieu?"

"My mother gave it to me."

"And now you want to give it to your second mother? Or are you his mother?"

Ned frowned. He was confused. Optimistic when he'd come into the room, he now sensed disappointment. The old man was mad with him and the anger was of the worst kind – cold, disdainful, and sarcastic.

"Dear Father, I can't quite follow what you're saying," Ned said with an earnest little smile. "It's a very small county. Piers needs somewhere of his own."

Edward's anger broke out of its coldness. "Stupid whore of whores!" he roared, grabbing Ned's hair in both hands, tearing out as much as he could. "Give away lands, is it? You who never gained any? As God lives, if it wouldn't break up the kingdom, I'd see to it you'd never enjoy your inheritance!" With all his strength, he threw Ned to one side and stood panting, holding onto the back of the chair.

"Why shouldn't Piers have some land?" Ned gasped, clutching his head. "You give away land to your friends."

"Is there room for anything else in your mind but that man?"

"There was no need to pull my hair out," Ned complained, looking at a handful of golden strands on the floor.

"I wish I'd pulled out your woman's heart!" Edward shouted. "By the Holy Mother, you're a trial to me!"

"I spoke to a lawyer who said if Ponthieu is mine to give, I can give it," Ned persisted, backing away. "I'm only asking for your permission out of courtesy."

The King raised his hands in the air, letting out howl after howl of grief, then began coughing uncontrollably. A few moments later he spewed on the floor. Ned watched, wide-eyed but unmoved.

Langton, who had kept as far away from the conflict as he could, came forward and took the prince by the elbow.

"My lord, it looks as though you have your answer. We can't get any further with this tonight," he whispered, helping the King back into the chair. "If I stay here and tidy up, will you go and find the physicians?"

The sky cleared within the hour. The wind stopped howling. Bright stars shone in the winter night. The chronicler paced the grounds, going from fire to fire, trying to control his excitement. His first instinct was to rush to his desk while everything was fresh in his mind, but three of the King's servants were billeted in his writing-room. They loved to feed him gossip, thinking they were helping with his chronicle. The last thing he wanted was more confusion. Versions of the incident in the warming-house would be all round the priory by now. History was already being distorted. Since the King's arrival at Lanercost over three months ago, his death had been rumoured several times. People claimed to have seen him dead and laid out. The sight of the King, if seen fast asleep, or in deep thought, could easily create these mistakes. Mere looking wasn't enough. True history was verified by expert *listening*.

The chronicler was the only one apart from Langton, the King and the prince, who knew the facts about the incident in the warming-house. He'd seen the King pulling the prince's hair out and cursing him. He'd seen the King vomit. He'd watched the Bishop of Chester cleaning it up. To this point, the chronicler was sure of what accompanying dialogue he'd heard and would be able to repeat on the page.

But while Ned was out of the room looking for the physicians, the King had spoken. The recall of his words worried the chronicler. Going over it in his mind, he couldn't quite believe what he'd heard coming from the King's lips.

"As God lives, and by the suffering of Our Lord, I see now that I can't impose that creature on my people. Where does his corruption come from? He's not mine, I tell you, not mine. I never had a hand in his making. His mother must have been a whore."

CHAPTER TEN

To make one man a fool above all others does not reduce the foolishness in all men," said Peter the Spaniard, papal nuncio, Cardinal-Archbishop of Santa Sabina, composer and sailor. A big, impressive man with large brown eyes, a wide, fleshy mouth, a wealth of chestnut hair, he sat on his horse like an oriental emperor, vast cloak spread out over its haunches, scarlet against the snow. Behind him trailed over fifty retainers in livery artistically designed by himself – sea-blue and gold, with a scarlet band around the collar embroidered with reef-knots.

"Consider the actions of Our Lord," he went on, gesturing expressively. "Everyone knew the Jews would kill him once he entered Jerusalem. Did that stop him? From some angles, judged superficially, that was sheer foolishness – divine suicide! Only by understanding it was for love of mankind can the foolishness – the foolishness of God! – be denied. In a much narrower context, the same can be said for your son."

"Huh?" Edward muttered tiredly, deafness making him unable to keep up. Peter the Spaniard was a man who began talking when he opened his eyes each morning.

"In the prince's case, the love of mankind is concentrated on one person. He only thinks of Piers Gaveston, who – for him – represents all mankind. Think of it that way."

King Edward was being carried in a litter to Carlisle cathedral to preside over the parliament which had been in session for the last fortnight. The old king had listened to a torrent of propositions from Peter the Spaniard, one on top of another. The man overflowed with initiatives – drowning problems rather than solving them – never pausing to obtain agreement on any issue, merely pressing on to the next.

The nuncio had arrived at Lanercost a week after the incident in the warming-house. As the gaudy cavalcade forced its way into the overcrowded chaos of the priory, Ned was the only one with sufficient status to welcome such an important guest. Both men took an instant liking to each other. Aware of the papal nuncio's power, sensing the universality in the man's character, Ned lost no time in appealing to him. Much of what the prince said was not news to the papal nuncio. He already knew a lot about Ned from the ecclesiastical intelligence network. Also, he had received a letter from Edward, which read, in part: *This difficulty of mine belongs as much to the Church as myself. We have received plenty of advice on what is said in Scripture, medicine and philosophy on this subject, but help from a recognised authority is needed. We hear you are such a man, wise, gifted and experienced, often employed by the Holy Father in these matters for your unparalleled diplomatic skills and expertise in the emotions of the young.*

The parliament, swollen by hundreds of extra clergy, nobles and hangers-on forcibly dragged out of the shires, was gathered in the cathedral. Objections to the King's demand for money had been beaten down by weeks of threats, cajolings and pleadings from the Exchequer's ministers and secretaries until, grudgingly, taxes had been agreed. By then fine weather through February and a general foreboding had drawn all government out of London, making Carlisle into the temporary capital.

Today Peter the Spaniard was due to address the assembled powers of England, fulfilling the stated purpose of his journey – reminding everyone of the advantages of the marriage between Ned and Isabella of France.

"You must be proud of your son," the nuncio said to Edward as the procession halted in front of the west end. "His Spanish blood from his mother comes through nicely. What a good impression he makes – handsome, good-natured and dignified, with natural authority."

Langton recognised Millstones, the man with the unaligned mouth. He was standing beside a tall figure who was attracting the attention of the crowd and everyone in the procession. Agog, they surveyed his erect, war-like bearing, the fierceness of his eye, his curly, abundant beard, the drooping lid of his right eye.

Edward was intent on getting off the litter, up the steps, and making a dignified entrance into the cathedral. When he heard the buzz of excitement around him, he stopped and cocked his head. All his life had been spent in crowds – armies, courts, parliaments. Antennae still operating in his atrophying brain told him something unusual was going on.

"What is it?" he asked Langton who had come to supervise his getting down.

"Look at the man over there, sire," Langton said, scenting a dangerous amazement of the crowd.

"Which man? Show me."

Edward looked where Langton pointed. His eyesight had deteriorated in recent months, and, not being a man ever to spend more time looking at himself in the mirror than was necessary, all he saw was a mob of beggars.

"Who are you pointing at?" he said testily.

"A man who looks uncannily like you did twenty years ago, sire," Langton replied, a catch in his voice.

Millstones waved to Langton, pointing at the tall man by his side. "This is Felix, the prophet of Dash, my lord! You said you wanted to meet him."

"What's going on?" Edward demanded.

Langton beckoned to Millstones over the heads of the crowd and shouted: "Bring him over here where we can see him properly."

Felix pushed through and stood before the King. If Edward's stoop could have been straightened out, the two men would have been the same height. Seeing them side by side created a sensation. There were hisses of superstitious wonder. Edward leant forward to examine Felix's features more closely. Langton broke down and wept. William Wild covered his face with his hands.

"The name of your father?" Edward whispered.

"He passed on to more important things fifty years ago," Felix replied.

His voice was Edward's with more strength behind it.

"Is your mother still alive?"

"She is."

"Bring her to me. Don't leave it too long."

Almost nose to nose, the two men smiled. On all sides people had been deeply affected, some going down on their knees in the slushy snow. Peter the Spaniard admiringly watched the scene. He adored pregnant confrontations. The choristers in his retinue had rehearsed a new motet he'd written – two parallel texts, one religious one secular – on the mystery of being. It had been his intention to have it sung before his speech to the parliament, but this was a much better occasion. Pushing his way back through the halted procession, he prepared the choristers to sing.

"Are those the Italian boys?" Millstones called as the motet started. "They're on our list of folk we must look at."

That morning, Gaveston had been given two months' notice to quit the kingdom. After a long meeting with Peter the Spaniard, the King had decided to break the deadlock of wills between himself and his son. A generous monthly allowance was made to Gaveston, provided he stayed out of England. A review of his case was promised at some future date. Mention was made of the possibility of a little piece of land coming his way as long as he behaved himself.

Ned and Gaveston were compelled to take oaths upon the consecrated Host in front of witnesses – Gaveston, to stay out of the country during the

King's pleasure – and Ned, not to receive or retain Piers near him.

After the oath-taking, Gaveston had immediately left Lanercost for the south. It was later discovered that one of the Italian boys had gone missing. A frantic, disconsolate Ned learnt from Peter the Spaniard that it was a girl in disguise – Fabiola, the most exquisite strumpet in Rome, brought hidden in the nuncio's retinue to put Ned's sexuality to the test. But, despite her best efforts, the Roman courtesan could find no gap to slide into between Gaveston and the prince. Ned had no passion for boys, or men, or women, or gods, or goddesses. His only passion was for Gaveston.

When, in desperation, Fabiola appealed to Peter the Spaniard for help, he arranged for the most powerful aphrodisiac known to Man to be put at the prince's bedside – wine made from tiny young gooseberries steeped in the blood of a newborn goat. When Ned obligingly drank the entire bottle to dull the pain of losing Gaveston, Fabiola revealed herself to him in all her seductive glory. Ned looked straight through her, thinking she'd come for his washing.

Ned's sense of betrayal deepened when Peter the Spaniard confessed to him that King Edward had been part of this attempted deception. He made the point that if a father went to such lengths to prove his son's manhood, it meant he had faith in its possible existence.

The nuncio followed up diplomacy with stern warnings, working hard on Ned's conscience. If he refused to confirm his maleness in some practical, observable way, the Anglo-French treaty would collapse. War would follow. Other nations would be dragged into the conflict. Christendom would be divided. The weakened West would fall victim to Islamic territorial ambition. Ned would be responsible for the collapse of civilisation.

For this great sin he would be excommunicated. If he came to the throne, he would be deposed by the Pope.

The next in line to Ned being but a child (Edward's ten-year-old son by Margaret, his French second wife), the boy's grandfather, the French king, would act as regent in England until the boy's majority. Knowing King Philip, he would probably break his word and usurp the throne.

England would become a province of France.

"Finally, it should be mentioned," the nuncio said solemnly, big brown eyes moist with tears, "if you should happen to die during any phase of this inevitable process, you will certainly go to Hell."

Bereft, feeling threatened, inadequate and inferior, Ned stood alone in the crowd outside Carlisle cathedral. Everyone was ignoring him. Instead, they marvelled at the meeting between his father and the prophet, Felix – a man who was the image of the father Ned remembered from childhood – the father who had deserted him just after his second birthday, taking his mother out of the country for three years. Within fifteen months of returning to England, Eleanor had died. Ned had hardly ever seen this lively, brilliant, much-loved wife but hollow mother. The place she should have occupied in his heart was empty.

His father had gone into a shell of mourning. Only war and the business of war could satisfy the grief-stricken Edward. The benevolent effects of Eleanor's influence faded away and the King became a testy tyrant. Ned's natural childhood had been sealed in the tomb with his mother.

Trapped in memories by the sight of Felix, Ned went into a spin of intensely painful self-pity. With Gaveston gone, he was nothing and there was nothing to live for. All that was left was the crown hovering in the air over his head. People only saw that, having no interest in the suffering man beneath.

The music rose around him. The sacred and secular texts of Peter the Spaniard spiralled upwards like chaffinches fighting.

The procession began to shuffle forward.

In the third verse of the motet, the harmonies went from two to three parts – the love of God in Latin, the love of Woman in French, the love of Man in English. Flashes of perfect harmony occurred when an identical thought was mirrored in all three texts.

The prince realised Piers was his mirror – the perfect man in whom he saw himself. Outside this emotional captivity, Ned was the dynastic mirror of his father and mother. My only chance is to be Everyman, he told himself, trudging along in the procession.

As the Italian boys entered the cathedral, their pure voices filling the great stone heaven in its gloom, the message in the music of the fourth verse unravelled and became simple.

It's all one, the motet said. Love one, love all.

Ned's heart lifted. A message of hope at last! The unison persuaded him that he could, perhaps, all being well, find a woman and prove himself. Peter the Spaniard's speech to the parliament – delivered in English as a compliment to the burgeoning importance of the language – was well received by the earls, knights and burgesses. When it was over, he was joined at the high altar by a phalanx of bishops. In part-payment for the absolute commitment Edward had given to fulfilling the Anglo-French treaty, *in all terms*, the nuncio conducted an intimidating ceremony condemning the souls of Bruce, the

Scottish usurper, and all his supporters, to eternal damnation for murdering the stooge king installed by Edward, and resisting English hegemony.

Langton did not attend. Upon entering the cathedral, King Edward had issued instructions for the arrest of Felix. This was to be done in the quietest way possible, then the prophet was to be taken to the castle nearby. This was easily achieved. Felix had expected it and warned his followers not to cause trouble.

When King Edward and Ned went to the castle, the litter had to be carried past the Beholders who were gathered outside. Millstones ground his teeth and spat as the King went by. He was promptly arrested and beaten. Edward had him brought over so he could talk to him.

"Does this prophet of yours teach disrespect to the Crown?" Edward asked him. "Somehow, I didn't expect that."

"Would a natural father have his own son arrested?" Millstones countered. "Would a natural man exile his mate because she's a Jew?"

"What are you saying? Have you lost your senses?"

"No more talking!" Millstones replied. "If they haven't already killed him, talk to Felix. Now let your bullies murder me so I can die in the grace of fulfilled penance."

When King Edward was carried into the torture chamber, he found Felix hanging upside down with his head in a bucket of slurry. The prophet was only able to breathe by keeping his head twisted up.

"I didn't ask for this!" Edward said.

"Nor did I," Felix answered carefully out of the side of his mouth.

"Cut him down and give him a wash."

Edward interviewed Felix privately in a small room with William Wild present. As they talked, passing pleasantries at first, Edward couldn't help staring at the splendidly regal specimen Felix was and torturing himself with the memory of Ned, England's future king, at breakfast that morning whimpering in sobs over his food.

Ned sat outside the room with Langton, wondering what was being said on the other side of the door. He listened to the raised voices and incoherent cries but couldn't make any sense out of what he heard, except for the pain behind it. That was reflected in his own soul, where, bereft of his mate, he grieved.

"I suppose you're very pleased with the way things have turned out," he said to Langton. "Does it occur to you I've lost my only inspiration? Without Piers I've got no idea what a king should be. What kind of example does my father set these days?"

"Strange you don't have a droopy right eye," Langton replied with an insinuating smile. "The King inherited his from his father. He inherited his from his father, King John, who inherited his from Henry the Second, his father. And so on back to King Arthur who is represented in art as a man with a droopy right eye."

Ned smiled patiently. "Let's put all our enmity aside, Walter. I'm very sad today. Let's be friends, shall we?"

The sound of repeated hard slaps came from the room where the interview was in progress.

"You knew my elder brothers, didn't you?" Ned asked.

"I had that privilege."

"Can you honestly say any of them came up to the standard of Piers?"

Langton pulled a wry mouth. "What standard d'you mean?"

"Any standard you care to think of. If I could choose an elder brother, I'd choose Piers. That's what he is to me. So, you see, Walter, my father has banished the perfect model of a son."

"Without admitting anything," Edward wheezed, beckoning the Irishman to stop hitting Felix. "Although it was a very long time ago, I confess to remembering a young woman who might be your mother."

"Praise the Lord for making you at least half-honest!" Felix retorted. "While you're at it, why not recall the whole truth? Before you start, answer me this: did you love my mother?"

The old king regarded Felix cautiously. "It was calf-love, if anything," he said, smothering a coughing fit. "I was very young."

"If anything?" Felix echoed bitterly. "If anything? What does that mean?"

"I was living in a hiatus – fifteen years old, married to a girl who was eight. I'd fallen desperately in love with Eleanor at first sight. The Church told me I had to wait until she was fifteen. Can you imagine that? Seven years of longing. Seven years of frustration."

"Never mind your seven years. My poor mother was only twelve when you made her pregnant. She had to wander the roads, cast out by her family, shunned as a fallen woman."

"Yes, we lost touch, unfortunately," Edward muttered. "What was in my mind those days? I seem to have been at the mercy of some kind of compulsion."

"God will punish you, I hope."

"I'd forgotten how young she was," Edward mused. "It must have been impatience with Eleanor. She was so slow to mature. If I encountered an underage girl who was precocious in that way, streets ahead of my wife, I obviously couldn't resist."

"You disgust me," Felix said hotly. "To have lived so many lies for so long and still be hanging onto them. You know as well as I do, my mother was part of a bargain your Exchequer for the Jews struck with her father."

"I don't remember that," Edward mumbled, eyes on the wide, snapping mouth of his tormentor, so like his own.

"Why should you recall one case? Negotiations between you and the Jews often produced this kind of deal. How many daughters did you deflower in this way?"

Edward's eyes glazed over as the enormous memory rose like a mountain from the sea of his mind.

"Jewish girls develop early…" he whispered. "Don't ask me why."

"How many bastards of yours conceived in this vile manner are wandering around England?"

The old king wiped his eyes with a handkerchief. His marriage to Eleanor had been perfect except for this one problem. Absolved by the marriage treaty from every carnal sin he had committed during the seven years of waiting, the constant drip-drip of paternity claims from Jewish mothers undermined relations with his wife to such an extent Edward had had to expel all Jews from England. The official reason given was that the children of Israel had run out of money and were of no use to anyone anymore.

"Who are you, precisely?" William Wild asked Felix, forcibly stepping in as he saw Edward drifting helplessly in reverie. "We need to know everything about your background."

"Everyone knows who I am! I can walk across the country from one side to the other and be recognised. God save the King! they cry. And everyone says I'd make a better job of it than that tartlet you've got lined up to succeed!"

Stung, Edward surfaced from his abstractedness. "Tartlet?" he yelled. "Tartlet? You dare call my legitimate heir a tartlet?"

"If I snapped my fingers, I'd have a popular following," Felix said with pride. "People naturally flock to me. Whatever I say, they believe. It's easy. In deference to you, father, I've only used this power on my followers, the Beholders, those poor, famished wretches outside the gates. They could flare up into a force to be reckoned with. You could have a major rebellion on your hands."

"Could I now?" Edward murmured. "I'd have to see about that."

"One word from me would do it."

"Leaving that aside for the moment, though I've made note of the treason," William Wild said evenly, "exactly where is your mother now?"

"I haven't seen her for seventeen years, but I know she's alive. I could find her if I wanted to. She'll back me up."

The Irishman glanced questioningly at Edward who was feasting his eyes on Felix. The old king lowered his eyes.

"I can't say I ever knew your mother," he said in a quiet, shaky voice. "In this cake-shop of a kingdom, no matter how I twist and turn, I know the tartlet must inherit. As for the two of us, my son, we can't meet again in this world."

"This is far less than I expected," Felix protested. "Think again! There must be something a father can do for his son."

"Life is the first gift we get. The second is hidden within it," William Wild said, tying Felix's hands behind his back. "You should have been happy with your obscurity."

The entertainment of the King's household, war-council, guests and friends throughout the winter finally broke the fragile economy of the Black Augustinians of Lanercost.

In April, the King was forced to look for other lodgings near the border with Scotland. Bed-bound, he was carried from place to place, ignoring the frantic pleading of those he wished to bestow himself upon. He was disgusted and repelled by their lack of charity and compassion. Hollow-eyed lords and abbots, rendered fearless by impoverishment, begged him to go elsewhere.

Ned was allowed to journey south to say goodbye to Gaveston – who'd sent a message from Kent with his travel plans. The old king made a special grant to help the Gascon on his way. Most of it was spent on clothes and armour for the French tournament season.

This generosity was triggered by an inspiring public pageant in Carlisle which had put Edward in high spirits for a few days. In early February, Bruce had become worryingly successful, penning up Henry Percy in the castle of Turnberry, pouring contempt on Edward as a dying tyrant. Then Bruce's two brothers were captured in Galloway and brought to Carlisle. Amidst huge celebrations, Edward was able to watch the prisoners being dragged through the streets at the tails of horses, hanged, decapitated, and their heads stuck on the castle tower.

On 5th May 1307 Ned saw Gaveston off at Dover. There were no tears. Ned behaved like a king with his subject. Piers was ordered to proceed to

Crécy where stores, provisions and money awaited him. Ned made a formal promise that when King Edward died – which couldn't be long now – Piers would be summoned back to England, and must immediately obey.

While Ned was taking the longest way back to the north, calling in on friends, Bruce defeated two English armies within the same week. The victories plunged Edward into a strange madness. On Whit Sunday, with two of his armies streaming out of Scotland in full retreat, he assembled the main invasion force and made the troops march decked in flowers and leaves, reviewing them from a stack of pillows on his sick-bed.

That night, in delirium, he instructed Langton to have Ned's confessor arrested and taken to Carlisle for questioning. Langton waited until the fit had passed, then checked to see if Edward remembered giving the order. He did, with particular clarity, and Langton was bellowed at for not obeying the order.

Brother John de Lenham, the prince's Dominican confessor, had first-hand knowledge. Listening over the years to Ned's sins, major and minor – the sins of a child, boy, youth, and man – he could make an informed assessment of the prince's character. It could safely be assumed that he knew more than anyone else what kind of man the prince was. A stern purist, de Lenham always demanded the truth from Ned in the confessional. He also refused several attempts by the King to prise those secrets out of him. When Langton offered a dispensation from his vows so he could reveal what he knew, de Lenham rejected it out of hand.

This sour, saturnine man was arrested in the middle of the night and taken to Carlisle to be tortured into revealing what he knew. The sophisticated cruelties of Norbert de Newcastle, a master-craftsman in pain who claimed he could separate any man from his sworn vow, were lavished upon him.

De Lenham didn't cry or groan. He said no prayers asking to be released from suffering. When asked questions, he spat blood and said nothing. Eventually Norbert had to admit defeat. He sent a message to Langton: *The reverend man's respect for the prince cannot be broken. The idea of death only makes him smile. You must find another way.*

When Ned returned from the south, his father was ten miles west of Carlisle, his invasion army gathering around him on the coastal plain facing the

Solway. On the next Sunday, de Lenham appeared – gaunt, pale, moving with difficulty. At Ned's confession, the Dominican asked for a new understanding between them: that, from now on, the prince should own up only to minor sins. The major ones would have to look after themselves.

CHAPTER ELEVEN

Edward's host of thirty thousand slowly advanced under high blue summer skies to the edge of the sea, beating the dried marshland into clouds of bronze dust. Burgh-by-Sands was a baked pan of sheep country, sand- and mud-banks of an estuary full of waders and marsh fowl. The coming and going of the tide through the gullies and channels was hardly noticeable against the surge of human movement as regiment after regiment entered the desolate landscape. From here it was only three miles west to Drumburgh where the estuary could be crossed into Galloway. Once over, the army would march fifty miles north to relieve Ayr which was being threatened by Bruce.

The army had covered only four miles in two days, with a day of rest between, moving at the pace the King's physicians would allow. At Burgh-by-Sands there was to be another day of rest. As the soldiers looked northwards to the far hills of Galloway, they doubted the invasion could take place under such conditions. To cross the Solway at low tide by the Sandywath route meant moving at speed. The King would not survive the strain of it all. He was falling to pieces, mentally and physically, his death rumoured by the hour, countered by hurried appearance at the entrance of his tent, propped up by attendants, waving feeble reassurances.

On the evening of 6th July, the King's cook opened a barrel of sturgeon sent by Ned to his father from Northampton where he was visiting his stepmother and half-brothers. The brined fish was off because it had taken ten days to come the distance. The cook interpreted the gift as a deliberate insult. Who, in his right mind, would send a barrel of fish a hundred and fifty miles in hot weather?

A letter accompanying the gift reported Peter the Spaniard had at last left the country – in his possession, documents to quieten the fears of King Philip of France. The papers proved that the Prince of Wales was definitely able to have sexual intercourse with a woman. This was attested by a personal declaration from Ned and a female. She was from a good family anxious to extend its land-holdings in western Suffolk.

Ned was supposed to set out for Carlisle two weeks after the sturgeon, obeying the general summons to join his father within three weeks of the

Feast of John the Baptist. But he was detained by hospitality. Ned saw no reason to hurry. The King had not appointed him to lead any part of the army and left his orders vague. He would catch up later. Meanwhile, the summer was sweet enough in the south.

William Wild had been spy and supervisor of the prince's household throughout the last eight months, sending in regular reports on his activities and expenditure. Ned abided the situation with as much grace as he could, but found it difficult not to resent the intrusion.

It took the prince some time after the incident in the warming-house in February to realise he'd won the argument by refusing to change what he couldn't change – his feelings. Nor would he betray them by resorting to duplicity and lies about his relationship with Piers. Even with Gaveston out of the country, the relationship flourished. It was, if anything, stronger. All the phrases conned from the royal writs and leaked by gossipy clerks – *undue intimacy, inordinate affection* – were meagre descriptions of a passion Ned pursued with single-minded steadfastness. It occupied a sphere of his being far beyond shame or politics.

Everywhere he went, Ned was open about his passion for Gaveston. The only nod he made in the direction of compromise was to call Piers his brother – but no brother was ever loved in this way. No matter what company he was in, high or low, he would declare how unbreakable the bond was between them. William Wild was forced to sit through countless drinking-bouts, listening to Ned's rhapsodies, then spend an hour writing them down for his report. The low company Ned kept – actors, musicians and the like – had to listen to Ned extolling Gaveston's virtues for hours on end. What emerged from the Irishman's reports was a love so supreme, so all-consuming, that it was obvious Ned valued it above everything – including his inheritance.

The Irishman also noted how the prince didn't presume to speak for Gaveston's feelings. He never said the Gascon loved him. There appeared to be no jealousy at work. Ned was happy with what there was. It was impossible for him to be hurt – except by Gaveston's absence.

These observations were conveyed to the King in succinct form, pared down to avoid upsetting him too much. An area William Wild minimised was the fact that all hope of reforming Ned had vanished. In spite of the Irishman's care, this sad information was inherent in the reports. Convinced all that could have been done with Ned had been done – with the exception of killing him – the King took the decision to see out his own time and leave the rest to chance.

There was, therefore, no longer any need for William Wild to send Edward accounts of Ned's misdemeanours, gaffes, debauches and ineptitudes. These days the King only took his son seriously as a cog in constitutional machinery. Ned would ascend the throne and satisfy the law. The terms of treaties and legal responsibilities would be met. The qualities required for kingship were no longer an issue.

With all these major concerns now pushed to one side, most of the later reports ended up being about Ned's extravagance and overspending. He was a chronic spendthrift and supplied enough peccadilloes to fill the reports, doing away with crueller reading William Wild could have supplied.

Just as the Irishman believed it was wrong to try and remove the central pillar of Ned's existence – an existence through which he must rule one day – he saw it as equally unkind to make the dying Edward acknowledge what he had unleashed on England. By his lack of direct action over his son's unfitness to rule, he had made the future a quicksand. But, so the Irishman reasoned, with a few planks and some courage, quicksands can be crossed.

If blame has to be allocated, he argued to himself, it must go to the blood, the family, the laws of belonging and inheritance. Other thoughts intrigued him. The future stability of the state was now in the hands of one man – Gaveston.

Without Gaveston, Ned couldn't live.

With Gaveston, he would be an impotent king.

After Edward's death, the Gascon would effectively be in control of the kingdom, disinheriting Ned from real power.

If so, why had Edward left Gaveston alive?

The answer William Wild gave himself was sobering. Edward had realised his son was being kept in one piece by a force which threatened the whole future and was prepared to let England's future be at its mercy. That was an antithesis of good kingship.

Edward's last days were being spent within his own incorrigible passion – conquering Scotland – which deserved at least as much understanding as Ned's. The Irishman had always hated that mean period in the life of old men when they lose sympathy with their friends of long standing and disappear into themselves. He wouldn't do this with Edward. After forty years together, they'd remain close right through to the end.

While the prince's household was in Halifax, the Irishman received a summons to immediately go to the King on Solway Firth. The same messenger carried orders for Ned to proceed to a part of eastern Scotland south of Edinburgh still under English control, to stiffen the resolve of local supporters and form the core of another army on that side of the country.

Within three days William Wild arrived at Burgh-by-Sands, ready for the worst.

The opening of the King's tent faced northwards so he could lie on his bed at the entrance and look over the estuary to Scotland. Every passing soldier – or Scottish spy – could see him and know he was alive. Banked around the tent were men from the most important families – earls and barons, generals and captains, senior clergy, men of the Chancery and Exchequer, all silent and watchful.

When William Wild arrived the King was snoozing, each rise and fall of his chest studied by the audience. A bunch of soft feathers suspended on a string moved close to his lips. The Irishman sat a little way off with servants and waited, watching the colours in the sunset strike through the dust and smoke of an army that knew it was going nowhere.

Distant cries of sea-birds and water-fowl heralded an incoming tide. Servants moved quietly in and out of the tent. While Edward slept, the great camp was in stasis. War was forgotten. All work and business were being held in suspense.

The Irishman begged food and drink from the King's cook and ate it on his lap, one eye on the invalid. Priests came to celebrate the Feast of the Translation of Saint Thomas à Becket with the King, but they were sent away.

Tired from his long journey, relaxed after wine and food, William Wild nodded off. He woke to find a servant pulling his sleeve. The King would see him now.

There was a buzz of resentment as William Wild left his place and walked through to the tent. Many among the assembled magnates had things of great moment to say to Edward, but this old Irish upstart, of no blood to speak of, had been chosen – an outsider who had always been an insider.

Edward lacked the strength to sit up. In the twilight, his head on the pillow was the colour of carved wax. It was an effort for him to speak.

"We'll cross tomorrow, Willy," he whispered.

"I'll be there."

Edward nodded. "Good," he murmured. "How's Ned?"

"I left him practising somersaults."

The old king's eyes became shadows as he turned away from the sun and sighed. "He's not my son," he said.

The statement hung in the warm air.

William Wild let the seconds pass, hoping what he had heard would ride away.

"He's your son, Willy. Don't deny it."

From experience in war, the Irishman knew the madness of the dying, the horrors and delusions, the lunacy of disintegration. Questions they asked themselves often belonged to a different reality, guilts rising up out of the depths of primitive fear. He adjusted his chair so he could see into those shadowed eyes, but they were closed.

"Eleanor told me," the King murmured with a bitter little snort. "I never did anything about it. That means I never really loved her, I suppose. It was all a sham."

Edward's voice was starting to break up. There was a rattle in his lungs. The Irishman looked around for a physician but the tent was empty.

"Admit he's yours. No one else need know," Edward went on, his breath brief and light. "It explains everything. Weren't your people in Ireland peasants? Ned is no more than a peasant."

"Edward..." William Wild said gently. "This is no time for this kind of talk."

"Say he's yours."

"You should have a priest."

"I can't be his father...I can't...He's nothing to do with me...If he was my son I'd have made a man out of him."

"If I thought you'd believe it, I'd say yes to comfort you – but you know it's not true."

"I've been going through the records. Look, here are the dates..." Edward scrabbled under his pillow and brought out a list of calculations. "At the time of Ned's conception, Eleanor and I were apart...she was in Castile. I was in Wales."

"If that was true – which it isn't – it's strange you didn't notice at the time."

"What a fool I must have been. Tell the truth, Willy. You won't be punished, I promise."

A long silence fell. Both men looked out over the estuary, avoiding each other's eyes.

"You should have told me. Think of the agony, the waste, the disappointment I've been through with that boy...that ditch-digging peasant boy!"

"I'm not Ned's father," the Irishman said steadily. "If you'd believed it for a moment I wouldn't be here to argue."

"Ned, Ned...my life has been nothing but Ned...oh, to be free of the bugger!" Edward railed, feebly hitting the mattress. "You committed adultery with Eleanor. If you weren't such a dear old friend, I'd have your head."

The Irishman turned away, fiercely upset. "I never betrayed you," he hissed. "Nor did Eleanor."

"She had too much power over me. We should be allowed one son of greater strength than our own, someone to eclipse us utterly!...to make us happy to die...just one...just one."

"I can't help you with lies," William Wild said, keeping his voice down. "Is this all you wanted to say to me?"

"Time after time you told me you loved her. Coming from you, it had a different meaning...something out of a long-winded Muslim book, something hard to understand...a man having many wives...a woman having many husbands."

Moved by his confusion, the Irishman reached over and took Edward's hand. Pent-up animal indignation rumbled in the spectators.

The hand was released.

"I did love Eleanor..."

"You old fool, the Welsh witch you've let into your heart is no more than a substitute for her."

"I loved Eleanor for what she was."

"And what was that?" Edward asked, sinking back, though his voice remained strong. "Apart from a whore."

"I loved her, and told you I loved her, because she was yours. Why did I give my life to you? I've never been sure where the lines between love and friendship are."

Edward frowned.

"What are you saying? You don't know the difference between a cunt and a handshake? You've lost me."

Night trumpets sounded over the sandbanks. Sentries were posted on the outer edges of the great army. A half-moon edged into the sky barred by a few thin clouds.

"Is there anything you want to pass on to Ned?" William Wild asked after a while. "When he finds out I was with you at the end, he may want to know what you said. So far, there's nothing I'd ever tell him."

"He won't ask...I don't matter to him any more," Edward muttered, abstractedly plucking at the linen of his shirt. "He thinks he's already free. But you can say this to Ned *from his king* – men must have leadership. To help him out while he gets used to the idea, my corpse is to be boiled to get the flesh off the skeleton. Tell him to have the bones made into a cross that can be carried at the head of the army. Our men will follow that anywhere."

Servants entered the tent with a tray of food, followed by three physicians. Elbowing the Irishman aside, they pulled Edward into a sitting position and supported him. In spite of his protests, one of the physicians spooned porridge into his mouth.

"It's the best thing for the bloody flux," the physician explained. "It binds up the bowels."

Edward started to choke.

The physician told the servants to hit him hard on the back.

The choking continued, frantic and deep.

"Harder, harder," the physicians cried. "He must get it up."

The King's choking got more desperate. Porridge spilled down his chin onto his beard.

The tent entrance was swiftly drawn shut against the surge of interested spectators.

"Go away! The King only sleeps," someone shouted from inside the tent. "Give him peace."

CHAPTER TWELVE

Once Edward was dead, officers emerged from a hinterland of government reserved for interregnums – chamberlains and servants, previously charged by the monarch with preventing panic, chaos and rebellion following on his defunction. The Exchequer and the Chancery continued working under the royal seals as if he were alive.

All exits and entrances to the tent were strictly controlled. Although no statement was made, no denials were made either. No one said anything on the question of Edward's existence. One rule ran the royal tent – to stay close. If anyone came and demanded to be told the truth, no information was given, but his name was taken as a doubter – only a hair's-breadth from a traitor.

Langton supervised this reign of the living dead. His instructions from Edward were: my death must be concealed from the enemy *and the army* until the transfer of power to my son is effected. The invasion host must not melt away.

Thirty thousand soldiers were assembling on the coast. Within a matter of hours, every man at Burgh-by-Sands felt he knew the truth, also the need for authority to go from the dead to the living. So they half-heartedly participated in the myth – but mourned all the same – sat on their haunches, playing dice and watching the ebb and flow of the tide in the estuary.

Meanwhile, a messenger rode towards Halifax to find Ned and deliver the news.

William Wild sat beside Edward's corpse, brooding and depressed. This was the worst part of being a bodyguard. Being confined in a tent with a cadaver in summer weather for days and nights of nightmare was sapping his spirits. This dark mood was exacerbated by a strange transference to him of Edward's anxieties in depth.

The moment had arrived. Ned was king.

The Irishman was glad he had something to read – a translation of Avicenna's *Book of Healing*, a vast philosophical and scientific encyclopaedia, which was in a locker beside the King's bed, a marker at page fifteen (where it had been for the same number of years).

For the days it took the messenger to return and announce King Edward the Second was coming north to receive homage and lead the army, William Wild read again what had once so disappointed him – the sum of human knowledge.

❧

The fact of death was only made public when Ned's messenger arrived at Burgh-by-Sands with his itinerary. Upon arrival on the Border he would go straight to Carlisle to receive the fealty of all those magnates assembled with forces in the main army, then to Roxburgh to do the same with the smaller eastern army.

These plans indicated the new king's intention to carry out his father's plan – an advance on Edinburgh in the east and a major invasion into Galloway, moving the army across the estuary.

On 18th July a mounted reconnaissance party was sent out to test the crossing. William Wild managed to have himself included by claiming expertise in this special area – referring the military commanders to his historical knowledge of King John's crossing of the estuary of the Wash a hundred years ago, done without reconnaissance, which had been a complete disaster.

High tide was forecast within three days, which would produce the furthest ebb for the longest period. To move an army of thirty thousand over three miles of hidden quicksands, treacherous gullies and mudbanks would need the two and a half hours' maximum time low water could provide. The planning of the manoeuvre must be precise and thought through in detail.

For William Wild, to be out in the huge space of clear, washed air after being cooped up with a decomposing body for ten days was a release. He delighted in the horse beneath him, the birds, the aromas of the sea, and the vista. In the surfaces of pools he saw where he would rather be – with his children, in his house, in his valley, by his river. It was a reasonable hope. Ned would not be asking him to stay on as captain of the bodyguard – of that he was sure. There was probably another, younger man who would be given the appointment. Also, the months as spy and supervisor had taken their toll on their relationship. Providing Ned didn't exact revenge, soon William Wild would be free to retire to the Wye Valley and farm his land.

It was while these day-dreams were floating through his mind he heard warning shouts from the riders at the head of the reconnaissance party. About twenty horsemen were pelting across from the Scottish side of the estuary, banners flying, sunlight sparkling on their weapons.

The leader of the reconnaisance party signalled his men to form a line abreast to meet the attackers head-on.

As the gap closed, the horseman at the head of the charge sheathed his sword and started laughing. All the riders behind him joined in, reining their horses to a walk.

When the leader took off his helmet, William Wild saw the mass of golden hair. It was Ned. The other troops in the reconnaissance party dismounted and knelt in the sand.

"I had you worried that time, Willy," he said, eyes gleaming with amusement as the Irishman got off his horse and bowed the knee.

"We took a diversion, wore their colours, rode through their camp – exactly how Piers would have done it, with style! It was such fun."

When the purpose of the reconnaissance was explained, the King seemed to take little interest. He said there was no point in continuing with it because his party had already ascertained it was safe by crossing the remaining distance. The reconnaissance turned back and both groups headed for Burgh-by-Sands.

William Wild rode alongside the King in the thrall of a strong memory from forty years past – Edward riding across the mouth of the Na'aman river south of Acre after a raid into enemy territory, Saracen heads swinging at his saddle, singing a psalm:

The King shall joy in thy strength, O Lord;
And in thy salvation how greatly shall he rejoice!
Thou hast given him his heart's desire,
And hath not withholden the request of his lips.

In the tent at Burgh-by-Sands, Ned spent a short time in prayer beside the body of his father. "*It* must go to Westminster," he said curtly to the chamberlain as he got up. "Speak to the monks. Do something about a tomb."

He went on to name those members of his father's household who would not be staying on – and those who would. Important among the latter were Tom, the fool, Matilda, the acrobat, Richard, the fiddler, Gregory, the bagpiper – and three wardrobe clerks who could also act in plays.

"And I want you to stay on as well, Willy," he added. "Life wouldn't be the same without you to keep me on the straight and narrow."

The question of the invasion supervened. Ned assured the commanders he intended to carry on with the existing strategy. The crossing would take place when judged best for the tide – in three days. He could only afford time to ride one day with his father's coffin on its long journey to London. Then he would have to double back for the homage of the magnates and lead the army into Scotland.

"You'll come with me, Willy," he said above the clamour his decisions created. "We can think about some more land for you.

Don't be shy. I'll brook no refusal. You deserve more than a smallholding." His eye caught a senior man of Langton's within earshot and he raised his voice, laughing. "Things are changing already! Willy Wild a baron! Who would have thought it?"

Embarrassed, the Irishman bowed and tried to withdraw as a crowd of petitioners surrounded the King. Towering over them, Ned kept his eyes on William Wild, a smile of mischief playing on his lips. "From now on we must see more of your Welsh concubine," he called above the throng. "Tell her Piers will be back in England shortly. He's always asking after her in his letters. Ah, those happy days when she came up to Wetheral! Remember? They got on so well together."

While close to death on the roadside near Nantwich in the spring, the Irishman had given all his stored-up faith to the woman struggling to preserve his life. She would live through the few decades it would take for William Wild to be completely forgotten in this world. Her own life, and the lives of their children, would carry his memory as far as it mattered.

Compared to the great desert faiths he'd explored, this belief wasn't much of a religion. A man of intellect should have been able to come up with something better. No texts, no ceremonial, no community, no symbols, no future – it would never stand up to scrutiny. Heresy was too elevated a description for this shanty of half-pagan ideas. All he could say (and, being wise, he wouldn't say) was – what I've worked out is mine. For me, beyond this truth, I've found nothing to sustain else.

There was one drawback. Its greatest weakness was its greatest strength. If he lost Valmai, he would lose everything. She was the lynch-pin of his private system.

Gaveston had been on good terms with her for the few months before his banishment, not paying her the respect due to a lady – which he paid to no woman – but giving her the recognition of one adventurous spirit to another. He made it plain he desired her – but that needn't be taken too seriously – he desired any attractive woman. Ned made it his business to stand to one side in these affairs, neither approving nor disapproving. But now he was settled in the seat of power with Piers at his right hand, he seemed intent upon providing the Gascon with all his needs.

On the day they both accompanied the King's coffin to Kendal, Ned mentioned to the Irishman how he'd taken the trouble to read all his confidential reports.

"Fascinating stuff, Willy," he said with the friendliest of smiles.

"It could have been much worse, I know. You protected me from my father's wrath. What I like is the acceptance of my ways, my character, my *foibles* – one of your favourite words – that comes through. We must always tolerate each other's *foibles.*"

Before Ned left the cortege and returned to Carlisle, he told William Wild to go to London as captain of the escort and assist Langton along the way.

"Piers will be in London by the time you get there," he added casually. "Help smooth his path, Willy. At this stage, he has many enemies. But everyone must learn to like him."

The Irishman asked if any one path above others should be smoothed.

"Most of the powerful people who resent him will be with me in Scotland. I'll deal with them while we're on campaign. That still leaves plenty of voices against him in the Church, and the City..." He shook his head as if in wonder at the hostility. "Why do they hate him so much? What has he done?"

"It will make things easier between us, my lord king," William Wild said flatly, "if we don't pretend the last ten years didn't happen. You know why so many people hate Piers Gaveston. He's your favourite."

"You were my father's favourite. Everyone doesn't hate you."

"Is there any real comparison?"

A cold pause ensued. The Irishman braced himself. If speaking out in this way meant making an enemy of the King, so be it. He could not envisage a future unconditionally supporting Gaveston's rise to power. The old king's failure to separate Ned's passion from politics didn't mean the argument was over.

"I want you to talk straight like that all the time, Willy. Always be brave and direct with me. It will be a great help," the King said, though there was a blue frost in his eyes. "Keep me in touch with what the haters are saying. Explain it to me, if you can." He paused, raising an eyebrow. "Well, let's start now. Can you explain it?"

"They're afraid of his power over you. They don't want to be ruled by him, through you. Why does he have to be a great man? What's he done to deserve it?"

Ned nodded as though in agreement. "Thank you, Willy. That was very clear. But you're describing ignorance and prejudice. How many times have I told them Piers is my *brother* – my closest family."

"But he isn't a member of the family. People can't be grafted onto it that way."

"Yes, they can. By law. When I marry that French girl she'll become a member of the family, won't she? Perhaps I should formally adopt Piers as my brother?"

❧

At Waltham Holy Cross ten miles north of London, Edward the First's body was lying in the Augustinian abbey after the long journey south.

A mass for the repose of the dead king's soul was being sung. Langton was present. The following morning he was due to go into London and make the funeral arrangements at Westminster.

William Wild was in the guest-house. Valmai had joined him at Waltham. Four knights arrived from the north, having set out from Carlisle after the King arrived to receive the fealty of the magnates. They carried a warrant of arrest for Langton.

The Irishman advised the knights to wait until the mass was over before making the arrest, which they gladly agreed to do – accepting food and drink from the canons. William Wild held them in conversation, without asking questions about Langton. As they relaxed, the topic naturally surfaced. The treasurer's career was over, the knights said – the incident at the warming-house had come back to haunt him.

"To arrest a bishop is quite a thorny business," the Irishman observed. "Where are you taking him?"

"To the Earl of Cornwall's castle at Wallingford."

Langton entered the guest-house, having returned from the mass. He carefully studied the arrest warrant, reading the charges out in a light, amused tone as if he had expected no less.

"Misappropriation of funds? This is all well done," he said with a terse laugh, taking a seat alongside the knights, "and I'm sure it won't stop you executing your warrant if I point out that a clergyman can only be arrested by an officer of an ecclesiastical court."

The knights affirmed it made no difference what he said. He was to be taken to Wallingford and delivered into the hands of Piers Gaveston, the new Earl of Cornwall.

"Well, what a mercy that will be," Langton said with a thin smile. "With such a witty man, I won't be short of things to talk about."

The knights were satisfied to remain overnight at Waltham but insisted on staying at the guest-house to watch over their prisoner. As the evening proceeded, it became increasingly convivial. Most of the knights' attention was on Valmai who was used to dealing with young men of this class. As they joked and flirted, Langton shared his thoughts with William Wild, whom he took to be a man in a similar position to himself.

"He'll get rid of everyone from his father's regime," he said resignedly. "Droves of Gaveston's friends and relations are already on their way over from Gascony. Gaveston will abuse the patronage system. He'll take revenge on anyone who's disapproved of him. Those will be the mistakes on which he'll founder. It's only a matter of time."

The Irishman said he couldn't imagine the King wanting councillors who'd only been doing their jobs to pay with their lives. That wasn't in his nature.

"We'll see what happens to me. I'm the first to go, as far as I'm aware. But I ask you – misappropriation of funds? Me? Everyone knows how honest I am. Dismissing me as royal treasurer is one thing, but to make Gaveston my gaoler? Perhaps he's being given powers of life and death. It wouldn't surprise me."

As Langton's assistant, it now fell to William Wild to shoulder the responsibility for arranging Edward's funeral. He took Valmai with him to Westminster, leaving the rest of the cortege in Waltham. The abbot of the Benedictines at Westminster had a message waiting for the Irishman from the King. The Bishop of Durham was to take over all matters pertaining to the funeral. Our trusted servant William Wild was to proceed *with his spouse* to Wallingford.

Fortunately, Valmai had been dropped off in Cheapside to do some shopping while William Wild went to the abbey. While with the abbot, he carefully made no mention of his wife's presence in London. As soon as he saw Valmai again, he told her what had happened. She would have to leave London immediately and return home. Because he had received the order in front of witnesses, he would have to go to Wallingford. If asked to explain Valmai's absence he'd say the message had been received after her departure for the Wye Valley.

Valmai was unwilling to be part of this subterfuge. She saw no point in disobeying Ned so early on in his reign. Although she couldn't imagine why it was so important for her to go to Wallingford, there was obviously a reason. The Irishman didn't enlighten her, anxious not to reveal his suspicions. "I'll tell them the truth – well, a portion of it – that you haven't seen your children since last April…" he said, ignoring her argument for obeying.

"The twins are well looked after by my mother," Valmai replied. "Why displease Ned if we don't have to? If he turns against you now, we can lose everything."

William Wild had no option. He outlined his fears.

Valmai listened in silence. He could see the impact of what he was saying. Gaveston's yen for her was not news.

"You don't struggle if you're in a net," he added finally. "You cut your way out."

She shook her head emphatically. "You know Ned. Except for one thing, he's completely inconsistent. As for Piers, he can fancy me all he likes. Don't you worry about him. I can take care of that."

It was a measure of Valmai's influence that he agreed, knowing in his heart it was a mistake. Valmai had argued that Ned was flexing the levers of his power solely in order to get the feel of running the country. The Irishman argued that should this be true, the design of corrupting a man's wife was mean, nasty and trivial. Ned was more intent on feeding Gaveston's whims than securing loyalty.

The political situation had been poised to change on Edward's death. Fear of how Ned would behave once off the leash dominated the thoughts of everyone in government. The indications so far were dismal. Ned would be a monarch only where the influence of his dead father lingered. The Scottish war had gone ahead. Ned was going to marry Isabella. In these decisions the old king ruled from the grave. But Ned's actions beyond his father's will were frighteningly random, subjective, and familiar – all expressive of personal emotion. His ambition was not that of a new king who took his function seriously. Inasmuch as he had a policy, it was to have his own way where it mattered to him. The rest could carry on rumbling along ruts worn down by his father.

CHAPTER THIRTEEN

I've been let off the annual tramp through the Scottish bogs, Willy. No Bruce-coursing for me this year," Gaveston said, a long fold of purple silk decked with raindrop pearls over his knee. "Ned realises how much work is involved in becoming an earl. Documents, documents, documents…cases, pleas, petitions. All new to me! I need a guide through it all."

Valmai was right, the Irishman thought, recognising face after face as men moved around the hall at Wallingford – this isn't about lust, but another deadly sin. McHunter and Gualberto had met him on arrival. A Frescobaldi banker was also there, in deep conversation with treasury men from the royal territories in Acquitaine. Gaveston was easy with all of them.

"You have Langton here, I understand," William Wild said as if by way of conversation. "Will he be joining us?"

Gaveston laughed aloud, handing the silk to a tailor who was standing by waiting to measure him. "Good old Willy. Always subtle in your enquiries," he murmured, flashing him a bright glance. "Langton is in my prison, as you're perfectly well aware."

"He's not going to make a contribution to…well, whatever it is all these finance experts are here for?"

"Bide your time, Willy. Where the King's business is concerned, it's best not to be impatient. All will become clear."

Gaveston stood up while the tailor's tape was put across his shoulders, then held out his arms for measurement.

"We travelled down from Carlisle together with the cortege," William Wild said. "It would be polite for me to say hello."

"Don't ask after his health. The bishop is recovering from some exercise he's not used to," Gaveston replied with a boyish grin. "Give him a few days to get over it. By the way, how does an old man keep the love of a young woman like Valmai? I always meant to ask you."

"She's obviously deluded," the Irishman answered with a straight face.

"She's wild. A real handful," Gaveston mused as he put his legs apart for the tape. "Any time you need her tamed, or she tires you out, send her to me. I love that black-haired, blue-eyed Welsh look."

Heart beating hard, the Irishman made no reply.

"You heard what I said?" Gaveston said with sudden harshness. "She interests me, but not as much as you do. I'm not the old Piers you knew. I haven't been wasting my time. I'm back to stay, Willy – and I've brought him salvation. While away, I've been working very hard so he doesn't have to spend his life scrabbling around for money."

"This isn't my kind of territory," William Wild said quietly. "Why do you need me here?"

"I don't. It's the King who wants you here, for reasons of his own."

"I didn't know you acknowledged he was capable of having reasons of his own," surged the reply out of the Irishman's mouth.

There was a chill pause. Gaveston frowned, looked hard into the Irishman's eye, then smiled.

"You really shouldn't cheek me, Willy, or you'll end up with Langton," he said casually. "And, by the way, where's Valmai. Ned told you to bring her with you."

"She's at home with the children, where she belongs," the Irishman replied with a touch of vehemence.

"Oh, stop being such a jealous old idiot," Gaveston chuckled. "I can see her any time I want. But Ned wants you here for the negotiations as his father's ghost. That's how he sees you. So, don't feel insecure, aged lover."

"Has the King expressed himself in that way?"

"Who knows his mind better than I do? We agreed you should be retained, and you should flourish. What man would hurt his father's ghost?" Gaveston smiled, reaching across to pat the Irishman on the his bald spot. "Calm your fears, captain. I swear on my blessed mother's grave an oath of friendship to you and Valmai, for that's all she is to me. But you musn't defy the King. We are both bound to obey him to the letter."

The Irishman slid out from under the patronising hand. Pale in the gills with suppressed anger, he forced a conciliatory grin. "My apologies for not offering you condolences." he said coolly. "I hadn't heard your mother was dead."

"Never mind her. Send for your wife. You're going to be at Wallingford for some time."

Gaveston's financial consortium was a ramshackle affair, but it had a certain freebooting vigour of imagination. With Langton under lock and key, his first step was to persuade Ned to let him empty the treasury at Westminster, add

Edward the First's personal money hoard of £100,000, and give everything to Emery de Frescobaldi as surety for loans to cover the cost of the Scottish campaign for double the amount. The Italian banker promptly shipped this loot to Gascony for safe-keeping. The second step involved obtaining a much greater treasure which would not only redeem that temporarily in possession of Frescobaldi, but give the Crown freedom from money worries for the foreseeable future – the huge assets of the Templars.

While banished in France, Gaveston had infiltrated the upper echelons of the order with the help of McHunter. Armed with contacts and introductions, he exerted his hard-nosed charm, offering control of the future king of England as a powerful bargaining counter. All the senior Templars knew they had little time to disentangle and disburse enormous deposits and caches of wealth throughout Christendom and Islam. What Gaveston suggested was a scheme whereby these funds could be invested in the English Crown – a legitimate, independent profitable business. Once the anticipated persecution abated, Templar veterans would be able to call on the royal treasury for financial help. It was essentially a pension scheme guaranteed by Gaveston's influence over Ned.

An approach had been made to Langton before the old king's death, asking for his approval of such a scheme. Immediately recognising the fingerprints of the Gascon all over the idea, Langton declined to answer.

On the evening of the second day after William Wild's arrival, Gaveston convened a meeting. Two hours before it was due to start, he asked the Irishman to visit the imprisoned bishop and outline the scheme to him again – roughed out for William Wild in advance – referring Langton back to the original approach.

"None of this unpleasantness need have happened, tell him," Gaveston said, ushering the Irishman to the guardhouse of the prison. "He never gave the proposal a chance. Stress the fact that this isn't pie-in-the-sky. We already know the location of a massive cache in Scotland which was buried by McHunter a few days before the Earn fiasco. Unfortunately, the site has been overrun by Bruce – who's ignorant of its existence."

"In doing this, am I in the role of ghost, or myself?" the Irishman asked. "You know I was a Templar once myself."

"Then you'll do what's best for your old friends – as well as praying for them, which they're going to need."

Langton sat in his cell in a filthy, bloodstained smock, a wreck of the man William Wild had been with less than a week ago. When the Irishman entered,

Langton shrank away.

"I thought better of you," he muttered.

"Don't misjudge me, Walter. Will you listen to what I've got to say?"

"As long as its nothing to do with mythical mountains of money," Langton sighed grimly. "That man is quite mad. Why have you been sent to see me?"

"Well, mythical mountains of money come into it," William Wild admitted, sitting down next to him. "But we can dispense with that."

"You're co-operating with that devil? He's out of his mind with greed."

"No, I'm not really helping him. But he's been talking to me about certain dreams."

"The hoard of the Poor Knights?" Langton said sardonically.

Out of interest, William Wild asked why the ex-treasurer – who had tried to control rolling royal debts for a decade – couldn't find any virtue in the scheme. "D'you doubt the existence of this wealth?" he asked.

"Not at all. I'm sure it's there," Langton replied. "Also, we know the order isn't going to survive. It lost its way years ago. One could say the Templars are only worth their money."

"In that case, why not put it to good use?"

Langton looked at his hands. The joints were swollen and inflamed. He held out his feet. The toes were black and blue.

"Lightly worked on by experts – pain administered only to an episcopal level," Langton said with a bitter attempt at a smile. "The Pope will hear of it – if that matters to these young fools. With no debts to hold them down they'd be as power-crazed as a pair of Mogul emperors."

"You don't think you should go along with their schemes until an opposition emerges?"

"And be taken for one of them? Then what would happen? Gaveston would pull me down with him – which is what will happen to you, if you're not careful."

The Irishman sat beside the wheezing prisoner in silence for a while, turning over what he'd said. When he got up to go, he offered what help he could – money to make things easier with the gaoler, clothes, food – if these were allowed. Langton shook his head and stared at the floor.

"Until I know where your loyalties lie, I want no help from you," he averred.

"How can I prove those loyalties? By being arrested? Then what use am I to anyone?"

"I've always served the Crown, not the person of the King," Langton replied with a sharp look. "You've always done the opposite."

"Have I? Where did that thought come from?"

"Have a look in the next door cell on your way out. Let that serve as my answer."

The Irishman shrugged and took his leave. When he stopped at the door of the adjoining cell, he could see nothing through the barred window. He asked the guard who the inmate was. The man whistled as though for a dog and the face of Felix the prophet of Dash appeared – stern, haggard and sad, wide-mouthed, heavily bearded, features framed in abundant matted curly hair – the tragic mask made slightly comic by a drooping right eyelid.

On arrival at Wallingford, Valmai was allocated separate quarters to her husband. She was put in to share with several women – all relatives of Gaveston from Bearn in Gascony. The Irishman had to make do with a corner in a room with other men.

On the morning of the final negotiations, William Wild called on Valmai before going into the meeting. As soon as he stuck his head through the door, the Gascon women stopped talking and eyed the Irishman.

Valmai steered him to a clear space by a window. "I'll have to tell you now, even though I'd have preferred to do it later, in private. Otherwise they'll tell you before I do. I'm pregnant."

William Wild stood stock-still. He was aware of the women watching him. With the hearing of owls, they'd picked up what Valmai was saying.

He made his expression glad, eying them defensively.

"This is good news," he said, taking her hand.

"They'll also tell you the child is Gaveston's," Valmai said, keeping hold of his hand. "It isn't. They're hill people who talk their own kind of nonsense. They believe Piers is the ram of the flock wherever he goes."

A lined, sun-brown woman of William Wild's age walked up to him and bumped her shoulder against his. "You should be with me, not her," she announced to the delight of the others. "I may be old but know everything there is to know about men. Let me show you, grandfather."

"Away with you," the Irishman said through shrieks of laughter. "Be more respectful, woman."

"No, no, no – you must respect *me,*" the woman declared, tossing her head proudly. "I'm the aunt of Piers de Gaveston."

In dark, sober clothes, long hair held back with a jewelled comb, Gaveston sketched out the Templar project to the meeting, explaining the predicament of the papacy, then in the process of being taken over by the French king and relocated in Avignon. The Pope, Clement V, was Bertrand de Grot, once Archbishop of Bordeaux in English Gascony. He was now a mere cipher of King Philip – but also titular head of the Templars. The rest of Christendom's reaction to the French take-over of the Church was fear and mistrust.

"We must move now," Gaveston finished by saying, "before King Philip takes everything the Templars own."

William Wild held up his hand. "May I ask the earl a question? If the order is dissolved, according to law what *should* happen to its assets?"

There was a flurry of amusement. Gaveston frowned and looked at McHunter. "Is there any law?" he asked. "I've not been made aware of any."

"There's nothing in the Rule dealing with the break-up of the order. It was assumed it would last for ever," McHunter replied. "This situation has never arisen before within the Church."

"So you admit the Templars remain within the Church?"

"We are part of the Church, and governed directly by the Pope, when he chooses to take an interest – but being under suspicion so long has driven us to rely only on ourselves."

"Then let's ask ourselves what would be right," the Irishman persisted. "Scripture's no help. You shouldn't have got so rich in the first place."

Gaveston got up and walked round the long table until he was standing behind the Irishman. "Willy, you're trying too hard," he said, putting his hands on his shoulders and squeezing hard. "Let's see to it the wealth of the Templars is distributed where it will do the greatest good."

This was well received. Gratified, Gaveston returned to his chair and clapped his hands.

"We need a diversion from all this hard talk," he said as a lutenist came out to join them with his instrument. "The King has sent me a song. He says it expresses everything he feels about me. The words are so moving, sincere and beautiful they might even have come from his own hand."

The lutenist sang, accompanying himself on his instrument.

No man's so accomplished he doesn't lack something.
Know my grief-stricken thoughts, my love.
You make me live so far from you.
Perhaps, at last, you've realised I'm not worthy.
If I come into your presence my heart is overcome with shame.

I'm of no account, uncultured, foolish and badly-mannered,
nor do I possess the intelligence, courage, goodness or beauty
to give your eyes any reason to gaze upon me.
I'm not fit to even think about you.
But what you have done and will still do for me
make me satisfied to go on living,
if there's hope of seeing you once more before I die.

There was a final flourish of notes, then the musician stood up to signal the song was over. The bemused meeting gave him a round of polite applause.

"What are we supposed to do – laugh or cry?" Gaveston said, comically rolling his eyes. "And all for little me."

Further discussions over the next two days dealt with guarantees for the Templars in exchange for the transfer of their funds to the Exchequer. In the middle of the knottiest negotiations, a messenger arrived summoning Gaveston to drop everything and join the King in Scotland.

"The dear fellow misses me," the Gascon said with scarcely disguised mockery, "and the war is going badly, which means he's running out of money. I'll have to leave you all to sort out the details of our arrangement. I want everything in place by December. No excuses!"

Gaveston's instructions from Ned were to leave by return with the messenger. In his haste to be away Gaveston gave William Wild no direct orders. Believing his duty sufficiently done, and his obedience established, the Irishman left Wallingford and took Valmai home to the Wye Valley.

CHAPTER FOURTEEN

It was a soft late summer afternoon when William Wild and Valmai approached Tintern Abbey along the north road from Chepstow. Fruit hung in the monastery orchards, wheat and barley stood golden in the fields. The cattle and sheep they saw along the way were fat. Down by the river racks of fish were drying in the sun. The only item missing in this welcoming sight was people. They spotted a few at work high up on the southern slopes of the vineyard in the distance but no one came out of the abbey or houses to greet them. As they crossed over the Wye at the abbey bridge a crippled lay brother they knew was waiting on the Gloucestershire side.

"I'm to give you a message," he said nervously, leaning on his crutch. "The lord abbot had news of your coming. He's told me to say no more than he's ordered me to say."

"Then speak up and let's hear it," the Irishman said warily, noting the man's apprehension.

"You cannot help but be offended," the cripple recited." My lord abbot would like to help but cannot get involved. This is a secular matter. He thinks it only right you should be warned. He advises your wife to come and stay in the guest-house until the worst is over. My job's done. I wish you well."

As the man hobbled back across the bridge, William Wild cried out to Valmai that she should go straight to the abbey, then spurred his horse towards Boldwood, calling his men to follow him.

No one was visible in the fields and orchards around the house at Boldwood. As he entered the yard he saw horses he didn't know in the stable paddock. Reaching the front door he remained in the saddle and breathed deeply, heart hammering. One of his servants whispered over his shoulder – reminding him of the abbot's advice to restrain himself.

Still no one appeared. The Irishman dismounted and went to the door and knocked.

The door was opened by Valmai's mother with the infant twins on their feet beside her. She gave him a warning look as he bent down to touch them.

"We're not hurt in our outer selves," she said, then stepped aside to let him in, whispering as she passed. "He's a plausible devil."

More than twenty people were gathered in the hall – armed men, women, children and servants.

Cold as ice, William Wild asked for a man to speak up and explain what had happened in his house.

"If you keep your sword where it is," a tall, bright-eyed man in his thirties said, stepping forward confidently. "I have no weapon, as you can see. Will you come into the open air? It's a better place for us to talk."

The Irishmen looked round all the faces to see if he could recognise anyone.

"There's no one here you know," the speaker said brusquely. "We brought all our own people. My name is Geoffrey March."

"You can burn in hell with your name and your people," the Irishman snapped. "What are you doing here?"

"Will you step outside?"

Once out in the forecourt of the house, the men of both parties faced each other over a distance of twenty yards while the Irishman and Geoffrey March stood between them.

"You see your infant daughters and mother-in-law haven't been ill-treated while they've been kept here," the invader said. "I had to hold them as hostages for the good behaviour of your servants."

"God's death, I should cut you in half now!" William Wild seethed, keeping his voice low. "Explain yourself while you're alive to do so."

"For your own sake, keep your temper. You should know we have full legal authority."

"What authority can you have in my house? Where are my servants? If you've harmed one of them, you're a dead man. I left sixteen here to look after my house and lands."

"They're waiting for you to decide their future. They had to get off the property."

Restraint was becoming almost impossible for the Irishman. He breathed hard through his nose and tapped the toe of his boot in the dust. "In as few words as possible," he said through gritted teeth, "give me the reason for this outrage."

Geoffrey March nodded and took a step back. "I am the steward appointed by the new owner..."

"I'm the owner!" William Wild shouted furiously.

"Please, keep calm..." Geoffrey March said, taking a further step back. "If you'll hear me out we can avoid unnecessary trouble. On the tenth of August, King Edward gifted this property to Raymond de Sauveterre. There is a deed."

His mind racing, the Irishman turned to one side for a moment to hold his rage and disgust in check. This was Ned at his worst. When he faced the steward again he was cooler.

"Who is this Raymond?" he asked.

"The captain of the King's bodyguard."

"That's strange," William Wild countered, staying in control though appalled and sick to the core, his feelings in a turmoil. "I'm the captain of the King's bodyguard myself, and I have a deed, and a charter from King Edward granting this property in freehold to me and my heirs for ever. So remove yourself and your people from my house and land before I destroy you."

"We stand by the law," Geoffrey March declared flatly. "You're the one who must leave."

"There's been a mistake. The King would never treat me this way. I'll drive you out."

There was a murmur from both groups of men facing each other across the forecourt. Geoffrey March held up his hands.

"Captain Wild, my employer's deed was issued under the seal of King Edward the Second, not the First," he said. "I have strict instructions. If you'll take a moment to look around you, a good reason will appear why you shouldn't force the issue."

William Wild looked round the forecourt. Archers with bows at the ready had appeared from the outbuildings and back of the house.

"With great Edward not yet in his tomb, this is done to me!" the Irishman cried, throwing his hat on the ground in helpless fury. "I'll go under this duress, but it will never stand in law, I tell you. It will never stand!"

In order to give William Wild time to find accommodation for his family, the abbot of Tintern let him use the guest-quarters – stressing he couldn't take sides in the dispute. Raymond de Sauveterre had already paid a formal visit to the abbey to register his status as the new owner of Boldwood. The abbot identified him for the Irishman as a neighbour of the Gaveston clan near Bearn in Gascony.

"Where will I find this odious man?" William Wild asked.

"He was on his way to Scotland," the abbot replied. "We only heard the old king was dead a week before he arrived."

Eventually the Irishman was able to rent a house near Tintern on high ground on the Welsh side near an unfinished church overlooking the valley. From there he could see his lands. The smoke from Boldwood's chimneys hung in the sky, mocking his anger. To bring the case to court would take an age. At the back of his mind he was not convinced Ned intended to cheat him in this way. A legal document would have to be translated out of Latin for Ned to understand it properly. A mistake had been made – a clerical error, a mix-up in the Chancery.

When he shared these thoughts with Valmai, she dismissed them as naïve. "Ned made a great show of asking you to stay on as captain of the bodyguard," she reminded him. "He told you he was going to make you a baron. This is one of his jokes. He had every intention of punishing you for being his watchdog and writing those reports."

"He asked me to stay on. There might be two positions now, one active and one reserve," the Irishman suggested. "Or he might intend it to be an honorary post in my case. You know how Ned gets everything back to front."

"It's because I do know Ned I think you're being naïve," Valmai said, a hard look in her eye. "He doesn't care what happens as long as he's pleasing Piers. He'll give him anything – even if it belongs to someone else."

"Then I'll have to speak to Piers. He can't be asking my advice one day and robbing me blind the next."

Valmai's reply was a pitying smile

The custodian of the small royal fortress of Saint Briavels up on the eastern ridge three miles from Boldwood was John Botetourt, a fast-talking, energetic man, some fifteen years younger than his friend, William Wild. They'd been on campaign together several times in Scotland and shared a liking for wide-ranging conversations, speedy greyhounds and Bordeaux wine. The Irishman received an invitation to spend a day hare-coursing with him. Botetourt asked him back to Saint Briavels afterwards for a chat.

Up to this point, Boldwood hadn't been mentioned. It wasn't in William Wild's character to solicit sympathy. His peers in the district avoided the subject if they met him. Botetourt broached it as soon as they sat down together for a drink, asking what action the Irishman proposed to take. What had happened was explained – how everything came down to conflicting gifts by different kings.

"I'm convinced it's a mistake," William Wild explained. "The King can settle it without us having to go to court, but there's no point traipsing around Scotland trying to find him. I'll have to go to London to attend the funeral shortly, so I'll wait and speak to him then."

"Don't be so passive! You're wrong-footing yourself!" Botetourt said scathingly. "You can't afford to wait. There'll be chaos and confusion in the King's household for months. The funeral, then the French marriage, then the coronation – one after the other – then all the Gascon upstart's interferences. You don't seem aware of the total mess we're living in. The only law we have at the moment is *possession.*"

William Wild drank his wine. Suddenly, he was tired of his ill-luck. He waited for the negative mood to pass before asking Botetourt to advise him further.

"Take Boldwood back. Then argue the toss from a position of strength."

"To go in and take possession will mean breaking the law," William Wild said. "Next minute I'll find myself asking the same law for justice."

"If this was in my jurisdiction – which it isn't – I'd say it's the new gift that must be proved, not the old. If this Raymond has a claim it should be made while you're in possession."

The Irishman was quiet for a while, looking into his cup.

"I wonder how many other cases there are like this," he said eventually.

"Quite a few, I'd guess – and more to come as that pair of jokers amuse themselves driving everybody mad."

The Irishman brooded, remembering the years he'd spent with Ned. The child had trusted and looked up to him. That had changed when Gaveston made his appearance, stealing all Ned's affection. Even then the Irishman had persuaded himself that he was still held in some respect. Now he saw how wrong he'd been. Ned and Piers had merely been laughing at him, as they laughed at everyone from inside their bond.

"It can't go on, Willy. This isn't government, it's clowning. Someone has to throw a bucket of water over those two."

William wondered who would have the stature to lead such opposition to the Crown.

"I know plenty of good men who aren't prepared to let the country fall to pieces. Patience will run out quite soon, you'll see. Does that sound like treason to you?"

"The older I get, the less I understand that word. Kings live off fear as well as popularity. Do these good men have reason to actually *fear* the second Edward?"

"There's no comparison with the old man. He was a terror, but an even-handed terror. What we have now are two harebrained boys off on a spree with the kingship. There's no need to be afraid of them."

The Irishman pursed his lips. "How can I fight a dozen archers?" he asked, returning to his own predicament. "That's what lost me the day. Without them, I'd probably have been able to drive the steward off."

"They're Welshman hired for the day – though the steward would like you to think they're part of the household," Botetourt said with a laugh. "You can find them any time cadging ale in the *Leaping Salmon* in Usk."

Three days later, Botetourt summoned Geoffrey Marsh to appear before him at the castle of Saint Briavels with his entire male household in order to ascertain liability for military service in Scotland, the hundred of Saint Briavels having not yet met its quota. The steward and his men were kept waiting for three hours while other cases were heard. When they appeared before Botetourt, a discussion with the sheriff took place about the boundaries of the hundred. On one of the documents, Boldwood was included, on another, it wasn't. Some idle clerk had been playing fast and loose with a pen. The enquiry was rapidly concluded. There had been a clerical error. Boldwood lay just outside the limits of the hundred. There were no liabilities of service.

Greatly relieved, Geoffrey Marsh and his company returned to Boldwood and found themselves locked out of the house. When the steward hammered on the door, the same dozen Welsh archers from Usk emerged and herded them off the property at arrowpoint.

The reoccupation of Boldwood created both happiness and anxiety. William Wild knew at some point in the future there would be a challenge from Raymond de Sauveterre. There was no guarantee it would be made through the law. Force had already been used by both sides. Until the King sorted out the dispute he had created, force would be the means of deciding the issue. From now on William Wild would be forever looking over his shoulder. Until the case was settled he would have no peace of mind over the safety of his property or family.

This worry failed to pull his spirits down, however. There was much for the Irishman to celebrate. The harvest was going to be a good one. The crops were still in the fields and on the trees, waiting to be gathered. The steward had not been a vandal – rather the opposite. Repairs and improvements had been made to the house and outbuildings. William Wild assessed the value of the work done and made a note. When the case was settled in his favour, the expense would be compensated.

As he got into his stride as a farmer, keeping his attention on what was immediately in front of him rather than speculating on the future, one thought kept plaguing him – had Valmai been unfaithful to him with Gaveston? The harder he worked, the more intensely the doubt made itself felt. It was as if everyday life and gnawing jealousy depended on the same stream of energy. Although he loathed the irrationality and saw dangers of allowing it to dictate his behaviour, he decided to speak up and risk the consequences.

He chose a time when the children, in-laws and servants were outside in the garden. Inviting Valmai into his work-room, he asked her to sit down at the table. She sensed something was afoot but said nothing until he put a package on the table and started unwrapping it.

"A present for me? Let me unwrap it for myself." she said, putting her hand on his.

The Irishman paused. "It's not a present," he said, disengaging his hand and removing the final layer. "It's a book."

Valmai examined the volume without much enthusiasm. "You know I can't read," she said. "But thank you for the thought."

"It's the four gospels."

"Oh, I see. Did it cost you a lot of money?"

The Irishman composed himself. "I borrowed it from the abbey library," he said carefully. "There's an oath I'd like you to take, Valmai. Swear on this book the child in your womb is mine."

Valmai drew a sharp breath. Her eyes froze for a moment. "Give it here," she said, pulling the volume towards her and placing both hands on top. "I swear by my soul and Jesus Christ and this sacred book the child in my womb was *not* fathered by Piers Gaveston." Taking her hands off the book she smiled up into the Irishman's face. "There, that's what you wanted me to say, isn't it?"

William Wild stared down at the table. A moment later, he sighed. "I'd like to go and hang myself now, if you don't mind."

"Oh, no, you don't get off that easy," Valmai said, getting to her feet.

"I've never felt more ashamed."

"Your trouble is – you think you know everything. You believe what you imagine."

He sat down at the table, lowered his head and rested it on the gospels with a groan. "You're right," he whispered. "I've offended what I love most. Hit me over the head with the book! That's all I deserve. But he is half my age, and God's gift to women, by all accounts – and we did all live cheek by jowl at Wetheral for the months when this child was conceived."

"Make your mind up what you believe," Valmai said lightly, as if it didn't matter.

"What can I do about jealousy?"

"It's a sin."

"You're all I believe in. How can I not trust you?"

"That's just the way you are. Anyway, having a man who's *a bit* jealous is better than having one who takes you for granted."

"I'll keep it down to a bit," he promised, taking her hand and kissing it. "You realise this means you can destroy me any time you like?"

"We'll leave the future where it is, if you don't mind. Think about Piers as you know him. He's something to look at, he flirts as he breathes, he struts, he challenges. It's not all show. He can do all the things he advertises – all the things men are supposed to do. He can amuse. He's brave. How does a woman deal with a man like that? We have to find our own way, *cariad* – or it's the convent for all of us. In many ways, he's the whole idea behind men, the men women are reckoned to like best. But he's shallow. He's got the money-sickness. When he's after something or someone he's got the patience of Satan. Meanwhile, as we've got the gospels here, you can swear an oath yourself."

"Name it!" he said, sitting up straight, gratified and bewildered by her analysis. "Not to be suspicious? I'll do it."

"I asked you a jealous question of my own a year ago when you were very sick" Valmai said, lifting his hands and putting them on the book. "We were on our way to join Edward on the Border. D'you remember?"

The Irishman nodded. "I remember," he admitted.

"Then you've known all this time how it must trouble me, you bad man. You didn't bother to give me an answer, did you? So your jealousy is not only unjustified but also unfair and selfish. Will you answer my question now?"

William Wild stood up with the book in his hands. "I've noticed how the more elaborate my plans are, the more I'm likely to be caught out by them. Tell me what I must swear."

"You know very well."

He pressed the gospels against his heart. "I swear on these sacred writings," he said solemnly, "and on the head of my unborn child, I was never the lover of Queen Eleanor and Ned is no son of mine."

That night was hot and humid. At two in the morning both of them were wide awake, lying splayed out on the bed. Wolves howled high up on the wooded ridge.

"Someone will have a sheep less in the morning," William Wild said, reshaping his pillow. "I hope it's not me."

Valmai made a sleepy sound. "It's too hot to talk," she whispered. "Don't keep waking me up."

"I love you too much for my own good," the Irishman declared, suddenly sitting bolt upright. "I'll have to reduce it somehow."

"What was that about sheep you were saying?"

"When I die, you'll go off with someone else.

The wolves howled again.

"They're nearer," he said, looking out of the window. "I should go down to the bridge in case they try to come across. Oh, Valmai, Valmai," he said, pacing up and down at the foot of the bed. "You've got too much power over me."

"Stop walking around. I'm trying to sleep."

"Today, did I give you all the answers you wanted?"

"Yes!"

"Will you come for a walk? It will be cooler down by the water. I want to talk to you."

"What about?"

"Eternal things."

Valmai sat up. "If it's eternal things, we're better off in the bedroom," she sighed. "What's the matter?"

William Wild sat down on the bed beside her. "If I explain, then we can lay it to rest. Eleanor…"

"You don't have to tell me anything more about Eleanor. You told me all I need to know."

"Let me explain once and for all. It was the effect she had on Edward that captivated me. She brought out the good in him. Otherwise, she was quite an ordinary woman."

"So am I," Valmai said, lying down again, "and I need my sleep."

"That's what I'm saying. You bring out the good in me – what there is of it – which, if there is such a thing as an eternal thing, must be an eternal thing."

"There's still time for you to be a priest if you want to," came the dozy response. "Don't let me stand in your way. Meanwhile, William Wild, if you don't lie down and stop talking, I'm going to feed you to the wolves."

CHAPTER FIFTEEN

After the successful crossing of the Solway with his army – not a man was lost – and a triumphal entry into Dumfries, Ned divided the host into three columns and sent them in pursuit of Bruce north-west, north and north-east to encircle him.

Meanwhile, Ned received the loyalty of those Scottish lords who would give it to him. He ennobled Gaveston at Dumfries *in absentia*, eliciting the support of magnates by bribing them with lands about to be conquered on the campaign. These men witnessed Gaveston's charter of enfeoffment as Earl of Cornwall. They did so without enthusiasm. Guy de Beauchamp, the Earl of Warwick – one of the magnates who loathed the Gascon most – was heard to mutter as his seal was put to the document: *a man makes his mark with one hand only.*

In mid-August, five weeks after his father's death, Ned was at Sanquhar in the valley of the Nith, thirty miles north of Dumfries, stuck between two ranges of guerrilla-infested hills, Carsphairn and Lowther, waiting for Gaveston in the rain.

The annual mass invasion in pursuit of a wily, mobile enemy who refused to fight a pitched battle held no allure for Ned. The gorgeous ceremonies at Dumfries over, he contemplated the slog through the hills with resignation. It would be a rerun of so many campaigns with his father – and it was only as a gesture to the past that he'd come thus far.

Bruce would never change his tactics. He would continue to wear the English down, his irregulars harrying overextended supply lines and sapping the original impetus of the invasion. This strategy had worked year after year.

With his father not yet buried, Ned couldn't withdraw so early in the campaigning season. Everyone knew the invasion had been designed and organised by the dead king. For it to be carried through was his last wish. But there was no need to go through with the whole plan from start to finish.

The conquest of Dumfries and Galloway would be enough for this year – a subjugation of one part of Scotland to impress the whole. A settled calm in this area would argue that people were happy to be a colony of the superior civilisation of the English. To prove this superiority, there would be feasts, games and parties. As soon as this notion took root in his mind, Ned knew Piers – that brilliant bacchanal – that festal god among dull men – must be at his side to show the Scots how to enjoy themselves.

They met on the bridge at Sanquhar. News of Gaveston's coming had gone ahead, announced by the new earl's trumpets along the way. By the time the two young men faced each other from opposite ends of the bridge, a crowd had gathered.

Both men wore purple – their colour of mutuality. While in his French exile Gaveston had obtained ostrich feathers dyed purple and brought them back in a long cedarwood box to wear at Ned's coronation. As he hurriedly packed at Wallingford for the journey north, he had decided to wear them for the reunion instead. This decision was questioned by the rain, but the symbolic value of these high, nodding decorations of self had become an *idée fixe*. In spite of the weather, in spite of the dye running into his hat and down his face, he wore the purple ostrich feathers.

"Brother!" Ned called through the rain that was hammering down.

"Noble earl! Come across." And he opened his arms for an embrace.

Gaveston bowed and walked forward, stopping at the centre of the bridge, ostrich feathers drooping. "My liege," he said, sinking to one knee.

Ned was unsure what to do. He couldn't keep his arms open for much longer without looking foolish. He had assumed Gaveston would come the full distance over the bridge, as any subject would. There was a long pause. Ned lowered his arms, then folded them, waiting for Gaveston to do the right thing. Instead, he remained on his knee.

Ned frowned and tapped his foot. The crowd was deadly quiet, abashed by the contretemps. Suddenly the clouds parted and a shaft of sunlight came down on the bridge. There was something about the sight of the beloved man kneeling humbly in the sun that wrenched Ned's heart. All protocol and stage-management was hurled aside as he bounded across his half of the bridge, conceding his ground. The onlookers growled in disbelief.

Gaveston did deign to kiss Ned's hand before being pulled to his feet and hugged. Ned whispered into his idol's purple-stained ear: "Who cares what they think? We must never be apart this long again."

In the large retinue following in Gaveston's wake from Wallingford was the lutenist who was on loan. He was rejoining the royal household of musicians, acrobats and clerks who doubled as an acting company. At the feast of thanks for his earldom given by Gaveston at Sanquhar, they performed an interlude with three characters – Greybeard, Face and Ape. This piece was a favourite of the old king's.

Greybeard was a strong, wise, well-balanced authority figure; Face, an alluring but irrational woman intoxicated by her own sexual power; Ape, brutality personified, vice-driven, mad and cruel.

What the elder Edward had always enjoyed so much was the co-existence of these forces within a simple story. No matter how often it was put on, it never failed to move him.

When the guests paused in their feasting to watch the interlude, the older hands among the English were disappointed to learn it would be the same old stuff. But they were interested to note the addition of a throne to the usual stage furniture. Having never seen the little play, the contingent of Scottish nobles who'd given allegiance to Ned at Dumfries were not aware of the change.

So far, the party had been a great success. Ned had made a special grant to cover the cost. Only the best was on the table. Since Gaveston's arrival, life had improved. Skies had cleared, bringing soft, warm winds from the south. The flooded Nith had settled back into its bed. Military stalemate forgotten, resentments transfigured into friendships by the magic of wine, the guests eased back their chatter to allow the actors to be heard.

When the dead king entered in his war gear it had a shattering effect on the Scots. A deep moan of susperstitious terror arose from them. The English froze, staring at the resurrection. Here was the strong man who'd ruled and held them together for thirty-five years. Bishops and priests paled and made the sign of the cross to protect themselves from this necromancy.

Felix paused by the throne, looked around him with a fierce, haughty air, flipped back his cloak, adjusted his scabbarded sword so it didn't get tangled between his legs, gave a pull at his long nose, and lowered himself slowly onto the throne.

Pandemonium broke out amongst the Scots.

The English had lied yet again. The old tyrant Edward was still alive. This was an offence against God and death. The cruelty of the deceit was beyond belief. Was there no limit to sassenach treachery?

Ned had to take the stage himself to calm everyone down. It was only a jest, he explained. It was only a lookalike.

"With your father not yet in his tomb?" demanded the Bishop of Glasgow, still shaken and upset. "What kind of a jest is that? I implore you, for all our sakes, be more serious. To attend this function, I was temporarily let out of prison. After this shocking display, I'd rather be back there."

The spirit of the feast was broken. People began slipping away. After a few vain attempts to reinvigorate the proceedings with music and dance, it was brought to a premature close.

In the small hours, Ned and Piers had a long conversation about getting married.

"I've got to do it, so it's only fair you should as well," Ned said. "There's a girl with enough prospects to tempt anyone – my niece, Margaret de Clare, the Earl of Gloucester's daughter. She's an heiress, with great lands…not bad-looking… passable at a glance. Well, a very quick glance…Knows her place. You'll get on with her."

"Is this an order?"

"I command your body, Piers. You will breed when I say so. The wedding will be at Berkhamstead the day after All Souls, it's all arranged."

Gaveston pulled a face.

"You had someone else in mind?"

"No – I simply hadn't thought about it."

"She's not someone who'll cramp your style."

Gaveston looked up and grinned. "Thinking about it, that's very good news, actually," he said with a laugh. "I'll be out of Scotland before the middle of October."

"Oh, long before then," Ned assured him. "I'm putting Aymer de Valence in charge of the army. I can't afford to waste any more time up here. I've got too much to do."

"You surprise me. Aymer was humiliated by Bruce only four months ago. He ran rings round him. He's certainly not going to terrify the Scots, is he?"

"That was a freak result. Sheer bad luck. It could happen to anyone."

"The man's a mediocrity."

"My father didn't think so."

"People who can't abide competition choose mediocrities to work with. That was your father's weakness. Langton was another of his stooges."

Ned looked at his fingernails. "Well, I can't argue with that," he said with a chuckle. "If ever there was a mediocrity it's Langton. We needn't think about him for a year or two. You've got him comfortable, I hope?"

"I don't know. I didn't bother to look. Ned, I do wish you'd consulted me before deciding on Aymer de Valence. I think you're making a big mistake."

"If you want the job of ruling Scotland for me, have it!" Ned blurted, upset. "I thought we were going to be able to spend more time together."

Gaveston laughed at the idea. "Leave me in Scotland? That's the last thing

I'd want. But I know these English lords, Ned. There's scarcely a soldier amongst them. Whoever you leave behind in Scotland must be a soldier."

"You're right. Some of them are contemptible."

"Giving Aymer de Valence the earldom of Pembroke was a disastrous decision," Gaveston added, "*Joseph the Jew's* already got more than he deserves."

"Stop saying Aymer's Jewish. He isn't!"

"Avaricious, oily, sly – doesn't that describe him? Why didn't you ask me what I thought before you made the appointment? And as for being given an earldom, well…it brings the honour into disrepute. I feel like handing mine back."

"I didn't give it him. It was my father, while you were away in France. Aymer kept asking and asking and asking. My father eventually caved in."

Gaveston shook his head. "Your father and his mediocrities," he said scornfully. "I'm a good judge of character, Ned, I know what people are worth. You talk to me about all promotions in future."

"That's what I want!" Ned exclaimed. "This is what we dreamt about – being able to run everything together."

Gaveston smiled. In his mind as he looked ahead he was balancing the joys and dangers of partnership, imagining how it could all possibly work. While in France he'd mixed with a new type of court politician, ruthlessly clever, hard-headed men, who, if let loose on Ned's immaturity, would strip him down to the bone. From exile he'd urged Ned to learn some statecraft, foreseeing the need for it in self-defence.

"Before we leave the subject, let me say one thing," he said gravely. "Delegating power is a delicate business. You need foresight and intelligence. The man you want in Scotland is Jean de Bretagne. He speaks the kind of language Scots understand."

"I've already told Aymer about the appointment."

"Then let him do it for a month, dismiss him and replace him with Jean."

"That will look bad," Ned said, dismayed. "It was supposed to be a promotion."

"Aymer's sure to fail. He's already lost us so much ground," Gaveston cried, his face suddenly flushed. "How dare he let you down! If it was up to me, he wouldn't get away with his life."

Ned turned their talk to a less important topic – William Wild and his wife. Ned was pleased to hear they'd appeared at Wallingford, as instructed.

"Seeing her wasn't as much fun as I'd hoped. She's going to have a baby," Gaveston said sourly.

"Piers, Piers, you only have to look at a woman and she's pregnant," Ned laughed. "Willy won't like that."

"She won't tell him – and I certainly won't."

"Giving his job and estate to your cousin won't please him either."

"Serves him right for spying on us."

"You watch out. That old Irishman will be looking for revenge."

"Willy's all mouth. It's about time he died and got out of the way. What are we talking about him for?"

The two young men looked at each other. A cloud of physical and mental amazement descended. They'd done it. It had all happened for them. Destinies, dynasties, wars, treasures, life, death, were tools in their hands.

As they hugged each other in sheer *joie de vivre,* ten years of waiting were swept away. They kissed like drunken emperors reeling on top of the world.

"You seem to have commanded my body yet again," Gaveston said. "Let's go and rest awhile."

In the following fortnight, the English column in the Nith valley managed to push on another sixteen miles and take the town of Cumnock. On 30th August 1307, Ned called a council of war there. Gaveston sat by his side, sharing a bench. Present were Aymer de Valence, Earl of Pembroke, Jean de Bretagne, Earl of Richmond, Henry de Lacy, Earl of Lincoln, Thomas de Vere, Earl of Arundel, Thomas de Lancaster, Earl of Lancaster, John de Warenne, Earl of Surrey, Guy de Beauchamp, Earl of Warwick and the marcher lords Mortimer of Wigmore and Hugh de Despenser, as well as the mace-bearing Bishops of Durham and Norwich.

Ned opened the meeting with a few words on the keeping of oaths. "It was my father, not I, you'll remember, who swore on the swan that his body would not be buried until Scotland was conquered. It's now fifty-three days since he died. That's too long," he said with a winning smile. "He must go into his tomb."

There was a silence as this information was digested. The earls exchanged glances. Was there any point in raising the issue of the player resembling Edward *père* who had shocked everyone at Sanquhar? He was still part of the King's household, travelling in a cage, chained like a bear. It was in bad taste, but the common soldiers liked to see him – relishing the terror his appearance had caused among the Scots.

Henry de Lacy took it upon himself to bring the matter up in a lighthearted sort of way, asking what the fellow's future consisted of – a good jest tending to pall with repetition.

"Remember what the old king told Ned to do, Burstbelly?" Gaveston said lightly. "Boil the flesh off his bones and carry them in front of the army. We can carry this lookalike instead."

The earls were unsure that they'd heard aright. Henry de Lacy was in his seventies, so corpulent his armour had to be specially fashioned to contain his paunch.

While the Burstbelly insult was being digested, the Earl of Warwick asked if the Earl of Cornwall had any observations of his own to make on the breaking of oaths.

"If I take an oath, I keep it," Gaveston replied haughtily.

"That's strange," Warwick said. "You swore on the consecrated Host never to return to England."

"Until recalled," Gaveston snapped, "if your memory will serve you."

"Recalled by King Edward *the First*," Warwick persisted, his dark face distorted by a severe frown. "Those were the terms. You broke your oath."

"Don't split hairs with me, Black Dog!"

Warwick stared, outraged.

"That's not my name," he said coldly, "and I take it as an insult."

"You're meant to, Black Dog. You know full well my exile is over. But if you want to make something out of me calling you Black Dog, Black Dog, we can arrange something."

The earls were astonished. It seemed Warwick's choice was either to draw his sword or leave. He did neither. For a moment he took the full brunt of Gaveston's arrogant, drilling blue eyes, then switched to the King's amused stare.

"Black Dog...Burstbelly...what next, sire?"

"Oh, leave it aside," Ned said offhandedly. "We have important things to discuss. My father's funeral, my marriage, the coronation, all make it necessary for me to halt this year's campaign. What territory we have, we will hold. Aymer de Valence is appointed guardian of Scotland. We will renew our efforts next year, God willing."

"And perhaps we can get some good fighting men with us, for a change," Gaveston added, eyes still darting blue fire in Warwick's direction, "instead of the lazy whoresons we've got here!"

"Christ's blood, how I hate them!" Gaveston railed, angrily drunk that night in Crumnock camp. "If we're to create a new kingdom, we must have a new aristocracy – real men, not eunuchs. No wonder Bruce is laughing at us. I spit on your useless earls! I spit on them!"

Ned made soft, placatory noises. "They're what we've got to work with," he said gently. "Don't hate them, please. You're one of them."

"What have they ever done for anyone?" Gaveston ranted. "Nothing! I'm not one of that gang. I tell you, Ned, I'm only an earl *for you*. If you died tomorrow I'd leave…walk away…become a hermit or something."

"You wouldn't be much of a hermit," Ned laughed.

"That's what Black Dog should be – a hermit in a kennel on a chain. When is that bloody man ever going to crack a smile?"

"Not tonight, I suspect. But seriously – we can't afford to alienate them all. We need friends."

"Oh, who needs that sort of friend?" Gaveston cried, catching Ned's hand. "Just be a king. My king."

On his retreat from Scotland with Gaveston, Ned decided to cross the Pennines by way of Wensleydale and visit Knaresborough, a castle on the plain of York near Harrogate, part of the landholdings of the earldom of Cornwall. The friends had agreed that this place would be their refuge from the world, somewhere to relax and play.

A messenger sent by Geoffrey Marsh to notify Raymond de Sauveterre, the new captain of the royal bodyguard, of the loss of his Wye Valley estate caught up with the cavalcade. Once Raymond knew the details of the repossession of Boldwood, and Botetourt's part in it, he complained to Gaveston.

After acquainting Ned with what had happened, Gaveston asked for Raymond de Sauveterre's release from his duties so he could go to Boldwood, evict William Wild, and reclaim his property. In addition, he persuaded Ned to discharge Botetourt from his post as *custos* of the royal castle at Saint Briavels.

During the conversation, Ned queried why Gaveston was so anxious to deprive his unborn bastard of a home. This was asked with no great seriousness.

"What's another child to those two? They'll find a way to look after it," Gaveston said. "She's grateful to be having a baby at all. She says Willy can't get it up any more."

Ned kept quiet for a while. "I wonder why she told you that," he said eventually. "She'd be making a fool of herself. Valmai's got twin daughters, both of them called after my mother."

"Well, that's news to me. She never mentioned them."

Ned regarded him with a curious half-smile. "Why would you bother to lie to me about something like that?" he said softly. "I don't need to be impressed by your conquests of women."

Gaveston shrugged impatiently. "What does it matter? I can't remember what they say half the time. But don't make any mistake. I've had the Welsh bitch."

"I rather hoped that would be so. If I know for certain you're not sterile, I'd like you to think about a scheme for dealing with this French wife I have to have. The proof of my virility we gave Peter the Spaniard was cooked up for the occasion, mainly to keep my father quiet," Ned said with an apologetic shrug. "I can't possibly get a woman with child – which is all this French marriage is about."

"Isabella is very beautiful, they say – the daughter of Philip the Fair is fair. Why not wait until you've seen her?"

Ned shivered. "The company of women, I enjoy – their bodies appal me," he stated, making a sound of revulsion. "It doesn't matter how beautiful she is, I know I won't be able to do it."

"How can you be so sure?"

"Because I tried it – while you were away in France. It was disgusting but I went through with it. I even made her pregnant. I've got a bastard called Adam."

Gaveston threw his head back and laughed. "Dear, mad-minded Ned! The things you come out with."

"The whole business was gross. I couldn't bring myself to please my father by telling him. He'd been so foul about the whole business. I didn't think he deserved to be made happy because I'd treated myself like a farmyard animal. He was better off with the affidavit – the lie he knew to be a lie. Besides, I knew I'd never do it again. It's far too messy – not right for a man like me." He paused, grinning at Gaveston's consternation. "Think of it – you'd father the future kings of England, maybe of France too."

"Ned, this is fantasy. We'd never get away with it."

"When you meet, she'll fall in love with you. They all do. I'll explain it to her. She marries me but you're her lover."

"Ned, this girl is a king's daughter. She's going to be a queen," Gaveston protested, unable to stop laughing. "Certain things will have to be right for her. Don't think you can palm her off with a substitute."

"She definitely won't want me. Women can tell when a man finds them repellent. She's young, very impulsive and adventurous, I'm told. I think it would appeal to her. With your co-operation, I think it can work."

Gaveston put his hands over his ears. "No, no, no, no," he moaned, still laughing. "No more, Ned. You'd be a traitor to your own blood, your own family."

"You're my family."

"*Par descente de heritage*, Ned! You can't break with your ancestors. You and your children belong to them."

"I belong to you and nobody else."

For the first time, Gaveston saw the true depth of the King's commitment to him. On Ned's side it was a blind force binding them together. Although feckless and often foolish, in this one thing he was a man above men, without fear, ready to take any risk. Gaveston's life had been precarious enough to know the consequences of living upon emotion. His own father had been driven from his lands because of a passion over a woman, escaping from the long reach of the French king with little more than his pride. That was all father and son had known while Gaveston was a child – the open roads of war, hand to mouth living made bearable by the belief something would turn up to redeem exile and loss.

If Gaveston was going to preserve his self-esteem and confidence, he had to match Ned's courage. Where that had come from, he couldn't guess – certainly not from his privileged, protected background. Not understanding its origin made the courage even more fantastic and powerful. If Ned couldn't care less what happened as long as they were together, neither would he. In this secret fashion, Ned was the true leader, he the led.

As they rode over the flatlands into Knaresborough, the grim, silent earls trailing resentfully behind them, the keep of Ned's massive gift towered ahead, dominating the landscape.

At the gates the earls were told the King didn't want them staying at the castle because he wanted to be alone with his *brother,* leaving them another twenty miles to ride to York to find alternative accommodation.

That night Ned commanded a performance of the interlude for Greybeard, Face and Ape. The audience of two shared a couch, legs entwined, feeding each other wine, trying to put the actors off by their antics.

Felix as Greybeard remained stern and severe, refusing to be dislodged from his role by their stupid lewdness. His expression was impassive, his dignity composed. As the antics on the couch became more heated and extreme, the flint in Greybeard's eyes was sharpened. When he spoke, his voice was the old king's. Now and again, when the sexual charade became utterly disgusting, it cracked.

By the time the interlude was over, Ned and Piers had forgotten the actors. As they left the chamber, England's king was being noisily buggered.

When Felix brained himself against a wall that night, he was still trapped in the role of King Edward, choosing to die a second death rather than live with such poisonous shame.

CHAPTER SIXTEEN

For three days and nights, Ned and Piers weren't seen outside the walls of their bolt-hole. The gates of Knaresborough were kept shut. Messengers and petitioners piled up, camping in queues, waiting for an audience.

At noon on the fourth day, Ned appeared on the castle walls overlooking the river meadows. He saw a line of harvesters working in a field of corn, scythes sweeping in slow rhythm as they brought down the crop.

Soon afterwards, the gates opened and Ned emerged arm in arm with Gaveston. Messengers with urgent business from the Chancellery, the Exchequer, the Church and the army in Scotland set up a clamour. Ned laughingly refused to listen to requests or receive documents, trotting off along a track with Gaveston towards the harvest field.

They arrived at the line of harvesters with a crowd of more than a hundred streaming after them.

The men stopped work, staring at this strange circus. Ignoring the uproar behind him, Ned took off his coat and shirt, gave them to Gaveston, held his hand out for a scythe, took a place in the middle of the line, then started cutting the corn.

By now the reapers had realised who was in their midst. Initial puzzlement changed to excitement. The sight of their magnificent young king expertly wielding a scythe, sweating alongside them, leading the rhythm from the centre, sent them into euphoria. They struck up a song. Ned quickly picked up the simple words. Soon they heard his baritone joining in.

Ned kept them going for three hours through the heat of the day. The waiting crowd sat on the stubble and watched with Gaveston who had been offered a scythe but refused, saying: "I'm only here to hold his coat."

As peremptorily as he had come, the King laid down his scythe and left the field. The harvesters faltered, then stopped, exhausted by the rate of work he'd set. No man amongst them had ever sweated so hard.

Gaveston wiped Ned down with his shirt, picking straws out of his hair. One of the harvesters came and asked if he could have the King's garment as a momento for the local people, which was granted. He went back to his friends thrilled, waving it in the air.

As they walked back, Gaveston was surprised to find himself envious. An unexpected instinct made him keep behind Ned instead of in his customary position, alongside. Used to attracting attention wherever he went, and glorying in it, he couldn't quite get over being ignored. The harvesters, messengers and petitioners had all been won over by a man who knew what he was doing, and could do it well.

The crowd with business for the King was thoughtful as it returned to the castle to wait again. People had seen something which would stick in their minds. To some, it was very close to Scripture – the Lord's anointed in the plenty of the harvest field, in tune and rhythm with his subjects – but to the more hard-bitten amongst the officials and messengers, the appeal of the image didn't survive the stroll back to the castle gates. By the time they got there, opinion had shifted: here was a king who compromised his crown, making serfs and sheave-stackers his peers, undermining his authority. Rubbing shoulders with the lower orders never helped maintain the law, collect taxes, or fight wars. No good would come of this fraternisation – a king must be a man apart.

This view was passed on to Ned, diplomatically and courteously, by William Greenfield, Archbishop of York. He had arrived with no pomp during the interlude in the harvest field. When he saw the reaper make off with the King's sweaty shirt, he sent men after him to confiscate it, knowing the power of superstitious reverence.

Seniority demanded Greenfield be admitted to the castle immediately – not kept waiting outside like the others. While Ned had a standing bath, with a team of servants pouring water over him, Gaveston picked straws out of his pubic hair. The stringy, pop-eyed old prelate watched in amazement.

"What can we do for you, Archbishop?" Ned said with a straight face.

Greenfield snapped out of his trance. He had a number of items he wished to discuss.

First – the coronation. Robert Winchelsey, the Archbishop of Canterbury, was still in exile in France, another victim of the elder Edward's passion for punishing the clergy. The honour of officiating at the crowning had fallen to Greenfield as the next senior man. However, there were so many prelates in captivity in England, or in exile, he felt inclined to raise the matter and protest before accepting. "Those who wield the powers of the Apostles should be judged solely by God and the Vicar of God," he finished by saying. "The Church asks you to free our brothers, if you'll be so good."

In the happiest of moods, pleased with life, Ned was at his most emollient.

He agreed to recall Winchelsey from exile immediately so he could officiate at the coronation.

This was not quite the answer the Archbishop wanted, but he quashed an impulse to advise Ned to turn the matter over in his mind at more leisure. Although the revocation of Winchelsey's exile was a major achievement, it meant Greenfield would not crown the King. Tempering disappointment with joy, he proceeded to the second item, which was thornier – a comparison which had struck him between the David and Jonathan story in the second book of Samuel, chapter one verse twenty-six, and the King's relationship with his favourite.

"The suggestion is, sire – there are some affections between men which are wonderful, passing the love of women. And what a king was David! Also, one has to think of the disciple John who Our Lord loved best. God, in his perfection, can only love perfectly. Divine love is shared out equally amongst us all. The gospel-writer merely makes the observation about John. He doesn't investigate, or comment. And the Church herself is obtuse on the question of this kind of love."

"As is the Koran, according to what I was told," Ned said. "Though I'm told what we're talking about is rampant in Islam, especially among shepherds."

"I wouldn't know about that," Greenfield replied huffily. "The point I'm trying to make, sire, is this – what matters with any relationship is the truth within it, and how that truth is given substance *by the behaviour of the participants.*"

"He's been talking to Black Dog and the others," Gaveston muttered, rubbing Ned's genitals briskly with a towel. "They sent him over to nag at you."

"Another issue arises," Greenfield went on, standing his ground. "We have been called to a parliament at Northampton in a month's time. Arrangements for your marriage are to be discussed. The Church offers a twentieth of the value of all personal property owned by the clergy, excluding land and buildings, if a certain guarantee can be forthcoming."

"A twentieth is a bit mean," Ned mused, stroking Gaveston's head which had been laid against his chest. "Make it a tenth."

"Isn't the King interested in what kind of guarantee we seek?"

"For a tenth, I might be."

"A fifteenth would be made available if sodomy, condemned outright in the Scriptures, continues to be an offence under the law, to be vigorously prosecuted in all cases."

"Is it on the statute book?" Ned asked Gaveston, holding his face between his hands and kissing him on the mouth. "I didn't know that. Did you?"

"I don't even know what sodomy is," Gaveston responded, fondling Ned under the towel. "Perhaps the Archbishop will tell us."

Greenfield blanched, his poise shaken. "Sire, I cannot believe you don't understand. The book of Genesis and its moral precepts were part of your education. We must offset Samuel's subtle understanding with the strict canon against homosexual coupling. It is an unnatural vice and a sin against God."

"Why have you brought this up with me?" Ned demanded, changing his mood. "If there's a law it should either be enforced, or, if it doesn't work, abolished. That's all there is to it."

In the face of the King's hostility and the clownish lovemaking performed for his benefit, the Archbishop floundered. Until now he had believed himself able to manage royal disfavour, having weathered the oppressive displeasure of the first Edward on a number of occasions. He was one of the few senior churchmen to have no prison record.

Greenfield respected himself as a man who always put God first, the Pope second, the secular power a long way third. Because of this reputation, the earls had chosen to send him to Knaresborough, appealing to his pride. "You can do it better than any man we know," the old Earl of Lincoln had said, an arm round his shoulder. "Your brave integrity is the admiration of us all." But the King had contrived a situation in which there was no room for Greenfield to manoeuvre. If his reputation, his religion, his office, his self-respect meant anything to him, he should speak out now and condemn the flagrant sin being committed in front of him.

The thought of prison sharpened his sense of what was practical. If he directly accused the King of being a homosexual, his head might be off before the sun went down. Leaving the Church in England without a leader at this crucial time would threaten its survival. His mind scurried in all directions.

"I raise the issue in reference to the alleged sodomitical practices of the Templars!" he cried, relieved to find an escape route at last. "Consider recent events in France! We have news of arrests for sodomy, blasphemy and heresy! The whole Order of Poor Knights appears to be infected."

"Well, we'd better discuss that, hadn't we, Piers? I didn't know they were up to those kind of tricks. You're not a bit of an old gossip, are you, Greenfield?"

"Sire, this information comes from the best possible source – our own Archbishop of Canterbury in exile in Poitiers."

"You're in touch with him? I thought people in exile were supposed to be out of bounds. You haven't been conspiring, I hope."

Greenfield gaped, caught off-balance. Denial hovered at the back of his throat but couldn't reach his lips. I'm making such a mess of this, he thought.

"Be fair, sweetheart – some of the best people have been exiled," Gaveston said, licking Ned's shoulder. "Mmmm, you're still a bit salty from all that sweat.

As I recall from my own sufferings in exile, gossip from home is a lifeline."

"How remiss of me to forget your absence abroad," Ned murmured. "If I remember rightly, your punishment was approved, amongst others, by the Archbishop of York here."

"Really?" Gaveston said, open-mouthed in mock astonishment. "I didn't know that. D'you remember what I was exiled *for,* your Grace?"

Abashed, Greenfield smiled and put his head to one side. "With most of those exiled under great Edward it was disobedience."

"Not in my case. I was exiled twice for loving my king. Do you love your king?"

"Of course I do."

"That doesn't stop you coming here to lecture me," Ned intervened. "Am I not to have friends?"

"Sire, circumstances have changed…" Greenfield whined.

"So they have!" Ned exclaimed. "And for the better! A new age has begun! Greenfield, dear old man, I appreciate the trouble you've taken coming to see me during my leisure. Whenever we get too brotherly we'll read the Book of Genesis, I promise."

Ned bared his teeth in a stage smile, dismissing Greenfield with a wave. The contempt in the gesture impaled the remnant of Greenfield's pride. In spite of his achievements in negotiation this day, he felt his power of contention with royal power had gone. The thought provoked a final attempt to recover some ground.

"Sire, as the servant of Christ and your crown," he said with an attempt at dignity, "I ask you to be more careful with the love of your people. To follow in the footsteps of a great predecessor is no easy matter."

"Oh, do be quiet, man," Ned sighed, "you tire me out. How can you be such a hypocrite? When my father was alive you did nothing but complain about his tyranny."

"Never, sire. He was no tyrant, only a hard taskmaster."

"Well, so am I. I like people to do their work – and I like them to be honest. Talking about honesty, Piers, you're keeping very quiet about your connections with the Templars. Is there any truth in these allegations we hear?"

Gaveston bowed his head, pretending to snivel. "Ah, you're so quick to spot my withholdings, sire. I confess I've been intimate with Templars and know a few worrying things about them."

"Be so good as to tell us what they are. The Archbishop is eager to know the details of any misdemeanour by Christians as pious as himself. What do they get up to, exactly?"

"Well, sire – they spend a lot of time on their knees," Gaveston replied, comically rolling his eyes.

"What's wrong with that?" Ned hooted. "We need good men to pray for our abominable sins"

Gaveston dropped the towel and knelt down, miming fellatio on Ned. Affronted and sickened, Greenfield turned his back on the appalling sight and lurched out of the room, their wild laughter in his ears.

On reaching the Wye Valley, Raymond de Sauveterre's first call was the castle of Saint Briavels. On Gaveston's request, Ned had empowered the Gascon incomer to serve a writ removing Botetourt from office and installing himself as *custos.* Botetourt was absent. Raymond served the writ on his deputy instead, and moved in, throwing all Botetourt's private possessions into the moat.

The deputy knew William Wild. He rode down to Boldwood with the writ and found Botetourt there also. He told the story of Raymond's takeover of the castle, and showed the writ to both men. In fact, it was a double writ – the second part incorporated the Irishman's estate into the royal demesne of Saint Briavels until such time as Raymond de Sauveterre was in possession; only then would it revert to a freehold. The effect was to make any resistance by William Wild an offence against the Crown.

Botetourt's instinct was to go immediately to the castle and remove the Gascon – the man's offensive high-handedness having put him in the wrong. William Wild pointed out the pitfalls of attacking a royal appointee whose rights were well known to both men because they had once enjoyed them.

The deputy asked to be forgiven in advance for what he was going to say next. He had sensibly bided his time, giving the Irishman time to recover from the shock of Raymond's reappearance. "He proclaimed certain things I'd rather not pollute my mouth with repeating," he said with trepidation, "but it would be wrong of me not to pass them on. If they remain unchallenged, worse might come of it."

Botetourt encouraged him to speak up.

"With respect, sir, it concerns the wife of Captain Wild. Coming from such a source, does he honestly want to hear it?"

The Irishman sighed, having worked out the gist of what he was about to hear. He nodded, nevertheless.

"Tell me," he said. "I might as well know."

"He brags that our women prefer Gascons because they're real men. He says your unborn child is Gaveston's and everyone at Court knows it."

Botetourt saw the terrible pain in his friend's eyes. "That's enough to end

Sauveterre's life," he declared. "Get on your horse, Willy. We'll go and do it now."

The Irishman sat down at the table, head in hands. "How d'you deal with people like this?" he groaned.

"What more d'you need? He must die today," Botecourt insisted. "You can't have this clown strutting around the valley spreading such lies."

William Wild burrowed his face into the palms of his hands, shaking his head as if to expel poison.

Valmai walked into the room, big with child.

"Go away," the Irishman pleaded.

"What's the matter?"

"Go away, go away. I'll talk to you later."

Valmai looked to Botetourt for help. He had tears in his eyes.

"If it's bad news, I should be told…" she faltered.

"Is the end of the world bad news?" William Wild snarled, leaping to his feet and knocking the chair over. "You swore on the gospels!"

Botetourt took his deputy's elbow and steered the appalled man out of the room, leaving man and wife alone together.

Hardly able to speak through his misery, the Irishman told her what had been said.

"You believe Gaveston before me?" she cried at the end. "How dare you!"

"All his relations are braying about it the length and breadth of the country! I won't be able to go anywhere without being laughed at!"

"Is that what concerns you – being laughed at? What about this child?"

"You must have done something you haven't told me about."

Valmai laughed, holding her belly. "Is this what you get for flirting? Come to your senses, idiot!"

The Irishman muttered under his breath that a good woman didn't call her master an idiot.

"I can hear you. I don't withdraw. If you believe this, you must be an idiot. You know Piers is a big-mouthed, arrogant fool. Do I like to give myself to big-mouthed arrogant fools? If so, what am I doing here with you?"

The Irishman chewed his lip. Valmai recognised the signs. One doubt was replacing another. "He's capable of any lie," she said, backing herself up. "He doesn't live under the same controls as we do. Ned's made him free to do and say as he likes."

William Wild held up his hands. "No more, Valmai. No more. I surrender," he said with a prolonged shiver and a shake of the head. "I'm not saying I have to believe you but, God knows, it feels that way."

"There's no proof I can offer you," she said, taking him in her arms. "Trust is hope, not proof. But be warned – even if the child is born looking exactly like Gaveston, the blood will be yours."

"You swear that?"

"I've done with swearing. I say it's so. From now that will have to be enough."

Botetourt sent the deputy back to his duties at Saint Briavels while William Wild and Valmai got themselves back onto an even keel. Chances were the deputy would be discharged and replaced with a member of Gaveston's family very soon. Botecourt estimated that he had no more than a week in which to act with the deputy's help.

William Wild emerged from the catastrophe in a philosophical mood. He was impressed with himself. To place Valmai at the centre of his world was one thing – to knock her off her pedestal then put her back up on it was another. The land, the house, the children were all secondary. If his belief in her hadn't been rebuilt, everything would have crumbled.

Botecourt was striding about in the forecourt at Boldwood, impatient for revenge. An all-consuming enemy let loose by the King, not by design but out of weakness and indulgence, had triumphed and must be put down. If corruption was to be cut out, a start had to be made somewhere. The Wye Valley was a microcosm of the kingdom. He guessed similar injustices were being perpetrated everywhere – swarms of Gascons taking over, advertising the prowess of their power-source and leader.

At the same time people of importance could feel the strong grip of the Crown lessening because the old king was dead. If there was a time to act it was now.

The Irishman prevaricated. From his close knowledge of the family system of government, relationships ruled over rights. At the moment, he was out in the cold. From experience, he knew his best hope was to be patient and wait to make a comeback.

"You're going to let him take Boldwood off you without a fight?" Botecourt demanded incredulously. "What kind of a man are you?"

"If I resist the writ, and someone is killed – which is more than likely – I'll have defied Ned not once, or twice, but three times."

"Make it ten times! What does it matter if the alternative is to lose everything? What about the slur on Valmai? Don't you care about that? If she was mine I'd kill any man who insulted her."

"That's just a sordid lie. It hurts but there's no protection from what people choose to say."

Botetourt was crestfallen. "This is sad, Willy," he said. "I thought you were a man after my own heart. If every individual who's been wronged as much as you have reacts this way, before long freedom won't mean anything in this country."

"At my age, I think it's a meaningless concept anyway," the Irishman mused sardonically. "My bonds – which are my woman, my family – mean more to me than freedom."

"Don't prefer bondage to freedom. Look at the King. He's in bondage to Gaveston. And the comfort of kin isn't enough, Willy. We need to be free men as well as husbands and fathers, to keep our weapons and our minds sharp."

"I can't win," William Wild stated resignedly. "We'll have to move – maybe into Wales, somewhere out of the way. Valmai has family we can go to until this blows over."

"And then?"

"We'll see what happens."

Botetourt was pensive for a while, scratching his chin. He asked the Irishman to sit tight and not make any irrevocable move.

"I'll be in touch again shortly. I've got some ideas on how we can get around this. I need to work them out in detail."

"If he arrives in force to evict us, I don't intend to resist," William Wild said with a shrug. "What can you possibly do to change things? You've enough problems of your own."

Botetourt mounted his horse. As he rode out of the forecourt he gave the Irishman a Parthian shot: "I'm surprised a man who's fought so many fights can become this faint-hearted. But you've opened my eyes to myself – I see now why I never married."

He rode hard to Tintern where a book-keeper monk was his cousin. From him he obtained a forged document in Languedoc French purporting to be the profit and loss record of a charcoal-burning business deep in the Forest of Dean, part of the royal demesne. Attached to the document was a map in case the new *custos* of Saint Briavels needed to pay a visit, also a short note from Jacques d'Oxelhaya, the chief charcoal burner, recommending a meeting at the works: *Returns are very high, and climbing,* said the forgery, *but I'm trying to keep it quiet because the Earl of Hereford thinks he has a cross claim. As custos of Saint Briavels you are entitled to half our profits, which could be doubled. We need whole trees, not just loppage, which is all you allow us. Also, I should say, while washing our equipment in a nearby stream, we found gold. A sample is enclosed. Unwelcome interest from outsiders at this stage could hurt us. If your lordship comes, bring only a very small escort. In my opinion, as your fellow-countryman – la Bastide Clairence is my birthplace – the fewer people who know about this the better.*

This package was delivered into the hands of Raymond de Sauveterre by a black-faced boy off a coal cart who could have been a charcoal-burner's apprentice. The job done, the boy went off a few pence richer.

Botetourt knew from bitter experience the paltry income Saint Briavels generated. Raymond would find this out before sleeping one night in the castle.

Using his working knowledge as *custos,* Botetourt broke into a royal hunting lodge in the forest and took five cross-bows and a supply of iron quarrels. These he transported by cart to the location of the non-existent charcoal-beds on the map he had provided. Once there, he dug a pit and made a fire in it, throwing on enough wood to make smoke visible. Loading the cross-bows, he hung them up in a tree where he could hide himself and see anyone approaching.

He sat there for three days and nights.

During this time, he meditated a great deal on William Wild's decision. Understanding arrived, alloyed by pity. The Irishman obviously loved Valmai in a different way to Botetourt, who adored her nobly from distance, honouring his friendship with her husband too much to do anything about it. But to be ready to kill in this way, underhandedly, from ambush, for her sake, helped him realise what lengths he would go to. He could only guess where it might lead.

On the afternoon of the fourth day, Raymond de Sauveterre appeared with one hunter beside him. Botetourt breathed a prayer of thanks. God, in his mercy, had decreed only one other soul would have to suffer. With successive shots he toppled them from their horses, climbed down the tree, cut their throats, and buried them in the fire-pit.

When Botetourt arrived back at Boldwood to advise the Irishman not to budge until the future made itself clearer, he found the family and household gone, the house a smoking ruin.

CHAPTER SEVENTEEN

Those who followed the slow progress of Edward the First to his long home in Westminster Abbey to lie under an unadorned grey slab inscribed, *Edward the First, Hammer of the Scots, Lies Here,* with no dates, no eulogising epitaph, realised that each farewell mass – and there were many – was an attempt to detain his warlike spirit and keep it a vital force in English politics. Even the Bishop of Durham and Patriarch of Jerusalem, one Anthony Bek, who conducted the last mass on 27th October 1307, wished the embalmed and eviscerated ten-week-old corpse of a monarch who had persecuted him and his brethren so relentlessly would rise up and terrify the people back into some form of order. A deeply secular man, happier with weapon in hand than prayer-book, Bek felt the slackening of state power. It was something he had often wished for as a Churchman. Now it was happening all around him, he regretted the weakness and futility it exposed.

For Ned's immediate family, and those who knew him best, the only hope lay in two girls – the thirteen-year-old Isabella, daughter of King Philip the Fair of France, due to marry Ned in three months' time, and the fourteen-year-old Margaret de Clare, Edward the First's granddaughter, heiress to great lands in the earldom of Gloucester, due to marry Gaveston five days after the funeral.

The arrangement of Gaveston's marriage was the personal work of the King. It was scheduled to take place only five days after the funeral. This was seen as a deliberate insult to great Edward's memory. And it was yet another undeserved gift of enormous power and wealth to Gaveston. The wedding was held at Berkhamstead where Ned and Piers both outshone the bride in the glory of their outfits. The groom's embraces were coldly formal for the girl, hot for his king and brother-in-love.

Ned and Piers were letting it be known there would be no pretending of passion. Minimal connubial duties would be performed, but, otherwise, the bond between king and favourite would be the stronger, far beyond the reach of normal rules.

Gaveston held a tournament at Wallingford a month after the wedding, ostensibly in honour of Margaret, his skin-and-bones, gawky little bride. She sat under furs and shawls in the cold wind off the Chilterns and watched her husband unhorse and beat down everyone who came against him. Many of these victims were her uncles and cousins. As the toast of the tournament, she had to present Gaveston with a succession of prizes, often with half-dead relatives being carried off in the background. As he insulted and jeered at the defeated earls, strutting around them when they fell to his superior strength and skill, she took refuge in contemplation. With her ears dinned by the clash of steel and the screams of wounded men and horses, she tried to sort out the bizarre experience of being married to Mars. War was his main interest and forte, as it was with most men in her class, but his ability exceeded everyone else's. The sheer energy of Gaveston amazed her. Knightly virtues of generosity and compassion in victory were absent from his nature. Instead, he scoffed at his humbled enemies, mocking them as inferior beings. She was glad her own inferiority was so absolute her husband need hardly bother to make anything out of it.

In front of the King and the whole Court, Gaveston hammered Guy de Beauchamp, the Earl of Warwick, to his knees with the flat of a battleaxe, smashed his armour, battered in his helmet so the vizor jammed over his face, kicked him as he lay on the ground, spurned him with his foot, called him Black Dog, a valourless idiot, and a weak fool.

The same treatment was given to the Earls of Surrey, Hereford, Arundel, Pembroke and Lancaster. Not one of them lasted five minutes of his onslaught. As he rained down blows and abuse, he created a mad *frisson* in the hearts of the spectators. This was not an imitation of war, but the essence of war. His contempt for his adversaries was that of an immortal. He was beyond courtesy, beyond honour. His power was so god-like it made shabby, feeble little men feel they hardly deserved to have the magic of life in their bones. As his opponents submitted, they were less shocked by his violence and skill than the aura of absolute unvanquishability he wore. The man had no fear, no conscience and no equal.

In the mêlée, when two teams of a hundred knights fought in a fenced compound in front of the ladies, there was always a tell-tale space around Gaveston as opponents drew away from his brilliant and berserk warcraft. Two knights died, suffocating in their armour under a pile of men stampeding to escape Gaveston's blows.

At dinner on the third day of the tournament, the King was absent, as were several of the earls who were recovering from their injuries. The remainder, bandaged and patched up, sat and glared aggrievedly at their host.

After a month of marriage, Margaret knew she couldn't count on having much time alone with her husband. Because the King wasn't at dinner monopolising Gaveston, and the battered earls were busy absorbing the anaesthetic available in the wine-jugs, she spied an opportunity to have a private conversation and ask some questions she wanted answered.

In her innocence, she asked why her lord husband took so much pleasure in other people's pain.

"Let's look at the life of Our Lord," he said, taking her hand and looking seriously into her eyes, "and the way we're asked to imitate his life."

"Our Lord would never fight in a tournament," Margaret said. "Nor would he insult people like you do."

Gaveston asked her to give him a little time to make his point.

"My father taught me that because we're imperfect, each of us can choose only one or two aspects of Our Lord to follow," he said, squeezing her hand. "I come with a sword as He said he would when He came again, and you choose to be sweet and obedient as He was to his father."

"No, I don't choose! That's what I'm told to be by *my* father."

"Now you're my wife, forget what your father says and listen only to me."

Margaret was quiet for a while, twisting a ring round her finger. "Tell me how I should behave as the wife of a man as mad as you," she said eventually.

"Mad? Me? Why d'you say that?"

"If my father came against you, you wouldn't hold back, would you?"

"If he comes to fight, why should I? If the Earl Gilbert wants special treatment because he's my father-in-law, he'd be a lot safer staying at home."

"There's only one man you'd allow to beat you – and his sport isn't tournaments."

Gaveston laughed. "You're very sharp, but wrong. I wouldn't hold back for Ned. But to answer your question as to how you should behave – the wife of a man like me should come out of the shadow of the convent wall and dazzle everyone. That's what I'd enjoy."

Margaret stared at him, annoyed. "To dazzle needs beauty, which I haven't got. You do enough dazzling for both of us."

Amused, Gaveston nodded approvingly. "A good answer," he said, "but I can't do everything for you. You must come up to my level somehow. By the way, I was sorry to hear that if I hadn't married you, you might have become a nun."

"You heard that wrong," Margaret replied. "What I said was – I'd rather become a nun than marry you."

"Why? Some say you've been rather lucky."

"Very young widows can have an awful life," she said, getting to her feet, "and having a baby when the father is dead is sad and burdensome."

Gaveston looked at her. She was so small and frail. Her head when she was standing up was on a level with his sitting down.

"So, you don't expect me to survive that long?"

"D'you care?" she piped, suddenly upset.

"Then while we can dance, let us dance," Gaveston said, giving her an unusually friendly smile as he got out of his chair to lead her to the floor. "As for babies, one is sure to have started in your womb already. I'll do everything I can to remain on earth until it's born."

Ned absented himself from the third day of Gaveston's tournament at Wallingford in order to attend a secret meeting with senior Templars in Oxfordshire. Present were William de la More, Master of the Poor Knights in England and all his commanders, McHunter from the Scottish Templars, and Imembert Blanc, commander of the Auvergne who brought with him a copy of the charges made eighteen days ago in France when all Templars were arrested. He'd been in England visiting when the swoop was made. Colleagues had despatched the document to him in the hope he'd be able to make good use of it enlisting support in England.

The King told the meeting he'd received a letter from the Pope telling him to arrest and interrogate all Templars. When this had sunk in, Ned ordered the charges against the Templars to be read out.

"They're too absurd, Your Majesty," Imembert said with searing contempt. "Reading them out loud would be too much to bear."

"We'll hear them, nonetheless."

"With your permission, Majesty, I'll ask my brother to do it," Imembert said, passing the document over to William de la More. "Good men are already dead because of this libel."

"How can that be? There's been no trial as yet."

"The Dominicans are using torture to extract confessions and many of our brothers have died rather than submit!" Imembert exclaimed passionately. "Besides, what use is testimony gained that way? Broken men will say anything!"

A frown passed over Ned's brow. He was having a struggle with the strong odour of so many Poor Knights gathered in a smallish room. The Order discouraged washing of the body.

"You'd do well to remember who instigated these charges," he said sternly, looking round the dark, scarred faces. "If the Pope, who is the head of your Order, didn't agree with King Philip, he would never have written to me demanding your arrest. The charges have to be taken seriously."

William de la More started mumbling in a low, embarrassed voice. Ned told him to speak up so everyone could hear.

"I was saying the present Pope is a Frenchman," he replied.

"Yes, he is – but a friend. We know him well from when he was Archbishop of Bordeaux in our Gascon territory. You'll reap no advantage by denigrating him. Read the charges."

"I cannot read, sire," William de la More admitted, lowering his head. "A clerk usually does that for me."

"But you can count!" Ned laughed.

"The Order has never encouraged learning, sire."

"Which might be the reason you're in so much trouble," Ned retorted. "Well, I'm not sitting here wading through it. Isn't there one amongst you who's committed the sin of being educated?"

The Essex commander could read the French the charges were written in. He crossed himself several times as he read.

> *Templars deny Christ, exchange obscene kisses, spit on the Cross and defile it. They adore a cat, reject the sacraments, worship a bearded male head and engage in sodomy. Brothers do not make charitable gifts, do not reckon it a sin to acquire properties by illegal means. They increase the profit of the Order in whatsoever way they can. Perjury is not reckoned to be a sin if done for the sake of the Order.*

As the list was read out, Ned had difficulty in keeping a straight face. The frowning Templars were kneading their foreheads and rubbing their eyes in disbelief at the insane conjurations of the French king's lawyers. The charges had their comic side, provoking a few snorts and guffaws. On the other hand, once the references to witchcraft and superstition were dispensed with as nonsense, the underlying message was plain.

"We're glad to have already discussed with some of you ways of dealing with this problem," Ned said quietly. "Acre fell sixteen years ago. There are those who think the Order has dragged its feet, ignoring the need for change. Who can say banking is any kind of substitute for the spiritual life? You turned away from your vocation, lost too much respect, and now you're paying the penalty."

"Sire, we keep to our vows and our rule!" William de la More declared. "We're Christian soldiers, not thinkers. How can rough fighting men like us be bankers? That requires a subtle, devious intellect like that of a Jew."

"In that case, it's no wonder we have no financial systems that work," Ned scoffed. "We'd better bring the Jews back."

"Will you at least give us the comfort of hearing you condemn these charges as false?" William de la More asked, age-lines on his forehead paralleled by abrasions from heavy helmets worn in the desert sun. "Our brothers have to defend themselves against this libel."

"The stuff about kissing, spitting on the Cross, sodomy and cats, I reject entirely," Ned said firmly. "That part has all the signs of being dreamed up. My future father-in-law has gone too far in that respect."

"I knew you wouldn't believe it! Praise God in his mercy!" William de la More exclaimed fervently.

"But as the son of a crusader, I have to say, once the Holy Land was lost, the purpose of your Order was also lost."

There was a chorus of protest.

"If the kings of Christendom would work together instead of fighting each other, Jerusalem could be recovered," Imembert insisted.

"What kind of world is it where the King of France arrests the Pope if he doesn't do what he wants?"

Ned smiled and shook his head. "We won't go into that, if you don't mind. Keeping the crusading ideal alive would have been the only means of saving the Order. But it's too late now. Answer me this – where do your loyalties lie? If there's no crusade, what are you doing with yourselves? In a war between England and France, who do you fight for?"

Someone whispered *Christ,* which made Ned even more scathing.

"My old tutor, Willy Wild, used to say when Christ fights on all sides he will always be a loser."

"Sire, we know something of that man," William de la More said disapprovingly. "He abandoned the Order. We place no value on the opinions of a vow-breaker."

"Willy has a brain. In your ranks, he must have been a fish out of water. But I can only deal with you as you are, as I know you. We're here to talk about two things – money and my ability to protect you from the Dominicans."

"Money, sire?" William de la More protested. "We're poor! Look at us, in our worn and patched clothes, our rusty mail, our scars!"

Ned chuckled. "What an act you put on, you simple soldiers. Templars have been running the finances of Europe for as long as anyone can remember. Are you telling me you've never made anything out of it?"

William de la More had known the old king intimately and fought by his side. At the funeral a month ago, he'd had a place of honour amongst the mourners.

"Protection has been mentioned," he said, carefully choosing his words. "Your father accepted our protection when he was in Acre. He would never have supported these trumped-up charges. As for asking who we are and whose side we're on, my predecessor was killed fighting for your father in Scotland."

"That's true," Ned agreed, "and there were Templars fighting on the other side. You're everywhere, and nowhere."

William de la More was left clutching at straws. "Defend us in our innocence," he pleaded. "Your father would have wanted it."

"I'll do much better than that," Ned replied with a workmanlike rub of his hands. "Providing you confirm our understanding, I'll personally write to the Pope expressing a few doubts about your guilt, and follow that up with a similar note to the kings of Castile, Aragon, Portugal and Sicily."

William de la More looked round the table. His brothers were beginning to look askance at the King's ambivalence.

Imembert spoke up, wondering aloud if it was safe for him ever to return to France. He might already be a refugee. In England an arrangement was possible, even likely, he ventured. He followed this observation with a thought: if everything else was to the King's satisfaction, would he be prepared to guarantee there would be no trials of Templars in England?

"These accusations were originally made in France," he carefully pointed out to the King. "They have no validity in your courts."

"If the Pope insists on having you charged here, I can't give such a guarantee," Ned replied. "He's your head, also the head of the whole Church. He argues that your misdeeds affect all Christendom."

"Misdeeds, sire? What misdeeds?" William de la More railed. "We have always served Christ."

"I should have said your *alleged* misdeeds," Ned acceded, "but if these charges are investigated by any papal commission in England, it will be supervised by us, controlled by our law. We may not own the Pope but we do own our courts where you'll find justice."

There was an appreciative silence. Encouraged, some of the commanders pressed for further concessions, especially a guarantee torture would not be used against them in England. William de la More silenced them. From experience, he knew it was time to stop and leave the grey areas to their greyness.

"We thank you for giving us hope, sire," William de la More said, signalling the others to be ready to leave. "At another time, I'll ask your advice on how we might live without any taint of corruption once our Order has gone."

"Live? What d'you mean?"

"We'll have no home, no income. After two hundred years of service we thought something might be done for us."

"Surely you don't expect *pensions*? You Templars have plenty put by for a rainy day."

"Lord Gaveston mentioned pensions at Wallingford."

"Oh, take no notice of Piers. He gets carried away with wild ideas. We'll look after you as best we can. Things will be better for you here than anywhere else. That's all I can offer."

Sickened, the brothers turned away. William de la More hurried to bring matters to a close. "Thank you for our lives, sire, if that's all we're to take away from this meeting. With your permission, we'll take up no more of your time. Bless your goodness."

Ned held up a hand. "Before you thank me too much," he said lightly. "I'm giving you forty days' notice that all Poor Knights in my territories will be arrested on 10th January."

There was a bubbling hiss like the last air escaping from a balloon. The Templars stole glances at each other like schoolboys in a lesson by a hated master.

"On the same day, all the Order's assets will be confiscated," Ned continued briskly. "To complete the business, I need an inventory – lands, buildings, movables, and treasure. Also, I believe McHunter can tell us where the treasure brought over from France to Scotland four years ago in anticipation of these sad events can be found."

McHunter looked uncomfortable. "Strathearn has been overrun, sire," he muttered. "The Scots control it now."

"Next year I'll get Strathearn back and you'll lead us to it," Ned told him. "On that optimistic note, let's close the Temple doors."

CHAPTER EIGHTEEN

John Botetourt was surprised to be summoned to accompany the King to Boulogne for his wedding. When discharged from his position as *custos* of the royal castle of Saint Briavels, he had assumed this to be a sign he was out of favour. He queried the summons to go to Boulogne and was told that all men of his rank – he was a baron by inheritance – could be called up for diplomatic service whenever needed. As for being out of favour, if he was so, the Chancery had not been notified.

There were three earls, five barons and a bishop in the wedding contingent, plus all their retainers. Botetourt took one manservant and his confessor.

During the Channel crossing, the main topic of conversation was Gaveston's appointment as deputy in England while the King was away in France getting married. This was taken as absolute proof that Gaveston was the second man in the kingdom. To many, his influence over Ned made him joint monarch.

Bitter comments were made behind the King's back: Gaveston had been left to sulk jealously in Kent, compensated for the insult of Ned marrying a woman by the temporary gift of unlimited power. This kind of crack was wide of the mark. The truth was Gaveston had rustled up enough common sense to refuse to be Ned's deputy on his wedding night. For this intransigence he was made deputy of England instead. This appealed to Ned's wayward sense of humour.

By the time the English arrived in Boulogne the wedding was not the main item on their minds. At the feasts and celebrations they talked politics. There was general agreement that Ned's first four months as king had been even worse than expected.

As Ned went to the couch with his very young bride and the English and French delegations quizzically faced each other across the chamber, it was Gaveston who occupied their minds. Under cover of the applause as the curtains were drawn on the marriage bed, the Earl of Lincoln turned to the Earl of Surrey and whispered: "All I can think about is our country lying completely at a foreigner's mercy."

Inside the curtains, Ned and Isabella listened to the hum of the audience around them. The sound was light-hearted enough, but anxiety was playing its wary music and prayers were being said.

Isabella sat up and leant on the pillow. "Making love under these conditions is disagreeable," she said in Ned's ear, showing him a small container. "If you don't want to do it, I've got some blood to put on the sheets."

Ned shook his head. "We must," he sighed. "It has to be done."

"We can jump about and make noises. That's all they want."

Ned was silent. Lying on his back and looking at the canopy of pink velvet above the bed, he'd noticed a bulge in the heavy pleats. It was moving.

He put his lips to Isabella's ear. "There's someone up there watching us," he said.

"Don't worry, it's only Hieronimo, my father's dwarf. He's been sent to spy on us. He's my best friend. He'll say what I tell him to."

"Oh, God," Ned groaned. "Why couldn't I have been born someone else?"

"If we're not going to pretend, let's get it over with, shall we?"

Ned looked at her hard. In the darkness, she flashed him an encouraging smile.

"It's alright for you," he muttered. "All you have to do is lie there."

The anxious note in the hum outside the curtains became more urgent. Pressure was being applied. The audience didn't want to hang around too long.

"We'd better do something one way or the other, I suppose," Ned said, lifting his nightshirt. "Kneel up."

"Like the animals?"

"D'you mind?"

"Not at all. It's my favourite."

"God's Mother," Ned murmured. "What have I got here?"

Outside, a dead quiet descended. Ned looked up and saw the dwarf's breathing had accelerated. Taking himself in hand he closed his eyes and worked a while, keeping his mind off dwarfs, fathers and duty while he prayed his flesh wouldn't let him down.

To help him through, Ned conjured up thoughts of another time and place. He'd been free and happy, at his ease.

While spending last Christmas with Piers in Kent he'd thatched a tiny one-room cottage on the estate. Roofing was a sensual pleasure. It moved him so much he'd spent a night there, sleeping on a bed of fragrant reeds, sneezing now and then – another sensation he found enjoyable.

Gaveston had refused to join him in the cottage, preferring the comfort of the manor house. Because Ned lacked the ability to question his own passions, he never asked himself why greater happiness came when he was alone with his own accomplishment – a happiness even exceeding what Piers brought him.

What Ned loved about the place – what had aroused him – was the fact that it was his creation. He had done it. If he ever found himself in that part of Kent and had the time, he would visit the cottage, turf out the family and spend a night beneath *his* roof.

❦

When the ship carrying the newly-married couple landed at Dover, the French men and women attending Isabella were astonished by the tableaux constructed at the land end of the gangway. Gaveston was on papier maché white cliffs dressed up in gold as King Arthur, wielding Excalibur. He poured a handful of shingle into Ned's hand saying: "I give *our* country back to you." Whereupon the King tossed the shingle overboard and embraced him. They disembarked arm in arm, completely immersed in each other, leaving Isabella to be welcomed by junior officials.

As the party passed through the villages of Kent people came out to look at the new queen. Much had been heard about her beauty – how she outdid her own father, Philip the Fair, in looks. But it was difficult for the spectators to identify Isabella in the large party. Veiled like a nun, head down as she sulked intensively but checked her wild temper, she hid in the middle of the procession.

Before London was reached, the first messenger was on his way to Paris with an itemised list of the humiliations she had already endured.

This intelligence wasn't sent with Isabella's knowledge. In spite of the demeaning treatment she was receiving, the girl's resolution remained intact. She made no complaint or protest, though the hurt burned in her dark Capetian eyes. As granddaughter of Philip the Bold, and great granddaughter of Saint Louis the Crusader, she was made of sterner, wilier stuff. Strong within outlandish contradictions, austere, sensual, pious and violent, she was prepared for life to be an ordeal as well as a pleasure, and under strict orders not to have her heart broken by any mortal man. These orders were severely tested at a banquet in Westminster Hall. In front of the French guests, Ned ostentatiously heaped all the wedding presents he had received from King Philip at Gaveston's feet, then retired to bed with him, leaving Isabella publicly humiliated.

Even this insult had to be absorbed. It was her responsibility to make the best of being the wife of this weak, reckless, self-indulgent man. From what she'd seen so far, Ned was bearable when he was with you, alone. He would chat to *anyone*, including his wife. On the ship he played the shipman, visiting a monastery he became a monk, in a marriage he might occasionally play the husband. What he refused to be was what he actually was – a king. This function was being given to Gaveston because it was his to give and he had no other use for it.

Unlike the men Isabella was used to, Ned set little store by her beauty, which was the marvel of the French court, nor would he share in the fun to be had out of a romance. Her father had warned her not to expect too much beyond a formal bond with Ned at first, but had promised that her lively loveliness and feminine strength would bring the man round. One day Ned would submit to her like King Edward had to his Eleanor. It was in the blood of these Plantagenets to do so – a line always struggling under the thumb of powerful women.

When Isabella arrived at Westminster to settle down after all the celebrations, the palace was shrouded in a river fog which didn't lift for several days. She busied herself establishing her household, altering the décor, changing the furniture, accustoming herself to the building. Ned paid her no visits. When he finally appeared, it was with Gaveston. They were both so drunk they could hardly stand up. She took it in good part, laughing at their horse-play, her dignity under severe pressure but unshaken as they made fun of her.

Even Ned's announcement that he was going to his manor at Langley for his honeymoon with Gaveston and leaving her behind didn't break her. She straightened her back, lifted her chin and looked him straight in the eye, though her tongue failed her.

But once the door closed and she heard them run down the passageway bawling with laughter, she collapsed into the arms of her servants.

The political statement agreed by the English wedding guests at Boulogne was taken home to be presented to the King once the marriage celebrations in London were over. The city fathers had gone to great expense with decorations. The theme was London as the New Jerusalem. No one in the delegation had the heart to spoil the relief following Ned's nuptial success at Boulogne. He had looked regal and magnificent, conducting himself with dignity throughout the proceedings – and he had got through the wedding night without any alarums.

When the time came to arrange for the political statement to be delivered, a nagging doubt arose in the minds of the delegation. What they had agreed on was…what? A statement? A plea? Or a warning? They couldn't decide. But even in its apparent imprecision, it was something they had agreed upon. Although it might not attract much attention from a king as thoughtless as Ned, it was all they had to show for the risk they were taking.

Their diffidence was misplaced. It was a truly revolutionary document. On the one hand, the signatories reaffirmed their oaths to protect the honour of the monarch as an individual man, and, on the other, to maintain the rights of the Crown. This formula drove a wedge between the person of the monarch and his authority, two previously unseparated ideals. An undertaking was also given to the people. Whatever oppressions troubled them must be lessened.

It had also been agreed in Boulogne that the King should have sight of the letter in draft before it was made public, to see if he had anything useful to say on its form and content.

The man put forward for this delicate task by Botetourt was his Dominican confessor, a man known to the King, who had kept silent for the entire fortnight in Boulogne, often going off on his own, visiting shrines and walking the harbour at night deep in thought. When people joked how punishing it must be to have such a serious confessor, Botetourt reminded them that there was plenty to be serious and silent about in this world, and Brother William kept him on the straight and narrow.

The gaunt Dominican was William Wild, aged by loss, sadness and not a little madness. When the Irishman tracked Botetourt down in London and presented himself, owning up to the arson of Boldwood, his own property, he was dirty, unkempt, without servants and on the edge of complete breakdown. Wanting to help, still with Valmai very much in mind, Botetourt took him to Boulogne in his retinue. As some equilibrium returned, the Irishman found a scrap of faith that if only he could speak to Ned, everything would be sorted out – even with the offence he had committed. On other days he talked obsessively of revenge. For a man of William Wild's experience and close knowledge of the life led by an English king, the logistics of an assassination were not too difficult.

Botetourt worked hard to bring his friend back to his senses – afflicted by his own conscience. He knew it would be assumed the burning down of Boldwood and Raymond de Sauveterre's disappearance were the work of the same hand. William Wild would be blamed for both crimes. He was a fugitive in risk of his life. What doubled the risk was his mental condition. But Botetourt could see it wasn't the threat of punishment that had driven his friend to the edge of madness, it was his love of Valmai and the agony of a jealous man.

She was somewhere in the mountains of Wales, soon to give birth to a child – but the Irishman couldn't bear to be near her any more, jealousy having got the better of him. Trust had become the victim of his moods. One day he had faith – the next, it had gone. Suspicion kept surfacing, leading to self-disgust, then anger. She could no longer help his unbelief because it originated in the essential character of his mind. He was still, in spite of himself, a man of religion. When he doubted his trust in her, it became a matter of theology as to how and why. In the time it took to speculate himself out of the doubt, the possessive impulses built up again, causing the same mayhem. She was his truth and his doubt. It was wise on his part never to fully communicate to Valmai how this blighted his life. If he had, she would have despaired of their relationship.

All Botetourt had been able to offer the Irishman as a refuge from all his confusion and pain was the closeness of a sympathetic friend. He might be able to use his disguise as a confessor until his derangement was corrected, using the priestliness as an aid to the spirit. Besides, if William Wild kept quiet and did as he was told, the time might come when his cry for justice was taken up by so many others, including the most powerful magnates in the land, he would cease to be a fugitive and emerge as part of a general protest.

His disguise remained intact throughout the trip to Boulogne. In fact, it calmed his troubled mind to play a man of God while high, heady politics swarmed around the English party.

News reached the Irishman on return to London that Valmai had given birth to a son. Her message ended in Welsh, a language she'd been teaching him. *Yn awr, mae gennym ddwy hwyaden yn ein teulu.* (Now we have two ducks in our household.) On receiving the letter, William Wild drew off his boots and stared at his feet which were webbed between big and second toe.

The child could only be his.

Jealousy was destroyed at a stroke. Faith, courage and hope were resurrected. William Wild would not only create a good life for his family and rebuild his home, he would also return to the project once shared with the first Edward – bringing Ned to his senses before blind folly brought him, and the nation, to disaster.

He offered to be the man to test the King's reaction to the Boulogne Declaration. Botetourt tried to dissuade him but without success. Happy, brave and sane again, William Wild was ready for any kind of self-sacrifice now.

There was fresh urgency to the cause of the Declaration. With the coronation set for two weeks ahead, a palace announcement, made the morning the Irishman left to see Ned, shook the great families and put them in a revolutionary ferment – Gaveston was to carry the crown, the highest of all honours at the ceremony. The aristocracy was in an uproar.

Unaware his risk had been added to, William Wild made his way twenty miles west to the royal manor of Langley.

The manor was full of the scourings of the nearby town of Slough. Ned had invited all the low-life friends he'd acquired in the district to come to a pre-coronation party. To his mind they were *the people,* or near enough. Giving them a good time occasionally was part of his responsibility. When William Wild arrived, the festivities had been going on for three days.

The Irishman's concern over whether he would be able to gain entry was unnecessary. The guards – some of them men from his old command – were mixed in with the partygoers, posts abandoned.

As he wandered around looking for Ned, William Wild stood out in his sobriety and soldierly bearing. He was wearing a mail shirt provided by the Boulogne men and his captain's royal surcoat, an article of clothing he took with him wherever he went. He was able to stride from room to room, transformed back to his old authority.

After a long search, he found Ned and Gaveston playing cards in a quiet corner. When Ned looked up, William Wild could see he was sober. Gaveston was so drunk he kept dropping his cards.

"Willy! What are you doing here?" Ned said, picking cards up off the floor. "I didn't invite you, did I? I thought you were over in Wales somewhere."

Gaveston cast a bleary eye at the visitor. "What've you done with my cousin Raymond?" he muttered. "No one can find him. His mother keeps sending me messages."

"Sire, I'm not here on my own account," William Wild said. "My hope is for a private word."

"Sit down, sit down," Ned sighed, making room on the bench. "We don't get much peace in this business, do we, Piers?"

"He murdered my cousin and burnt his house down," Gaveston slurred. "Throw the old rat into prison."

"Is that what you're here to talk about, Willy?" Ned asked him.

"No, sire. I'd rather we left that for later."

"I bet you would!" Gaveston shouted, trying to get to his feet and falling over.

"It's a bit cold outside, Willy, but let's take a walk and leave him to sleep it off," Ned said, putting a cushion under Gaveston's head. "What a pleasure to clap eyes on your dear old self. How long is it since we last saw each other?"

"Six months, sire," William Wild replied, telling the white lie. In Boulogne and on the ship, Ned had never noticed him under his cowl in the crowd.

"Is that all? When I saw you standing there it was like stepping back into ancient history! And, d'you know, I found that rather pleasant."

They went into the grounds, strolling along a path towards empty vegetable gardens waiting for spring. A giant naked vine, buds showing, was trained along a brick wall.

"Sire, you once said my function was to be the ghost of your father," the Irishman said carefully.

"Did I?"

"I know this is a time you've put aside for yourself, but I've been asked to bring you a letter. If you choose to read it, everyone could benefit."

An expression of fleeting exasperation crossed Ned's face. He silently held out his hand. The Irishman took the document from under his surcoat and gave it to him. Ned walked on a little, read the text, then returned it with a shrug.

"My father warned me to expect this kind of thing," he said wearily. "Every time there's a new man on the throne, they try it out. No one likes paying taxes, Willy. That's what it comes down to. As for the oppressions of the people – look around you."

The familiar blandness worked again. It was so hard to fight it. Even with the catastrophic effects on his own life, the Irishman could still find no real answer. Indignation petered away into a kind of awe.

"Sire, what I brought you to look at may be the beginning of something more serious," he said. "The grievances haven't taken root yet. They're at the theoretical stage. Ideas are more capable of adjustment than armies."

"Think how many ideas my father adjusted with armies," Ned laughed. "The men who've made use of you, Willy, want to see what they can get away with. They don't like to be ruled by someone who knows what he wants."

Standing beside the huge spreading vine, William Wild realised he'd been set up. The text of the draft letter made no mention of Gaveston. Now the general political case was dispensed with, it was left to him to lodge the real protest.

In order to do that he had to abandon the advantage of all his past service. He was no longer teacher, guide, mentor and *locum parentis.* As his king, Ned now had those powers. The tutor must ask the questions as pupil, not master. The greater risk lay in losing the advantage of Ned's ignorance of the events at Boldwood. He obviously knew nothing about what had happened. Gaveston had probably used the royal seal to give his relative the property.

"What plans have you for Piers, sire?" was the Irishman's cool presentation of the issue. "People would like to know."

"You can't have plans for someone like him!" Ned chortled. "He's a natural force, like a storm or an earthquake."

"Are you aware how unpopular he is?"

"Oh, that's just envy," Ned replied quickly. "When he's had time to show what he can do, they'll take him to their hearts."

The Irishman chanced one final interrogation, which had to sound as if it came from innocence.

"In what direction do you think his talents lie?"

"Come on, Willy – you've known him long enough. Someone as capable as Piers must have a hand in government."

"I didn't know he was all that interested."

"Don't sound so surprised. Not only is he a first-rate leader of men, but he's also very good at finance, which I'm not," Ned enthused. "Thanks to his hard work we've funded this Scottish campaign, and probably the next. And he's got a very practical idea how to get our hands on the huge arrears of tax we're owed. We're going to use ex-Templars to work on late-payers and defectors. Be sceptical if you like, Willy," Ned said as the Irishman raised an eyebrow, "but his ideas work. I've had a lot of trouble with parliament turning down my requests for money. They even refused to provide what's needed for my coronation. Now, thanks to Piers, the problem is solved."

Ned outlined another of Gaveston's schemes which was already a success. All the assets of Walter Langton, the imprisoned bishop, had been confiscated to pay for the coronation.

"He robbed my father for twenty years as royal treasurer," Ned added with a grin, "and paying for me to be crowned will stick in the old thief's gizzard."

Gaveston entered the walled vegetable garden at the head of an unruly gang shouting, "Where's my boy? Come on, you've been talking to that old cuckold long enough. On your way, Willy!"

"Oh, he's woken up," Ned said, giving the Irishman's elbow a squeeze. "I'll have to go. Give my love to Valmai. How is she, by the way?"

One eye on Gaveston, William Wild told him of his sadness.

"Deformed, you say? How?"

"Certain features of the boy are those of a bird, sire. But we'll learn to live with it."

The King gave a vague, troubled smile. Piers had something to do with this misfortune – but misfortune and Piers never went together in his mind. The information was already being edited out. He'd provided Gaveston with so much material fulfilment in these few short months it was impossible for him to keep the detailed repercussions in his head. It was like a man broadcasting corn trying to remember one grain of the thousands hitting the earth.

"I'm so sorry," Ned mumbled. "We're both very fond of her. Bring her to the coronation. We'll make a fuss so she forgets it all."

"Sire, until the suffering fades, I daren't take her anywhere," William Wild said as Gaveston shouldered him roughly aside. "It's probably best if we keep to ourselves for a while."

"Willy and Valmai have had a bird-child," Ned informed Gaveston. "Isn't that terrible? These things always happen to people who don't deserve them."

"Serves the witch right!" Gaveston laughed. "One of her spells obviously bounced back on her."

❀

The Irishman was half-way to London before he realised why the Boulogne Declaration might as well be torn up. The old king would have reread the draft twenty times by now, poring over every detail. Lawyers would already be on the job, bishops would be drafting excommunications, warders sweeping out cells. Ned's lack of interest in this first tiny mushroom of opposition indicated an isolation of mind that had actually increased since his accession. Being king had pushed him further away from reality.

Two myths were at work inside the golden bubble the pair occupied. The more these myths were integrated into the relationship, the stronger they would become.

Gaveston would rule because he was born *to* it.

Ned would rule because he was born *in* it.

But by reason of Ned's peculiar nature, he constantly made Gaveston the gift of himself. As a result of these outgoings, a gap appeared where a king should be. For the last four years of his life, the first Edward had known of this strange transfer of self into a void. Surrender to his son's oddness was the greatest failure of his reign and an indictment of all inherited power.

Such a vacuum must eventually swallow everyone's rights. The longer Ned and Piers were left to believe they could run the country double-handed, the more the fallacy would gather momentum. What life, or impression of life, it had would be the spasms of a disabled and disabling power taking a very long time to die.

Ned was still young – only twenty-four.

He could live another fifty years.

Fifty years of Ned and Piers. It was a nightmare.

If things weren't altered, rule from an inner sanctum that was no more than a rumpus-room cut off from this world would transfigure the politics of the age.

CHAPTER NINETEEN

Valmai's uncle, Gethin, ran russet sheep near Pant Mawr on the eastern slopes of Pen Pumlumnon. The house was long and low, built of grey stone, slated, well hidden beside the Bidno, a plunging tributary of the Wye. From rising land a quarter of a mile from the back of the farmhouse, the village of Llangurig and the road to Rhayader were visible.

With her twin daughters and baby son, plus her mother, Valmai was aware she might overstay her welcome, even though her uncle – with four working sons to feed – never broke the code to suggest as much. He knew the kind of trouble she was in, and sympathised because he took a poet's interest in the wider world, whereas Megan, his red-haired, shrewish wife, was impatient with her niece for bringing trouble down on the family by taking up with the Irishman, tool of the hated English king.

Pen Pumlumnon was remote but not unreachable. There was a road along which English power could come from Hereford any time. To Gethin, this was a lifeline out of isolation as well as a threat. He encouraged Valmai to talk about her time with terrible old King Edward on the Scottish border, especially the stories of Ned's infatuation with Gaveston and the struggle with the father, which appealed to Gethin. After twenty years with Megan, any man struggling for independence was an ally.

"If, as you say, no good can come of his weakness, then it will be to our political advantage, surely," Gethin said to Megan during an argument at dinner with his four sons listening. "When the new king loses control because he has no *self*-control, the English will draw back to fight amongst themselves and leave us alone."

"That's not how it works, you ass!" Megan snapped back. "They'll spill over and bring their wars here, like they always do. This king will want Welsh help to put down any rebels. And where will they rebel? Here, on the marches, where they can do what they like. And who'll get it in the neck? We will."

Gethin smiled ironically at Valmai. "We have no Prince of Wales now your friend Ned is king. If you could bring back Llewellyn the Last, what would you say to him apart from don't repeat your old mistakes?"

"Ned will end up having to make peace with everyone," Valmai replied, "but for the wrong reasons. Willy thinks Bruce will run rings round him in Scotland. If there was a Welsh equivalent, now would be the time for him to think about doing something adventurous."

"Go and tell that to Llewellyn's headless body rotting down the road," Megan sneered. "God knows why, but they always come here to do their fighting. The sad part is there're no men left in Wales. The girls should take up arms, with Irish help, eh, Valmai?"

The men round the table laughed. The barb was aimed at Gethin, not them. His long, meditative look over the horizon into the greater world annoyed her. She attacked his pacifism daily.

"Don't laugh too much, boys," Megan said. "If the English come here looking for Valmai, you might be forced to strike a blow for Wales. Think about that. It would be the first in forty years!"

Her rough, jeering laughter outdid that of the men. Gethin sadly shook his head, disliking the inference on both counts.

"We haven't been bothered here for a long time," he reminded his wife. "If what Valmai tells us is right, the chances are we'll be left alone. Besides, she's not a fugitive. She's committed no crime."

"The English don't care about crime. All we've got to do is be Welsh and they destroy us. And although you mightn't think it sometimes, Valmai's Welsh like the rest of us, but she's Welsh trying to be English – her and those half-breed children of hers."

"Megan, shut your insufferable mouth!" Gethin commanded. "You make me ashamed!"

"Let her make up her mind who she is! I don't mind getting into trouble on our own account, but I don't see why we should protect people who've turned their backs on us."

"That's enough!" Gethin stormed. Turning to Valmai he bottled up his anger so he could talk to her. "I apologise for what she said. These barbarous opinions aren't shared. You're welcome in this house."

"Don't you apologise for me! If you want to apologise, make it because you don't put your own family's interests first!"

Although Valmai's expression was pained, it was obvious to her that Megan's rant – which was only a part of her congenital indignation against the world and life in general – wasn't having too much effect. What mattered was Gethin's support, which was always rock-like.

"You'll let her stay for ever, I suppose," Megan said scornfully, picking up a bowl and carrying it towards the door. "We're tenants of an English lord, you dreamy idiot! His bailiffs will come sniffing round before long. All they've got to do is look at her to realise the bitch isn't off the farm."

Next morning Megan said, in passing, she was sorry for calling Valmai a bitch.

"I don't take back everything I said, but I take that back," she declared with a toss of her head as they supervised the servant girls filling water containers from the stream. "I shouldn't call you names. To be honest, you're a bit too lovely for the boys to deal with, and that gets on my nerves. They can't deal with it very well. Anyway, what's going to happen if your husband doesn't come for you? You can't marry again until you know he's dead. If you stay here much longer Gethin will fall for you completely. He's had enough of me, and who can blame him?"

"We'll move on as soon as we can, I promise you," Valmai said without rancour. "Willy will come soon, I'm sure."

"God knows why you fancy older men. You shouldn't encourage Gethin. He'd be no use to you, take it from me."

"He's my uncle," Valmai replied levelly, a note of exasperation creeping into her voice.

"Poets should only marry beautiful women. If they don't, they sulk and take it out on people like me," Megan said, aiming a kick at a girl struggling up the path with a brimming pail. "I'm like this one here – a beast of burden. You? You're a beast of the bedroom."

"You've got the wrong idea about me."

"If your uncle falls for you any further, and my sons become your slaves more than they are already, poor drooling colts, I'll skin your looks off with a knife."

"I hope you don't mean any of this, Aunt Megan."

"I do. These are my men. They serve me, not you. If they betray me because of you, I'll kill you, then them, then myself!"

"You're mad!"

Prodding the last of the servant girls up the slope with a stick, Megan laughed and said she could only agree. To live in such a place with an impractical dreamer would be a test for anyone's sanity.

"I'm the real farmer, you realise that? If I wasn't here to keep him steady, he'd have gone under years ago. But if you want him you can have him. I'll become a nun and take it easy."

Megan's cackle made the labouring water-carriers turn on the path ahead and morosely look back like cattle barked at by an ankle-biting dog.

William Wild's report on his meeting with the King was delivered to the men of the Boulogne Declaration two days later. When he finished telling his story, the meeting went into lamentation tinged by disgust and anger. They had been treated with contempt. No intelligence whatsoever had been applied to the question they'd raised by expressing their theory of the separated entities – man and Crown. The King had been given his chance to head off trouble and now must be brought up against real opposition backed by stronger arguments before the situation worsened.

"This Edward isn't crowned yet," Aymer de Valence, the Earl of Pembroke, pointed out. "We should use the coronation itself to bring him into a proper discipline. He has to make three promises – to protect the Church, the Law and the People. We should add a fourth."

"To alter the coronation oath isn't in our power," someone interjected. "Its form is laid down by sacred tradition."

"Then who can alter it?" Aymer de Valence asked. "Who decides what happens at coronations?"

"It's a religious ceremony, first and foremost. The Pope should be consulted."

There was murmur of disagreement. It would take too long to get a response from the papacy, and such a move would only muddy the water further. Ned's outrageous treatment of Isabella was already producing a crisis. King Philip, her father, was letting it be known throughout the chancelleries of Christendom how insulted he was, and likely to take action before long. A rumour was already in circulation that he had instructed the Pope at Avignon to annul the marriage – treaty or no treaty.

As the meeting went on, the idea of using the coronation to make a political statement took hold. The major advantage was the timing of the event. It was scheduled to take place soon. Something could be achieved quickly, and publicly.

"If we look around the men in this room," Henry de Lacy, the senior earl said, "what do we see? Men who know the Church, the Law and the People. We have as much right as anyone to propose this change. A parliament can't do it because there isn't time for the King to summon one – even if he wanted to, which is unlikely – before the coronation, which is to be held next week. We'll have to do it."

"Well, as it happens, I've got a rough text to hand," Aymer de Valence admitted. "I didn't entertain much hope for William Wild's mission. It struck me we'd need a document we could work on and agree today."

Everyone concurring, the draft fourth promise was read out. In it the King would swear to uphold those rightful customs granted to the people of England by former monarchs *and chosen by the commonality.* The vagueness and ambiguity, Aymer de Valence explained, would make it palatable to the King.

"You mean, he won't notice?" Guy de Beauchamp, the Earl of Warwick, said sardonically.

"His lawyers will – but we can talk to them beforehand."

"Why be so unclear? We need something we can hold him to."

"Believe me," Aymer de Valence urged, "there's room for interpretation in that phrase *chosen by the commonality.* If we get that past him we legitimise our opposition. We can say – you agreed it's the people who decide what's a rightful custom and a wrongful custom."

Guy de Beauchamp – Gaveston's *Black Dog* – thought the new oath a farce because it made no attempt to deal with the power of an upstart favourite.

"Then let's make him swear not to have one," Henry de Lacy said, "and mention Gaveston by name?"

"It's our rightful custom in this country not to be ruled by a favourite," Aymer de Valence said keenly. "As far as I know, in all our history we've never had a king with a favourite like this before. The fourth promise gives us the power to stop it."

Voices were raised doubting the value of any promise made by this king. Someone said the life Ned led with Gaveston was a separate existence governed by a law of its own. William Wild backed this up, glad to hear an opinion so close to his own.

"What is that law they live under?" Guy de Beauchamp demanded contemptuously. "Can a normal man with a natural mind understand it?"

"If you'll bear with me a moment, I'll try to explain," the Irishman said. "I met a Dominican called Durandus while I was in Boulogne. For me, he's the only thinker who throws light on the state of Ned's mind. He argues relationship itself is a form of existence."

There was a strained silence. The earls hesitantly looked to Anthony Bek for a response. As a Churchman he might have some idea what this was about. Bek, sinecured son of a noble house, with scanty education, cleared his throat in a mildly intellectual way.

"Go on," he urged, folding his arms and looking at William Wild attentively. "That sounds very promising."

"Durandus says three forms of being must be admitted – being in itself, being in another, being becoming another. To my mind, the second and third categories explain these two young men."

"They're being in another and becoming one another," Botetourt said with bitterness. "I think we can all follow that."

"The rest of us aren't part of that twofold transitional being; we're stuck in being in itself which is ourselves and excluded," the Irishman continued, scanning the perturbed faces around him, "but I'm not sure how useful you'll think this is."

Guy de Beauchamp laughed and hit his forehead with the heel of his hand. "What am I doing here?" he declared. "I thought we came to talk real business not chop logic."

"Could we invite Durandus over to talk to the King?" Henry de Lacy asked. "It might help him understand himself."

"I tried very hard to get Ned interested in philosophy, but it passed him by. Besides, Durandus is still at the Sorbonne in Paris, studying for his doctorate. He isn't even qualified yet."

"Then what's the point of wasting our time telling us about him?" Guy de Beauchamp sneered.

Henry de Lacy was more supportive. "I think we should try everything, go down every avenue. He sounds promising to me," he said warmly. "I've got a glimmering what he's talking about. There's a hermit living on some land of mine in Herefordshire who thinks his being is God. I've had several conversations with him. He's not saying he *is* God, you understand, that would be heresy and I'd have him out, but the experience of being is the experience of God's power is what he's saying…or something like that, if you see what he means."

There was another silence. Anthony Bek looked towards the door. Guy de Beauchamp sniffed and tapped his foot.

William Wild moved smoothly into the silence, anxious to save the impetus he had created by moving the discussion into a more reasoned and philosophical arena. "My lords, the task is a hard one. We have been given a king – and a man. Everything possible was done to prepare him for the throne. But birth with its gifts and flaws is not part of education. Many of us have unchangeable natures." He sat back, saddened. "I have always wished it were otherwise."

"I can't believe Gaveston isn't aware of the dangers of this relationship," Anthony Bek said suddenly. "He'd have to be even more stupid than he is."

"Have you seen him fight?" the Irishman said. "He doesn't care about dangers. The man believes in two things – first, that he leads a charmed life, and second, that the King loves him. If he was king, and he loved someone, he'd behave just like Ned but for a different reason – because he *chose* to. Ned doesn't choose to be like he is, but nor does he want to change. I have to add, Gaveston doesn't understand how Ned loves him because he couldn't love anyone like he's being loved. It's a mystery to him."

"Well, thank you for tying us in knots, Captain Wild," Henry de Lacy said drily, smiling. "I'm totally bemused."

"I wish I could come up with a magic cure but there isn't one," the Irishman admitted with a shrug. "I've known Ned all his life, taught him, helped bring him up, looked after him. In many ways I'm the last person you should ask. If his father can be blamed for the way he is, I bear part of that responsibility. All I would say is – both Ned and Piers are completely devoid of imagination. As is the case with all people who suffer from that deficiency, even if they love each other they can't understand each other because they can't begin to guess what it's like to be each other."

Guy de Beauchamp let out a low groan and put his face in his hands, muttering: "No more! No more! This is our king we're talking about, not some girl. We're supposed to respect him."

"Beyond ceremony and usage, Ned doesn't really know what respect means," William Wild said flatly. "That is the core of the problem. He can *show* respect, when he likes, but that's a trick he's been taught. What he can't do is feel it."

"Then how do we make them see things differently?" Anthony Bek asked in frustration. "Are you saying that it's hopeless? That fiddling around with the coronation oath is a futile exercise?"

"Not at all," William Wild asserted. "Everything should be done to break down the King's isolation of mind before it's too late."

"A sword would do it," Guy de Beauchamp said in a voice that darkened every mind in the room. "I'll not live under that Gascon brat much longer – it will be me or him."

The fourth promise was slipped into the coronation oath by Woodlock, the Bishop of Winchester, who officiated at the ceremony in place of the exiled Archbishop of Canterbury. The ancient prelate, wobbly with exhaustion from his journey back from his own long exile – another victim of Edward's penchant for sending senior clergy out of the country – didn't have the strength or flair to run such a big occasion. He was uncertain, vague and imprecise.

As it was nearly forty years since the last coronation, no one remembered the exact form of the ritual. When the relevant archive documents were dug out, they were found to be scribbled over and confusing. When it came to the swearing of the oaths and the fourth was sneaked in, the King's lawyers stood behind pillars, well out of earshot, bribes having secured their collusion.

Once the fourth promise was made, its significance was overtaken by the jumble of resentments that had gathered round Ned's kingship. Most people weren't listening to what the monarch actually said that day. Their eyes were on

Gaveston, the gorgeous star of the proceedings, who wore a magnificent purple robe with cascades of pearls as he carried the crown against his heart on a cushion of matching hue. If Durandus had been at the ceremony, visual proof of his theory of the three states of being would have been provided – the monarch's power transferred from himself to another who was the ideal warrior-king form of himself.

Conscious of the intense feelings being aroused by the crowning of such a controversial king, the monks of Westminster had constructed lath and plaster walls on three sides of the throne area to keep gogglers from getting too close. As the heavy crown was taken off Gaveston by the geriatric bishop and shakily lowered onto Ned's head, the barons and clergy sighed and pressed forward as if expecting a sign. The temporary walls collapsed, bringing down the high altar, knocking over the throne with Ned on it, and crushing to death Sir John de Bakewell as he crawled inside the barrier, reaching out for a touch of Gaveston's magical beauty.

The throne had to be moved clear of the debris. The remainder of the ceremony was hurried through. Ned had to cradle the orb in his lap while clutching a handkerchief to a cut on his forehead.

That night the Benedictines of Westminster broke their disciplined silence as they tidied up the mess. Their conversation was about the justice of God, how amazingly strange it was. He felled his enemies when they least expected it. Anyone hoping catastrophe would strike at this coronation might think the victim – in terms of desserts – would have to be Gaveston, that superb blasphemy of a man who had stolen the good king's heart and mind. But no – the Lord never does the obvious. Instead of focusing on the greater evil, under cover of its magnitude He punishes those sinners overlooked by scandal and the public eye.

On the abbot's instructions, the monks had often prayed for Sir John de Bakewell to be utterly destroyed because he was a single-minded, viciously mean opponent involved in a land dispute with the abbey. As the monks washed down an Anglo-Saxon queen's tomb on top of which Bakewell's bleeding corpse had been laid after the disaster, they enjoyed an innuendo fashioned on the spot by one of the brethren and later spread all over London – that this was the closest Sir John had ever got to lying with a woman.

CHAPTER TWENTY

William Wild thought he'd done all he could for king and country. The time had come to look after himself and his family. But before making his new life in Wales, he felt it incumbent upon him to witness Ned's coronation. He hoped it would be the final act of his own public life. After the doomed crowning was done, he would revert to being a private individual, all his old dreams and ambitions demolished. For his own part, he shared the guilt of making this tragedy. He had used body and brain in the service of what he'd known to be fatally flawed. The sense of impending strife was now as natural to him as mortality itself.

When he first caught sight of the ramshackle shanty erected in the abbey around the throne, a peculiar numbness had taken hold of him. The crude, artless screen was an unavoidable metaphor of the first Edward's folly in allowing Ned to succeed him. The boy's education and preparation for power had been no more than these flimsy walls – a weak shield against the brawling pressure of the world. When the structure fell down, and the fourth promise had to be cheated into the service through a cloud of plaster dust, the Irishman couldn't bear the cruel ironies any longer. He fled the abbey and took the road to Wales, to spare himself further pain.

In the explosive mutterings he poured out between his horse's ears during the westward journey, a broken-hearted phrase in two parts kept recurring.

Love supersedes all wisdom and learning, it went, *and bad blood inheritance brings forth the day of the people's wrath..*

The thirty-three days between the coronation and the parliament of 28th April were a strange mixture of repercussion and presagement. Up until this time there'd been a hope that Ned's wild oats might be sown right up to the last minute, but once the clamp of the crown was on his head, the golden oil smeared on his breast, the mighty, reverberatory oaths sworn, there would be an overnight reformation. He would, as Saint Thomas à Becket the libertine had, be refounded in character by the power of his great office and, perhaps, become a miracle of a king.

People watched for signs.

Ned had shown a preference for peace. He would rather mow a meadow than go to war.

The model of warrior-king and lawgiver created by great Edward wasn't popular at all levels. The wars and the laws cost a great deal. Scattered amongst the three million English were those who perceived Ned's only flaw to be excessive affection – something government was short on.

If he ignored everything his father had taught him, he might become a new kind of king – not one more brutal descendant of William the Conqueror – the blood-bolted monster lodged in the English people's memory.

Radical homespun thinkers prayed at home and in church that Ned might become another Edward the Confessor, who loved God excessively.

They forgave their new king his youth and all his early mistakes. The benefit of the doubt was freely given. Ned was not seen as one of those who sought to expand royal power. He simply wished to be left alone to live his life. Thought of that way, he was much like everyone else.

While at Wallingford, Gaveston's aunt got to know the prisoner, Walter Langton, very well. She was allowed to visit him as often as she liked. Their conversations turned on the workings of money, an interest common to both of them. A sanguine man, he viewed the disappearance of his entire fortune into the royal treasury with limited regret, knowing that if he was ever let out of captivity his skills in finance would soon recoup these losses. He also had a strong feeling he'd be returning to office at some time. His acumen would be needed.

It was either Gaveston's aunt or Langton, or both together, who first came up with an idea which became the germ of the life insurance business. Following the mass arrest of Templars, many were imprisoned at Wallingford. They subsequently took part in discussions with Langton and Gaveston's aunt to develop the original concept.

Gaveston's aunt was popular amongst these men. Her unfeminine directness coupled with a gambler's personality endeared her to them. By means of her strong, earthy persuasiveness, she was able to sweep males along.

This powerful peasant woman became addicted to the company of the prisoners, spending more time in the dungeons than her own apartments. She was the only member of the family not to attend the coronation. Instead, she remained behind with the captives, putting the finishing touches to proposals she would lay before the house of Frescobaldi.

Her meeting with the Italian bank took place in London in early April. Coming straight to the point, Gaveston's aunt said she wanted to make a bet on how long her nephew would live.

The Frescobaldi agent was Gualberto, the ex-Templar, a much-changed man, now very hard of head with a mercenary glint in his dark eye. He had been arrested in the swoop, then rerouted into the finance house within a fortnight to help with the complex transfer of the Order's assets to the Crown.

Taking his cue from the aunt's frankness, he prefaced his reply by passing on gossip about her nephew. The news from the Inns of Chancery was that Henry de Lacy, known as the most moderate of the earls, was now so inflamed against Gaveston he was drawing up a document of protest against his influence.

Gualberto observed how this was the second protest document in as many months – the third if the altering of the coronation oath was included.

With this in mind, he said, what kind of odds was the aunt hoping for?

The art of the actuary being yet unborn, there were no tables to consult, nor past practice to refer to. Gualberto mentioned Julius Caesar. On the Ides of March, Mark Anthony would have taken one bet on the length of the dictator's life and Brutus another.

Gaveston's aunt brushed Caesar aside. She wanted to bet her nephew would live another five years. That was worth odds of 20 to 1. Gualberto hummed and hawed, thinking aloud. At present, it looked as though the opposition to Gaveston was prepared to go through legal channels. This could change to direct action if the King ignored the peaceful protest. He mentioned the parliament called for three weeks' time. Henry de Lacy's declaration of grievance could form the foundation of more radical protest by the members. If they decided to attaint Gaveston without trial and demand the full penalty of life and members, he could be dead by May Day.

So Gualberto argued that 20 to 1 might be better odds for a bet on Gaveston's *survival,* taking into account the power of the King to protect him. But with things as they were, a bet on his death was no long shot. Given his capacity to annoy the baronage, and the King's absolute blindness to his faults, 5 to I might be nearer the mark.

Gaveston's aunt laughed in Gualberto's face. This was a true Gascon they were talking about – a lucky fellow, blessed with all the natural talents a man could wish for. To kill him his enemies must first catch him. Given the blundering style of his opponents, their lack of style and flair, their gutlessness, chances of success were very low.

The amount of money to be laid on the bet was brought into the negotiations. In spite of being stripped of all their assets, the inmates of Wallingford prison had come up with a sum large enough to surprise Gualberto. He asked Gaveston's aunt to dine with him next day so he could have time to consult his principals.

"This is a new venture," he said. "It would be a pity for us to destroy such a good idea by making a huge loss the first time out. We need to think this one through very carefully."

At their second meeting, Gualberto produced the leaked document of grievances drawn up by Henry de Lacy's lawyers. Students at the Inns of Court, with their customary irreverence, had called it *Burstbelly's Complaint.* Gualberto pointed out how natural it was for the young to admire anyone prepared to flout the old guard. To the students, the antipathy of the barons towards Gaveston was a recommendation. If there was an insurrection in London, the students and apprentices might take Gaveston's part and even up the odds.

At the request of the aunt, Gualberto went through the argument, beginning with the revolutionary statement that there is a clear distinction between the person of the King and the Crown. It is to the latter that homage and allegiance are due. Should the King not be guided by reason (here Gualberto sighed with sheer admiration at the twist) *his subjects would have to put him back into the dignity of the Crown.*

Although impatient to get down to business, and suspicious of constitutional concepts *per se,* the aunt asked for an explanation.

Gualberto told her it meant that the King would have to be taught a lesson in kingship by the earls. Many were now arguing that it was impossible for Ned to reign properly if Gaveston remained by his side. He read her more of de Lacy's declaration: *There is a person close to the King,* the document said, *who is a man not to be endured. He impoverishes and disinherits the Crown. He is a promoter of discord between King and people; an enfeebler of legitimate government. The destruction of the Throne is in his power. His misdeeds make him the sovereign. Since the King has agreed to support him unreasonably against every man in every respect, this person cannot be judged or attainted under the law, whereupon* (here Gualberto smiled with pleasure again at a fine jump in the argument) *the people consider him judged and attainted because he must be a robber of the kingdom, traitor to his liege lord (whom he has disequilibrised), and an enemy of the realm. The King is bound by the fourth promise of his coronation oath to accept the laws the people choose. He must implement the decision of the people against this person.*

"Why don't they just come out with it and say who this person is?" the aunt asked when Gualberto had finished.

"It would be discourteous to a friend of the King."

The aunt chuckled, slapping her broad knee. "Oh, the English! Their courtesy is no more than cowardice."

Gualberto let her talk in this vein for a while, then, choosing his moment, he made the offer. Taking all relevant factors into account, and in a spirit of experiment, the Frescobaldi would accept a bet of 3,275 marks at 5 to 2 that Piers Gaveston would be dead *by violent means* in two years or less from 1st May 1308, inclusive, the stake money to be paid on that date or sooner.

Gaveston's aunt was shocked by the meanness of the offer. It was a long way from what she and her Wallingford colleagues had hoped for, but Langton had warned her that the Frescobaldi would be tight.

When Gaveston's aunt returned to Wallingford she found her nephew had arrived with the King the day before. Once she had apprised the prisoners of the Frescobaldi offer, she decided it was her familial duty to speak to Gaveston about what she had learnt in London. Leaving him in ignorance of what might evolve into an actual design upon his life exceeded even her robustly business-oriented ethics.

To give a full account it was necessary to explain how she had come by the information. Only the amount collected for the bet was adjusted in the telling, knowing this might excite avarice.

Gaveston was amused by the idea of the wager – Ned less so.

"Oh, come on," Gaveston chided him. "They're only playing the game for what it's worth. So is friend Gualberto and the Frescobaldi. We're big enough to cope with that."

"This document Gualberto referred to," Ned said with a worried frown. "Did he say when we might receive it?"

The aunt said the forthcoming parliament had been mentioned. She was then dismissed wondering if she'd done the right thing.

"If Henry de Lacy is the man behind it, you must have upset him a great deal," Ned said to Gaveston once the aunt had left. "Deep down he's very loyal. He stood by my father through thick and thin. Can you remember anything you might have said to upset him?"

"He's senile, for Christ's sake!"

Ned winced. "Is that what you said to him – that he's senile?"

"He *is* senile! What's the point of telling someone who's senile they're senile? They're too senile to understand!"

"No one likes being called that, even if they are," Ned muttered. "We should avoid getting on the wrong side of people like him."

"Is this is a king speaking?" Gaveston sneered. "To hell with mediocrities. They'll drag you down to their level."

Ned walked up and down, arms folded. He didn't want a row. They had just returned from a very happy time in the solitude of Knaresborough. Some mornings had been so sunny and blissful Ned had been forced to make himself a little sad so he could be practical and deal with the day.

"Would it be too much trouble for you to talk to him?" he said after a while. "I don't want things to get out of hand."

"Apologise to old Burstbelly? Never!"

"I didn't say apologise. All you need do is pay him a little attention…charm him."

"Placate, placate!" Gaveston snorted. "Why should I charm someone I don't respect?"

Ned shrugged and looked out of the window. His father and William Wild had given him a grounding on how to distinguish a genuine, heartfelt grievance from the everyday moans and groans of the governed. This learning drifted back into his mind. If Henry de Lacy was alienated enough to invoke *law* against his king, there would be worse elements – less honest, less open – active behind the scenes.

"What shall we do now?" he said in a lighter tone. "We've a couple of hours before dinner."

Gaveston beamed him a triumphant look.

"I was just thinking about my aunt's bet. Why don't we race those punters in the prison? They need to be let out now and again for a breath of fresh air. Let's show we can be as sporting as they are."

Ned clapped his hands in delight. Piers had a knack of brightening up any day.

"They're all priests and monks in there of one kind or another," Gaveston added. "The godly chase us to the grave. We should give them a taste of their own medicine."

An hour later, Langton and eight ex-Templars were lined up naked on the grass (racehorses run naked, Gaveston argued). Bets were made, and the whole contingent of guests and staff watched, as the prisoners set off to sprint round the castle.

As Langton fell by the wayside, purple in the face and clutching his chest, Gaveston caught Ned in a moment of worried melancholy, the smile gone from his face. Putting an arm round his shoulders, he asked what the matter was.

"If you died, I wouldn't want to live," Ned whispered. "We must do something."

"Let something be nothing," Gaveston replied. "You're not my nursemaid."

"I can't understand why people hate you so much."

"It's not our business to please them. That's been your mistake. Ignore them all from this day forward. Let's trust to our own instincts."

The race fell apart, the unfit prisoners unable to complete the circuit. Their eyes beamed detestation up at the battlements where Ned and Piers stood gazing at each other in a moment of union, the spectacle forgotten.

That night a Chancery messenger arrived from Westminster with leaked copies of letters sent by King Philip to the earls. In these he declared himself in favour of any protest they might make against the evildoer, Pierre de Gaveston, promising to bring pressure on his son-in-law, the King of England, to drive the culprit out of the country. He added that if anyone supported Gaveston in any way, he would become the mortal enemy of the King of France.

A Chancery note informed Ned that gifts for the earls had accompanied these letters – an immense sum of 40,000 pounds altogether. King Philip's sister, Margaret, the widow of King Edward, Ned's stepmother, enraged by the wholesale transfer of her property to Gaveston after her husband's death, had made a substantial contribution. Also, the earls in receipt of these letters had been sent large amounts of French wine.

"Why does everyone blame you?" Ned said after Gaveston had read the letters. "They don't know you at all."

"You're sacred and I'm not," came the tart reply. "If you ever need to sacrifice me, I'll go willingly."

Ned threw the letters on the floor and stamped on them; then, in tears, he embraced Gaveston. Once he'd recovered, he told him things would certainly come to a head at the parliament. Everything was building up to that.

"See if I care," was the insouciant reply. "What's a talking-shop to me?"

Ned confessed that he'd been holding information back, not wanting to upset his loved one. The Church had secretly joined in the protest.

"We only have each other? Is that what you're saying?" Gaveston said harshly. "We'd better think this out. We have no army? We have no allies? We're powerless?"

"Of course we're not powerless! If I want, I can call people to their obedience and they'll come," Ned told him. "But can I afford to put them to the test? With King Philip waiting for a chance to destroy me...Bruce to invade...the earls, the Church...what a risk I'd be taking!"

Gaveston put his hands behind his head. "Well, if I were you, I'd feed me to the lions," he said. "Please don't have a bad conscience on my account."

"That I'll never do," Ned declared, stemming tears. "All I'm saying is – civil war is something my father warned me against. It was his nightmare."

"So was I his nightmare," Gaveston quipped.

"Don't be flippant. Help me!"

"Whose life is being threatened?" Gaveston snarled suddenly. "If I choose to smile at it, that's my privilege!"

"Don't get angry with me. What must I do?"

"I'll tell you what you must do," Gaveston said, calming down. "Ask yourself what you believe in."

"I believe in you, of course."

"That's not the right answer. You should have said – I believe in *us* – because when it comes down to it, you don't."

"I do! I do!"

"You don't believe in us at all."

"I do! Is it my fault nobody else does?"

"Frankly, yes," Gaveston declared, moving away. "You've made no effort to explain. When I'm mentioned, all you talk about is your feelings. I've never heard you defend me."

This was new mental territory for Ned. He stared at Gaveston as if seeing him for the first time. "I've never considered you as someone who needs defending," he said.

"How can you say that? I was exiled twice, remember?"

"But we knew you'd come back. Every time you fight, I know you won't be hurt. You're never ill. You do what you like. You say what you like. Piers, you're one of the immortals."

"Tell that to my aunt."

"If you think I should defend you – and you may be right – how do I go about it?"

Gaveston thought for a while. "We should have seen this coming," he said eventually. "Put forward some arguments. People understand brotherhood. Brotherhood is everywhere – in families, in armies, in the stories of the Round Table, in the monasteries. Tell them we're simply a brotherhood of two."

Ned was stirred, but his mind was elsewhere, hastening to catch up with the danger they were in. He found the strength to suppress his emotion. He had to think clearly. Threats to his happiness had coalesced into a huge rugged lump poised to roll down and crush him. Its ugly presence dominated the immediate future. Even though Piers appeared indestructible, he was now targeted by experienced political combatants who knew their business. Blow by blow, Ned's father had taken him through the baronial revolts led by Simon de Montfort against the Crown – civil wars fresh in the memory of seventy-five-year-old Henry de Lacy, the earl Ned thought he could count on.

Ned's grandfather, Henry the Third, had become the slave and prisoner of his opponents. This had happened – so Ned was taught – because the magnates never understood anyone's needs but their own. A two-way sympathy was essential to sane government.

Ned remembered the deaths of traitors he'd witnessed – or men identified as traitors for the convenience of law – William Wallace of Scotland and David Llewellyn of Wales dragged to London to be disembowelled and hacked to pieces. He imagined Gaveston being destroyed this way. If it ever happened, he would die himself.

The use of the word *traitor* in Henry de Lacy's list of grievances gave rise to the greatest fear. If they could make it stick to Piers, no love could save him. Between the millwheels of being a traitor to England and an enemy of France, he would be ground to dust.

"They want me to be lonely, like my father was," Ned brooded. "We should never have let Willy Wild go. We're going to need him on our side with that brain of his. I'm going to apologise and say what you've told me was done to him was all a terrible mistake. I'll give him everything back and a bit more."

"What can he do? He's nothing," Gaveston protested. "Forget Willy Wild. You're clutching at straws. Appeal to the Pope."

"The Pope?" Ned echoed incredulously. "Have you forgotten who controls him?"

"Try Oxford, then, or Cambridge! They can work something out for us. It'll give them something useful to do."

"No schoolman will win this argument," Ned retorted. "Willy still has status as the man who was my father's closest friend. Don't you understand? He knows about friendship. He knows about being a favourite. We have to find a justification somewhere."

"Oh, try asking the Devil in Hell," Gaveston snapped, turning abruptly away, pessimism sending a shaft into his confidence for the first time. "Justify *ourselves?* What's this? You've been having a weak moment. Pull yourself together."

Ned was crestfallen. He roamed round the room, big body slumped at the shoulders. "What can I do if you won't face facts?" he wailed, shaking his head.

"Have you no right to choose your friends?"

"It's the influence you have over me…" Ned uttered the words unwillingly, looking at Gaveston to gauge their effect. "That's what they resent most."

"Do I have an influence?"

Ned laughed outright, waving his hands in the air. "Do you have an influence? What else is all this about?"

"Then we don't need any outside help, do we?" Gaveston said in masterful mode, grabbing Ned's shoulders and shaking him. "We work together. Wake up! This is a new time. We're ruling this country in a different way – through brotherhood."

"That's what they don't like," Ned mumbled, hanging his head. "You know I can't pick and choose how I rule. There are traditions and precedents."

"Well, with that attitude, you're beaten before you start!" Gaveston said huffily. "Why shouldn't there be adjustments when a new man comes to the throne? When there's a strong queen, do they complain about her influence over the King? How does she do that? Through love. If I have influence over you it's through love, isn't it?"

Unable to follow the argument further, Ned sank into an even deeper confusion.

Gaveston softened his tone. "They'll be disagreeing amongst themselves before long. Let them come crawling to us to make their case officially. When they do, pretend to be surprised, as if we know nothing."

"Perhaps we do know nothing," Ned said with pathos. "I honestly thought one day they'd all find it easy to accept you."

"What a disappointment I must be!"

"They're the disappointment. I'll never forgive them for putting you through this."

Gaveston knelt at Ned's feet and took his hand, placing it on top of his own head. "I am your creation. Like God with Adam, you've literally given me the earth," he said without a hint of irony. "Do with me as you will."

Stated this way, Gaveston's gratitude went beyond thanks for the splendid gifts he'd received. To Ned's role as brother was added father. His power had made Gaveston great. When able, at last, to give everything, Ned had found a new happiness, a release from himself. The reaction of outsiders to this generosity was beyond him. They seemed to live in another land where sharing was sin and love lukewarm.

CHAPTER TWENTY-ONE

Although Ned had plenty of warning of what he would face at the parliament of 28th April, he obeyed Gaveston and did nothing to prepare. When the representatives arrived in London, the retinues of the earls and barons were armed. Ned was given a false report that a rebel army was coming in from the south-west. In fright, he ordered the bridges over the Thames at Kingston and Staines to be broken down to hinder its progress.

When the members of parliament assembled, instead of using the palace chambers where the meetings took place, they went over to the abbey instead. Ned refused to join them, remaining in his palace a few hundred yards away. Eventually Henry de Lacy had to go over and present him with the list of grievances agreed by all the earls, barons, knights of the shires, burgesses, bishops and judges of England.

He told the King it was only a short walk but a long way for him, personally, as a loyal subject, to come so far.

In the room, Gaveston was sitting in a window seat with his feet up against the wall. He had pointedly remained where he was when the old earl tottered in with his document rolled under his arm, panting from the stairs.

"Are you not ashamed to be doing this?" Ned whispered in Henry de Lacy's ear, nodding in Gaveston's direction. "How can you, a valued friend and counsellor, lead an attack on our dearest friend?"

"Make him crawl!" Gaveston muttered loud enough to be heard. "God's soul, he should prostrate himself and kiss your feet!"

Henry de Lacy had been hoping for a chair but Ned kept him standing. Unbuckling his sword belt he supported himself on the scabbarded weapon. "This is the only use I have for my sword," he puffed, holding out the roll. "This is the consensus of all the people over there. In order to live in peace and obey our lawful king, we must have these demands met."

"What does it say in here?" Ned asked, holding the roll in his fist like a baton. "You tell me in your own words."

"A lot of trouble has been taken to express the way we feel, sire. Please read what your people say."

"It's my head you want, Burstbelly," Gaveston called out from the window.

"Why aren't you man enough to come out and say so?"

"I'm here to talk to my king," the old earl replied stiffly, his eyes fixed on Ned.

"You came here full of hatred and envy!" Gaveston shouted, banging his fist on the seat beside him. "The King will rule in spite of traitors like you!"

Henry de Lacy put his sword-belt back on and spread his feet a little wider. "Am I to say anything on my return to the parliament, sire? Do you have a message for your people?"

Ned walked across to Gaveston. "We know what's in it," he whispered. "Perhaps we should talk to him? It's easier dealing with one of them."

"No," Gaveston whispered back. "They might have changed it from what was leaked. We have to see exactly what's there. Send him away."

Ned returned to Henry de Lacy and smiled. "Well, if you won't tell us what it says, I suppose we'll have to read it."

"That would be best, sire," the old earl replied with a weary grin. "It's an important matter. The members wait upon your answer."

During the rest of the day Ned sent for each of the earls one by one. Once in front of the King each man struggled to conduct himself with restraint. While each interview was taking place, Gaveston sat in the window seat, pointedly reading the text of his condemnation. Ned had hoped to uncover signs of disagreement between the most powerful magnates – men who relied heavily on keeping the hierarchy in place. While Gaveston impugned the motives behind the attack on him, scoffing at the document, the earls maintained a steady, serious front, refusing to be provoked. Each man confirmed his support for the demands being made, at the same time affirming his loyalty to the Crown.

"I'm not a crown, I'm a man," Ned burst out at one point when John de Warenne, the Earl of Surrey, was in front of him. "I have my heart, I have my life, I have a brother, as you do! Why should I deny myself his company?"

John de Warenne suffered from a speech defect – a rolling, guttural lisp that had afflicted every generation of his family. A big man with a barrel chest, the sound of his voice reverberated in a deep, growling torrent. Sometimes his tongue seemed too big for his mouth and he showered spit as he spoke. While he laboured to make a guarded reply, Gaveston imitated him word for word, spluttering and spraying. Finally, the earl lost his temper.

"We will not be wuled by your bwuther!" he said, jowls quivering with indignation. "We are wesolved on that!"

Gaveston tumbled out of the window seat, holding his sides. "Bwuther, is this all we're up against? A waterfall?"

"My brother doesn't rule you," Ned said, signalling for Gaveston to be quiet. "Tell me, John – what will happen if I say no?"

John de Warenne looked uncertain. He had often stood before the old king and been dressed down. It was no new experience for him to be held to account for protests and complaints, even defiance. Controlling his anger was something he did well.

"If he stays, we will not be wuled by you. Until you weturn us to our whole allegiance by getting wid of him, we will wule ourselves and wait."

"You will rebel – is that what you're saying?"

"Until that man goes, we will not be wuled by you," the earl repeated doggedly, his courage holding. "He's sitting over there, listening to what I say. If he was your twue bwuther, and loved you as we do, he'd go of his own accord."

"You should die for that, my April shower," Gaveston seethed. "How dare you dictate to me! Bring your sword into the yard."

John de Warenne looked questioningly at the King, appealing for permission to take up the challenge. Although twice Gaveston's age, and having been hammered to the ground by him at the Wallingford tournament only a few months ago, he was fired up and ready to fight.

"We're not here to start a war," Ned said, frowning. "Behave yourselves, both of you."

"Bring them all into the yard one by one or all together and I'll see there's no rebellion," Gaveston said, walking around the earl, leaning close to glare into his eyes. "My sword would wule you, wet John."

"You tapeworm hanging out of England's arse!" the earl spat, his features suddenly contorted in loathing. "I wegret we've given our word to cure our ills only by law. You should be stamped on as a pawasite!"

The King's last visitor was a man close to death and indifferent to danger. Robert Winchelsey's ill-health and frailty had rendered him incapable of officiating at the coronation as Archbishop of Canterbury. Years of exile for defying the old king's power had give him a far-reaching, independent perspective. Once the mitre was on his head, spurning earthly glory and pouring contempt on secular values had become his chief pleasure. His hero, Saint Thomas à Becket, beckoned him towards a martyr's crown.

When he was carried into the King's presence in a chair, Ned asked why he'd come. No summons had been sent for him. The interview had been granted in the hope Winchelsey might have a different, more enlightened attitude.

"Sire, the parliament believes you've had time to study their demands,"

Winchelsey quavered, eyes bright with the thrill of tackling the whelp of his old adversary for the first time. "What I have to say has a bearing on the person alluded to – who, so I'm told for I've never met him, is that young man over by the window."

Gaveston stood up and bowed. "What have you got to say to me, old fellow," he said with a curl of his lip. "Don't let not having met me hold you back from speaking your mind – if it's still working."

"I don't deal with playthings," Winchelsey replied haughtily. "The members are merciful men. I've spoken to them and they'll accept the exile of this person instead of his death."

"How good of them to let me live!" Gaveston said with a flick of his fingers to show his indifference.

"But the lands you gave him must be returned to the Crown," Winchelsey continued. "He may retain his title of earl during his lifetime. Money may be granted to him for the sake of his wife."

"Oh, these are generous men!" Gaveston shouted, stalking around the room with arms aloft. "You sound as though you're the King! This is the King! He decides!"

"Once this person goes, he must never return. If he does dare come back, the Church will immediately excommunicate him."

The message delivered, a small smile of satisfaction appeared across Winchelsey's face. He'd done well in his bearding of the despot's whelp. "Now, if you'll forgive me, sire, I'm very fatigued and would like to be dismissed."

"You weren't invited in the first place, Judas!" Gaveston ranted, giving the carrying chair a shake. "Get him out of here!"

Ned made a gesture, commanding calm. "How long were you in exile, Robert?" he asked.

"Twenty months, sire."

"A mere twenty months. In a life as long as yours that's very little time, isn't it?" Ned said sweetly. "It's virtually a holiday."

"Every day was an agony."

"Ah, you missed your family and friends, your home…how sad. And it's made you poorly."

"I was never so miserable, sire. It was a martyrdom."

"Remind me of the offence for which you were exiled," Ned murmured, scratching his chin. "What was it you did to upset my father so much?"

Winchelsey was silent. He sniffed and looked at the rings hanging on his fleshless fingers.

"You can't remember? No matter. It all comes back. You were suspected of conspiracy. Were you guilty?"

"No, sire!" the Archbishop declared, lifting his head. "I was not!"

"You think yourself innocent. Yet you wish to condemn my friend, who is also innocent, to an entire life of exile."

"The people are determined he should go, sire."

"Only if being precious to me is a crime can he be guilty of anything!" Ned bellowed suddenly, eyes flashing indignantly. "How can you, of all men, the leader of our Church, go along with such irreligious cruelty?"

Winchelsey sighed and sat back in the chair. "Sire, what have you been doing for this person since you came to the throne?" he said patiently, pointing a long finger at Gaveston. "What was in your mind when you raised him up?"

Ned was taken aback. He glanced at Gaveston who had turned away.

"There was nothing in your mind? You can't remember?" Winchelsey went on, leaning forward intently. "If that's the case, the protest we make is against your thoughtlessness. Whether you intended to or not, the parliament is certain you've a made him a *quasi* king, thereby diluting your own authority – which you are not entitled to do without their assent."

In pain of mind, Gaveston rocked backwards and forwards, holding his head. "He'd send my soul to Hell without a second thought. For what? Sheer envy!"

Ned went over and held Gaveston's head against his chest to quieten him down. Looking over his shoulder, he told Winchelsey that if he, as king, was to blame for acting outside the law, he was the one who should be punished, not the faultless man in his arms.

Ned kept them waiting for three weeks. The armed bands of the magnates and parliament members wandered around London in a state of drunken anxiety. There were show-downs between old enemies, bloody fights – but it was all sporadic and inconsequential compared to the issue waiting to be resolved. Rumours of armies being raised by the King came in daily. The space between the palace and the abbey was full of people hurrying, gossiping, speculating, looking up at the windows for a glimpse of the beleaguered pair. They kept to their quarters trying to marshal support through the machinery of the royal household, appealing to friends and traditional loyalties. When these efforts produced a picture of alarming weakness, a crack appeared in Ned's resolve that got wider by the day. He hinted there was no alternative to adopting a succumbent attitude – for the time being. To avoid civil war, his darling Piers must go. This decision was presented to Gaveston as if it formed part of an overall strategy for reforming parliament and reducing its powers.

"By the time you get back, everything will have changed," Ned assured him. "I'll sort them out so it can never happen again."

"It's surrender! Don't dress it up! You take all my lands from me and call it a tactical withdrawal?" Gaveston cried. "It's only eight months since I came back from the last exile! This is the third time you've let me down!"

"While you're away, it will become obvious I'm a much better king with you than without you."

"How will that be accomplished? They don't listen to a word you say."

"By being much tougher on them, reminding them what life was like under my father. They'll realise the advantage of our way of doing things."

Gaveston looked doubtful. "To lose all my lands is a terrible loss," he grieved. "I've only had them for a short while. Can't you do something about that?"

Ned spied his opportunity. Gaveston's pride was sagging. The hatred of the entire community had done its work.

"The last thing you should worry about is land," Ned said softly.

"Even if you lose the Cornwall possessions, you have what your wife brought you, also my stepmother's portion, all the other bits and pieces…and whatever else I can find. We'll discuss that later."

"Thank you, brother," Gaveston said, secretly very relieved but preventing himself from appearing too pleased. "No matter what happens, I know you'll always look after me."

"The way I look at it is this – they haven't had enough time to get accustomed to the changeover from my father," Ned told him, a teacherly edge in his voice. "He reigned for thirty-five years. I've only been on the throne for nine months. People are still getting used to me. It's ridiculous to expect them to take it all in at once. So, instead of exile, I'm going to see if I can get away with sending you to Ireland."

"Ireland? It's worse than Scotland."

"You'll be my lieutenant. When you've shown them what you can do, running it for me, no one will dispute your right to be by my side."

"Will you come and see me?"

"Of course. As for lands – I'm giving you property in Acquitaine worth £2,000 a year, an assorted parcel here to make another £2,000, for you, and your expenses in Ireland. There – is that so bad?"

Gaveston blinked, delighted by the news but keeping his face straight. This wasn't as bad as he'd thought. "They won't object?" he asked.

"They'd be mad to. Also, I think a pension is appropriate, and one for your wife…you can have some blank charters under my seal, fill them in yourself…What else? A lieutenant should have his own treasure. We'll get some to take with you. "

"And I definitely won't lose the title of earl?"

Ned shook his head. "Never. You're one of nature's noble creatures," he told him.

Ned could see Gaveston was pleased. To be in Ireland where he wouldn't be hated by the people as an individual, only in his role, was a big attraction. So far, his lack of function in the English state had been a stumbling-block.

"Over there, you'll be me. Think of it like that."

Gaveston was taken with the idea. He plumed himself like a child given a lead part in a play. Ned's heart flooded as he watched him brighten up.

Such regeneration was a king's work. He felt proud of his own achievement. By his own wits and judgement, he had hit upon a solution. The thoughts had flown into his mind like doves. Everyone could be happy – except Richard de Burgh, Earl of Ulster, who had been appointed lieutenant in Ireland the day before.

No matter, Ned thought, as the inspirational idea slotted into the framework of government starting to form ghost-like in his mind, we can get round that. I'll give Richard de Burgh something else to keep him quiet.

"Don't be too happy in Ireland without me," Ned said to Gaveston who was visibly overtaken by relief, "and don't imagine you'll have an easy time."

"Who said I wanted an easy time?"

"People who go to Ireland for too long become more Irish than the Irish. Don't do that. Stay as you are," Ned went on. "You'll have to be tough on them. Don't judge the Irish by the ones you meet over here. They're on their best behaviour. At home they're another race of men – still quite primitive." He then recalled how his own father – who'd known a thing or two, he realised – always said travel refreshed the soul. "I'll come over on a visit when the dust has settled," he added. "By the time this business is sorted out my soul will need some help. I can only get that from you."

Apart from the Earl of Ulster, everyone whose life was being paralysed by the *impasse* was happy with the arrangement to send Gaveston to Ireland. To serve in the bogs had long been considered a form of punitive exile. The protesters discovered their overhelming need was to be rid of the problem rather than inflict punishment.

When news got out of the huge compensatory gifts being showered on the favourite, there was revulsion but it was muted by resignation. Secure in his animal self again, still with no real sense of possible failure, Gaveston's bravado re-emerged, its vigour only slightly moderated, but the jokes he cracked weren't aimed at the earls, and his haughtiness had a learned edge. When, in a late June heat wave, his enormous retinue set out from Langley for Bristol to take ship to Dublin, a revelling crowd of locals saw the new lieutenant off, admiring his magnificent green and gold costume – designed by a tailor whose remit had been to clothe the Emperor of Hibernia.

The crisis solved, Ned's commitment to his lover elevated the affair into realms only occupied by heroes. In the public mind, who else could turn the tables on the envious, over-powerful earls but men who lived beyond common reality, men witty and brave? That hot, humid summer the love of Ned and Piers became a mystery with supernatural overtones, their life together a zone of godlike invincibility.

Dreams and visions of the pair cropped up among humble people. Three separate parishes in Lincolnshire reported Ned and Piers appearing as Siamese twins joined at the navel and mouth, under a shared mane of flaming hair. An angel informed an anchorite in Ludlow that the King and Gaveston were charged by God with building a new world.

In universities and monasteries, libraries were searched for evidence of any king in history whose overfondness had been of benefit to the people. Only King Arthur's love for Lancelot bore a faint resemblance. Henry the Second's love for Thomas à Becket in their early friendship was more promising. An abbot suggested Gaveston be made Archbishop of Canterbury for a couple of years. It might cool the King's passion and provide a second great martyr for the Church.

As Gaveston disappeared into the mists of Ireland, the honeysuckle of myth curled round his name. Whatever else you say about him, the sages averred, like the Trinity, the man wields power through love. Who are we to understand it? Look at the desert fathers in their lice, their strangeness, their relationship with the invisible Lord. The love of God passeth all understanding in both directions.

So does the love of men.

Having removed Piers from danger, Ned set out to repair all the damage done. He paid court to Isabella as if they were starting all over again, treated her kindly, showed her the sunnier side of his nature, trying manfully to get her pregnant, and giving her gifts of land, castles and money. At the same time, he humbly approached her father, King Philip, assuring him that the whole Gaveston episode was over. Finally, he wrote to Pope Clement V questioning the usefulness of the pendent excommunication, which still stood in its original form. He asked for it to be relaxed, arguing circumstances could arise where his lieutenant in Ireland needed to come to England for consultations. This request was accompanied by a bribe of £1,500. The bribe was pocketed by Pope Clement but no decision emerged. The threat of excommunication was held in reserve in case of future disagreements.

His bridges partly rebuilt, including Kingston and Staines, Ned set to work on the earls. He went to them open-handed, gave them everything he could in terms of redress of grievances, showed willing in every department. When the earls were softened up, starting to question the morality of their hatred of a mere youth, he worked on their guilt with new-found skill. Into their self-doubt he slipped the notion that they could make amends by giving Gaveston back the lands of the earldom of Cornwall. There would be a condition, of course. His lieutenant in Ireland – who was doing dramatically well over there a mere two months after his appointment – would treat the magnates with more respect. There must never be any repetition of his arrogance and insults. That Gaveston would have to be with the earls in order not to insult them was overlooked.

The earls treated these approaches with caution. Though heady with relief that the nightmare was over and glad to extricate themselves from opposition, they kept their actual experience of the man Gaveston clearly in mind. They ruefully accepted Ned had outmanoeuvred them: once Gaveston's appointment in Ireland was allowed to go through without complaint, they could hardly insist it also constituted punitive exile. A king's lieutenant was not a criminal or a traitor.

Only a few voices were raised in dissent – Black Dog's amongst them, but even his growl was subdued.

CHAPTER TWENTY-TWO

The unusual heat of the early summer made tensions worse in Gethin's household at Pant Mawr. While he struggled to keep his sheep from dying of pneumonia – the animals were overheating in the humidity by day and getting chilled by mountain air at night – his sons became increasingly useless to him, fighting amongst themselves over Valmai, encouraged by Megan.

On the day William Wild arrived, there was an outbreak of fighting at breakfast. Valmai ended up locked in the barn with her children until things settled down. Confronted by Megan who had blood on her hands from patching her sons' cuts and bruises, the Irishman introduced himself.

"Boys, you can make friends now," Megan announced, "her husband's come at last."

Valmai and the children came blinking out of the barn. The Irishman held his son for the first time, checked his feet and rejoiced.

"We should move out as soon as possible," Valmai said in his ear, looking over towards the five men of Pant Mawr who were glaring miserably at the reunion. "They've been very kind but we've become a burden."

Within the hour William Wild found himself roped in to gather sheep carcases off the hillside. The flock was being decimated by pneumonia, the surviving animals gasping in any shade they could find, choking on their own blood-stained snot. Death-rattles sounded in the humid air. As the farm visibly slid towards ruin, the Irishman found it difficult to negotiate the withdrawal of his family. To leave while help was needed would be ungrateful.

Megan spotted his hesitation.

"Don't you worry about lending a hand," she said brusquely as Gethin marked out a burial pit for the carcases. "We'll work better if you get your wife and children out of here."

"We could do with help digging," Gethin said, unwilling to accept the idea of Valmai leaving. "If we all pitch in it will be done sooner."

"There are other things I'd like done sooner," Megan flashed back at him. "I'd like some peace from having her around. You left her with us too long, William Wild. She's had a bad effect on this family."

"Please ignore my wife," Gethin said, sweat running into his eyes. "We've loved having Valmai here. But if you want to leave, don't let us stop you."

"A few hours won't make much difference," the Irishman said, aware of the charged atmosphere. "I'm sorry to find you in the middle of such a disaster."

"That's Nature for you," Gethin replied, driving a pickaxe into the stony ground. "The weather comes when it wants."

As the men and women worked side by side digging the pit, three horsemen rode up the lane to the farm. They had tracked the Irishman down, following his trail from London.

They were hirelings who had served with Ned and Piers in the Scottish campaigns, surplus sons of families who would have no inherited fortune. With the decline of law enforcement since the death of the old king, they had supplemented their incomes by crime until the opportunity arose to go and serve Gaveston in Ireland where pickings might be better. He had sent the party over to Wales.

Their work in this case was to fulfil a blood feud. Gaveston's aunt had pressed her nephew for full formal vengeance on William Wild for the disappearance and assumed death of her sister's son, Raymond de Sauveterre, and the destruction of Boldwood. An additional reason for killing the Irishman was to convince those who made enemies of Gaveston's tribe they did so at their peril.

By late afternoon the humid heat at Pant Mawr was overwhelming. The killers were forced to lead their exhausted horses up the gradient for several miles from Llangurig. When they arrived, no one was in the farmyard. They saw a long pit being dug into the hillside nearby and piles of dead sheep.

When Megan came out of the house, sure in her mind they were the landlord's men come to collect dues, she flew at them in a fury, pointing up the slope at the carcases. "If you want paying, there's plenty of mutton there, you heartless wolves," she screamed. "Take it all for his lordship's table! I hope it chokes him!"

The killers told her they didn't want sheep, but a man.

"Can't you see how we're suffering?" Megan yelled, beside herself with heat and indignation. "Go on, fuck off and find someone else to harass, you Saxon swine!"

When he heard Megan's strident abuse, Gethin trotted down to the farmhouse, believing the same as she had – that bailiffs had chosen the worst moment to come.

Megan's voice was raised to an even higher pitch. "William Wild? Who the fuck is William Wild?" she screamed. "What kind of name is that for a Welshman, you donkeys! Get out of here!"

Megan's harangue stopped suddenly. Gethin entered the courtyard in time to see her skewered on a spear. As he leapt across to her, he was cut down.

Up on the hillside, the Irishman recognised the sudden silence. It shimmered in the heat like a fanning hawk. Violent death was detectable to his soldier's senses. It made an impact on the air. He listened for a few moments, his heart going cold. Assuming all his old battlefield authority, he stopped the sons following their father to the house.

"It's someone looking for me," he told them. "Take Valmai and the children and servants up the bed of the stream and hide. I'll come for you when the coast is clear."

He then walked towards the farmhouse armed only with a spade.

"Who are you?" the three killers asked as he came round the corner. In answer, he held up his spade. "I work here. I'm no one of account," he said, in Welsh.

His eyes took in the two bodies on the ground.

A moronic grin came to his face. He squinted, smacked his lips and tugged the lobe of his ear.

Covered in dirt and sweat, he looked like a serf.

"*Dim Saesneg,*" he said, slurring like an idiot defective. "No speak Saxon."

"Who's this?" one of the killers demanded as Gethin was turned over to show his face "What's his name?"

The Irishman scratched his head, grinning like an imbecile.

"Name! Understand, you stupid Welsh cunt? What's his name?"

"Oh, poor William Wild," came the slow, laboured answer.

One of the killers grabbed the Irishman by the throat and shook him. "If your lord asks any questions, tell him the King's lieutenant in Ireland has right of revenge on this man under the laws of that place. The woman's tongue brought her own death. Understand?"

William Wild nodded his head as the killer loosed his grip. He picked up a bucket and held it up to them to prove he had understood. While he went to the stream, the killers rested in the house, too hot and fatigued to bother looking for something to rob in such a poor place. When William Wild returned with water he was sent back for more. For half-an-hour he fetched for them and their horses, grinning vacantly, saying nothing. As he staggered into the courtyard with the eleventh bucketful, stupid grin fixed in readiness, he saw them leaving.

He stood and watched them go, the heavy bucket hanging from his arm. When they were out of sight he became aware of the weight of the water and lowered the bucket to the ground.

Bending over to do this, he glimpsed his own distorted reflection in the moving surface – the dirty face of an old, grey-haired man. Only the intelligent anger in the eyes gave life and dignity.

He went to his knees, supporting himself on the rim of the bucket, staring at his image in the water.

By quick thinking he had saved himself. In the process, he had taken everything from these people. If he had never come near them they would be living now. He'd brought death and the devils of Hell.

Guilt and self-disgust choked him.

An hour later, everyone from the house came down from hiding on the slopes of Pen Pumlumnon. They found William Wild on his knees still staring into the bucket. As the bodies of Gethin and Megan were discovered, the sons ran amok, howling, Valmai, the children and servants scattered from the sight. For a while the Irishman couldn't explain what had happened. The words wouldn't come. The four sons challenged the Irishman as he knelt at the bucket, demanding to know why he'd sent them to hide. Although none of the sons were trained in arms, they could have put up a fight.

"They came looking for me. Your mother and father got between me and them," William Wild managed to say. "If I hadn't sent you away they'd have killed you all."

The sons said that would have been preferable. As men, they would never be able to hold up their heads again. How could they live having stood by while their parents were butchered? Their anger was surly, threatening and poisonous. They circled him, accusingly. "This is all because of you. You couldn't look after your own family. Why couldn't you leave us alone? How will you pay? How will we get our pride back?"

Unable to look at them, the Irishman covered his ears, leant forward and laid his head on the bucket, offering his head. He waited, eyes shut, the sons yelling, "If it wasn't for your wife we'd kill you!"

Under the stinging lash of their hatred, William Wild took a personal oath. This time, Gaveston would not escape retribution. He would have to die.

As the rage in the farmyard subsided into keening, he bent down and kissed his own image in the water, drinking from its lips.

Valmai lay in the night-cold of the farmhouse with her husband, too drained of energy to chase the servants to build a fire. As the Irishman dozed, she dragged all the details she could out of him, trying to interpret his ice-cold state of mind.

"Leave it till tomorrow, I'll try to answer," William Wild said finally. "Too much has happened today."

Two servants had run away, terrified of possible repercussions to the murders at Pant Mawr, for which they might be blamed. Although no protection was ever given by the marcher lords this far west, they were always quick to bring people into their courts for justice.

Gethin and Megan had to be buried alongside their sheep because of the heat. The clergy would have plenty to say about that. In the days to come there would be trouble of the worst kind. The farm felt like a place abandoned by luck. Murder, heat and misery had transformed it into a branch of the infernal regions. Children, men and women, having sweated in a cauldron of tears by day, lay on a rack of ice by night, frozen by the mountain winds, wondering how much worse life could get.

"Give me room," the Irishman said, pushing Valmai away as she renewed her efforts to warm him in the depth of the night. "If I need you, I'm the weaker for it. Stay away until it's all over."

She refused to be put off, coming back to him. "I don't understand you. What have I done?"

"My faith was only in you, which was wrong. You're just a woman."

"What does that mean?"

"When I fought in the Holy Land I was strong in the Lord. I need that strength now." He held her at arm's length. "You weaken me, woman. Who are you, in truth?"

"You know who I am."

"Do I? In those days we knew our enemy. You could see him a mile off. All you've done is blur the edges. The man who shed this innocent blood today is someone you find attractive."

"Don't go back into all that," Valmai sighed. There was no point in arguing any further. Jealousy, guilt and anger had merged.

As the Irishman lay sunk in his misery, the smells of her body came to him in the cold air. When he heard her quiet weeping, his heart relented. Stroking her hair in the dark he allowed his broken mind to wander, telling her Palestine wasn't the only Holy Land. Another lay to the west – Ireland, his country, where he was born.

He told her how an additional horror had emerged. Piers had a licence to ruin Ireland.

"This is a trick you're playing on yourself," Valmai said, recovering from her tears. "It sounds like a madman talking."

"Without the influence of Ireland's saints, the brutes who call themselves Christians would be a hundred times worse. I must go back. Everything I've spent my life looking for was in the place I was born. I should never have left."

"If you intend to go to Ireland, we go together. From now on, wherever you go, I go."

"This war is not for women."

"What war? There is no war."

He dismissed what she said with a rough laugh, tapping the side of her head. "God leaves the repair of an imperfect creation to men only. Stay with your children."

Valmai shrank from him, hurt and confused. "I don't know what you're talking about," she said.

"If I'd trusted my instincts, Piers would never have corrupted Ned. One blow is all it would have taken. I could have done it for Edward…and Ned. Now I'll put that right."

He turned away from her. Raised as a child amongst people who idolised seers and prophets, and being one who'd yearned for revelations all his life, he wasn't going to release his hold on the vital meaning made clear to him. He'd been given a sign and permission to act.

After a while, Valmai was able to take him in her arms, hoping the guilt-ridden madness had subsided a little. They slept fitfully as the horror slid into the immediate past.

William Wild wept in his sleep. Valmai thought it was because of dreams, but she was wrong. It was the impact of the certainty – the release from long, tortuous prevarication.

The greatest of all blessings had been granted him.

He knew what he had to do.

CHAPTER TWENTY-THREE

Gaveston knew nothing about Ireland. The speed with which the decision had been taken to send him there gave little time for preparation. Its reputation had been falsified by those prejudiced against it because they'd been sent there, and by those prejudiced in its favour because it belonged to them. In his retinue were men who had lived and worked there – administrators, clerks, soldiers and priests. They knew how much he would have to learn if he was to be a success in Ireland – the first thing he must understand was the passion for revolt. Of all the provinces of the English empire, Ireland contained the most contradictions – the sharpest being that England ruled Ireland by hardly ruling it at all.

Being the man he was, Gaveston quickly recovered from the stress of recent dangers. On the voyage from Bristol, his confidence increased day by day.

With the coast in sight, the ship was becalmed in hot, humid weather. The men who knew Ireland and her ways sat and sweated, waiting to be consulted by the new lieutenant. They knew he was a soldier. They knew he could fight. But they also knew he didn't know the Irish in Ireland. At home, on their own turf, they were a different race.

As a child of the south, Gaveston suffered the heat less than his fellow passengers. He was in no hurry. For hours he sat with his feet up on the bulwark, drinking wine and dreaming. Thoughts any ordinary man might have after surviving such a tidal wave of hate were absent. The self-doubt which had broken through his mental barriers during the crisis at Westminster didn't reappear. What he saw over the calm sea was a land of opportunity.

Unlike his earldom, it wasn't only there to be enjoyed. There was a task and glory to win. From conversations with Ned at Langley, he knew rebels must be seized and chastised, malefactors caught and executed, alliances with collaborators strengthened, the country opened up for transport and trade. Inside the Dublin pale, English rule was little more than a blister on Ireland's eastern side, pressed against the sea. Nine-tenths of the island was in the hands of warring chieftains.

It was another Scotland – without the power of a Bruce holding it together. The rebels in Ireland weren't organised in a common front. They fought each other as much as they fought their conquerors. With all English armies driven out of Scotland and Ned unwilling to undertake the annual invasion until he could be more certain of loyalties nearer home, Gaveston was the only English general with a chance to achieve anything positive that year. The sooner he could notch up victories against the King's enemies in Ireland, the sooner he could return to London in triumph.

Gaveston decided to delay asking too many questions of the old Irish hands. They sat watching him on the deck, fanning themselves – pity in their eyes. *So you think you're different? That you're going to achieve something? Think again, boy.* He smiled at them, often. The time would come for him to absorb the hard facts – the real briefing – but not yet. He'd relax a little longer before immersing himself in the dark pool of Irish politics.

In Gaveston's experience, if too much knowledge was accrued in a short time, fear would start to ferment. The more intensively people learnt, the more they guessed at the future, and the more they allowed it to oppress them. Salient, natural forces created his responses. I own. I take. I fight. I live.

I lose. I give. I live in peace. I die – these were stamped on the sides of coins he never turned over.

He would put Ireland into shape – show everyone what he was made of and what his partnership with Ned was made of. Opposition had only succeeded in making Gaveston stronger – and clearer in his mind. Soon his genius for war would be flourishing again. Under the auspices of Ned's genius for love he would cover himself in fame.

Whether anyone else understood didn't matter. It was their mystery – and they would make it work.

When an east wind blew and the ship could move, he sailed into Dublin in his green and gold, trumpets sounding, drums roaring.

The last time William Wild was in Ireland – forty-five years before – he had lived under the name he was born with, Theodosius Lanagan, the son of wanderers. There was no home town, no base for his family. The whole island was their natural territory. His nomadic young manhood in the Mediterranean and Near East was an extension of this itinerant childhood. Now he was back in Ireland, the instinct returned. He became a Lanagan again.

His attempt to settle down in the Wye Valley with Valmai had been destroyed. Now he was an outsider with no king to protect him. When he caught up with Gaveston and killed him, he would die himself, purging the shame of having let his life become a mere instrument used by other men.

Valmai had to let him go. Deprived of reason and self-respect, he couldn't live much longer eaten up by guilt and hatred. If he was successful it could change him. Certainly, it would change a world poisoned by Gaveston. Valmai had to be satisfied with a remote chance of future happiness – if her husband killed Piers, who was everyone's enemy, it might make their fortune again. This was all the hope she could find in the situation. She returned to live quietly in the Wye Valley with her children to wait for his return, or news of his death, or the deep silence of his disappearance.

The four sons of Gethin abandoned the farm at Pant Mawr and escorted Valmai to Tintern. In a matter of weeks they had been forced into a tough, embittered manhood. Grimly, they said goodbye to her, their adoration of her beauty stifled by what had happened. Beauty was not part of their world any more. They couldn't help blaming her for the destruction of their family, even though her involvement arose from innocence and need. But it was the sort of blame she knew would be forgiven in time.

They wanted to go to Ireland with William Wild to exact revenge, but he advised them otherwise. He said they should find employment as soldiers in the private armies of the English earls who most hated Gaveston. If the Irishman's mission failed and there was a war over the favourite, the four sons of Gethin would be better placed to find some form of vengeance.

On the day William Wild stepped off the ship in Dublin, his Boulogne acquaintance, Durandus, the radical thinker, was dragged from his bed in Paris by agents of the French king and taken to Calais where he was handed over to agents of the English earls. They took him across the Channel to Dover, refusing to answer any of his panic-stricken questions as to why he was being taken to England.

In London, he was lodged with Henry de Lacy, the Earl of Lincoln, who treated him kindly. He was given a letter from King Philip containing instructions to provide all possible help to the English earls as they might specify.

Ned was at Langley, resting after his conciliation labours. Having spent so many months working on the rehabilitation of Piers, he was suddenly very lonely. There was no one he could talk to about Piers. All the hours of cajolery, flattery and bribery Ned had spent on the rehabilitation of the loved one had kept him in mind as a problem, not a joy.

When Durandus was ushered into the royal presence by Henry de Lacy, Ned was lying back in a chair emotionally exhausted after composing his forty-fourth letter to Gaveston. Not a single reply had been received in return, only dry, impersonal reports and accounts. Convinced Piers had forsaken him, Ned was surprised to find himself in the throes of an agonisingly powerful outbreak of sexual feeling – all of which had been poured into the letter.

When Durandus entered clothed in the black and white of the Dominicans, Ned was so shaken by the sublimity and darkness of his passion he took him for a confessor and groggily fell to his knees.

Prevented from making his prepared introduction, Henry de Lacy hesitated. No one could interrupt the King's prayers. Believing he'd briefed the young French philosopher all he could, the old earl wished him luck, left him to it and withdrew.

Ned remained on his knees, his letter to Gaveston in his hands.

He offered it to Durandus with a heart-rending sigh.

The Dominican took it to the window and read it carefully.

"Execrable slime!" he snarled when he'd finished.

Ned was shocked. He looked up, eyes red-rimmed, cheeks inflamed, lips hanging loose. "I can't help myself," he muttered, wiping his eyes with his sleeve. "I love him so."

Apart from his intellect, the reason for Durandus's choice of philosophy as a career in the Church was to control the power of his black temper. It had to be kept under the strictest control, its furnace-like energy channelled into his work.

Much of his discipline had gone under the pressure of the last few days of captivity in Henry de Lacy's house. The sight of Ned on his knees with the ink of carnal filth on his fingers had blown the cap off his anger.

"Are you so deep in your dunghill you imagine I'd be taken in by that excuse? You can't help yourself! You don't deserve to live in a Christian country, never mind be the ruler of it."

Ned studied the man standing over him. "Are you new?" he asked tremulously. "I'm not used to being spoken to this way."

"It's about time you were. Your soul is a sewer."

"Perhaps."

This semi-submissive response provoked even greater indignation. "Don't play games with me! The whole of Europe feels sorry for your people!" Durandus shouted, crouching down to thrust his face into Ned's. "Beyond your abominations, what are you? Call yourself a king?"

"Go on, go on. I'm listening."

"You set a disgusting example. You defile! You contaminate!"

"Yes, Father – I see what you're driving at. But why did God make me like this?"

"Blaming God for your sins is the worst sin of all."

"I didn't create myself – nor did I choose to be myself."

That word *be* – central to Durandus's special subject – wrought a change. He was able to rein in his temper and adopt a different tone. "That's a specious argument," he said in a more moderate tone. "However, without conceding anything, we can take a look at what you're saying."

For several years Durandus had been writing his doctorate. He was out of the habit of hearing confession. Deep down, he missed the human contact, the rawness. Ned's vulnerability was interesting. There was something in his attitude that appealed to the Frenchman.

"Does the concept of free will mean anything to you?" he said equably. "No one is a slave of God."

Ned was silenced. He went back on his haunches, looking at the ceiling as if for inspiration. "I'm not sure where that leaves me," he said eventually. "If I'm free, and I've chosen all this trouble, then there's something the matter with my mind."

"Be in no doubt – homosexuality in practice is a heinous sin," Durandus said. "It's also a crime, even in England. Are you above the law?"

"I think so," Ned replied, "though it doesn't feel like it."

"What possible excuse can you have for holding your kingdom to ransom on account of one relationship?"

Ned thought for a while before answering. "England had a happier time when my father was happy with my mother. Why shouldn't the same be the case with Piers and me? We love each other like they did."

Durandus frowned. "I don't know the background, but that sounds like a sophistry. You know the unnaturalness of your offence. If you carry on as you've been doing, there'll be catastrophe and war. D'you want that on your conscience?"

Ned got up off his knees. Guilt and passion were easing off, but he didn't want the Dominican to stop the discussion. This priest would tackle anything.

"I need a confessor who'll be straightforward," he said. "My sins have been the same for years. I never chop and change and I never get any help. The men who listened didn't apply their minds to what I was saying or consult anyone about my problems."

Durandus was becoming aware he'd landed himself in a disturbing predicament. Ned was a devious man as skilled in dodging responsibility as ignoring it. His initial excuses were being consistently maintained. It was not his fault he loved Piers, nor was it his fault so many hated Piers.

For Durandus to admit that he was not a confessor but a tool of King Philip and the earls meant the outspoken criticism he'd made could be taken as an insult. He needed the customary protection a confessor received.

"Even if we knew from the confessional that a king was Lucifer on earth we couldn't make use of the information," he said, mind racing.

Ned put his head to one side, blinking vaguely as he absorbed the denial of his case. "Come to think of it, your accusation that I'm holding my kingdom to ransom is a sharp one," he said. "Is that your own idea or did someone put you up to it?"

This man's mind shifts very quickly, Durandus thought to himself. He's starting to ask himself questions about how I got here.

The unfinished doctorate on the three states of being was on his desk in Paris. It must be completed.

"Your Majesty," the Frenchman said, smiling in a calm, professorial way. "I'll elaborate on the question of one relationship holding an entire realm and its people to ransom. Without going too far out of context, it could be argued that the relationships between the Father, the Son and Holy Ghost, all male you notice, hold our whole universe to ransom."

Awed, Ned puffed out his cheeks. The towering comparison had left him strangely satisfied. Here was a religious parallel of real substance. But now wasn't the time to pursue it. He was tired. He needed a drink – several drinks. "Let's leave all that aside until we know each other better," he said, bestowing a disarming smile. "Meanwhile, run along and tell them I want you to be my regular man."

News of Gaveston's military successes began filtering back from Ireland. He'd caught and hanged the seditious outlaw William Macbaltor, killed the rebel leader Dermot O'Dempsey in a skirmish in Kildare remarkable for its strategic brilliance, and subjugated the untameable O'Byrnes of Leinster in a lightning campaign through the Wicklow mountains. He was also conquering hearts and minds with his generosity, good-nature and style – bringing a breath of European style and fashion into the primitive lives of the warlords.

His splendid appearance became a feature of the new English presence. Superb good looks, magnificent clothes, valiant deeds, a singer, a lover, a sportsman, he overwhelmed the populace. People walked miles to see the King's lieutenant pass. When the debonair outlaw, William Macbaltor, was commenting on the ugliness of the man appointed to hang him, he asked Gaveston to do the honour of being his executioner instead, saying he'd rather be done to death by a peacock than a crow.

Wherever he went, Gaveston was accompanied by his barber, Flanagan – a quiet, ravaged, balding man with a hare-lip who kept a careful eye on the coiffure of his master, always on hand to repair the work of the wind. Although

Flanagan was dumb, it was noticed he seemed able to comprehend the meaning of a number of languages.

The previous incumbent of the post of lieutenant's barber had resigned his position and, for a good sum of money, recommended Flanagan, who was William Wild in his new manifestation, and he had been accepted at face value by Gaveston. The Irishman's old self could not be recognised. Half his body-weight had been withered away by his cares, his cheeks were sunk, his military bearing gone. As part of the arrangement, the outgoing barber had also taught the Irishman the basic skills of hairdressing and performed the minor operation on his lip with a razor to complete the disguise.

Neither kind nor cruel, Gaveston only took note of the existence of servants inasmuch as they were functionaries. If they failed to do their work properly, his reaction was immediate and severe. In the first week of William Wild's new barbering career, as his hand trembled with the razor close to the jugular, he nicked the skin and drew blood. Without looking, Gaveston knocked him off his feet.

Discovering he was so safe from detection, the Irishman regretted the mutilation of his lip. Convinced he would never kiss again, he'd worked on the principle that the mouth is what most people focus on in a man's face.

The Irishman wasn't indecisive about killing Gaveston. Nor was he coldly savouring his revenge. Once in a position to commit the murder, he saw no need to hurry. There was a strange excitement in being so close to his victim. He was at the centre of Gaveston's power, within his aura.

Each morning he shaved him while the daily letter from Ned was read. To rest his blade against the mover of history's fair cheek became addictive. One slash of the razor and Gaveston's magic would disappear.

When the deed was done, he knew his own life would be over. But now he was back in the swim of adventure, part of life rather than death, he wanted it to flow on for a while. During this time he would come to terms with failure on the larger canvas of his whole life. For someone who had battled his way through Christian and Islamic death-worship and rejected both, total cessation as a concept – absence multiplied by non-being multiplied by nothingness – was not to be embraced in a hurry.

These days he found it hard to think about Valmai and the children. How he could continue to love life knowing he would never see them again, he didn't know.

He was surprised to find he managed it, somehow. This he put down to an idiosyncratic flexibility of soul.

Serving Gaveston in Dublin Castle, or in the Wicklow mountains, William Wild saw life from a new perspective and found it instructive and entertaining. As he watched the Gascon taking decisions, leading his men, making things work, prejudice fell away. Then the shambles in the farmyard of Pant Mawr would come back to haunt him.

He would tell himself to wait until the perfect moment to strike – without specifying in his mind how that might come about, or how to recognise the time when it came.

It would have to have poetry and be apposite. As a turning-point in the affairs of men it would garner its own fame for him, which would also be his epitaph.

Not one of Gaveston's successes in Ireland could be accounted a major victory. As in Scotland, the Irish saw to it no full-scale battle was ever fought. Although the measures he took made sense in terms of keeping trade routes open between Dublin and its hinterland, once a traveller was fifty miles out of the city he entered the territories of Irish chiefs who followed the ancient Brehon code rather than English law.

As Gaveston's modest, workmanlike achievements became known in England, the political imagination of the earls was stirred to alarm. Those eager to be friends with the King again gave quick approval to what was being accomplished. It became obvious that any sizeable triumph of Gaveston's in Ireland would put the opposition to him in England on the wrong foot. No one was likely to outshine the Gascon at home. The earls were of indifferent ability as military men, and knew it. Besides, the lack of a Scottish campaign this year meant there were no other opportunities to demonstrate what little talent they had.

The convinced anti-Gaveston men turned their attention back to family business – examining the webs of land and property ownership within their class. The King's stupendous gifts to his favourite had made a gigantic hole in their expectations. Patronage, marriage and connections brought in more long-term profit than war, and the market was shrinking because of one man.

To maintain their position they needed either the King's good will, or influence over him. They began to realise how important it was to consolidate the extra power accruing to them since Ned's accession. Demands could be made on him that would have been madness to attempt with his ferocious father. If the old king had ever been besotted by a favourite – the name of William Wild sometimes surfaced in these speculations – the land would have been reduced to ashes before he permitted anyone to influence such a relationship. But by the pressure of the magnates, Gaveston had been levered out of England. At their dictation, the lovers had been separated. Even bearing the compromise of the Irish lieutenancy in mind, real power had been exercised by the opposition. It could be used again if necessary.

Only a few of the earls remained outside the circle of those brought back into the royal good graces. Amongst those who appeared won over, there were cynics far-sighted enough to guess how long it would be before the crisis flared up again. They used the time of royal affability towards them to extract benefits out of the King, anticipating another collapse of cordiality in the future.

During this interlude anyone trying to read the future and guess at the dominant influences over it could only come to one conclusion – whatever the sphere, everything was still contingent upon the life of Gaveston.

CHAPTER TWENTY-FOUR

Durandus had an opinion on most of the truly knotty questions encountered in a man's life. During one of his chats with Henry de Lacy, the French friar admitted to having thoughts on the essence of the godhead when only four years old.

Age had encouraged the use of reason in the venerable fighting earl. If the King could have his feelings for Gaveston explained rather than condemned, he might be able to control them. The business of philosophy was to propose explanations and oppose condemnations – so William Wild had said at the meeting when Durandus's name had first cropped up. This attitude seemed right for any study of Ned. Henry de Lacy had known the King since birth and looked upon him, even after all the unpleasantness, with avuncular affection. He remembered the time of the miracle birth – the time of hope when Ned was the golden child. Also, in the privacy of his own mind, the old earl considered fondness for a male friend not outside natural law. When taking pleasure in male company, he'd often thought: what is friendship but one of the degrees of love?

In the days following their first encounter, Ned and Durandus talked about love in all its forms. Because Ned's particular form was such an epic and public problem, it initially composed the background rather than the foreground of their discussions.

Almost accidentally, Ned revealed his attitude to women – which was not entirely hostile (quite fond of my sisters, aunts, stepmother, *sometimes*). This woolliness elicited nothing but scorn.

"Women are unsatisfactory," Durandus said emphatically.

"Why be so hard on them?"

"The uterus dominates their lives too much. Only men struggle to improve within the bonds of their humanity. My ideas are essentially predicated on maleness."

"Piers has got to meet you as soon as possible! You must go to Ireland," Ned said, glowing with enthusiasm. "To be thought about constructively would do him so much good."

"Ireland?" Durandus breathed. "Land of saints! Oh, yes please!"

"Talk to Piers in the same way you've talked to me."

"There's a place that would be perfect for us to meet – a famous holy island, a spiritual powerhouse where I've always wanted to go."

"Go wherever you like," Ned said with an encouraging smile, gliding away from any further headwork. "I'll pay all your expenses."

The yearning Durandus had to visit Ireland originated in his studies. Casting about to find a society which demonstrated how the state of being created by relationships could take precedence over individual being, he had come across the early Irish Christians who had starved themselves within a hair's-breadth of death on great sea-rocks out in the Atlantic, suspended between earth and sky.

For some reason, this image had lodged itself alongside his suppressed sexuality. When he contemplated the vivid sufferings of these men, imagining their strange, terrified ecstasy as towering storms sent waves to pluck them off their roosts, it was very close to a romance. There was a doodle in one of his folders showing naked men flying, holding hands in a line as they were blown off a pinnacle towards the cauldron of a raging ocean. A marginal note said: *Who would think to ask what these creatures feel for each other at the moment of death? Could it be: "I hope Heaven includes my friends."*

An important ingredient in the romance was Ireland's position at the western edge of the known world. Those human limpets on the great rocks facing the wild Atlantic were literally at the outer limit of human life, facing the unknown where God was still at his drawing-board. Durandus loved them for that. Deep in his heart, he craved their superb faith, and brave dicing with suicide, the great sin so adjacent to the inner logic of the Gospels. Conversely, he wondered if any of these Hibernian ascetics had, by near-death fasting, visions, and negotiations with God, ever made what must be the greatest sacrifice of all.

Greater love hath no man than this; that he lay down his soul with his friend. Was this not what Ned was doing?

Study of this supremely destructive but virtuous relationship and ultimate conquest of self – based on hypothesis, admittedly, as there were no means of verification even if it had happened – underpinned all his research. He hoped the modern tendency to attack the ideas of Thomas Aquinas would leave cleared ground for such a radical proposition. At present, merely playing with the concept could only be accounted heresy. *I do no deals*, said the haunting voice in the night. *I am what I am and you are what you are.*

In the late spring of 1309 Gaveston was busy with construction work. The fortifications of Newcastle McKynegan and Castle Kevin south of Dublin were being rebuilt and a road pushed through to Glendalough.

Pleasures such as this had been foreign to him until now – the laying down of stone, the raising of towers and gatehouses, the driving of highways through wilderness. It was creative whereas his soldiering had only taught him destructiveness. Gaveston discovered how much pride could be taken in watching builders erect something permanent. Now and again, when a letter arrived from England while he sat in the sun with plans on his knee, he would imagine Ned stripped off in the sun, happily sweating alongside the men with pick and shovel.

It was such a day when the letter arrived from London telling him to join Ned and a friend on the island of Skellig Michael off the coast of Kerry on 9th June .

Gaveston was immediately suspicious.

Once the Irish chieftains beyond the Dublin pale worked out how Gaveston had come to be their ruler, they infiltrated his communications, sending forged love-letters purporting to come from Ned. Gaveston had been invited to trysts. Obscene temptations were offered with lavish details. These masquerades were so ill-written and outlandish, so obviously composed for scurrilous amusement out in the bogs, none had received serious attention.

The summons to the Atlantic rock – the home of sea-robbers for four hundred years, a dangerous place a hundred miles outside English influence – had every appearance of authenticity. Gaveston pondered over the seal and the scribal hand, both familiar. He wondered if the Irish could be getting better at counterfeits. But it was the annoying absurdity of the summons which had him worried. No king of England had ever visited Ireland. If there was a sound political reason for this to happen, it should be to Dublin, not some rock stuck out in pirate-infested waters. And to ask him to sail there from Dublin incognito – as the letter instructed – was madness. As soon as his ship left harbour it would be shadowed. There was no such thing as incognito in Ireland.

He threw the letter on the ground. A sea-breeze blowing over the battlements rolled it a few feet away before the barber paused in his ministrations, stepped over and put his foot on it. As he returned the letter, he bowed.

Gaveston shook himself out of indignant thoughts and patted the bald patch on the barber's head. "You're no advertisement for the guild of haircutters, Flanagan," he joked. "But you take good care of me, which is all that matters."

The following day another letter arrived from Westminster, delivered by Flanagan, as usual. (Gaveston's household officers found this the most convenient method of getting correspondence to their energetic lord as he had to sit still for a while.) The letter was surprisingly deep in content. Once again, Gaveston had cause to be suspicious. Ned was an effusive and affectionate lover and he sometimes said far too much, but paragraphs beginning, "Single being is an inferior mode to doubled being. The perfect state, however, is trebled, as between God and two loving brothers, provided their human love is equal in all aspects. What d'you think of this?" were untypically complex from someone whose natural tendency was towards lightheartedness.

Further on in the text Gaveston encountered something which made the authorship certain but also proved there was another hand in the composition: "How often have I predicated my entire existence on our bond as brothers? But it's been too one-sided. Why have you never been articulate about your feelings for me? Do I live at this extreme of feeling alone, isolated? If so, then what is the essence of our relationship? What defines it? If you should die, my being would be destroyed. If I should die, what would happen to your heart? The time has come to be honest."

Sitting on a newly-constructed wall in the sun at Newcastle McKynegan having his hair cut, Gaveston listened to the gentle snip of the scissors and pondered. Disliking the new tone and content in Ned's letter, he nevertheless made an effort to answer the question: If Ned died, would I miss him?

Never mind that – do I miss him at this moment?

He caught a whiff of the priesthood and their cant behind the letter – a scent he found repulsive. What do paid virgins know about how men feel? Beaten whores have a better chance of understanding. They know what hit them.

The letter was tossed onto the ground. This time it lay still in the quiet air until Flanagan finished trimming and picked it up.

"Talk, talk, talk, talk..." Gaveston mused aloud. "I don't see what good it does in the long run."

When he glanced at Flanagan for a reaction, there was the hideous hare-lip smile and the steady eyes. Gaveston's memory – never his strong point – sent a dim signal: you've been looked at this way before, by someone. Then he dismissed the thought, deciding it must have been the barber at another time.

"To hell with them all, we say, don't we, Flanagan?"

The barber drew his finger along his upper lip and worked the scissors in the air.

"Moustache needs attention? Then I'd better stop talking, hadn't I?" Gaveston said with a grin. "What a good man you are to have around."

When the King's lieutenant sailed south out of Dublin he was far from incognito. There were four ships, all flying his flag. His retinue was large and armed to the teeth. He was sailing into enemy territory.

The June weather was warm, the winds kind. Keeping twenty miles from the coast, the ships passed Cork, the Old Head of Kinsale, Clear Isle, Bantry Bay and the Kenmare estuary. From all the inlets they passed, pirates emerged like stoats poking their noses out of their holes, but once the strength of the fleet was appraised, they slunk back into their havens.

Sixteen miles off Bolus Head a pair of great rock islands rose sheer out of the sea. The ships headed towards them. A watchful eye was kept on the coast.

It was the middle of the afternoon. A gentle on-shore breeze drew the vessels closer. One of the islands was inhabited by thousands of seabirds. As Gaveston looked up at the twin peaks and saddle of the larger island which was hung with enormous swags of sea-campion flowers, he marvelled at Ned's poor judgement at choosing this as a rendezvous. Except in perfect conditions – a calm sea and modest wind, as today – getting ashore on Skellig Michael from the seaward side looked impossible.

The ships sailed slowly round the rock. On the landward side there was a horizontal formation that looked as though it might offer a landing to a small boat. As no other ships were in the vicinity, Gaveston had to assume Ned hadn't yet arrived. He decided to wait. There being no anchorage, the ships circled the rock.

After an hour a sharp-eyed sailor reported spotting someone waving on the highest peak. Gaveston couldn't believe Ned would have landed and sent his ships away. He sent four men in a small boat to reconnoitre. They were clearly visible as they found harbourage and disembarked, climbing up to the saddle by what appeared to be a stairway. Gaveston watched them explore the western end, then traverse the saddle along to the peak, whereupon one of them disappeared, leaving the others to wait. It was half-an-hour before he emerged alone and the group began to descend.

When they returned to the ship Gaveston was told there was a Dominican friar called Durandus waiting for him in a cave right at the top of the pinnacle. He had a document under the royal seal summoning the King's lieutenant to meet him, alone. Only one servant could attend. He must remain below the peak during the discussions, which must be absolutely private.

Keeping his chagrin at Ned's non-appearance to himself, his suspicions now acute, Gaveston questioned the four men about the rest of the island and what had been found. They reported that at the western end were several strange beehive-shaped stone buildings which Durandus had told them belonged to an ancient monastery, long deserted.

It was trap – of that Gaveston was certain – but what kind of trap? To bait it with a Dominican demonstrated the trapper had little knowledge of his quarry. He had heard how the chieftains were noted for ornateness of mind, loving to weave subtly patterned plots. But they would never leave the execution of such a complicated trick to a serious man of religion, which they respected unduly. Something told Gaveston this was a new Ned putting him to the test – a Ned under someone else's influence.

As the oars creaked and a sliver of moon appeared beside bright Venus in the western sky, Gaveston looked over the rower's bald patch to the peak. Never a man to share emotional secrets, having none to all intents and purposes, when he looked around for someone to take with him onto the rock, he'd encountered the steady gaze of Flanagan. The man was loyal, reliable, discreet as all barbers have to be, and trustworthy. Also, being mute, whatever happened up there, he'd keep quiet about it.

Instead of waiting for his guest to climb up to the pinnacle, Durandus came down to the little rock harbour. Gaveston had been able to watch him descend the steps from the saddle for some of the way. When they came face to face, the Dominican made no bow. Instead, he offered his hand as an equal. Gaveston noted the move, shook the cool hand, and said nothing.

Flanagan had been tying up the boat. As he climbed over the slippery rocks, Durandus called out: "How good to see you again. What's happened to your face?"

Gaveston's hand went to his sword.

"We had such a good time in Boulogne together at the wedding," Durandus said, taking the Irishman's arm. "Have you been ill? You're much changed, my friend." Turning to Gaveston who was frowning hard, he said, "He was by far the most intelligent and interesting of the guests from England."

Gaveston looked hard at his dumb barber.

"What were you doing at Boulogne?" he demanded.

William Wild could see Gaveston's eyes stripping away his disguise, finding the face behind the face. He decided to speak.

"You paid to have me murdered, Piers."

"I should ask for my money back, wouldn't you say?" Gaveston said icily, hand still on his sword. "What happened to your lip, Willy?"

"Too much grieving."

Durandus stepped back, puzzled and alarmed. "If there's bad blood between you, settle it elsewhere. I hope you, a Dominican, aren't involved in anything sordid, Brother."

Gaveston laughed and shot the Irishman a frowning look.

"He's no Dominican. Who were you spying for in Boulogne, Willy? Who was it this time?"

"I was trying to get over the ruin of my life," the Irishman said bitterly, "which is all your work."

"This man's working for my enemies. He's a mere paid assassin," Gaveston declared.

"I find that difficult to believe," Durandus said.

"In Boulogne I was an imposter, I'm afraid," the Irishman admitted. "I'd prefer not to go into the reasons right now, if you don't mind."

Durandus gave a grimace of disapproval. "In France it's a capital offence to impersonate a priest. This reason of yours must have been very powerful."

"If you two have quite finished your *tête à tête*," Gaveston snapped. "I was summoned here by my king. Where is he?"

"He meant to be here but events have taken over. He had to remain in London. Another crisis has arisen, associated with yourself, which I'll describe later. However, I know the King's mind on the main issue."

"And what is this main issue?" Gaveston asked with a twitch of annoyance. "If it's to do with me, I'd like to know."

"That was conveyed in some detail by the letter which called you here, my lord."

"If I decide there's been a conspiracy between you two, your lives are over."

"We haven't been in contact with each other for over a year," Durandus assured him, taking a few steps along the harbour access. "I don't pretend to know what's going on between you, nor do I wish to. My mission takes precedence over your squabbles. We only have limited time. A ship will call for me tomorrow at noon. When I get back to London, the King will be given a full report on our meeting."

"He'll get one from me as well," Gaveston glowered. "Taking me from my work for this charade! What does he think he's doing?"

"If we were in London right now, you'd understand how nothing, nothing, is more important than *this charade*, as you call it. Your work – anyone's work – will have no meaning if we don't succeed," Durandus said, picking up his skirts to climb over the rocks. "Dear friend – will you remain here while I take his lordship away for a talk? It's of the utmost importance. Perhaps we can squeeze in a little time together in the morning."

"Oh, no," Gaveston said firmly. "As soon as my back's turned he'll escape in the boat and leave us stranded."

Durandus gave the Irishman a beseeching look. "Help me. If you give your word you won't take the boat, that's enough for me."

"But not for me!" Gaveston said, sitting on a rock. "We can easily talk here where I can keep an eye on him."

Durandus emphatically shook his head. "That's out of the question. I haven't travelled all this way and made my preparations for nothing. We must climb up to the top. That's essential. If you insist on mistrusting him, then he'll have to come with us."

"Well, what a day I'm having with one and half Dominicans," Gaveston snorted. "Lead the way. You go behind him, Willy, and I'll bring up the rear."

The three men traversed a level path cut through the rocks beside the little harbour, went round a buttress and reached the bottom of a stone stairway which went straight up a steep slope. From the bottom it seemed close to the vertical. They began to climb steadily.

"Any time you want to throw yourself off, don't let me stop you," Gaveston said after a while, poking the Irishman in the back. "Tell me, Willy, I've been thinking – you had hundreds of opportunties to cut my throat. Why didn't you do it?"

William Wild brushed a hand over his brow. "I was biding my time, perhaps," he said over his shoulder. "I did occasionally get the feeling that if I got rid of you, worse things could happen as a result."

"Come on, Willy, you were gloating. You enjoyed the feeling of power over me."

"No, I wouldn't say that," the Irishman panted. "It would be nearer the truth to say I became too interested in my intended victim – which is always a mistake if you have to kill someone."

Gaveston snickered, giving the Irishman another poke in the back. "Same old Willy. Nothing's ever straightforward with you, is it? Come on. Up you go."

"I will kill you, Piers. I have to for the sake of my soul."

"How will you manage that?" Gaveston mocked. "You're not in good condition. You're getting out of breath. Your heart's failing. Besides, I'm going to kill you first. What a nasty piece of work you've turned out to be. But I'll miss you as my silent barber. Oh, yes, I liked you as my barber."

CHAPTER TWENTY-FIVE

Durandus, William Wild and Gaveston sat crammed into a shallow hermitage excavated in the rock. It was virtually at the pinnacle of the island. The access was a cleft in the rock they'd had to squeeze through. On a ledge beside the cave two stone basins had been chiselled out. Grooves up the rock face guided rainwater into the basins.

"You see below there, on that little terrace," Durandus explained, "that's where he grew his vegetables. He would sit on the outmost edge, weather permitting, or even weather not permitting, in meditation, the universe at his feet. Imagine him under the stars at night, enthralled. Have you ever been in such an inspiring spot?"

Once they'd arrived after the long, hard climb, even Gaveston's run of tart comments and complaints were silenced. His indignation at being brought so far out of his way for what would probably amount to no more than a sermon evaporated. Suspended between sea and sky in this grand simplicity, the three men shared a sense of wonder that drew them together.

"I heard so many stories about the power of this wonderful place when I was a novice," Durandus said. "I always wanted to come and experience it for myself."

William Wild had heard such stories himself. How all the soil had to be brought over in skin boats. How there was no fire on the island. How the people on the mainland kept the monks going with gifts. How the ocean sent terrible storms and tidal waves as high as the peak itself. How a man had fasted and fasted, hoping to become as light as a feather so the wind would blow him off into bliss. How desire to be with God struggled with self-murder. How the monks had finally abandoned their holy island.

"Different times produce different men," Durandus said, smiling at Gaveston. "The monks who first discovered this rock were looking for a desert place, not beauty. The community below, the hermit up here, lived with beauty for centuries until it was no longer what they wanted. I'd like to have heard their debate before deciding to leave. What would they have said? God doesn't live here any more?"

The allure of the shining space between sea and sky deepened as the sun dropped towards the western horizon. Gaveston was caught between letting his spirit revel in the sensation of peace and finding out exactly what Durandus had been sent to tell him. He was about to put this question when he was pre-empted.

"Come what may, the King wants you back in England by 27th June. He'll meet you at Chester," Durandus said. "But there has to be a new understanding. His existence depends entirely on his love for you. But as a king his strength relies on being alone, which he cannot bear. Would you like to comment on what I've said so far?"

Gaveston huddled against the rock and was silent. He was taken aback by a strong sense of disappointment. He didn't want to leave Ireland. As for the rest, it hardly registered.

"The King has worked very hard to get everyone to accept your return," Durandus went on, "but the price is high. There are moves to curb his power because of you. As soon as you step on English soil again, he knows there'll be objections. The position of the Crown will be altered – because of you. The nature of government will be altered – because of you. He can no longer pretend your relationship is a private matter. It has always been everything to him. Now it's everything to everybody. I ask you again: would you like to comment on what I've said so far?"

Gaveston watched the gulls arcing through the perfect light. The Dominican's voice was having a tranquillising effect. He saw the problem spread right across the gleaming horizon. It was a painful dream. He heard nagging, decrying voices in the din of the seabirds: Gaveston must go. In his nostrils he suddenly caught a whiff of wet mortar. A half-completed road ran through his mind – work, achievement. If he went back to England he would lose his new happiness.

"Very well, if you've nothing to say, I'll proceed to the next stage," Durandus murmured with a glance at William Wild. "Constitutional change is going to arise as a direct result of your relationship with the King. In many ways, that relationship will become part of the way the people are ruled. He's ready to accept that, to reduce his freedom of action and his authority, but he must know..."

Gaveston looked away from the gulls as Durandus hesitated.

"Will you always love him?"

The Gascon's laugh scared all the gulls. They rose in a cloud from the rock, screeching.

"Why laugh?" Durandus demanded, annoyed. "The question is more than reasonable. Put his mind at rest. Give him an answer – and let it be absolutely true."

"Ned, Ned..." Gaveston muttered ruefully. "What a thing to ask. I belong to him. Isn't that good enough?"

"I'll repeat the question in the form he insisted it must be put: will you always love him?"

"Who can say? He might change – drive me away from him. He might go mad. I might go mad. But yes – I'll always love him."

"Thank you. I'll tell him that. The King also asks: can he, with confidence, build an entire state on what exists between you?"

"What else is there?" Gaveston demanded. "If I'm to be recalled because he misses me so much, what's the difference? Or does it depend on my answer whether I go back or not?"

"No, it doesn't – but whether the King sacrifices his power in order to keep you does," Durandus said flatly. "I must tell you what you already know – the King is not an intelligent man. Neither are you. Also, from what I've learnt, when you act together you appear to have less than the sum of your joint abilities."

Gaveston found this candour annoying. "If that's the case, why are you here? What's the point of talking to a simpleton?" he said, peering over the edge at the slow swell of the sea round the rocks below. "Why don't we just let things happen and see where it takes us?"

"The mood in London is this, my lord," Durandus said, leaning forward, finger drawing signs in the air. "It seems this relationship, this being you've created between you, cannot be destroyed. Very well. The country must live with it as best it can. A *modus vivendi* is needed. I'm here to persuade you to be more sensitive, more aware of other people's feelings. All the earls, Queen Isabella, King Philip, and His Holiness, the Pope, know about this meeting and approve what I'm trying to do."

"I've obviously been turned into someone else!" Gaveston sighed, holding his head in his hands. "My life isn't my own any more!"

Durandus leant back against the rock wall. "To my next point, my lord. The kind of Christianity once practised here on this island gave me the idea on which my whole work as a philosopher hangs: the concept of *anamchara,* the soul-friend. Elevate your relationship with the King to that level and you'll find all your problems will fall away."

"Never heard of it," Gaveston said, evincing no interest whatsoever.

"You must learn. I can help you understand. And another thing: you must never insult the earls again and call them names. They don't like it. The King wants you to be friends with them as well."

"Soul-friends with that ghastly crew?" Gaveston murmured, standing up. "Impossible."

Durandus dodged a white mess dropped by a passing gull. "Since you left England, the King has got himself an African lion. I know he's written to you about it but you've never bothered to reply. He sits and watches it pace up and down in its cage. It's name is Piers."

Gaveston admitted he'd read as much in one of the King's letters. What could he say about such a compliment?

"The day he can walk his lion *on a leash* amongst the people will be a happy one for the King. What he doesn't want is for his magnificent, proud animal to become such a nuisance it has to be put down."

Unnerved, Gaveston put his hands against the rock to steady himself. "He's threatening me," he said shakily. "I never expected that."

"He wants to be proud of you – to be able to enjoy you," Durandus continued. "That's the best way your relationship can work."

"Oh, thank you, thank you," Gaveston effused suddenly, grasping Durandus' hand, "I see what he means! Thank you, thank you for coming all this way to help me!"

Durandus smiled with satisfaction. "Good," he said. "I seem to have got through. We can leave it there. Now, if you can look after yourselves on your way out, I'm going to spend the rest of my time in this fabulous place fasting and praying."

"This has been a turning-point in my life," Gaveston said humbly.

"I leave you with a message from an old Roman playwright: *Beneficium accipere libertatem est vendere.* To accept a favour is to sell one's freedom. Bear it in mind."

At this point, the four ships of the Dublin fleet sailed into view, slowly circling the island looking for their commander.

"Your men are anxious," Durandus said, waving. "Show yourself so they'll know you're safe."

Gaveston got to his feet and waved both arms in the air, then turned to the Irishman. "Come on, Willy. Let's leave this genius to his prayers."

A weird, tortured cry came from William Wild. "No, no, no, we can't have this," he groaned. "You musn't get away with it. Why didn't I cut your throat when I had the chance?"

"From now on everything will improve," Gaveston said soothingly. "And I'd like to thank you for holding back and letting me live in spite of all the evil I've done. I see it all so clearly now"

"So do I see it clearly!" the Irishman shouted, eyes fiery as the sinking sun. "I see war and famine! I see chaos and anarchy! I see disaster upon disaster."

"Dear Willy, you've heard what's been said here today. Everyone wants peace. Let's be friends again, soul-friends if you like," Gaveston oozed, holding out his arms. "I'll forgive you if you'll forgive me."

The Irishman leapt to his feet, gave a howl of despair, and hurled himself over the precipice, plummeting down seven hundred feet, bouncing off rocks like a rag doll before splashing into the sea below.

CHAPTER TWENTY-SIX

Guy de Beauchamp, Earl of Warwick, gnawed on a leg of mutton as he watched Gaveston approaching along the table in a cloud of green and gold net, poking a trident onto people's plates as he passed. This was the Gascon sense of fun and must be tolerated. The earl prepared himself to smile and be courteous. He had been impressed by Ned's diligence in reconciling Gaveston with the great families. By his persistence, the King had not only won over the earls, but the Pope, the King of France, and the parliament. Bribes of land had been given, gifts of jewels and money. Bishops had been released from prison. All round, the result appeared to be beneficial.

Guy de Beauchamp's agreement to forgive Gaveston and accept him back in England was given once he had been rewarded with a gift of four former Templar manors.

"Enjoying your bone, Black Dog?"

The earl choked. Malignantly he raised his large, dark eyes, blinking.

"Is one bone enough? Surely a dog deserves several when he's been very good for his master. Here, have a few more."

Gaveston scraped gnawed bones off other guests' plates onto Guy de Beauchamp's plate.

There was a silence. Gaveston pushed himself onto the chair beside the amazed earl and prodded around on his plate with his trident. "You obviously have sharp teeth, Black Dog. You don't leave anything behind when you gnaw. Let me see your fangs."

He reached out to touch Guy de Beauchamp's lip. The earl recoiled violently, eyes bulging.

"This is so pleasant, Black Dog. What a grand sight to see all our friends at the trough," Gaveston continued. "You've all done rather well out of me, haven't you? He waved at the Earl of Leicester further down. "How are you, Potbelly!"

"Burstbelly, actually," Henry de Lacy called back with a humourless smile. "Do get it right."

"Old Harry can take a joke much better than you can, Black Dog," Gaveston chuckled, slapping his victim's shoulder. "Even though his face is so red, I think the old glutton might die tonight – not before time. My God, Joseph the Jew's gone very grey since I saw him last. Doesn't suit him when he's wearing yellow. Yellow doesn't go with grey, Black Dog. Remember to avoid it when you're dressing up. How's life, whoreson? Come on, give me a smile! He's going quite purple. We've got all the colours of the rainbow tonight."

"So much for change," Guy de Beauchamp said in a deadly calm voice. Blood had drained from his dark face leaving it cast in a sick pallor. The King's eye was on him. He had given his word. He had taken the bribe. But this was too much.

"What changes?" Gaveston taunted him. "A greedy dog is a greedy dog."

Ned smiled at them from the end of the table. He raised his wine in a toast. He had heard the insults, observed the torment in the faces of the earls, but had no remedy.

"Why are you doing this?" Guy de Beauchamp blurted. "The King has risked everything for you."

"Everything is nothing if it means I have to stroke a dog I don't like," Gaveston drawled. "Are you afraid to be detested? Come, come, you must be used to it by now."

Guy de Beauchamp spat out his food and left his seat, sick with rage. He walked up to the King and asked for a word in private. Ned refused to quit the table, laying a hand on the sleeve of the incensed man.

"It's only a joke. You know Piers when he's been drinking," he whispered. "It doesn't mean a thing."

The earl withdrew. The good cheer at the dinner vanished. All the other earls gravitated to a part of the table furthest from the King.

Gaveston went up to join Ned and lounged beside him, making lewd gestures with his trident. The earls sat staring at them in furious bewilderment. The silence was only broken by occasional guffaws from Gaveston. Suddenly the earls got up as one from the table and marched out, fuming.

Later that night there was a row in the King's chamber. Ned and Piers screamed at each other for an hour, fought until blood was drawn, then fell into each other's arms and slept.

In the morning a servant came in to clear up the mess. He moved sideways, like a crab. These days it was understood by the households of Ned and Piers that the first man into a sleeping chamber shared by the King and his lover had to be this one particular servant who understood their ways.

One-eyed, asymmetric skull permanently tilted to one side, only a few teeth left in one side of his mouth, a leg rigid from hip to ankle, hare-lipped, William Wild scuttled around the room on a silver crutch.

When fished out of the water by Gaveston's men after his jump from the pinnacle of Skellig Michael, the Irishman was found to be little more than a sack of fractured bone. Gaveston took him back to Dublin, hired three doctors to set all the breaks and had him nursed round the clock for three months. He also paid for masses to petition God for his survival, employed priests, nuns and monks to pray for his recovery, and visited him in the infirmary of the Benedictines every day. The Irishman's recovery was a miracle. While it was happening, he realised inside his suffering, that it was the revelation he had always lusted after. Every miracle is a revelation, he reasoned as life pulsed in his shattered body. I've been granted my greatest desire.

But he would be in pain for the rest of his time on earth. All that remained unwounded was his mind – now sharper, more erect and defiant, a brilliant stained glass window intact in a broken ruin.

Since Skellig Michael, he had received nothing but kindness from the man he hated. It was the only genuine change Durandus had achieved. Gaveston had altered in one detail – instead of revenge, his treatment of the crouchback cripple who was now his body-servant (the old king's favourite as much as he had ever had one) was exemplary. As for the rest of Gaveston's promises to reform, they had been cast mockingly into the wind.

On the ship William Wild was in a coma. He fully revived after a week in the infirmary, emerging into a consciousness of terrible pain. At first, this could only be relieved by alcohol, but the amounts he had to take worsened his condition.

One of the doctors was a veteran of the Holy Land who, like William Wild, had studied the Persian physician-philosopher, Avicenna. He was conversant with the Islamic author's advice on the treatment of severe battle-wounds in his book, *al-Qanun fi at-tibb,* the Canon of Medicine.

When he examined the Irishman, he recognised the skin of a man who had been cooked in rusty chain mail under the hottest sun – a soft, pink-streaked whiteness except where it had been exposed. Below the wrists and above the neck it was dark and seamed like fossilised wood. On scars showing the points of stitching, the design was that of Arab healers.

The doctor asked William Wild if he had been in the Holy Land. To answer, the patient was told to blink – once for yes, twice for no.

Did he know the power of opium to ease the greatest suffering? Had he ever taken it? If he had, had he kept the balance of his mind?

As soon as the doctor had his answer, he sent to the pharmacy of the Knights Hospitallers nearby for the pain-killing drug. Fed on barley cakes baked with thickened juice of the white oriental poppy, William Wild won the struggle to keep his sanity. The agony was kept at bay long enough for his body to heal naturally. So many people told him that he'd defied medical science by surviving, it seemed he hardly owned his own life. It belonged to Gaveston, his saviour.

When the patient had mended sufficiently to talk – his jaw, broken in three places, had been slow to knit – the first thing he said to Gaveston, his regular visitor, whose retinue crowded into the room each day to catch a sight of the indestructible in conversation with the irresistible, was – why did you save me?"

With delicate gentleness, Gaveston touched a fingertip of the splinted, twisted hand. "You showed me the Fall of Man, Willy," he said with a lovely smile. "You flew." And left it at that.

The Irishman entered the darkened room. A thin shaft of light from a rent in the heavy curtains caught his strange, shuffling shadow. "Pooh, this room smells foetid. How are we, children?" he said, one hand on the draw-rope. "I have to wake you."

"Don't !" Ned groaned as he heard the curtain rings rasp on the bar. "No light, please, Willy."

"You can't lie in your filth any longer. The earls are outside," William Wild announced, pulling the curtains back as far as they'd go. "Their mood is thunderous."

"Ignore them" Gaveston mumbled from the pillow, shielding his eyes from the glare. "Castrate them with rusty razors."

"The guard has been called. A confrontation's been going on for the last half-hour."

"I'll have to go and apologise, I suppose," Gaveston sighed, getting out of bed. "What a way to start the day. Tell them I'll be down after breakfast."

"They'll tear you to pieces," William Wild said, opening the door, wafting it backwards and forwards to get air into the room. "After your well-chosen words at dinner, all Ned's hard work over the last year has gone up in smoke."

"I can't help it. They do something to me."

"They'd like to do something to you."

"One look at them, so petty, so worthless, and all I want to do is prick their balloons."

William Wild rang a hand-bell for breakfast to be brought in, rubbing his trussed hip which was hurting.

"How should we deal with these dreary parasites? Put them in the Tower? Ned can do that, if he likes. It's easy. Or he can throw me in. That would solve his problem."

"My advice is for you to leave by the back door," the Irishman said. "Don't let them catch you while they're in this state."

"I never use back doors."

William Wild grinned, shaking his head, making loose vertebrae in his neck grate. "You create risks for Ned," he said, picking up fallen furniture.

"Oh, the earls would never harm a hair on his head, as they're always saying," Gaveston jeered. "They're true to their king."

There was a long pause. Gaveston winked at William Wild, who didn't respond. Ned stared out of the window.

"Please, shut up," he said eventually, his voice weary. "Willy, you know them. Surely, by now, they realise the way Piers is."

"The way Piers is! The way Piers is!" Gaveston chanted. "Who is this odd person? Tell me, was I like this in Ireland? D'you know why? Because those bastards weren't there!"

Ned sighed and walked about the room. "I have to think about them all the time. I have to think about you all the time. There's no time for myself."

"Poor old Ned!" Gaveston burst out laughing. "So put upon by everybody."

"They don't blame their king directly," William Wild said by way of consolation as he collected clothes scattered around the room. "Every one of them has put himself in your place."

"When they've got me to blame, why blame Ned?"

"That's a good question," William Wild said, fixing his one good eye on Gaveston. "But your reason for holding them in such contempt escapes them. You're supposed to be a family member."

"I loathe families. I detest that kind of duty. It's servitude under another name."

"That's the crux of the whole thing, Piers!" Ned shouted. "I've made you hugely rich, given you power, but you can't accept the responsibility."

Gaveston pissed into an earthenware pot. "Should we worry about the earls?" he mused. "Deep down they're nothing but peasants. They hoard everything, including their hatred. If I wasn't here, what would they have to talk about?"

William Wild sat on the bed. A vile pain came through the base of his neck, shooting down into his lungs, making him breathless. "Tell me, Piers – if Ned was foolish enough to let you go down and face them, what would you say?"

"Sorry. And not mean it."

"Sorry wouldn't be enough, even if you did mean it," the Irishman wheezed. "They made that clear."

Ned pulled on a gown. "I can't keep making excuses for you, Piers," he said, a quaver in his voice. "It's so humiliating. I'm running out of things to say in your defence."

"Then don't say anything. Give them what they want – get rid of me."

"See how cruel you are? You know I could never do that!" Ned cried. "But they're quite right. We can't go on like this."

"The way they see you is through me," Gaveston said, going to him. "Their envy of me is how they know you."

William Wild watched them closely, bald head cocked as he listened, an unearthly gleam in his eye.

"If I wasn't here for them to hate, they'd hate you," Gaveston breathed in Ned's ear. "No one likes to be governed. In their hearts, they always resent it. The earls know their envy is a sin. That paralyses them. Have I got it right so far, Willy?"

With the embroidered counterpane in his hands, the Irishman nodded almost imperceptibly, then threw it over the bed.

"Everything possible has been done to destroy what we feel for each other," Gaveston continued, giving William Wild quick, little approval-seeking glances. "But do I blame you, Ned? When I'm condemned, exiled, excommunicated, do I say it's your fault? And, in your heart of hearts, do you blame me for the trouble I cause?"

"No, no, no," Ned groaned. "I blame myself for not being able to do without you, that's all."

"Thanks!"

"Integral to our animal selves is the law of desire," William Wild interposed. "To disobey it is a form of death. To live, we must follow the compulsion implanted by God."

"When did you join the priesthood?" Ned said bitterly. "What's happened to you? You keep coming out with all this useless tripe! Why?"

"Don't be hard on Willy. At least he thinks on our behalf and expects nothing for it. He knows us better than anyone."

"I expect so," Ned owned up, wearily abashed. "I'm sorry, Willy. I get so embarrassed at the idea this all has to be profound. If everyone would only leave us to it, that would be enough."

"There's no chance of that now," William Wild said, scampering in pursuit of a half-dead rat being dragged across the carpet by one of the palace cats. "You should have gone overseas with Piers, gone to live in Cathay or Moscow or somewhere, never accepted your inheritance. But it's too late now." Taking the rat off the cat, he swung it by the tail and killed it against the window-ledge.

"What's left to the earls now?" Gaveston mused as the Irishman slid the bleeding rat into the earthenware piss-pot. "If they kill me, they're killing the King's love…for his people. Because, like it or not, I'm your people, Ned – your only people. The earls and the others aren't your people. They're their own people, living for themselves."

William Wild nodded. A tender, reflective smile touched his mutilated mouth. "In spite of all the shit, all the problems, Ned, only love is worth while," he said, flexing his thumbless left hand. "I've known you since you were born – infant, boy, prince and king – and after all this time, what I say to you is..."

Ned covered his ears. "No more!" he said, flaring with impatience, broad shoulders straightening. "You two are losing touch. If I have to be king I must have someone. It happens to be Piers – a weakness I'm prepared to admit. When I talk to those hard-hearted bastards, I'm going to say so."

When the meeting with the earls finally took place the mood was sombre. Ned had made them wait several hours. The presence of a group of lawyers expert in constitutional questions alarmed Ned. On his own side, he had brought minimal support from his administration because the subject was not one he wished to share too widely.

There was no display of anger. The earls were impassive and dignified. Ned noticed the absence of Guy de Beauchamp. After a few minutes he realised a metamorphosis had taken place. The heat of protest had become the ice of intention.

"Sire, the papal bull of absolution for Piers Gaveston is in your possession," Henry de Lacy said levelly. "We have allowed him to return. He has been reinstated as Earl of Cornwall, with all his lands, and more. We have kept our promises."

Ned nodded nervously, hardly listening. His confession of need was uppermost in his mind. Gaveston's inability to sustain good behaviour had hit him hard. One day the Gascon would be sweet and charming – the next, offensive with such deliberate intent he seemed unstable – a wild man anxious to start a war. When he was in this mood, no argument or appeal penetrated his mad compulsion to provoke. The reason Ned would give the earls for this strange trait was that it was a malady common amongst Gascons.

It was the accusation of evil influence Ned feared most. Under cover of this fallacy, the Church could create an image of Piers as the Devil – a part he loved to play. With relief, and some surprise, Ned noted the absence of bishops and priests at the meeting.

A further surprise emerged. After the opening statement, Gaveston wasn't mentioned again during the five hours the discussions lasted. Instead, an enormously long list of grievances was produced – forced loans, royal constables throwing their weight about, rapacious foreign merchants, fluctuations in the value of the currency, the sale of pardons to criminals, illegal seizure of lands by Crown agents. Every one of these legal, ecclesiastical, fiscal and military matters needed immediate redress, the earls insisted. At the forthcoming parliament – which the King would undoubtedly be calling soon – these outstanding issues should be settled once and for all.

Meanwhile, it was proposed wise men, called Ordainers, would supervise all government and help run the country, protecting the Crown from the excesses of the man wearing it. They would take action against extortion, waste, dismemberment of administration, loss of conquests, and the stealing of the King's treasure.

There was no need to mention what the consequences would be if the monarch refused his consent to this abjuration of his authority. The blow would fall where the weakness lay.

In the freezing courtesy shown at the meeting was the message: Have *at our hands* what you want most, the passion you prize more than your power – but the price is your power.

CHAPTER TWENTY-SEVEN

Since his great leap from Skellig, William Wild had worked his way through several theories about himself. One was that he was, in fact, dead. What had survived the fall was his imaginative soul, capable of dreaming pain and suffering, but not living as life is lived. The wreck of his body was there for the purposes of punishment. One sin above all others had put him in this position: he had lost his faith in God and put it in a woman. His continued existence in the nightmare of his body was a reminder of the choice he had made. The completeness of his punishment was that Valmai would never want him again – a broken cripple whose servants took an hour to dress him, straighten out the stiffness of his limbs and set him on his feet each day.

When he looked at himself, he wanted the flesh to disappear. These are the feelings of a dead man who cannot escape from life, he said to himself. I must never see Valmai again. That's death, near enough.

And the Gaveston he had met after the fall? Was he real? By binding the Irishman to him, stealing his heart, Piers had forced him to turn against his old self. Vengeance was now an impossibility.

It was obvious now that Ned and Piers were set on a course of destiny. A blind Fury had them by the hand, leading them on. And they were godlike in their indifference to the danger – so it ceased to be a danger. To them, it was part of being together. All Ned wanted was to be with Piers, at any cost. All Piers wanted was whatever Ned gave him – treasure, the earth, palaces, power, and fanatical devotion.

The Irishman had been disappointed when Durandus couldn't quite bring himself to admit the parallel with Jesus. To sacrifice everything for love – when you have everything – is an imitation of Christ who, as the son of God, had everything.

The Ancient Greeks might have made a play out of it, in which Ned and Piers were metamorphosed into rams charging headlong side by side towards a precipice, seeing only each other because that's how the eyes of sheep are set – to the side.

Once Ned accepted rule by the Ordainers, they went into conclave, shutting him out. They let him know the takeover would be slow and painstaking to disguise its revolutionary nature from the people. Every aspect of his kingship would be expertly scrutinised. Lawyers would pore over Magna Carta, spinning new restrictions of royal power out of its imprecisions. While a young, slow-witted and weakened king was on the throne, trapped in his feelings, the opportunity to get things right in government had to be used to the full.

Assured Gaveston could remain by his side at least until the submission of the Ordainers' findings – it was estimated the investigation would take a year to eighteen months – Ned decided to invade Scotland and give himself a chance of glory, putting the triumph of the earls in the shade. To go to war was, as yet, within his royal prerogative.

William Wild said his piece. He was by now the spider at the centre of Ned's intelligence network – a function he had often carried out for great Edward in the old days. He advised against leaving London in the hands of the Ordainers, now headed by Guy de Beauchamp, the Earl of Warwick, Gaveston's implacable enemy. Ned decided to appoint Henry de Lacy, the previous leader of the opposition, as *custos* of the realm for the time he would be away on campaign, thinking the old earl's credentials as a reasonably intelligent moderate would serve both sides.

"When the Ordainers deliver their verdict, you know what it will mean as far as Piers is concerned," the Irishman insisted, taking the opportunity to speak openly while Gaveston was absent. "Piers will have to go. Why not pre-empt them? Let him return to France and visit often. Divide your time."

Ned rejected the idea as defeatist. "When we conquer Scotland and get our hands on the Templar treasure in Strathearn we can buy everyone off."

"Take what treasure you've got and go somewhere else. Find a place where no Englishman can ever track you down. Live in peace. Go to the edge of the world, if necessary – but don't stay here."

"That wouldn't do," Ned said, though it was obvious it had some appeal. "I can't give up my inheritance."

"Not for what's the most important thing in your life? That doesn't make sense, Ned."

"Who said Piers was the most important thing in my life?"

William Wild's jaw fell with a clack. "I can't believe I heard you say that," he protested. "If he isn't, what's all this been about?"

Ned frowned and rubbed his eyes. "If one of us got bored of the other, or met someone else we liked more, we'd have to call it a day. So it's impermanent, but being king is permanent. Also, the day I stopped being king, Piers would lose interest in me."

William Wild sighed in a kind of rapture. He wanted to take this broad-shouldered, blonde ox, this lumbering beast of emotional burden, in his arms and congratulate him.

"Was that a moment of illumination, Ned, or have you always known it?" he asked gently. "You're quite right about Piers."

"If I abdicated, he'd offer himself to the next man on the throne, whoever that was. If it happened to be a woman, he'd offer himself to her."

"How long have you known this?"

"I'm not a complete fool, Willy," was Ned's sharp answer, "and never have been."

Having an eye to the rigours of war and the Irishman's precarious health, Gaveston was prepared to do without William Wild on the Scottish campaign, but the Irishman refused to be left behind. From now on he must be integral to everything that happened, missing no part of the action. It was all that was keeping him together in death-in-life. Without it, he would evaporate in the boiling pot of his own pain.

Gaveston had a chariot made for the Irishman that catered for all his handicaps, including a Z-shaped bed to fit his twisted spine. William Wild was on his knees in the courtyard at Westminster admiring the ingenious handiwork in the suspension of the vehicle when he looked up and saw Valmai standing over him.

Beside her were two little girls and a boy toddler in walking-reins.

William Wild pulled himself further under the carriage, put on a voice and told her all visitors to the palace must report to the guard.

"Come out of there, *cariad*," Valmai said, crouching down and putting out her hand. "Don't hide from me!"

"Go away and leave me alone!" he pleaded, trembling with shame.

"Children, this man is your father. He's been in the wars."

"Don't make them look at me," the Irishman begged. "It'll make them sick."

Valmai grabbed hold of the scruff of his neck and dragged him out from under the chariot. "Is this the greeting I get? Stand up! What do we care what you look like?"

When Gaveston could see the Irishman was intent on going to Scotland, he'd sent someone to find Valmai in case he never returned.

Since his return to England, Gaveston had encouraged William Wild to let Valmai know where he was, even to join him in the household, but this hadn't been acted upon. The Irishman believed his wife was better off without him.

They had a week together. The children couldn't help staring at his phenomenal ugliness. Sometimes, they laughed. When this happened, he limped away, cursing – only to be brought back by the hand. Gradually, he realised they were intrigued rather than repelled.

When Valmai held him in her arms, she was in touch with someone she knew, working off memory. He watched her persuading herself, remembering, transferring, winning the war against aesthetics. Now and again she wept in the night. When he asked her what was the matter, she pretended to be asleep. He realised this was true, in its way. She was putting a part of herself to sleep. At first he couldn't believe this could be achieved by an act of will – but he was wrong. Her new tenderness overcame regrets and revulsion.

Each day he was with his family, his disbelief was reduced. Somehow, they had the means to love him. The mirror told him this was extraordinary.

When the time came for Gaveston to leave for the north, he gave the Irishman the chance to change his mind about coming on the campaign. He had told Ned to restore Boldwood to him, with a grant and a pension. The family could settle down together until the end of the Irishman's days.

The temptation was great. But, in a thousand years, he would never be able to explain to a woman of Valmai's beauty, a woman who could have any man she wanted, why he couldn't accept this gift straightaway, and go back.

He must see it through with these young men who had been his friends, his enemies, now his friends again as brothers often are in the strange rhythm of instinct. They weren't his kin, but they shared the blood men have, the blood which is there to be shed, often for the most foolish cause. To be absent at the death of an age you have helped to define is not to have lived to the limits of its truth.

He was amazed when Valmai took it so well. She sat and listened intently as he struggled to explain. Eventually, she asked him to stop. Brotherhood of this kind was beyond her. It could only be understood from inside a man's marrow, not his mind. They would wait for him at home, she said. She knew he'd come back. There was no one else. It wasn't duty. It was choice. There was plenty to do, rebuilding the house, getting the farm sorted out, bringing up the children. When he returned, they'd have plenty of time together because William Wild was obviously designed to live several lives, and had the scars to prove it.

The Scottish summer of 1310 was warm, sunny and temperate – perfect for the outdoor life of war. The English army basked on the lowlands, challenging the Scots to come down and fight. From the bogs and mountains Bruce sent back ambivalent, mocking messages alluding to Ned's parlous position at home, suggesting he was only in Scotland because he wasn't welcome in his own kingdom.

Bruce knew Ned's military resources were too stretched to achieve anything in terms of occupation. His invasion was no more than a reminder, a gesture. He would wander around in a futile pursuit until the winter came, then have to retreat back across the Border.

All the earls except Gloucester and Surrey had refused to bring their forces, claiming their critical work as Ordainers kept them in London. Their flagrant disobedience was what neutered the whole effort of the campaign. Hampered by inadequate strength on the ground, Ned drifted in desultory search of Bruce, happy to be with Gaveston, not thinking too much about the future.

The preliminary report of the Ordainers was brought to the King in the field. They stressed it was only a taste of what could be expected in the final draft. A character called *Peter,* instead of *that person*, appeared for the first time. Whenever a reason needed to be given for severe limitations of royal power, Peter was given as the reason.

Ned pushed these warnings out of his mind. In the wide spaces of the north he felt freer and more relaxed. Time spread itself over the long summer in a haze of possibilities. The endless lottery of politics would come up with a prize. A pattern of dependence would shift. A potentate would die. A famine might intervene. A prophet could arrive, howling for a new crusade. There was no point in despairing when so much was a gamble.

In the Scottish war – scarcely deserving the name – nothing was achieved. There were occasional parleys and negotiations with the elusive enemy. However, being away from the south and the persistent poison of discord kept the omens at bay.

Reality was suspended whenever Ned and Piers were together. It was a season of enchantment. The summer went through in glory to harvest and they were still untouched. Between themselves they agreed to stay in the north right through the winter, keeping as far away from London as possible.

In October, the English army was at Biggar, heading for Glasgow. Spies had laid information Bruce was at last ready to do battle before the bad weather came. Scottish irregulars harried the flanks of the columns every day, picking off stragglers. During one of these raids, William Wild was captured in his chariot and driven off. The next day he was brought before Bruce, who was eighty miles away from where spies said he would be.

Bruce was of Norman blood, dark and difficult. At thirty-six, he was a past master of deception, a man who knew how to bide his time, how to feign madness, how to strike a blow from which no recovery could be made, how to charm. William Wild knew everything there was to know about the man who smiled at him with such charitable courtesy.

"Stand up! We have a legend in our midst, gentlemen," he said to his companions at the table as the Irishman was ushered into the room. "This is William Wild, the man who could have been earl of anywhere he liked under Longshanks, God rot him. What's happened to you, sir?"

The Irishman leant on his silver crutch and made what bow he could. "My lord, that's a long story," he said with a grin. "Let me sit down. Treat me kindly and I might tell you the story."

Bruce came round the table and ejected a man from one of the chairs, brushing down the seat. "Indeed, you will be given the best of everything. That much you'll be used to, working for the King's sweetheart. What ransom d'you think he'd pay for a man of your standing? A thousand pounds was on my mind."

William Wild whistled through his few teeth, good eye blinking as he calculated the odds. "A mighty sum," he murmured, accepting a cup of wine. "I'm not sure I'm worth it."

"Eat with us. Who knows what any of us is worth? We'll see what lord Gaveston comes up with," Bruce said, returning to his place. "Now we'd like to hear what happened to you."

William Wild listened to himself telling the story. He heard Piers Gaveston shielded from the worst, and praised for the best.

Bruce was sincerely interested. "What kind of man can do this?" he asked when the tale was finished. "If I met him, would I be able to make sense of his character?"

The Irishman warmed to the curiosity. Wine was easing his pain. The men around him were amiable and respectful. He had no idea whether the staggering sum of a thousand pounds would be paid, or whether he cared all that much if Gaveston refused.

"Let's dispense with the myths about Gaveston," William Wild said, propping himself up on one elbow. "Witchcraft, duplicity, manipulation…they don't apply. Also, forget about right, forget about wrong."

The Scots laughed appreciatively. Bruce said he approved the lack of moral judgement. "Everyone stopped thinking in those terms about that pair a long time ago. It's a matter of taste. But what intrigues me is why everything in England is being allowed to slide to destruction because of this one man."

"What Piers did for me when I was in great pain may be what he does for the King," the Irishman said. "That's as near as I can get."

"It's not the same, surely."

"The worst thing about pain is the absolute loneliness it creates. Ned's in pain all the time if Piers isn't there."

The Irishman's voice trailed off as he saw the hurt of understanding in Bruce's eye. Slowly the Scot shook his head.

"Who'd be him?" he muttered.

Four days later Bruce's hostage envoys returned with a thousand pounds from Gaveston. They reported no haggling, no hesitation. The sum was agreed without demur.

William Wild was returned to the English army in his chariot, under escort. He carried a gift from Bruce to Gaveston – a ruby worth a thousand pounds, with a note recommending he should hold it up to the light for the heartsblood colour and be glad.

By January 1311, Ned had moved as much of his administration as he could to York – the Exchequer, the courts of law, the Chancellery and his household – stripping London of the machinery of royal government.

When the Ordainers protested, claiming this was nothing less than shifting the centre of power to the north to keep it out of their hands, Ned referred them to the practice of his father who'd done the same thing when a major Scottish campaign was in progress. He promised once the Scots were brought to heel everything would be moved back to London again.

Up until this point the campaign had been funded by the abolition of the Templars and the sales of their lands and property. This money now started to run out. The Ordainers in the south began putting obstacles in the way of the collection of taxes, dues and levies, slowing down the King's income to a trickle.

Desperate for money, knowing if he stopped the Scottish campaign he'd have no reason not to return to London and the whips of the Ordainers, Ned decided to send an expedition to recover the Templar treasure in Strathearn. McHunter, the commander whose men had been accidentally massacred eight years before as they returned from the task of hiding the treasure, had recently been taken prisoner while fighting for the Scots.

At first he refused to co-operate, insisting the treasure was part of the tranche of minor assets moved to the Hospitallers when the Templars were abolished and he would not break his vows to his new order. When Ned sent him to be tortured, it was noticed he was severely scarred from other work done on him. He confessed this was from Bruce's men who had been trying to obtain exactly the same information.

William Wild was asked to use his influence. Without introduction, he went into the room where McHunter was being kept. The Scot, who had got to know him well in Saint Johnstone eight years before, didn't recognise him. When the Irishman identified himself, tears welled up in the tortured man's eyes. Sympathy soon developed between the battered veterans. This companionship of suffering loosened McHunter's tongue.

They were in the castle of Berwick-on-Tweed where the King was spending the dark months of the winter. Every evening they reminisced over a drink. McHunter recalled his French brothers and what they had been through.

"Strappadoed, jerked on ropes with weights fastened to their balls...red-hot irons in every orifice...molten lead poured in the ear...all the perverted cruelty of the human mind...and we think we've had it bad," he growled. "They sawed their feet off. Made them eat hot shit. Burnt them alive. For what? So the King could have money. Well, he got the money – but he didn't get the books."

The Irishman looked puzzled. "What books?" he asked.

"All that's hidden in Strathearn is books."

The Irishman didn't press the point but maintained a quizzical silence until he thought McHunter was ready to go further.

"If that's the case, why didn't you tell Bruce and save yourself all this trouble?" he said after a while.

"Because he's ignorant! Rex illiteratus! And this king of yours is another! I won't serve ignorance any longer!"

William Wild poured more wine for them both and toasted the inviolable power of the ignorant. McHunter laughed.

"Shall we go and recover the books, you and I?" he said with an ironic grin. "Two wrecks together. We can make it. My problem is, you'll have to tell me what those books say. All I know is what I was told by Jacques de Molay, our Grand Master, when he sent me to Scotland to hide them. He said the books were worth more than the treasure of Alexander the Great, Genghis Khan and the Vatican rolled into one."

The Irishman's eye was bright with interest, but he expressed doubt as to whether the value of the books could be realised in terms of money – which was what the King wanted.

"Ask him straight – has knowledge any price? If not, where are we going? What are we doing?" McHunter groused, waggling a tooth loosened by the pliers of his tormentors.

William Wild advised against telling the King the whole truth at this juncture. All Ned needed to know was McHunter had agreed to guide an expedition to the treasure. If Ned knew it was merely books, he was perfectly capable of selling the information on the whereabouts of the treasure to Bruce, and duping him. Even if the books had a commercial value, they might have deteriorated after being buried so long. The Irishman recommended they should get permission to go to Strathearn, recover the books, find out what was in them, and take it from there. For the Grand Master to have taken such pains to preserve these volumes was enough of a guarantee they were worth something.

"They won't have deteriorated, I promise you," McHunter assured him. "We didn't bury them. They're well wrapped up and in a dry, safe place."

A week later, in cold, bright weather, a force of two hundred men left Berwick-on-Tweed under Gaveston's command to go to Strathearn. The Scots had withdrawn from the eastern lowlands and the road to Strathearn was free. Within four days McHunter had led them through the wilderness to the shores of Loch Earn. That night, they made camp under a light fall of snow. William Wild chose a dark freezing hour with owls giving their eery cries, to tell Gaveston what he knew about the treasure. By agreement with McHunter, he added the lie that he'd only just been given the information himself.

"We don't know what's in these books," he said, observing the gloomy disappointment with which the news was being received. "It might consist of more wisdom than wealth, or wisdom which could also be wealth."

"If it's not gold or silver or jewels or pearls or coin, it's of no use," Gaveston sighed.

The Gascon was in a strange frame of mind. The folly of the campaign was obvious. Bruce was laughing at the English, sliding away from confrontation. Bringing him to battle was impossible because every plan laid was communicated by sympathisers within the lordships which had nominally accepted, usually with Bruce's encouragement, English rule. There were no chances for Gaveston to shine, to acquire plaudits to cancel out the propaganda the Ordainers were using against him.

By each Chancellery post from York to Berwick, Ned was provided with clause by clause leaks from the revolutionary document being drawn up in London. It had reached the stage where he couldn't bring himself to tell Gaveston what these clauses contained.

Faced by yet another futile enterprise, Gaveston looked at the few swirling snowflakes falling into the fire and came out with the first melancholy thought the Irishman had ever heard from his lips.

"This is very similar to the time Ned's father sent him into the wilderness with you and a dozen archers hoping to get rid of him."

Hardly visible in a fur robe clutched round his shoulders, William Wild refused to be drawn.

"Think how much trouble would have been avoided if the ruse had worked and Ned had been killed on that foray. No Ned. No me. It would have been better for everyone, perhaps."

The Irishman's good eye glared out from the fur, which was quivering as he laughed. "You've chosen a fine time for these meditations," he said mockingly. "The die is cast, Piers. We must soldier on."

"I wouldn't put it past Ned to arrange for Bruce to capture me," Gaveston declared, speaking above the wind. "That would solve all his problems."

The fur shook violently and William Wild's bald head emerged. He was laughing so much he'd run out of breath. "He'd beggar the entire country to pay your ransom!" he said. "Sell his birthright, his kingdom!"

"Which is his undoing. Why can't he see the truth?" Gaveston paused, lifting his eyes to the swirling flakes. "I should do something about it, but I can't."

"D'you mean, you can't think what to do, or you can't do what you think is right?"

"When you look at everything I've been accused of, it's all true, in a way," Gaveston confided. "I do influence him more than anyone else. He does give me everything he can, even now when he's so desperate for money. I have a free pass to the Treasury. I can take what I like. There's no point in refusing. He won't let me. If I point out he's only making things worse, it doesn't get through."

The Irishman's skinny hand emerged from the folds of the robe in a calming gesture. There was a cough and a clearing of the throat. The hand drew back into the warmth. "Piers, it's too late to torture yourself with these questions," the Irishman remonstrated gently. "You live in a civilisation which claims to give love first place. We have a religion that says love is above all things. We claim to live and die by it. We don't. We're cruel and cold. We lie about our beliefs. Our Church is a place any self-respecting god would refuse to enter. Concern for our own souls sickens me. Any love that doesn't live for itself but for someone else is magnificent in my book."

"And doomed," Gaveston chipped in, sadly. "Thank you, Willy. Knowing I've got someone with me who understands makes it bearable."

A sound came from the depths of the fur robe akin to a cat's purr. The Irishman's misshapen shoulders shifted as he sucked a reddish lozenge of pain-killing opium, spitting occasionally at its bitterness, watching the pink saliva arc through the firelight to hiss in the flames. The good eye closed contemplatively, opened again, sending Piers a warm beam of consolation. Down from the high hills swept a sudden wind, shaking the camp and moaning over the loch.

"Can't wait to look at our treasure tomorrow," the Irishman sighed with a little smile. "Knowing my luck, all we'll find will be recipes for onion soup."

CHAPTER TWENTY-EIGHT

On the northern shore of Loch Earn is a hill called Sron Mhor. To the east of the hill is a valley with a stream rising from six sources. In the summer of 1303, Commander McHunter and his Poor Knights, under vow not to examine the contents, wrapped six large sewn bales in clean wool, sealed them with pitch, cased them in timber, excavated a cavity to fit each bale in the nearest notable rock outcrop to each of the six tributary burns, then replaced the broken rock as if it were the work of Nature.

The books had been divided into six sections when they were crated up for despatch in Marseilles. The morning after their arrival at Loch Earn, McHunter showed Gaveston and William Wild the tattoo of a spider on his left thigh with a letter at the end of each leg: A, B, H, G, I, R.

"I've had to explain that a few times," he told them with a grin. "*Aunty Betty emits great indigo rhapsodies* was one of my best."

Sentries were posted around the rim of the valley and along the shore while the bales were recovered. When all six were safely in a covered waggon the expedition set out on its return. At Saint Fillans where the river Earn leaves the eastern end of the loch, an early camp was made in the deserted village, the inhabitants having fled.

The six bales were taken to the wooden church. With Gaveston and McHunter present, William Wild carefully opened the bale marked A, cutting through the skin of pitch with a knife.

"I can't do this with you two looking over my shoulder," he said as the bale split. "Why don't you leave me to it? As far as I know, neither of you can read much."

Gaveston and McHunter agreed and left. Only half an hour later, the Irishman emerged, demanding a drink before he'd say anything.

"Well, what have we got there?" Gaveston demanded. "Is it worth anything?"

William Wild gave a curt laugh. "First and foremost, politics," he told them. "This library was given to the Templars for safe-keeping by Pope Boniface the Eighth just before he died. It's the Vatican's collection of pornography – Assyrian, Babylonian, Egyptian, Greek, Indian and Roman. *A*unty *B*etty *E*mits *G*reat

*I*ndigo *R*hapsodies. I think the idea was the Templars should be caught with it when the persecution started and the accusations of obscenity and sodomy were first levelled against them – but the wily old Grand Master had other ideas."

Gaveston put his head in his hands. "Of what use is that? We've had a wasted journey!" he moaned.

"There's an index in the first bale," the Irishman said, blowing his nose free of ancient dust from the documents. "Some of the authors are the very best. From what I can see, the definition of pornography used was so wide it was virtually meaningless. Other people might call much of it literature."

Gaveston cheered up. "Now you're talking," he said enthusiastically. "You can get good money for literature."

William Wild mentioned Ovid, Catullus, the texts of Dionysian fertility-rite plays and the antics of stick-figures in Egyptian hieroglyphs. "The Vatican officials who got the collection ready for despatch overlooked a whole archive of learned works by doctors of the Church attempting to lay down what constitutes pornography," William Wild said, looking at some notes he'd made. "The most interesting I found is by Photius during the pontificate of Nicholas the First..."

"Yes, Willy...I'm sure it's fascinating," Gaveston muttered, still in the grip of his disappointment. "But it's not going to keep me out of my bed. We've a long day tomorrow carting this rubbish back to Berwick."

"It's been gathered together over centuries for the purposes of research and study and worth taking seriously. The definition of pornography is still open for discussion. Perhaps the present Pope would buy the collection back..."

Gaveston and McHunter drifted away, leaving the Irishman alone. He shrugged and stared into the fire, pulling his fur robe tight. They had wanted a conventional treasure – gold, jewels, coin and the rest. But his time with the rolls, bundles of parchment and palimpsests had set him thinking. Efforts to control sexual power by political power never succeeded. His last conscious thought before nodding off was: political power inherited through blood originates in sexual power. Pornography is a cartoon of wild animals trying to live together while squirming beneath the heel of instinct...and so on.

During the night the Bishops of Glasgow and Saint Andrews arrived with their retinues at Saint Fillan's. When the English awoke next morning they found themselves surrounded.

On the return of the bishops from imprisonment in England Bruce had told them that rededication to the spiritual life was essential to the health of the Church in Scotland. Whilst in the south they had been contaminated. Set at liberty as part of the deal engineered by Ned to get Gaveston's excommunication revoked, the prelates had returned to Scotland with an inflated idea of their own importance, seeing themselves as major figures on the international stage. A month in the cell of Saint Fillan – an eighth-century hermit known as *The Faster of Earn* – was designed to put both bishops back in touch with the values of an independent, de-Anglicised Scotland.

When the bishops discovered who was in charge of the English force they were dismayed. As noblemen, they had been treated with courtesy in England, often let out on parole to attend tournaments where Gaveston had been in action.

As experienced soldiers, the bishops knew the inspirational effect on troops of fighting under the banner of a great warrior. The two hundred English needed to be respected as if they were double in number.

Given the chance, the Scots would have withdrawn at the end of the first parley, giving Gaveston a free road out. But a blizzard descended from the north, forcing the bishops to sue for an immediate truce. They asked the English, as fellow Christians, for the use of the village as shelter. Cheek by jowl, the men of both sides huddled down to see out the fierce, freezing storm. In the wooden church built over the cell where Saint Fillan mortified his flesh, the Bishop of Glasgow and the Bishop of Saint Andrews sat on the pornography of the Popes playing dice.

It wasn't long before all the fuel in the village was used up. As the temperature dropped, everything that would burn was put on the fires. The cold worsened further, freezing the horses to death outside. The carts of the bishops' baggage-trains were broken up for firewood, followed by William Wild's chariot and the treasure waggon.

In the depth of the night, with the wind screaming, all the men dug their way out of the houses and made their way through chest-high snowdrifts to the church where the last fire was burning. Scots and English sat pressed together to find what warmth they could.

The bishops had treated Gaveston with great deference so far. In order not to provoke him, they'd asked few questions. As the fire sank down into ash and the cold assumed a murderous grip, they plucked up courage.

"My lord, the only wood left is the church itself," the Bishop of Glasgow said politely, trying to stop his teeth chattering. "If we start breaking up the fabric of the building, eventually we're going to freeze to death anyway. May I ask whether what we're sitting on, which may be valuable to you, is flammable?"

There was silence in the icy gloom. The embers of the fire began to powder into ash. Death by cold spread its preludial sleepiness. Then someone echoed: "May I ask whether what you're sitting on, which may be valuable to you, is flammable?" and chuckled ironically, repeating the question until it took hold, chanted by all the men as they elbowed Gaveston, William Wild and the bishops aside, ripped the six bales apart and began to feed the fire.

"You should give thanks the treasure wasn't what you hoped it would be," the Irishman whispered to Gaveston as the pitch skin of the packaging combusted in leaps of warming flame. "If it had been, we'd all have been dead by morning."

William Wild returned to Berwick in a litter carried through a snowbound landscape. As the column floundered over hill and dale, the Irishman encouraged those who carried him by reading aloud from a few manuscripts he'd saved from the flames, translating as he went along. Most popular was Sappho of Lesbos whose love poetry spurred the men on to heroic exertion, even though it was written by a woman who loved women. As the Irishman observed to the Bishop of Glasgow, who was hostage for the column's safe-conduct: "What they like about her is the lack of cynicism. She gladly goes to the utter limit, a stranger to shame."

Henry de Lacy became seriously unwell. Although *custos* of the kingdom in Ned's absence, he was still at the heart of the opposition, helping the Ordainers all he could from his sick-bed, checking draft clauses for irrationality and immoderate rant. Some days he drifted into antagonism towards his hapless king; others he lapsed into nostalgia, remembering promises given to *Edwardus Primus.*

Everyone came to see him who had a problem, seeking advice from a dying man whose judgement, though impaired, was valued above all others. He never became impatient, but every other visitor he received was a priest.

The magnates paid him court during this final phase, aware of the major shift in power his death would bring about. His son-in-law and heir was Thomas, Earl of Lancaster – a surly, dogged opponent of the Crown and Ned. Five earldoms would converge on Thomas when the old earl passed on – Lincoln, Derby, Leicester, Salisbury and Lancaster – making him Ned's strongest vassal. The leadership of the opposition would naturally devolve upon him.

When the time to die arrived, the old earl was fully prepared.

In case he forget to mention something, or weakened, his confessor read his death-bed speech for him. It was a long, rambling meditation. Disenchantment with philosophy was evident. Durandus wasn't mentioned by name, but the Three Relationship Theory of Being took some hard knocks. There were hard-hitting political sections. In the most important of these he exhorted his son-in-law to free the people from vexatious exactions. Henry de Lacy's place in the history of thought rests on his dictum – *in politics it is always the people who have most to lose.*

Towards the end of the speech, the dying earl chimed in urging Thomas of the five earldoms to remove evil from the King's side. He expired with the name *Peter* on his lips. When the clergy put out a resumé of this most Christian death, Peter was identified as the keeper of the gates of Heaven, not a certain Gascon adventurer.

Compelled to swear fealty for his new lands before they could legally be his, Thomas went north with a large retinue to Berwick. He stopped on the southern bank of the river Tweed, which was the border, refusing to leave England in case he fell foul of his feudal duty to serve in the Scottish campaign. From the castle on the northern bank, Ned made his own stand, refusing to cross the bridge to the south bank to receive the earl's pledge of loyalty. Threats were exchanged. The earl's retinue swelled in numbers until it could be accounted a small army. In spite of Gaveston's strong advice to the contrary, Ned crumbled and gave in, saying he couldn't be bothered to argue any more. He agreed to meet Thomas on English ground ten miles south of the river at the castle of Haggerston.

For the first time in their relationship, Gaveston suspected he was being punished by Ned, who had hinted that his surrender to Thomas of Lancaster had been triggered by his disappointment over the Templar treasure. The story brought back from the expedition was unconvincing. Knowing Gaveston's immense appetite for riches, Ned suspected a share-out with the Scots.

This suspicion enraged Gaveston. William Wild produced his manuscripts from the collection and verified the account of what had happened. Ned said he had to believe what he was being told but, nevertheless, it left a bad taste in his mouth.

At the ceremony where Thomas of Lancaster vowed to serve his liege lord, with life and limb as long as he lived, in exchange for his colossal inheritance, Gaveston was insulted in the most public manner. Thomas refused to greet him. The offence was so deliberate, performed right under the King's nose, it was taken as proof of Ned's connivance in the insult – the motive being to signal some form of separation between himself and his favourite. By allowing it to pass, Ned allowed Piers's dignity as Earl of Cornwall to be traduced. When Gaveston took Ned to task, demanding to know why he had been exposed to such humiliation, Ned said he was imagining things. To be ignored by the charmless Earl of Lancaster was something to be thankful for.

In Scotland, however, the Earl of Cornwall had his dignity amongst the people, even though it was the dignity of an enemy. In July, when Ned, stripped of funds, was forced to go back to London and face the Ordainers, he left Gaveston behind as his lieutenant, or, as the Gascon sourly deemed it, his midwife to an aborted campaign.

A second cause for suspicion on Gaveston's part came with the launch of a massive raid by Bruce into northern England as soon as Ned left. The ravaging and looting was accompanied by derisive messages to Gaveston, teasing him for always being in the wrong place. There was a knowing edge in the messages that smacked of collusion. Someone with intimate insights was feeding jibes to get under the Gascon's skin. As Gaveston was forced to retreat before the swarming attacks until he was in Bamburgh Castle, thirty miles south of Berwick, he shared his suspicions with William Wild, who found them absurd. As an exponent of ridicule yourself, he told him, learn to take it as well dishing it out.

Feeling more alone than ever, licking his wounds and waiting to hear the outcome of Ned's dealings with the Ordainers, Gaveston shook off the suspicions. He sported and hunted along the coast, rewarded the Irishman's good sense by building him another chariot, took some pleasure in the news his wife was pregnant. The news that his old enemy Walter Langton was to be the treasurer of the royal household again – an appointment forced on Ned by his enemies – gave him no pleasure at all, however.

When the final verdict of the Ordainers reached Gaveston from London, it had a familiar ring: exile for himself, but this time all his relatives, employees, and associates were included. He was labelled a symbol of royal corruption, injustice, rapacity, untrustworthiness and mismanagement. Everything wrong with the government of the country, the King and his household, the law, the Exchequer, was laid at his door.

Ned resisted the demands for two months, arguing the proposed reforms for cutting back his authority made kingship a nonsense. Also, he insisted the charges of corruption against Gaveston were unjust, containing no shred of evidence.

Purposeful rejection of his defence on all counts was the response. As London was full of armed retainers belonging to the Ordainers, Ned offered agreement to the programme of reform *in toto* provided the demand for Gaveston's exile could be dropped.

This climb-down was taken as final proof of the evil power Gaveston had over the King. If, as Ned alleged, the reforms made kingship a nonsense, his acceptance of them was evidence of his readiness to sacrifice everything and anything to keep his lover. Voices were raised saying such an infatuation was too deep for absence and time to cure. Only Gaveston's death would do.

Gaveston was deprived of his lieutenancy and summoned back to London.

Sick at heart, he journeyed southwards, calling in at Knaresborough where he'd had such happy times with Ned. On his arrival at Westminster, he was intercepted before he could see the King and officially notified of his perpetual exile, not only from England but all English possessions. All his lands were taken back into the possession of the Crown. A pretence of legality for the sentence was made – when exiled by Edward the First four years ago, he had returned without proper assent. Gaveston mocked this excuse. A dead king could not revoke his exile, but a live one could. There was no law in this matter, only prejudice and hatred. He was ordered to leave from Dover by 1st November 1311, on pain of death if he ever returned.

❧

"He's an innocent from the beginning of the world – Adam before the Fall, Eve before the apple, the angel in the serpent, the wilderness before the Garden of Eden," William Wild said to his old friend and ally, John Botetourt, who had worked long and hard with the Ordainers over the last eighteen months. "Your mistake is to use Piers Gaveston negatively. You justify a corrupt system by excluding him from it. He knows no law stemming from what we call government because his mind belongs to Nature and the time before law."

"He represents everything government has to control – greed, anarchy, aggression..."

"How wrong you are. Piers is very conventional. He's what all your colleagues are in their secret dreams. The accusation of envy is justified. If Piers was king, he'd be very like great Edward was at that age – cruel, thoughtless and overbearing..."

"Enough, Willy," Botetourt said, covering his ears. "I'd heard you'd become his man but this is too much."

"How can I be anyone's man? Look at me!" the Irishman laughed. "I'm not even half a man any more. But I can be a conscience."

"Then you're not a good one. He's as arrogant as ever. Think back over what he did to you!"

"I didn't say I was *his* conscience," the Irishman retorted. "Piers is a challenge, I agree – to those who need to extinguish, to destroy life. They can't allow him to flourish. His fire must be put out – instead of thinking how to adapt his genius."

"Genius? What genius is this?" Botetourt protested. "The man's an appalling parasite!"

"Given the choice – who would you rather be ruled by? The dull dogs you've been working with or someone with his flair and energy? Ned frustrated the natural independent talent in him. There could have been a different story."

"Don't mention dogs," Botecourt muttered. "No animal has ever been so talked about in committee."

William Wild laughed quietly, satisfied with the unsettling effect his defence of Gaveston had made on his old friend. "Although I wasn't present, I can guarantee that not a single word has been said in his favour throughout your deliberations. No Christian has stood up for him, in charity – no soldier as a comrade-in-arms, no relative by marriage has tried to protect him. His condemnation has been universal – with one exception, two if I include myself. As I remember, the case was similar with Christ."

Botetourt recoiled, covering his ears. "No more, Willy. You're too good an apologist for a simpleton like me. What will you do when he's gone?"

"Go with him, of course."

"What about Valmai? Go back to the Wye Valley. Let her take care of you. Retire!"

"She'll join us, wherever Piers settles. I think we'll establish a new state…give some of Plato's ideas a chance. You've heard of the philosopher-king?"

"Only from you."

"I can make Piers into a passable philosopher-king. He listens to what I say. There must be a little country somewhere in need of a ruler…some duchy where the line has become extinct and they value natural power in a man."

Botetourt's eyes narrowed. "You're pulling my leg," he said. "Either that, or your brain didn't escape injury when you had that fall."

In the ten days left before the exile came into force, the Ordainers did all they could to keep Ned and Piers apart. Meetings were called, crises declared, plots uncovered, rumours of war started, cooled and restarted. Whenever they were able to see each other, they were watched. Earls, barons, bishops and burgesses hovered, waiting for an opportunity to get between them. The functions of the officers of the royal household had been so reduced by the reforms they were powerless to keep these invasive spies at bay. The King's privacy had disappeared along with his authority.

Queen Isabella resented this loss. Heavily committed to the anti-Gaveston party, she had never wanted to see the King's power and dignity whittled away. The strange situation arose whereby it was only in her apartments Ned and Piers could be together, but in her presence. Under these conditions, they knew anything they said to each other could not be confidential.

The most important item they needed to discuss was where Gaveston would go once he left England. King Philip had already let it be known there'd be no welcome in France. As for going home to Gascony, that was an English possession and therefore closed to him.

When Isabella saw Ned in such a state of mental exhaustion, sapped by surrender, beset by a devouring aristocracy still hungry for more of his power, she began to believe the monarchy could disappear altogether. All that appeared to be holding him upright was his love of Gaveston. If the favourite went to live somewhere far beyond his reach, Ned might lose his will to live along with his will to fight.

Her suggestion for Gaveston's place of exile was Flanders. It was near, politically friendly, connected by trade and migrant Fleming communities to England and Wales. Communication was easy. For Ned, incognito visits would be feasible.

Isabella had reached the stage where she accepted the twist in her husband's make-up – not with any real grace or understanding but from a strong, pragmatic instinct. If she blamed anyone for her predicament, it was her father and Ned's father. The boy's proclivities had been consistent. Everyone had known what he was like. Yet the marriage had gone ahead, regardless. To gamble on a change of his sexual personality was not an error – it was a deliberate sacrifice of her and his happiness. Although the bed of dynastic marriage was an ice-bound place, it was not as cold as the minds of the men who had tucked her up in it. Compared to them, warm-blooded, stupid, purblind, passionate Ned was recognisably human. His errors were understandable within his severe limitations. She was already convinced he would never alter or improve.

"Bruges comes to mind," she said to Piers with only a week left to decide where he was going. "As the crow flies it can't be more than a hundred and fifty miles from here. What's that? The distance to Somerset."

Ned nodded, raising an eyebrow in Gaveston's direction. "The duke's married to my sister, Margaret. He's amiable enough," he said. "We've helped him in the past. Shall I write to him? We haven't got much time."

Still numb from the helplessness of recent weeks, Gaveston shrugged, evincing no enthusiasm. "Let it be Bruges, if they'll have me. What does it matter?"

"It has a big English community – merchants, not boring barons. Artists love it, musicians flock there…the food and wine are excellent…wonderful buildings, canals…they call it the Venice of the North," Isabella enthused. "I think you'd like it there."

"Are you trying to get rid me?" Gaveston said with a wry laugh. "Will you really come and visit, Ned? You didn't come to Ireland."

Ned glided over that issue, preferring to emphasise what a good idea Bruges was. "We'll see you have plenty of money, a lot of money. Make a big splash. Don't hide your light under a bushel. Enjoy yourself. Make some new friends…" He paused in his prompting. "Didn't you go there with my father just after we first met?"

"Yes, to fight – if you'll forgive me, Isabella – against the French. Your father was being more impossible than usual. Yes, I vaguely remember being in Bruges."

"If you go there, don't spend any time fretting. As soon as you've gone, we'll set about changing things. We'll have you back before long," Ned promised. "The barons have already started disagreeing amongst themselves. People will see how unfairly you've been treated."

"That I don't believe!" Gaveston stormed suddenly. "When I go it will be for good. I won't be coming back. Perhaps you should ask yourself – is that what I really want?"

Troubled, Isabella gave an odd little grimace. Unable to stop herself, she touched his hand. She had always known Gaveston for what he was – a true, deep-dyed Gascon with all the verve and nuisance value of that race. The upsurge in his feelings was both natural, and orchestrated – a hot wind blowing by command.

"Don't suggest Ned would ever betray you," she whispered. "He couldn't even if he wanted to."

"There's something I'd like to say to Ned alone, if you'd be so good…" Gaveston mumbled. "It's especially difficult."

"Be careful what it is" Isabella replied as she withdrew. "At the moment all you two have is each other."

Once she'd gone, they avoided each other's eyes for a while. Ned sat by the window, looking down at the busybodies haunting the courtyard.

"What is it you want to say?" he asked.

Gaveston sighed with exasperation. "I still can't believe this has all gone so wrong," he said. "Are you clear in your mind what you want?"

"Clear about what?" Ned asked, perturbed.

"Whether it's been worth it…You've had to climb down from such a height… to give away so much."

"I like to give things away. As for climbing down, I watch those rats climb down huge distances whenever they want something for themselves. What's the difference?"

"So your surrender was insincere?"

"When they've cleared out of London and gone home, I'll find a way to release myself from every agreement I made. Forget all their clauses and committees – it was the knife at my throat that persuaded me, and they know it."

Gaveston frowned, still unsure. Suspicions he'd experienced in the north returned. Ignoring Isabella's exhortation to be careful in what he said, he told Ned about his suspicions that he was being used as a scapegoat. "I know you have to manipulate me as well as everyone else," he added, "but if any of those suspicions were justified, it might be best to admit it so I know where I am."

"Suspicions?" Ned hissed, staring at him, outraged.

"I need to know where I stand."

"Know where you stand? You're here! Here!" Ned screamed, thumping his heart as he leapt out of the chair. "And I can't get you out! If I had any sense I'd chop off your fucking head and be done with it! God's arse and entrails, you disgust me! After all I've been through for you…"

Drawn by the uproar, Isabella came running back into the room to intervene.

"This ingrate has said some terrible things, Isabella," Ned shouted. "I can't believe it. Oh, how you've changed, Piers! You've let them win!"

CHAPTER TWENTY-NINE

Piers left England four days late, and not from Dover, as ordered, but from the Thames by dusk in a ship laden with baggage, servants and horses. Opponents watched him go, glad the farce of chasing, cajoling and hastening his departure was over. He had tested their patience to the limit, making excuses by the hour, hanging on to the King's indulgence until the Ordainers were frantic with disgust. Fists were raised and curses hurled as the vessel slowly made headway on an ebbing tide. Guy de Beauchamp said it was vomit from England's throat.

Margaret, the exile's wife, watched from Blackfriars with her brother, Gilbert, the young Earl of Gloucester. She was six months pregnant.

Gilbert found dealing with such deep hatred for someone closely tied to him by marriage bewildering. The family couldn't approve Gaveston's attitude to the earls, nor could they share in the communal hatred their peers had for a senior member of their clan. Gilbert had tried to take up a position outside the conflict, but that proved impossible. Nothing was straightforward about the relationship the de Clare family had with Gaveston. Although locked to him by law, the pressure of other families to recognise the madness of the King's infatuation made the de Clares admit there were faults in Gaveston. Gilbert resolutely argued the shortcomings of his brother-in-law could be remedied, but when death was mooted as the only cure, he was quick to accept exile was the solution.

Margaret wondered aloud whether the child in her womb would ever see its father. Since their marriage four years ago she'd seen little of him. Lately, her knowledge of his character had been shaped more by calumny than her own experience. A woman isn't expected to hate her husband for any reason other than her own, but people couldn't resist looking to her for confirmation of his evil nature. She was pitied as the wife of a heretic is pitied – not for her own opinions but for the misfortune of her subservience in marriage.

Gaveston left her in the care of her brother and Ned, cousins in blood but no longer in mind.

❧

Once out of the Thames estuary, the ship turned west in the thick November night, heading for the Channel, instead of setting a course for Zeebrugge, the port serving Bruges. Twelve hours before leaving Westminster, intelligence had been received from Ned's sister, Duchess Margaret, of rumours being spread by agents of the Earls of Lancaster and Warwick among the English wool merchants in Bruges. Anyone who befriended the exile would suffer. Gaveston was to be ostracised. Under these conditions, she advised looking elsewhere for asylum.

A decision on where to go had to be made quickly. There was no time to seek permission from foreign governments. The Irishman suggested Piers should come with him to the Wye Valley, posing as a servant, until an alternative place of exile could be negotiated. In spite of the danger to Piers should he be caught in contravention of the terms of the exile, this idea had appealed most to Ned because it defied the Ordainers.

"If you had any hair, Willy, I could be your barber," Gaveston remarked ironically as the vessel began to pitch and roll. "That would be appropriate, considering our history together."

"A labourer would be better. Ned would like to think of you digging a few ditches..." William Wild replied, folding himself into a bulkhead corner. "Could you manage something simple and down-to-earth? We have to hide you, somehow."

"Whatever you say, Willy. I'm in your hands now."

"We'll do a bit of barbering on you for old time's sake. Cut your hair short. Get rid of the moustache. I'm afraid labourers wear rather rough, unfashionable clothes. An accent will be needed for when you have to say something – which should be infrequently. What kind of character can we create for this hard-working lad? We don't want him to draw too much attention to himself."

"A clod is what I'll be," Gaveston declared bleakly. "It'll be fun for me to be a clod."

William Wild raised the problem of the servants. There were twenty-two on the ship.

"Well, that ruins everything. One servant can't keep a secret, never mind twenty-two," Gaveston said bitterly. "My career as a clod is over before it's started."

"We tell the servants what's happening. It's all we can do. If we put them ashore, they'll talk. If they know the deception is for your good, which is their good, they'll keep quiet."

Piers raised the issue of Valmai – she would react badly to his presence, bearing in mind the past.

"We won't tell her who you are. You won't be living in the house with us – however much of it they've rebuilt, which won't be a lot. I'll find you a suitable hut."

"A hut?"

"From what I remember, there are huts. If they've all gone, we'll build you one."

"Don't enjoy this too much, Willy. Remember how downfall feels."

"Piers, I want you to win. Those who hate you claim to be the people. They're not. They pretend to be the victim when, in fact, they're the oppressor. You *be* the people, for a while. Hide among the people. It will do you good."

"Oh, spare me. Why don't I go to some desert and lose myself? My life's over."

William Wild frowned with annoyance. "If we're going to beat these hypocrites, we won't do it with a long face," he said vehemently. "Live the part of a simple, ordinary man. A cup of water, a handful of oatmeal, a turnip. Enjoy the experience. And if, as your master, I need to come down to your hut occasionally and give you a thrashing – not a pretend thrashing as they're always unconvincing – I expect you to take it like a man."

The Irishman chuckled slyly, his imagination spinning. All the risks were dwarfed by the notion of Gaveston, whom he had seen in his greatest glory, living the life of a serf. It had a mighty moral and spiritual appeal, a theological grandeur. His feeling for the young man would be reinforced and escalated. Dying with him – which he saw as inevitable and to be desired – would be an honour tinged with sublimity.

Gaveston leant forward and touched the Irishman's twisted hand, bringing him out of his reverie. "If I have to pretend to this degree, why don't I go the whole hog and be a woman?"

William Wild's eyes glittered. The suggestion filled him with delight. Taking his young hero's hand, he kissed it.

The arrival of Captain William Wild, home from the wars with a large retinue and vast amount of baggage, was an event impossible to play down. Agog, the community of the Wye Valley watched as three flat-bottomed trows were dragged up the tidal river from Chepstow by men in harness. It was a popular homecoming, though saddened when people saw the old man disembark, having to be carried off the vessel like a babe in arms.

No advance notice of their coming was sent. Alerted by neighbours downstream as the flotilla was hauled up past their properties, Valmai took the children down to the landing, wondering what had brought the Irishman back in such style. The last news Valmai had received was from London a week before the exile became effective. Bruges was then the destination. Now here he was, loaded with goods and treasure, accompanied by a host of servants, in sparkling form, it was said – but no Gaveston, or news of him.

The welcomes over, explanations promised, he hurriedly inspected the works on the house – which had progressed well, already providing good shelter for the family – and hastened to look at the accommodation available for the servants.

"We'll need more huts," he told Valmai as they watched his chariot being unloaded.

"It only takes a day to build a hut. If you'll slow down for a moment and let me know what's happening, I'd like that," Valmai said quietly. "Where's all this stuff come from?"

"I'll tell you later. Great events need patience to understand. Trust me."

"Willy, a lot has been achieved here. Now you're back, it's perfect, like a dream. I didn't expect to see you for years, perhaps. But, if there's some kind of trouble, I need to know what it is."

"Come and have a ride in my chariot," he said, seeing the tears in her eyes. "I'll tell you everything I can."

The lie was essential – so the Irishman told himself. Valmai was led to believe Ned had arranged for Piers to be taken off the ship at sea and taken to the Canary Islands. He was to live there quietly until he could safely be recalled. All his goods, baggage and servants would be kept and looked after for him, and given back when the time was right.

In her half-finished house, surrounded by strange servants, her husband in the thrall of a dark excitement all his own, Valmai clung to her dream and asked no further questions, but she wasn't persuaded all was well. Within a few days so many problems had arisen with Gaveston's entourage, Valmai had no time to dwell on her misgivings.

One female in particular – Alison, by name – was causing havoc in the huts down by the river. Men were travelling from all over the valley to hang around in hope of seeing her. Wherever she went, males followed, doggedly seeking her favours. At night her hut had to be guarded.

Eventually, Valmai said the woman must be brought into the house where an eye could be kept on her. William Wild insisted there was no fault to be found in Alison's behaviour. She wasn't encouraging these attentions. Her power to attract was a natural gift beyond her control. The poor woman had even taken to walking with a stoop and keeping her face dirty to put off the mob. But after several fights down at the huts between competing males, and the death by drowning of a rejected fifteen-year-old, he was forced to agree to the transfer.

The suggestion Alison should become one of Valmai's personal maidservants wasn't approved. Instead, she was put in the kitchen to help the cook.

Christmas-time in the lower Wye Valley was wet. The river rose, flooding the meadows, bringing down banks, drowning stock, sweeping bridges away. All building work exposed to the elements had to be curtailed. As the rain-clouds came in from the Bristol Channel yet again, information reached William Wild that searches were being made in the south-west for Piers, the earls having got wind he was somewhere back in England.

For the last six weeks the entire household had gone along with the Alison myth. The first time Valmai went into the kitchen and encountered the bold grey eyes under the unkempt blonde hair, she knew what had happened. No words passed between them, but a mutual intuition recognised the danger of breaking Gaveston's cover. Also, the cook worked out the sex of the underling when she found her having a piss round the back.

By unspoken agreement, the truth was kept confined. No one told William Wild or Gaveston the game was up. From a mere mile away, Tintern Abbey dominated life – a giant celibatic iceberg. The idea of having the most powerful sexual magnet in the region as part of the household was something the servants didn't want to lose. It had become a matter of pride.

On New Year's Day 1312, a messenger arrived by night with a verbal message from Ned. Gaveston was to join him at Nottingham on the 10th January, without fail. He must bring everything – household, baggage, treasure. Together with the King, the Lord Gaveston, Earl of Cornwall – all his lands restored to him – would go to the north. It was recommended the first part of his journey to Nottingham should be by sea to Boston on the Lincolnshire coast to avoid those scouring the south-west for him.

"What does he think he's doing?" Gaveston complained to William Wild. "He seems to think we can create a new kingdom in the north. It's a mad idea."

"Now's the time to disappear, if that's what you want. Once you join up with him and the whole thing's out in the open, it'll be too late to back out."

"Advise me, Willy. Within myself, I know what to do. Go out there and defy them. But there has to be a chance of success."

"Ned may have found a lot more support. The moderates may have moved to his side, not wanting the Crown belittled any further. Isabella could have talked her father into helping Ned against overpowerful opposition and keeping the idea of kingship alive. The Church generally doesn't like a weakened central authority because that's what it works through…How can I possibly advise you when I don't know what's been happening in London? Ned may be going to fight the

Scots with all the earls at his side…but he's told us nothing. Take your pick, Piers. Take your pick."

Gaveston thought for a while. It was the first clear night for weeks. A perfect half-moon rode over the Black Mountains to the north. He looked at his hands, rough and hardened by work in the kitchen. "What the hell, I'm ready for a fight," he muttered. "I was born for a better life than this. It's time we had a bit of luck. You'll come, I hope?"

"Try and stop me."

It took two days to arrange for the trows and a ship to be waiting at Chepstow. The voyage back down the Channel and up to Boston would take at least a week, giving only a day for the thirty-mile journey to Nottingham.

On the last evening before setting out, Valmai insisted on talking to Gaveston and her husband together. The cripple and his lord sat side by side. In a few hours they would ride to Chepstow to meet the trows which had already gone downriver, and supervise the transfer to the ship. Gaveston was no longer the girl in the kitchen. Resplendent in green and gold, a sword at his belt, he gave Valmai a child's smile.

"I'll bring him back in one piece," he promised. "Next time I won't have to be anyone but myself."

Valmai gave him a searching, sardonic look. "Piers, whoever it is you are, or wherever you are, there's trouble. Tell me something – d'you ever dream of living in peace?"

Gaveston's smile changed from innocence to mock affront. "Me? Peace? Come on, Valmai – you know me better than that!"

"In front of you, Piers, I want Willy to explain why he's not staying behind," Valmai said levelly. "That's he's forgiven you everything you did to him is a point of pride to me. Very few men are big enough to forgive that much. By his example, I've found it in myself to forgive what happened to my family at Pant Mawr, thanks to you – something you hardly thought about, I expect, but it still gives me nightmares."

Gaveston looked puzzled. "Pant Mawr? That doesn't mean anything to me," he replied. "Should it? Did I do something unpleasant to Willy? If I did, then I regret it bitterly."

"Let's leave it in the past. I shouldn't have brought it up," Valmai said, picking up the glance of intense affection he directed at the Irishman, which couldn't be anything but genuine. "He's determined to go with you. That much he's told me. But we need him here. He should be with his children. Whatever he says, he's no longer equipped to fight wars or take your kind of risks."

Gaveston turned and looked at the Irishman. "You must answer, Willy. Change your mind if you want to. There's no duty I can possibly hold you to. If I had a woman like this, I'd think about it very carefully."

"If it's your wish to have me older than I am, Valmai, I can't help you," he said coldly.

"Look at you!" she cried. "How can you run? How can you defend yourself?"

The Irishman pulled a dismissive face. "Valmai, a man in the midst of his second life doesn't run. There's nothing to run from. How often have we talked about what we cherish in this world? D'you think all the things I said weren't meant?"

She made a gesture of impatience. "You always talked too much! How can I remember everything you said?" she retorted, avoiding his eye. "And don't give me a lecture now, if you don't mind."

"Let me ask you a question..."

"As long as the question isn't a lecture!"

"In your experience, Valmai, of the men you've ever met, who is the most hated and reviled, the most envied, and the most loved?"

Valmai snorted and turned her back.

"You daren't answer because he's in front of you, large as life," the Irishman scoffed softly, a light in his one good eye. "Haven't you ever asked yourself what makes people feel so intensely about him?"

Valmai's shoulders slumped. She asked in a low voice to be allowed to miss the rest of the nonsense he was going to talk.

"I'd be a bird on Christ's shoulder if I could, watching how he works his miracles," he went on, ignoring her request. "I'd sleep alongside Mahomet in his cave and share his dream. I'd be sad in both cases, because, ultimately, they failed in their attempt to take over the world. But I have my saviour to lead me to the knowledge I seek."

"I'm a Christian, as everyone is in this house, including Piers, as far as I know!" Valmai snapped, crossing herself. "Keep your blasphemy to yourself!"

William Wild laughed, untroubled by the accusation. "You've always known what I'm like. Pain has made me even more impatient with sham and deceit. Faith is submission to ignorance. In Piers we have the essence of our animal selves. His magic has proved itself. It has real power because we don't have to believe in it. It's already there, controlling us, confounding us."

Gaveston chuckled, raising an eyebrow in Valmai's direction. "Don't worry too much," he advised genially. "He goes on like this when he's upset. He's going to miss you. He always misses you."

Valmai gave him a withering stare, then transferred it to her husband.

"There we are then, Willy," she said icily. "You hear that? Piers doesn't think much of your chatter either. It doesn't mean anything."

"Sweetheart, I use what brains I have. What you find overreaching in me is what I live with, and have to use. After my fall, the real questions were all I had left, and the one real answer I'd ever found – you, Valmai – couldn't answer them."

"So, I'm to be punished for that? You'll go away and die, leaving me here because I can't answer questions no one can answer?"

Painfully, the Irishman edged himself over to Valmai and clung to her. "No, *cariad*," he said. "This young man reinforces the answer you gave me but on the grand scale. I have to stay close to him to the end. Forgive me."

CHAPTER THIRTY

Gaveston's ship was held back in the Channel by contrary winds. He missed Ned at Nottingham and had to follow him up the Great North Road to York.

As soon as the ship touched Boston, his armed retinue and baggage train openly flying the Earl of Cornwall's banners, he was shadowed. Messengers were sent to alert the Ordainers and the country at large that Gaveston was back.

On 18th January Ned publicly defied the opposition and declared Piers Gaveston to be a good and loyal subject whose banishment was against the interests, laws and customs of the realm. All his lands were restored to him.

This was followed by another public declaration saying only reforms not prejudicial to him as king would be observed.

Ned then wrote to the mayor and citizens of London ordering them to guard the city while he fortified castles in the north against the Scots.

The Ordainers gathered men and horses in preparation for war. Gaveston's wife, Margaret de Clare, was given safe-conduct to come to York to give birth to her child. The waiting for war merged with the waiting for the baby.

When the child was delivered, Gaveston sat in a chair with the bundle in his arms looking into the red, wrinkled face, saying nothing. His expression was puzzled. He didn't know what to make of it. Someone told him it was a girl. He grimaced and said it was more like a monkey. His wife asked if he was disappointed it was a girl. *She* had hoped for a son. Gaveston said blood was blood. Any child of his, male or female, would have to contend with who did the fathering – an evil monster by all accounts. When this girl grew up she wouldn't want his name. Extinction of his real self, his good deeds, the meaning of his life, would be the punishment for his sins.

It was his darkest moment. No one dared intrude on the savage melancholy. He sat with the baby in his arms until she cried. When Margaret offered to take her from him, he was reluctant to let go.

❧

The Ordainers were slow to act, but there was no hurry. Right was now entirely on their side. An axis between the Church and the magnates was forged. Archbishop

Winchelsey of Canterbury excommunicated Gaveston. Thomas of Lancaster was chosen as the new leader.

The country was then divided up into four regions: the Earls of Hereford and Essex to protect the east; Thomas of Lancaster and the Marcher lords, the west; the Earl of Gloucester (Gaveston's brother-in-law and Ned's cousin), the south; and the Earl of Northumberland, the north. The Earls of Pembroke and Surrey were given the task of capturing Gaveston.

All the magnates in opposition swore to be loyal to each other. The bishops gave their full support, threatening excommunication to anyone who worked against the general effort. Having covered themselves with every form of legality they could, the muster of armies was undertaken. It was time for everyone to choose which side they were on.

As the weakness of his position became clearer, Ned wrote to various Gascon leaders, commanding them to raise troops. These orders were ignored.

Like a juggernaut in pieces being brought to an assembly-point, the opposition forces slowly moved towards convergence, taking their time, disguising their movements by holding tournaments. There was no need to rush. The longer they waited, the more obvious the King's powerlessness and isolation would become.

As his enemies approached, Ned abandoned York and went further north to Newcastle, the combined baggage trains of the royal and Gaveston's households taking up more space on the road than their paltry army.

For the first time in his life, Gaveston fell ill – his previously unbreakable health undermined by Ned's retreat into his northern fantasy. From his sickbed Piers saw the domination he still exercised, how everything was being lost because of him – and how, to Ned, there was no choice. Love was all, and the world well lost.

To cure Gaveston's perplexing illness, Ned supplemented the ministration of the doctor by giving the patient more and more treasure, lands, income, honours, everything he had left to give. It was the only medicine he understood. In the courtyard of the Newcastle fortress, gold, silver and jewels were daily transferred from the royal treasure waggon into Gaveston's.

Both the doctors and Ned claimed success in bringing about a full recovery, but the real credit was the Irishman's. He never left his lord's bedside, paying Gaveston back for saving his life. He persuaded Gaveston that despair was for other beings, beings who could not be loved in the grand manner. Hope should never be abandoned by a star. For a natural hero to do so was denial of his gifts. If destiny decided death was part of this fatal hope, so be it.

Ned was intrigued by the solicitousness of the Irishman. It recalled parts of his own childhood when stories were told, thoughts shared, by this same man, but in his prime. Whenever Ned visited Gaveston on his sickbed, William Wild retreated, giving him room. On one occasion Ned asked what a disabled old bodyguard of his father's could possibly have to talk about day after day. Gaveston replied that it was a pity such a bright man should be reduced to bedside prattle, but he was glad of it.

After three weeks Gaveston was well enough to answer the emergency when the armies of the Earls of Lancaster and Northumberland appeared a few miles south of Newcastle. No time was given for the King to negotiate. Ned was forced to flee with Gaveston to the port of Tynemouth, abandoning both baggage trains on the quayside because they wouldn't fit in the ship. They set sail for Scarborough ninety miles down the coast.

At Tynemouth, sitting on the harbourside, the pursuing earls found an embittered Isabella, pregnant and discarded because there was no room for her either.

At sea, his authority tattered as the sails of the leaky ship he had commandeered, stripped of the greater part of his retinue, Ned was criticised by a resurgent Gaveston for abandoning their joint treasure. They would need it to fight the war. If Ned intended to merely shuffle around the country in shame, he must do it alone. There was no dignity in being a refugee. Ned's order for him to openly defy the Ordainers and return from exile had achieved nothing but humiliation. Once safe in Scarborough's royal castle, a firm grip must be taken. He was still the King. The country must be rallied to the cause.

Ned took enough time off helping the crew sail the vessel to sit down and agree with everything Piers said. As he practised a few knots the shipmen had taught him, he promised he would make a better job of everything. But the weather was glorious, the wind fair. He couldn't lose heart simply because of a few setbacks. He told Piers to look on the bright side. They hadn't enjoyed such fine days together for ages.

Gaveston had insisted William Wild's chariot must be taken on board in spite of the valuable space it took up, causing a dispute with the ship's captain on the quayside. Eventually it had to be towed in a boat behind.

As Ned continued his refusal to face facts, Gaveston became increasingly flummoxed. Try as he might, he couldn't fathom Ned's mind at this point. It was an opaque jelly, quivering but holding its form. The England they could see as they sailed along the coast had lost its king. The intervening water had more solidity than Ned's future. Tormented by frustration, Gaveston jumped overboard, swimming underwater as long as he could so Ned would think he'd drowned. When he surfaced, Ned was swimming alongside him, laughing: "It's not at all cold, is it?" he said. "Race you to the little boat and back."

Once in the castle at Scarborough, which was lightly garrisoned by his own troops, the King went to York to see if he could raise additional men, leaving Gaveston in charge. While Ned was in the city, Thomas of Lancaster put his army between Scarborough and York, cutting Ned off and isolating Gaveston in the castle. He then called the other earls to join him in setting a siege. Helpless in York, Ned sent messages to the earls, demanding they remove their armies from the area. These were ignored.

The best defence Piers had was the Crown. When he was within its aura, there was protection. Conversely, it was this relationship that enraged the earls against him. In their minds, the separation of the Crown from its wearer was now almost complete. By leaving Piers in Scarborough, Ned had taken away a final flimsy layer of protection.

William Wild had argued strongly for Ned to make a stand at Scarborough and negotiate. After forty years in royal service he knew the protective power of kingship. The throne stood in a sacred grove. Whoever sat there was guarded more by myth than Myrmidons. The King's physical presence radiated sanctuary.

Gaveston and the Irishman watched from the battlements as the preparations for the siege were made below.

"After all the campaigns I've been on, all the sieges I've been at, it's an odd thing to realise that I've never been on the receiving end before," Piers said. "I've always been on the besieging side."

William Wild was silent. With the supplies and men available he knew there was little chance of holding out longer than a month. He had never imagined dying in a siege. The prospect was an uncomfortable one. There was something too passive about it.

Offers to parley came from the besiegers at regular intervals. The Irishman advised against entering any negotiations. Long sieges became bad-tempered, bloody-minded affairs. Leniency evaporated to zero the longer a siege went on. He wanted a final catastrophic bloodletting raised as a possibility in the public mind. With Ned powerless on the sidelines, the siege of Scarborough would act on the conscience of England, focusing attention on the fundamental issue: do we want to keep our sacred king or be ruled by a gaggle of greedy mediocrities?

Cooped up in the castle was a symbol of a new age – Piers in all his stardom and celebrity. Besieged by destructive forces which had beaten the meaning out of natural life, poisoned religion, and broken the back of philosophy, this symbolic youth would shine above the mire and smoke of corrupt times. If the siege was lifted by public demand, Piers would be saved by *the people* and elevated beyond the reach of envious minds.

When Gaveston's treasure waggon was opened on the quayside at Tynemouth in front of Thomas of Lancaster, this fabulously wealthy man was staggered by what he saw. The amount of gold, silver and jewels was beyond even his imagination.

The physical manifestation of the King's love for his favourite glittered in the sun. When the assembled earls gazed at it, they were speechless. Draining the royal treasury was one of the accusations levelled against Gaveston. Their suspicions had been right, but their estimates well below the mark. As they marvelled, someone compared the vast heap of wealth to the ransom paid by the English to Duke Leopold of Austria for the release of King Richard Coeur de Lion. Later, they realised that the comparison with Richard wasn't valid. Politics had demanded his ransom be paid. What they feasted their eyes upon had been given not to free a man but to bind him.

In spite of their misgivings, the earls were impressed and their cupidity aroused. Although they represented the forces of law and good government, the existence of such enormous amounts of wealth and Ned's open-handed use of bribery altered their mood. They had taken over the government. Its wealth and income could follow. If the King wanted to buy his way out of the crisis, he could – if the price was right. But whatever happened, money or no money, the reforms would remain.

This honeyed compromise spread over what the earls saw as their high moral intentions. When Gaveston secretly met Aymer de Valence, the Earl of Pembroke, his *Joseph the Jew,* and bargaining began in earnest, William Wild was in the depths of a pain-free hashish sleep, having one of his recurring dreams in which he was a mounted Roman gladiator, the *andabata,* who fought blind in a helmet without eye-holes, the lunging horse beneath him sole guide to a maddened, murderous world.

When the negotiations were completed, which took a week because Ned was involved, participating via messengers from York, Gaveston told William Wild what had been agreed. At first, the Irishman was dumbfounded. He couldn't believe what a mess this classic confrontation between light and dark had become. It was now a befogged quagmire.

"What does Ned think he's doing?" he railed. "Once they've got you in their hands, they'll make you die the death of a common miscreant."

"My personal safety has been guaranteed. From here we'll go straight to York to meet Ned with all the earls involved. A deal will be struck, don't worry."

"All you're doing is putting off the evil day! D'you think they're going to exile you *again*?"

"That was Ned's fault. He ordered me back. I've been thinking – there're plenty of places I can go…"

The Irishman folded his hands and leant his chin on them, glaring into the Gascon's increasingly bland smile. "Underneath all that show, you're nothing," he said. "Why couldn't you have died in battle? This is sordid!"

"At twice my age, it's easy for you to say that. How many times have you ducked the issue and run away?"

"And who noticed? Who cared?" the Irishman insisted, his voice shaky. "But when they bring Piers Gaveston down into the mire it's the loss of an argument we can't afford to lose."

Gaveston put his hands on his head and walked up and down the room. There were lines on his face which hadn't been there a year before. He breathed the air from the window as if roses were growing outside.

"What else is there but life itself?" he said. "You know as well as I do it's all we've got."

On 19th May, after ten days of desultory siege, Gaveston surrendered himself to his enemies on magnanimous terms. Ned had sent a thousand-pound bribe from York to the Earl of Pembroke to ensure Gaveston's actual person would be safe from all harm.

The besiegers entered the castle to take over and arrest Gaveston. At the formal ceremony in the courtyard, guarantees were given. The defenders were laying down their arms when William Wild appeared on the tower, shouting and waving his silver crutch.

The ceremony was halted.

"Who's that?" the Earl of Pembroke asked, squinting into the morning sun.

"Old Willy Wild," Gaveston said with a smile of regret. "His mind's gone, I'm afraid."

"Would you go up and talk to him? We have to get on with this business."

"I've spent too much time talking to him already. There's nothing more I can say."

The Earl of Pembroke frowned. "He was a good servant to the old king. I wouldn't like any more harm to come to him. Ask him to come down, will you?" he said.

Gaveston's agreement to do this was given grudgingly. He sighed before he looked up.

"Come down from there, Willy!" he shouted. "We must get on with the business."

"I hear you, lord!" came the reply. "When the darkness comes, dazzle them."

"Come on down!" Gaveston called back. "You're holding us all up."

The men below watched in silence as the Irishman dragged himself between the crenellations of the battlements until his legs hung over. Two soldiers were sent up the tower to stop him but it was too late. Before he let himself go, the Irishman cried: "The second Fall of Man will be worse than the first."

As the body hit the ground, Gaveston looked away, his eyes on the open gate. "Dazzle be damned," he whispered. "This isn't over yet."

As a suicide William Wild was buried where the people of Scarborough put their unshriven dead – in a grave dug on the high line of the tide when the ebb was flowing. As his broken body was lowered into the water gathered at the bottom of the grave, Gaveston was entering York. Instead of being taken to the Abbey of Saint Mary to meet the King and be part of the negotiations, which is what he expected, he was put in the castle prison and manacled like a felon.

At Scarborough it had been negotiated with the Earl of Pembroke that should no agreement be reached on Gaveston's future by 1st August – more than two months hence – he would be brought back to Scarborough, which was still a royal fortress. The garrison and stores would be maintained against his return. If the Earl of Pembroke failed to keep this part of the bargain, all his property would be forfeit.

While he was in prison heavily guarded and kept completely incommunicado, gossip was fed him by underlings – the King had offered to give Gascony to Pope Clement and/or the King of France in return for help in securing his favourite's freedom…a special parliament was being summoned at Lincoln with only one item on the agenda, *Peter, Peter, Peter*…a cult had emerged worshipping him… people were queueing to offer themselves as his executioner…his child could already speak but only to curse his name…a hundred graves had been dug for him all over the country…vigils were being kept in churches for the security of his flesh and the good of his soul.

His treatment ran counter to the agreement reached at Scarborough. It was as if he'd become a forgotten relic of an old dispute. On 4th June he was brought out of prison and told he was being taken south for his own safety. With so many private armies wheeling about in the north, an outbreak of civil war was very likely. His captor, the Earl of Pembroke, on whose word his life was guaranteed, would escort him to a secret destination until the situation eased and anarchy was avoided.

When Gaveston asked to see the King to complain that every agreement with Pembroke was being broken, he was told things were so bad, the chaos so deep and widespread, there was virtually no law. All agreements of any kind were at the mercy of the earls, who were arguing amongst themselves over who should have what. When the dust settled, and the courts started up again, people would remember who'd started it all.

Gaveston asked his informant if the King himself was a prisoner.

"You should know, *Peter?*" came the repy. "You've had the poor bugger in chains for years."

Once outside the city of York, the Earl of Pembroke released his prisoner from all the humiliations of captivity. He was given clothes from his own baggage, one of his personal servants was permitted to attend him, and he rode side by side with Pembroke in the middle of a phalanx of men-at-arms. Gaveston used every ounce of charm left at his disposal to try and wheedle news from his companion, who was determined to give nothing away. The broken Scarborough agreement was kept to one side. Although Gaveston had no wish to alienate the man who had him prisoner, he did harp on the 1st August date when he must be returned to Scarborough if no agreement was reached between the King and the Ordainers.

Pembroke smiled and nodded. "That's my understanding, certainly," he said. "All this will be sorted out by August the first, I believe."

Questions about the actual whereabouts of the King were given vague replies. The last Pembroke had heard was that the King was going south for the same reasons as themselves – because it was safer. But he wasn't completely sure that was correct. There was some sense in the King staying in the north because a parliament was to be held at Lincoln in a month's time. Parliament as the highest court in the land would probably try Gaveston. But the truth was no one knew anything for sure. The best way was to wait and see.

Pembroke's column reached Deddington in Oxfordshire. The majority of the men-at-arms left for duties elsewhere, leaving only a few to guard Gaveston in the rector's house in the village. When the prisoner questioned the wisdom of this Pembroke assured him the danger had passed. They were in safe territory now and could relax. That evening he was going to meet his wife at Bampton, one of his manors nearby. He'd like to take Gaveston along, but he hadn't seen his wife for months and they wanted to spend some time together.

Gaveston pointed out how vulnerable the rectory was to attack. With so few men it was impossible to defend. Pembroke stood on his dignity. "Everyone knows I've sworn an oath on the Lord's body no harm shall come to your person," he said solemnly. "Why doubt me now after I've carried you such a distance in complete safety? You're tired and anxious. Who can blame you? Take as much rest as you can. Tomorrow I'll return early and we'll take you to your own castle at Wallingford. You're to live there on your own parole until called to give an account of yourself."

Pleased and relieved to learn his destination was his own property, Gaveston let Pembroke go with no more objections. Later that evening he asked the rector how far it was to Bampton. He was told it was the best part of twenty-five miles away.

The remaining guards kept close watch at the door and windows of his room that night. His servant was kept away. When Gaveston queried this he was told the earl had given strict instructions that he should be tightly protected and prevented from making an escape.

Bemused and chilled by the peculiar atmosphere in the house, Gaveston tried to sleep, but couldn't while his mind swarmed with dangers. He missed Ned's royal magic around him – a bright ring of untouchability.

Unable to sleep, he heard occasional noises – the random hunting cries of nocturnal birds and animals. Now and again he heard the guards moving about, talking in whispers. A shallow, fitful sleep came in the hour before dawn.

He woke with a start. The clatter of hooves and shaken steel filled the courtyard. A voice yelled, "Get out of bed, traitor! You're taken!" When he looked down, Guy de Beauchamp, Earl of Warwick, was standing in his stirrups, rapping on the window-ledge with his sword, glaring up at him with a savage grin.

When Gaveston put his head out, Guy de Beauchamp howled like a wolf.

CHAPTER THIRTY-ONE

Guy de Beauchamp had ridden through the night from Warwick in order to arrive at Deddington with the dawn. At half-past four, Gaveston was dragged out of his room and down the stairs past his sheepish guards, who had surrendered without a fight. The rector was nowhere to be seen.

A rope was put round the prisoner's neck. His arms were tied behind his back. In the underclothes he had managed to throw on before the soldiers burst into the room, he was led out of the courtyard on foot. Trumpets blared, bringing villagers out of their houses. The news that Gaveston was taken was shouted to them. As the procession left the courtyard and went down the street, the villagers cheered.

Guy de Beauchamp got off his horse, took hold of Gaveston's hair and pulled him along. "Look at the lovely boy, meek as a baby! England's pestilence has such a pretty face! But that won't save him."

Gaveston smiled patiently and asked to be treated according to his dignity as Earl of Cornwall. Incensed, Guy de Beauchamp spat straight into his face. "That for your whore's dignity, and your earldom, and your perfumed arse!" he screamed.

"Pembroke guaranteed my safety on his oath!" Gaveston cried above the noise of the crowd. "What you're doing to me breaks an agreement with the King."

"Am I Pembroke? Do I look like Pembroke?"

"How did you know where to find me?"

"I can smell you," Guy de Beauchamp sneered, sniffing like a hound. "You know how good I am with my nose!"

"When the King hears what's happened here today, it won't be forgiven."

Throwing Gaveston to the ground with a roar of disgust, his captor dragged him along on his face, choking him with the rope.

"We need no forgiveness!" he snarled. "Begin to hate yourself and your sins. Tell the rector to ring the bell! Let everyone know England's agony is nearly over!"

Men were sent ahead to announce the coming of Gaveston and bring out the people to line the road. He was put on a horse so the column could move faster. In towns and villages he was taken off the horse and made to walk so he could be reviled and jostled at closer quarters. In this way he passed thirty miles westward through Chipping Norton, Moreton-in-the-Marsh, Snowshill, Aston Somerville and Sedgebarrow to Warwick's castle at Emley in Worcestershire, which was reached as the sun was going down.

Exhausted, he lay in a dark cell seeing colours on the stonework. To hold his mind together he had kept his eyes on roadside flowers.

He was in a trance, numbed by what had happened. The stench of spittle that had dried on his hair and clothes couldn't reach him. Honeysuckle was in the air. All would be well. Ned would find him. There was no prison door in England the King couldn't open.

He was left without food or drink for two days. When he shouted no one answered, though he could hear men outside. During this time the full effect of the degrading journey from Deddington took its toll. The part of Piers able to fight so brilliantly, defying death by ignoring it, shrank into nothing. He lived only in the ruins of broken arrangements, rebuilding them in his hopes. As he worked on the possibilities, William Wild kept coming back into his mind. He had completely reconstructed this man who had hated him, brought him back to life, made him love him. He remembered what had been lifted from the sea – a wreck, shattered flotsam. A new man had been nursed out of that mess, able to live and be fulfilled. In the frantic mental repairs he was making to himself, Gaveston drew a veil over the Irishman's despair and death at Scarborough. He was still somewhere at large in his chariot.

They would meet again. The forgiveness exchanged between them would infuse the future, setting an example to the earls.

He would make the earls love him.

On the third day, he was taken out of the cell, fed, allowed to wash, given clean clothes, and taken twenty miles to Warwick castle under heavy guard. Towns and villages were avoided. The curious were driven away. Gaveston learnt from his escort that the earls were in a meeting at Warwick to decide his fate. Pembroke was elsewhere, supposedly asking for help to recover custody of his prisoner. If any harm came to Gaveston his lands would be forfeit.

What he had worked out with Guy de Beauchamp was a way to break the agreement and not lose everything. Nevertheless, everyone knew he was party to what was happening now.

Gaveston asked the officer in charge of the escort if there was any word from the King. Would he be attending the meeting?

The officer shrugged. No one knew where the King was.

"He'll come..." Gaveston said, eyes on the nodding white heads of the cow parsley as the horses brushed past. "Nothing can be done without him."

Five days after his capture at Deddington, still in borrowed clothes, Gaveston stood before a tribunal at Warwick castle. When he asked what legal court it represented, the reply was: Thomas, Earl of Lancaster, and Guy, Earl of Warwick, are your judges, acting on behalf of the people. They are invested with powers accepted by the King at the time of your exile, which you broke, thereby incurring the sentence of death.

"The King ordered me to return. I had no choice."

"This is a simple matter," Thomas of Lancaster declared. "You were exiled by us, not the King. The offence is against the people and it is the people who demand your death."

Not permitted to plead in his defence, Gaveston was taken away. In spite of all the mention of death, no actual sentence was passed upon him. The next day he was brought before two royal justices and they condemned him to hang as a traitor, but set no date for his execution.

For the rest of the day, the earls wrote letters of mutual support to each other which could be produced later to show how they shared the responsibility for what they were about to do.

That evening Guy de Beauchamp came to see Gaveston alone. All risks had been laid off between the earls, guarantees against loss issued by the richer to the poorer, undertakings given in as many areas of future danger as possible. To meet the vengeance of the King with a united front was the principal intention. But in spite of all the negotiated mutual insurance, Guy de Beauchamp was nervous.

Before coming to see the prisoner, his final act of self-preservation was to persuade Thomas of Lancaster, the most powerful magnate, and the King's cousin, to have Gaveston killed on his land.

"You're troubled, my lord?" Gaveston said after a few minutes silence during which his visitor sat and stared at him.

"While you live there'll be no peace," Guy de Beauchamp muttered eventually. "I'm a civilised man but you compelled my hatred. You insisted upon it. Why?"

"My lord, you took me too seriously. I can be a fool sometimes. Can't you forgive a fool?" Gaveston argued with a smile that stayed fixed in place as he continued in a different vein: "But you should realise that all this pretence of legality won't convince the King. Let me go and I'll persuade him to forgive *you*."

"No, no...that's all decided. We can't go back. It troubles me you have to die without the comfort of the Church."

"Let my exile stand. I'll leave the country immediately and never see the King again or make contact with him."

Guy de Beauchamp shook his head. "No one believes you'll ever change. It would be better if you cursed me like you used to. Be that same man again, please."

Gaveston laughed drily. "Now I have nothing, you want everything from me. Why should I make things easy for you? What will I achieve by being the man I was? That's how I got here."

"You should never submit. It's not credible to us."

"What you interpret as submission is merely trusting to agreements and the word of honourable men. The King can sort this out."

Guy de Beauchamp sighed heavily and stirred. "No notification of our decision has been sent to the King," he said. "He doesn't know what's going to happen. And even if he did, he's in no position to do anything about it."

Gaveston looked away. "When you say I can't change, you're wrong," he said quietly. "I've learnt my lesson."

"It's the King who can't change."

"He'll never forgive you. His revenge will be terrible."

"All that's been taken into account," Guy de Beauchamp said, getting to his feet. "We're ready for him, whatever he does after tomorrow."

"Tomorrow?" Gaveston groaned, covering his eyes. "So soon? Give me more time to prepare."

"We've decided to grant you a nobleman's death, which you don't deserve. Instead of being hanged you'll be beheaded."

"I should never have surrendered Scarborough!" Gaveston seethed, jumping to his feet, striding up and down the cell. "Willy Wild was right! Why didn't I listen?"

"I leave you to look to your soul."

Gaveston stopped his agitated pacing, wrapping his arms around himself, eyes closed. "God protects the innocent," he said, letting out a long breath. "His grace isn't only in the hands of priests. Oh, Ned, hurry, hurry, hurry."

In the morning, Guy de Beauchamp stayed in his quarters. The prisoner was led out of the castle on foot, arms tied behind his back, and made to walk several miles along the Kenilworth road to Blacklow Hill – land belonging to Thomas of Lancaster.

The other earls were careful to watch the proceedings from behind a line of demarcation, staying on Warwick land.

Thomas of Lancaster was waiting on the roadside near a bend. He introduced the condemned man to his executioners, two young Welshmen in his service, one carrying a sword, the other an axe.

"These men are brothers. They've asked for the privilege of ending your life," Thomas of Lancaster said. "It seems you were responsible for the deaths of both their parents at a place called Pant Mawr in Wales."

Gaveston looked at them dully, without interest. "That means nothing to me," he said.

"You sent men to kill William Wild," one of the sons of Gethin said, "but they killed our mother and father instead. We lost everything because of you."

Gaveston became more alert at the mention of the Irishman's name. Aware his nobleman's death was a sordid roadside killing shorn of any dignity whatsoever, he straightened up and lifted his chin, trying to make the best of it. "William Wild loved me. It sounds like a mistake someone made," he said with a vague smile, his eyes on the bend ahead as if expecting someone to come round it.

"Let that be your epitaph," Thomas of Lancaster said, giving a signal the work should be done.

"Wait! I'm not ready!" Gaveston cried as he was released to stand by himself in front of the brothers. "Give me time to pray."

The sons of Gethin hesitated. The trussed man twisted and stumbled in front of them.

"Get on with it!" Thomas of Lancaster commanded.

One brother ran Gaveston through the heart with the sword and he fell back, releasing the blade. The other stepped forward, turned him over until he was face down, then hacked off his head with three blows of the axe.

There was silence for a while, broken by steel being cleaned, skylarks singing on the hill, a breeze disturbing the roadside flowers. The earls watched the body empty of blood onto the summer grass, commenting on the copious amount and its bright colour. There was a flow of muted chatter. Finally, Thomas of Lancaster ordered everyone to disperse, leaving the body and head where they were.

A few bystanders crept back once the main party were out of sight. They stood idly around, entranced by the magnitude of the event. One of them, who fancied himself as a poet, began putting together saleable doggerel. After a while these people went their ways, taking what they wanted for their memories.

Later on, four shoemakers from Warwick came along the road and found the body. The bonds round the arms were a puzzle. This stretch of roadside wasn't a traditional place of legal execution. They assumed a traveller had been murdered by robbers. Not aware of the exact line of demarcation between the two properties, they erroneously assumed the Earl of Warwick would be responsible for investigating the matter. They borrowed a ladder off a nearby farm and took it upon themselves as good citizens to carry the body all the way back to Warwick to give it to Guy de Beauchamp.

After receiving confirmation it was all over and Gaveston was dead, Guy de Beauchamp had spent the rest of the morning in anxious contemplation of the immediate future. His part in the killing meant the King was now his enemy. The antipathy would be absolute. His lands, life and family were in extreme danger from now on.

He was appalled to see the shoemakers arrive in the castle courtyard with their bloody burden. He ran down and drove them out, screaming they must take the corpse back to exactly where they'd found it on Thomas of Lancaster's land.

A few hours after the shoemakers returned the body, Dominican friars came along the road from Kenilworth. By then local people were gathered round the corpse, chattering excitedly and speculating. Once the friars knew the identity of the victim, they realised the King would thank them for any respectful treatment the dead body of his favourite received. They carried the body fifty miles by cart to Oxford and sent a messenger ahead to London to inform the King what had happened. As an excommunicant, any kind of Christian burial, temporary or otherwise, was denied Gaveston. The friars eviscerated and embalmed his body with spices and balsam, sewed the head back on and waited to hear.

The earls sent Ned no official word of Gaveston's death. At the time, the King was on the coast of Lincolnshire digging sea-defences to keep out the same tides rocking William Wild's bones further up England's moving coastline. In his isolation, Ned was taming the greed of the land-grabbing sea, shovelling mud and stone, an easier task than running the country – but it was enough to make him think he was doing something useful. As he sweated in the heat, he held down all his real problems, using what mental energy he had to hope against hope Piers would be returned to him.

No one in the royal household was allowed to mention the chaotic state of the country. The officers and clerks did their work in an unreal atmosphere. Decisions made inside this confusion had little effect on the malfunctioning machinery of state. It bumped along worn grooves, guided by hapless hands. Since the surrender at Scarborough, the King had lost control of his kingdom.

He had no means of protecting Piers from his enemies. Everything he could offer, he'd offered. Every sacrifice he could make had been made. He could do nothing but what the earls allowed, and trust to their magnanimity. He couldn't believe they'd sufficient vandalism in their hearts to kill what he worshipped.

Piers had never suffered battle-wounds and injury in war or tournament. It was said he was miraculously protected from harm. Robust, tough, vital, virile, fortunate, favoured, he was a symbol of the best manhood had to offer, the essence of an active creation.

Everyone should know how to love such a man.

Ned comforted himself with the thought – Piers still has his charm – when he chooses to use it – his looks, his valour, his enterprise. Somehow or other, he'll always come through.

He'll be alright.

At first Ned couldn't accept the fact. His mind went backwards. Life is Piers. If he's dead, why am I still here, left behind?

The power of his grief made him ill. He lay in bed for days, refusing to see anyone. Piers pulled him towards death. Priests came in and counselled him, coaxing him away from despair.

Following their advice, he tried to connect with Piers as a freed soul. But of what possible use would the world of the spirit be to such an earthbound god? It would stifle him. The thought of Piers in heaven was pointless. He was heaven in himself. To imagine him wandering in some vague afterlife was to diminish the lustre of what went before.

A week later, Ned travelled to identify the body along with those people who needed absolute proof Piers Gaveston was dead – Margaret, his wife; Queen Isabella; the young Earl of Gloucester, his brother-in-law; the Earl of Pembroke who had been the guarantor of his safety and had now come out in opposition to the faction that had murdered him, and Gaveston's aunt (who had lost the bet with the Frescobaldi by two years and nineteen days) representing his family.

When the viewing party gathered round the coffin, Hugh Despenser, a young Marcher lord who had recently acquired the knack of consoling the King, was close by to help.

The body was draped with heavy cloth of gold. The King asked Hugh to remove the covering from the face.

When this was done Ned shook as he saw the botched, clumsy stitches at the throat, then the rouge on the lips, the brushed blonde hair, the eyelashes. Out of the corner of his eye he saw Margaret cross herself. Beside her Isabella pursed her lips and nodded in her first thought: That's him. He's dead. Take a look, you men. We don't want to go through all this again. Her second thought would have surprised Ned if he'd possessed the power of looking into other people's minds. Isabella was looking at Hugh Despenser and thinking about fish. Taught to angle as a child, she harked back to something learnt on the banks of a stream in France

– if a trout is caught in a hole amongst the rocks, a couple of days later another will have taken over its territory.

"Let me see the hands," Ned said, balking at the painted, unbelievable face. He couldn't accept this garish mummy, tarted up by the friars to please him. It was impossible to believe the perfect being had dwindled down to this sad sham.

Hugh parted the cloth over the breast. The hands lay folded over each other, tied at the thumbs with string. No cosmetic work had been done on them. Hard skin from sword-use jutted in a little ledge at the rim of the right palm. Any caress for the King had always come from the left hand.

"They have murdered the brother of my heart," Ned whispered, leaning on Hugh Despenser's arm, "which means they have murdered a half of me. How will I ever live without him?"

FINIS